Hawkwing knew he was young; he hadn't lived through SkyClan's most trying days. Still, the Clan meant more to him than he could possibly say. *We look out for each other,* he thought now. *We put the Clan first, and ourselves second. That's important.* He paused, looking up at the narrow moon and his ancestors twinkling in the sky.

We have to save our Clan.

Every hair on Hawkwing's pelt began to tingle, but this time it was not with fear. He felt a fierceness run through his body, powerful as flame, a determination to make sure that the worst would never happen.

As long as I'm alive, SkyClan will never be exiled. We will always survive!

WARRIORS

THE PROPHECIES BEGIN

Book One: *Into the Wild*

Book Two: *Fire and Ice*

Book Three: *Forest of Secrets*

Book Four: *Rising Storm*

Book Five: *A Dangerous Path*

Book Six: *The Darkest Hour*

THE NEW PROPHECY

Book One: *Midnight*

Book Two: *Moonrise*

Book Three: *Dawn*

Book Four: *Starlight*

Book Five: *Twilight*

Book Six: *Sunset*

POWER OF THREE

Book One: *The Sight*

Book Two: *Dark River*

Book Three: *Outcast*

Book Four: *Eclipse*

Book Five: *Long Shadows*

Book Six: *Sunrise*

OMEN OF THE STARS

Book One: *The Fourth Apprentice*

Book Two: *Fading Echoes*

Book Three: *Night Whispers*

Book Four: *Sign of the Moon*

Book Five: *The Forgotten Warrior*

Book Six: *The Last Hope*

DAWN OF THE CLANS

Book One: *The Sun Trail*

Book Two: *Thunder Rising*

Book Three: *The First Battle*

Book Four: *The Blazing Star*

Book Five: *A Forest Divided*

Book Six: *Path of Stars*

A VISION OF SHADOWS

Book One: *The Apprentice's Quest*

Book Two: *Thunder and Shadow*

Book Three: *Shattered Sky*

Warriors Super Edition: Firestar's Quest

Warriors Super Edition: Bluestar's Prophecy

Warriors Super Edition: SkyClan's Destiny

Warriors Super Edition: Crookedstar's Promise

Warriors Super Edition: Yellowfang's Secret

Warriors Super Edition: Tallstar's Revenge

Warriors Super Edition: Bramblestar's Storm

Warriors Super Edition: Moth Flight's Vision

Warriors Super Edition: Hawkwing's Journey

Warriors Super Edition: Tigerheart's Shadow

Warriors Field Guide: Secrets of the Clans

Warriors: Cats of the Clans

Warriors: Code of the Clans

Warriors: Battles of the Clans

Warriors: Enter the Clans

Warriors: The Ultimate Guide

Warriors: The Untold Stories
Warriors: Tales from the Clans
Warriors: Shadows of the Clans
Warriors: Legends of the Clans

MANGA

The Lost Warrior
Warrior's Refuge
Warrior's Return
The Rise of Scourge
Tigerstar and Sasha #1: Into the Woods
Tigerstar and Sasha #2: Escape from the Forest
Tigerstar and Sasha #3: Return to the Clans
Ravenpaw's Path #1: Shattered Peace
Ravenpaw's Path #2: A Clan in Need
Ravenpaw's Path #3: The Heart of a Warrior
SkyClan and the Stranger #1: The Rescue
SkyClan and the Stranger #2: Beyond the Code
SkyClan and the Stranger #3: After the Flood

NOVELLAS

Hollyleaf's Story
Mistystar's Omen
Cloudstar's Journey
Tigerclaw's Fury
Leafpool's Wish
Mapleshade's Vengeance
Goosefeather's Curse
Ravenpaw's Farewell
Spottedleaf's Heart
Pinestar's Choice
Thunderstar's Echo

ALSO BY ERIN HUNTER

SEEKERS

Book One: *The Quest Begins*
Book Two: *Great Bear Lake*
Book Three: *Smoke Mountain*
Book Four: *The Last Wilderness*
Book Five: *Fire in the Sky*
Book Six: *Spirits in the Stars*

RETURN TO THE WILD

Book One: *Island of Shadows*
Book Two: *The Melting Sea*
Book Three: *River of Lost Bears*
Book Four: *Forest of Wolves*
Book Five: *The Burning Horizon*
Book Six: *The Longest Day*

MANGA

Toklo's Story
Kallik's Adventure

SURVIVORS

Book One: The Empty City

Book Two: A Hidden Enemy

Book Three: Darkness Falls

Book Four: The Broken Path

Book Five: The Endless Lake

Book Six: Storm of Dogs

THE GATHERING DARKNESS

Book One: A Pack Divided

Book Two: Dead of Night

Book Three: Into the Shadows

Survivors: Tales from the Packs

NOVELLAS

Alpha's Tale

Sweet's Journey

Moon's Choice

BRAVELANDS

Book One: Broken Pride

WARRIORS
SUPER EDITION

HAWKWING'S
JOURNEY

ERIN
HUNTER

HARPER

An Imprint of HarperCollinsPublishers

Special thanks to Cherith Baldry

Hawkwing's Journey
Copyright © 2016 by Working Partners Limited
Series created by Working Partners Limited
Map art 2016 by Dave Stevenson
Interior art 2016 by Owen Richardson
Manga text copyright © 2016 by Working Partners Limited
Manga art copyright © 2016 by HarperCollins Publishers

www.harpercollinschildrens.com

Library of Congress Control Number: 2016949972
ISBN 978-0-06-246770-6

17 18 19 20 21 CG/OPM 10 9 8 7 6 5 4 3 2 1
❖
First paperback edition, 2017

ALLEGIANCES

SKYCLAN

LEADER
LEAFSTAR—brown-and-cream tabby she-cat with amber eyes

DEPUTY
SHARPCLAW—dark ginger tom

MEDICINE CATS
ECHOSONG—silver tabby she-cat with green eyes

FRECKLEWISH—mottled light brown tabby she-cat with spotted legs

WARRIORS
(toms and she-cats without kits)

SPARROWPELT—dark brown tabby tom

CHERRYTAIL—tortoiseshell-and-white she-cat

WASPWHISKER—gray-and-white tom
APPRENTICE, DUSKPAW (ginger tabby tom)

EBONYCLAW—striking black she-cat (daylight warrior)
APPRENTICE, HAWKPAW (dark gray tom)

BILLYSTORM—ginger-and-white tom (former daylight warrior)
APPRENTICE, PEBBLEPAW (brown-speckled white she-cat)

HARVEYMOON—white tom (daylight warrior)

MACGYVER—black-and-white tom (daylight warrior)

BOUNCEFIRE—ginger tom
APPRENTICE, BLOSSOMPAW (ginger-and-white she-cat)

TINYCLOUD—small white she-cat
APPRENTICE, BELLAPAW (pale orange she-cat with green eyes)

SAGENOSE—pale gray tom

NETTLESPLASH—pale brown tom
APPRENTICE, RILEYPAW (pale gray tabby tom with dark gray strips and blue eyes)

RABBITLEAP—brown tom
APPRENTICE, PARSLEYPAW (dark brown tabby tom)

PLUMWILLOW—dark gray she-cat
APPRENTICE, CLOUDPAW (white she-cat)

SANDYNOSE—stocky light brown tom with ginger legs

FIREFERN—ginger she-cat

HARRYBROOK—gray tom

STORMHEART—ginger-and-gray she-cat

MISTFEATHER—gray tom with amber eyes

QUEENS   (she-cats expecting or nursing kits)

BIRDWING—black she-cat (mother to Curlykit, a long-haired gray she-kit; Fidgetkit, a black-and-white tom-kit; and Snipkit, a black she-kit with white patch on her chest)

MINTFUR—gray tabby she-cat

HONEYTAIL—pale ginger she-cat with long fur

ELDERS (former warriors and queens, now retired)

PATCHFOOT—black-and-white tom

CLOVERTAIL—light brown she-cat with white belly and legs

FALLOWFERN—pale brown she-cat who has lost her hearing

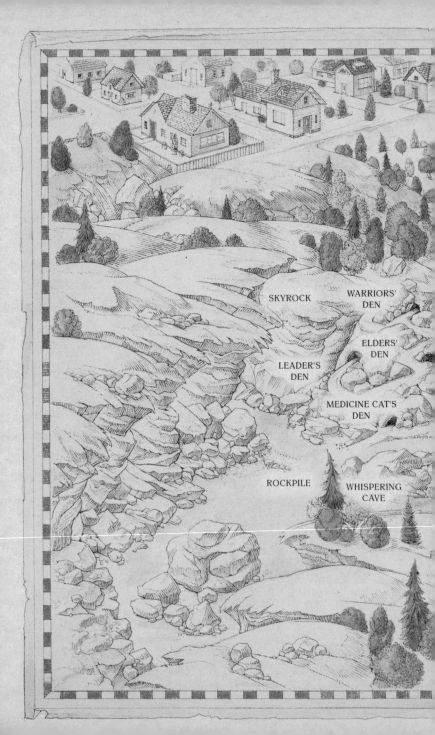

SKYROCK

WARRIORS'
DEN

ELDERS'
DEN

LEADER'S
DEN

MEDICINE CAT'S
DEN

ROCKPILE

WHISPERING
CAVE

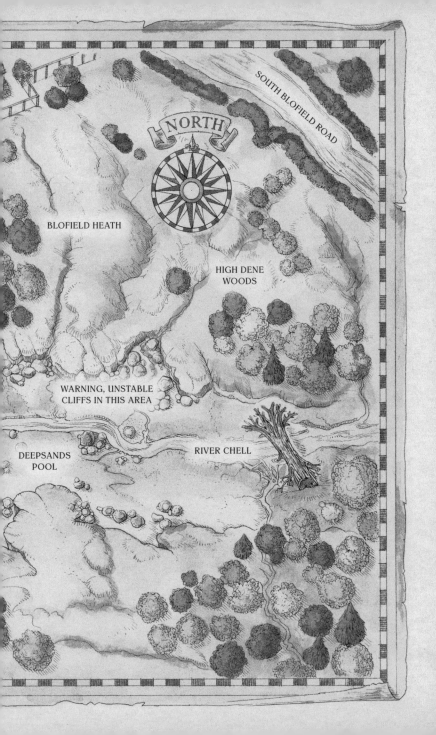

PROLOGUE

Sunlight poured into the gorge, bathing the sand-colored rocks in a warm glow. On either side the walls plunged down sharply until they reached a narrow valley at their foot. In the depths, water cascaded from a black hole beneath a pile of boulders, and became a stream that wound its way through the gorge until it was lost to sight among bushes and trees. A gentle breeze carried the enticing scents of prey.

A powerful tom, his pale gray fur patched with white, sat on top of the pile of boulders, gazing downstream. A frosty glimmer of starlight clung to his pelt, and stars shone in his blue eyes.

After a while, the stillness of the gorge was broken as a brown tabby emerged from a den near the foot of the cliff and padded purposefully over to the rocks, scrambling up until he could stand beside the gray-and-white tom.

"Brackenheart," the gray-and-white tom meowed. "Have you thought any more about this vision?"

"I have, Cloudstar," Brackenheart replied, dipping his head. "And I have no idea—"

He broke off as a third cat appeared at the top of the gorge and came bounding down the trail to join the other two on top of the boulders. Stars flowed like water through his gray pelt and gave an icy glitter to his claws.

Cloudstar rose to his paws; he and Brackenheart bowed their heads in profound respect. "Greetings, Skystar," Cloudstar mewed.

Skystar returned the greeting with a brisk nod. "Well?" he asked. "Have you come to a decision?"

Brackenheart shook his head, while Cloudstar looked troubled, replying, "No. What we have seen is too terrible. There are no easy answers."

"But an answer must be found." Skystar stood up straighter and gave an impatient lash of his tail. "All three of us have seen the scourge that looms over SkyClan, a danger more dreadful than the heaviest, darkest storm cloud. It could black out the sky and put an end to the Clan I founded forever. I could not bear that."

"SkyClan will never end!" Cloudstar's blue eyes glittered fiercely. "We have suffered great losses before, only to rise and thrive again. When we were driven out of the forest, so many seasons ago, we persevered. We found a home in the gorge, and even when the rats destroyed and scattered most of the Clan, a few cats kept the memory alive until Firestar came to restore what had been lost."

"But Firestar is dead," Brackenheart mewed somberly. "And his StarClan is far from here. He can do nothing for SkyClan now."

Skystar looked thoughtful. "Then we must speak to SkyClan directly," he insisted. "They must be warned."

"True, Skystar," Brackenheart responded. "But what kind of warning shall we give? What can we tell them to *do*?"

"We must tell them to fight," Cloudstar mewed decisively. "They are strong, brave cats, deeply committed to one another as a Clan. They will win if they believe they can."

Brackenheart let out a sigh. "But not even Firestar himself could fight this scourge. This battle is unwinnable!"

"Precisely. The time has come for SkyClan to leave their comfortable territory," Skystar declared.

"What?" Cloudstar's eyes stretched wide in outrage. "After so many cats struggled to keep it? After so many cats *died* for it? You want them to just leave—without putting up a fight?"

"Everything comes to an end, sooner or later. SkyClan has been its own island for too long." Skystar leaned forward, his brilliant blue eyes fixed intently on the other cats. "When I founded SkyClan, it was one of the five petals of the Blazing Star, and all of the Clans thrived because they worked together. SkyClan must take a lesson from its history."

Cloudstar gave the ancient leader a puzzled look. "Then you're saying that SkyClan is *meant* to leave the gorge?"

"That's exactly what I'm saying. Leaving the gorge will only be the first paw step on a much longer journey."

"No!" Cloudstar's neck fur began to bristle. "My Clan and I had to struggle to make our home here among the rocks. Firestar risked his life to reunite us after we were driven out the first time. And now you suggest throwing all that away? Have you got bees in your brain? They must *fight*."

Brackenheart nodded in vigorous agreement. "I was

SkyClan's last medicine cat before rats drove us out of the gorge. After all we went through, how can you expect me to stand by and watch as my Clan is driven out a second time?"

Skystar listened impassively to Cloudstar's heated outburst and Brackenheart's desperate protest. His voice was quiet and steady as he replied. "No. Every cat knows what our Clan has suffered, but there is a time for our claws to grip hard to what we own, and a time to let go. The threat SkyClan faces is just the beginning. Only by joining with the other Clans can they clear the sky."

Brackenheart drew in a wondering breath. "All five Clans, together again . . ." Then he gave his pelt a shake. "But how can this be? Where will SkyClan live, if they rejoin the other Clans? There is only so much territory. How do we know that the other Clans will accept them peacefully? How do we know that the cats of SkyClan will *want* to join the others? They have only ever known Firestar, and he is in his own StarClan now."

"And Sandstorm," Cloudstar reminded him.

Skystar nodded. "Yes. And she is a brave cat, but her path is dark to me. It is to Firestar's kin that SkyClan must look now. For when fire dies down, there are still sparks that remain. And you are right that SkyClan's path will be long and difficult. That is why they must start now." He paused, staring into the distance.

"They must find those sparks, or their future is terrible indeed. . . ."

CHAPTER 1

❧

Hawkpaw let out a drowsy purr, enjoying the sensation of warm sunlight on his pelt. He lay curled up at the base of a rock, his dark gray tail wrapped over his paws. His whiskers twitched as he sank deeper into sleep, imagining himself stalking prey among the bushes at the top of the gorge.

"Mrrow!"

Hawkpaw startled awake as a bundle of ginger fur landed on top of him and paws prodded him sharply in the ribs. He breathed in the familiar scent of his littermate Duskpaw.

"Get off me!" Hawkpaw yowled, pushing Duskpaw away as he sat up and shook out his ruffled fur. "What's gotten into you? I was enjoying my nap!"

"Well, it's time to wake up, lazybones!" Duskpaw meowed. "Cloudpaw and Pebblepaw and I have come up with the best plan ever!"

Still half asleep, Hawkpaw narrowed his eyes in annoyance. *What is it this time? Duskpaw is always bugging me with some amazing plan, and usually it's, "Hey, we're going to steal some Twoleg food!"* Since he was a kit, Duskpaw had loved the taste of Twoleg prey, and was often willing to do some very silly things to get it. *Honestly,*

Hawkpaw thought, twitching his whiskers. *I think he must have bees in his brain.*

"Okay, then," Hawkpaw murmured, then stretched his jaws in a massive yawn. "What's this great plan?"

"Pebblepaw saw some Twolegs carrying woven twigs to the Twoleg greenplace," Duskpaw explained, bouncing up and down on his paws. His eyes rounded with excitement. "And you know what that means, right?"

Hawkpaw gave a weary sigh. *I saw this coming.* "Twoleg food."

At the same moment, Duskpaw let out an excited squeal. "*Twoleg food!* It's been a while since Pebblepaw saw them," he continued. "They must be long gone. But their leftovers will still be there!"

"I think you're going to turn into a Twoleg if you're not careful," Hawkpaw teased, grinning. "Your fur will get thin, except on top of your head it'll be all puffed up and messy, and you'll start walking on your hind legs and riding about in monsters. . . ."

"Don't be a stupid furball!" Duskpaw protested. "Like that would ever happen!"

"You're so crazy about their food, and it's not even that exciting!" Hawkpaw responded. "Besides, how do you plan on getting away without Waspwhisker finding out? Not to mention Billystorm and Plumwillow. They won't like their apprentices sneaking off without permission. Ebonyclaw would rip my pelt off if I was idiotic enough to join you."

"They won't find out," Duskpaw mewed with a dismissive wave of his tail. "All the warriors have stuffed themselves with fresh-kill, and now they're snoozing at the bottom of the Rockpile—just like you were, a moment ago. We're going straight there and we'll be right back, before our mentors even wake up to miss us."

Hawkpaw noticed that his sister Cloudpaw and the speckled white she-cat Pebblepaw were standing a few tail-lengths away, just out of earshot. Pebblepaw was scraping impatiently at the ground, clearly tired of waiting for Duskpaw.

"Get a move on!" she spat. "Let Hawkpaw stay here if he's too much of a scaredy-mouse."

Hawkpaw growled deep in his throat at the insult. "Like I'd go if *she's* going."

"Look, I know you don't like her," Duskpaw meowed, lowering his voice and casting a quick glance between Hawkpaw and Pebblepaw, "but you should get to know her better. You know, the two of you are a lot alike. You're both as difficult as a fox in a fit. So are you coming or not?"

Hawkpaw let out an irritated hiss at the thought that he was anything like *Pebblepaw*. She had to be the most annoying cat in the whole Clan. *She struts around like she's so great, when she's just an apprentice like the rest of us.* "No thanks," he snapped. "Just leave me alone, okay?"

"Keep your fur on!" Duskpaw protested. "Your temper will get you into trouble one day."

That made Hawkpaw even more angry—being scolded by the brother who spent so much time messing around. "No, *you're* the one who'll get into trouble, for sneaking out to steal Twoleg food."

Duskpaw shrugged, his eyes sparkling with mischief. "It's worth it! Twoleg food is delicious. But you can suit yourself. We're going."

"Fine!" he huffed. "Have fun." *And good luck explaining when you get back.*

Hawkpaw let his annoyance ebb as he watched his brother scuttle off with Pebblepaw and Cloudpaw. He yawned, reflecting thankfully that at least his other sister, Blossompaw, had the good sense not to get involved. Curling up again, he wrapped his tail over his nose and closed his eyes. *Maybe now I can finish my nap in peace.*

Some time later, a stiff breeze rustled the branches of the trees at the top of the gorge as Hawkpaw followed the paw steps of his mentor, Ebonyclaw, through the undergrowth along the SkyClan border. The sun was dipping down below the topmost branches; Hawkpaw fluffed out his pelt against the sudden chill.

Ebonyclaw's lithe black figure halted and she glanced at Hawkpaw over her shoulder. "Wait here while I renew the scent marker," she instructed him.

Hawkpaw did as he was told, his ears pricked for the sound of prey. He wondered what had happened to Duskpaw and the others; they hadn't returned from their expedition by the time he and Ebonyclaw had left camp.

Probably they were so excited by the food that they lost track of time. Mouse-brains.

A secret thrill crept through Hawkpaw at the thought

of Duskpaw getting into trouble. *He's always fooling around and bending the rules! I love him, but he needs to get serious if he wants to be a warrior.*

It didn't seem all that fair to Hawkpaw that he always worked as hard as he possibly could, but Duskpaw kept getting away with his stupid behavior. *Maybe if he has to deal with the elders' ticks for a few days, he'll decide to make more of an effort.*

When Ebonyclaw returned from setting the scent marker she was sniffing the air, a suspicious expression on her face. "Can you smell that?" she asked.

Hawkpaw opened his jaws to taste the air, and an unfamiliar scent flowed into his mouth. "Great StarClan! What *is* that?" he exclaimed.

"I don't know."

Hawkpaw blinked in surprise. *I thought Ebonyclaw knew everything, even if she is just a daylight warrior!* "Do you think there's some new kind of animal near the gorge?" he asked, trying not to let his voice quiver with the sudden apprehension he felt.

"There could be," Ebonyclaw replied. "I've picked up this scent once or twice before, near the place where my Twolegs put their rubbish, but this is the first time I've caught it on our territory."

"What are we going to do?"

Ebonyclaw's ears twitched. "Nothing, for now. You can't fight a scent. But we'll report it to Leafstar, and tell all the others to be on the lookout for a strange animal. You never know—it might not be dangerous."

Stinking like that, it can't be good! Hawkpaw was drawing in more of the tainted air, trying to commit the scent to memory, when he noticed another smell, something strange and bitter, that made his nose wrinkle. Glancing at Ebonyclaw, he saw that she had her ears perked up and her nose stuck in the air.

"What's that? *Another* animal?" he asked.

Ebonyclaw shook her head. "I think it's fire, but I hope it isn't." She sniffed the air again. "It must be coming from the Twolegplace. They're such mouse-brains, they always like to start fires to stick their food into. We should go check it out to make sure they have it under control. Follow me."

Anxiety fluttered in Hawkpaw's belly like a whole nestful of birds. *That's where Duskpaw and the others went! Will they still be there? Surely they would have left by now . . . right?*

Hawkpaw had never seen fire before, but he had heard enough stories from the elders to know that it could be a serious threat. "Will it reach the camp?" he asked, padding alongside Ebonyclaw as her paws turned purposefully toward the Twolegplace.

"Probably not," Ebonyclaw reassured him. "The Twoleg-place is quite a way from the gorge. But the scent is quite strong, so it's best to make sure that we'll all be safe."

As they emerged from the bushes, Ebonyclaw picked up the pace until she and Hawkpaw were racing across the stretch of dry grass that separated their territory from the Twolegplace. The scent grew stronger with every paw step, and Hawkpaw's flutter of fear grew stronger too.

I really hope Duskpaw has gone back to camp!

To his surprise, Hawkpaw spotted movement in the grass

and realized that small creatures—mice and shrews—were pelting through the stems toward them, away from the source of the smell. One mouse practically ran into his paws, then veered away at the last moment.

Hawkpaw's jaws watered. "Hey, look, Ebonyclaw," he mewed. "Easy prey!"

"There'll be time for hunting later," Ebonyclaw told him, racing on without a pause. "Right now we have to make sure that everything's safe for our Clan."

As they drew close to the Twoleg greenplace, the air grew thick with a gray swirl that billowed around the two cats. The acrid scent was overwhelming, catching Hawkpaw in the throat so that he had to cough.

"Stay back," Ebonyclaw warned him.

At the heart of the gray swirl, Hawkpaw could just make out a red glow that began to grow as he watched it, reaching up into separate licking tongues. He stared at the scarlet flames as they spat out gray puffs of air. They seemed to be feeding like some greedy animal on a kind of Twoleg rock made from flat sticks. Hawkpaw had sometimes seen Twolegs sitting on it with their kits, eating the weird food Duskpaw was so crazy about. Now the fire blazed up, crackling orange sparks leaping up into the low-hanging branches of a tree.

Duskpaw, Cloudpaw! he thought, gazing around in terror as he looked for his littermates.

But there was no sign of them. *They must have left by now,* Hawkpaw reminded himself. *I wish I could leave, too!*

The gray air was making his eyes sting, and his lungs burned with every breath he took. "Ebonyclaw, can we—" he began.

Suddenly the gray air swirled again. The wind shifted, blowing harder from the Twolegplace. The fire surged, and the low-hanging tree branches burst into flame. For a few heartbeats they blazed, then with a loud crackle the lowest branch fell right next to the burning Twoleg rock.

Ebonyclaw let out a gasp, and pushed Hawkpaw back. Every muscle in Hawkpaw's body tensed. He had never heard a warrior sound so terrified before, let alone his own mentor.

But Ebonyclaw's gasp was instantly drowned out by the sound of terrified yowling from beneath the Twoleg rock. It was hard to hear over the rushing and crackling sounds of the fire, but the yowling sounded dreadfully familiar to Hawk-paw.

"*StarClan, no!* There are apprentices in there!" Ebonyclaw screeched.

Oh, no! Hawkpaw felt as if his belly was dropping out. His littermates were still there—and in grave danger. *Duskpaw . . . Cloudpaw!*

"Stay back!" Ebonyclaw snapped, then raced toward the fire and smoke, her belly fur brushing the grass and her tail streaming out behind her.

Hawkpaw crouched, staring at her, his claws digging hard into the ground. The shrieking came again, louder than before, and now he could make out separate voices. *Duskpaw, Cloudpaw, and Pebblepaw are all in there!*

Ignoring Ebonyclaw's order, Hawkpaw sprang forward and hurled himself toward the blaze. "I'm coming!" he yowled.

As the smoke thickened around him, Hawkpaw found it hard to see what was going on. The gray tendrils stung his eyes and caught him in the throat. Coughing, he groped his way forward until he spotted Cloudpaw trapped between the burning branch and the Twoleg rock. A heartbeat later he managed to make out Pebblepaw crouching underneath the strange rock, while Duskpaw scrabbled on the ground at the far side of the blazing branch.

Guilt flowed over Hawkpaw, hotter than the flames. *I wanted Duskpaw to get into trouble—just a bit—but not for something like this to happen!*

Then Ebonyclaw appeared through the smoke, fighting her way to Cloudpaw's side. Hawkpaw froze for a moment. *Do I try to help Duskpaw, or Pebblepaw?*

Pebblepaw seemed to be in more danger. Flames had burned through parts of the Twoleg rock, and pieces were starting to fall off; Pebblepaw cringed away from them, letting out a wail of terror.

Beyond her, Duskpaw was still scrabbling around as if he was trying to get to Pebblepaw. He yowled something. Hawkpaw couldn't hear the words through the roaring of the fire, but when he saw his brother turn his head, he understood.

He wants me to help Pebblepaw.

It did look like Pebblepaw was in more danger—but Duskpaw was his kin. *I wish I could ask Ebonyclaw for advice, but she's busy saving Cloudpaw!*

Hawkpaw thought he had been standing motionless for moons, but it couldn't have been more than a few heartbeats before he flung himself through the flames toward Pebblepaw. All his instincts were telling him to run for safety in the other direction; burning grass scorched his paws and hot sparks landed on his pelt. But he kept going until he reached Pebblepaw and grabbed her by her scruff.

"This way, furball!" he growled through a mouthful of her fur as he dragged her away from the fire and onto a clear patch of grass.

Ebonyclaw approached as Hawkpaw let Pebblepaw flop to the ground, pushing Cloudpaw in front of her.

But where's Duskpaw? Hawkpaw couldn't understand why his brother hadn't followed them out of the blaze.

Peering through the smoke, Hawkpaw saw that Duskpaw was still where he had been, next to the burning branch. But now he was slumped over, unmoving.

A chill of terror gripped Hawkpaw. *"Duskpaw!"* he yowled.

With Ebonyclaw at his side, Hawkpaw raced back through the smoke and flames. When they drew closer, Hawkpaw saw that one of his brother's paws was trapped underneath the thicker end of the branch, where the fire still hadn't reached. For a moment he felt his heart stop, and he couldn't take a breath.

Duskpaw wasn't telling me to save Pebblepaw: He was asking me to help him!

Together Hawkpaw and Ebonyclaw thrust at the branch with their forepaws until it rolled off Duskpaw in a billowing cloud of sparks. Then Ebonyclaw grabbed him by his scruff and dragged him out to where they had left Pebblepaw and

Cloudpaw. Hawkpaw followed, pushing his littermate from behind. Duskpaw's legs were limp and his head lolled; he didn't seem able to help himself.

Pebblepaw and Cloudpaw still lay slumped on the ground, coughing and letting out whimpers of pain. Hawkpaw could see that patches of their fur were scorched, giving off a strong scent of burning. But to his relief, neither of them seemed to have life-threatening injuries.

However, Duskpaw was hardly moving. Now and again he would feebly try to lift his head, and let out a weak cough, but then he would slip back into unconsciousness. Hawkpaw gazed at him in horror, and shook his shoulder with one paw.

"Duskpaw! Duskpaw, wake up," he begged.

"*What* were the three of you doing out here?" Ebonyclaw demanded.

Cloudpaw let out a mournful wail. "Duskpaw said we should sneak over here and look for scraps of Twoleg food."

Hawkpaw couldn't take his eyes off his unconscious littermate. *And I might have been with you—if I hadn't said no.* He remembered his earlier hope that Duskpaw would get into trouble with a shudder of shame.

Ebonyclaw didn't seem to notice. She lashed her tail at Cloudpaw, clearly frustrated. "If Duskpaw told you to jump off the cliff, would you do it?"

"I know it was our fault too," Cloudpaw whimpered. "But when we got here, the fire was just over there, in that shiny thing." She pointed with one paw.

"The trash can, yes," Ebonyclaw meowed. "And you didn't

have the sense to go back to camp and report it?"

"It seemed safe enough then." Pebblepaw continued the story. "Duskpaw said that the fire must have driven the Two-legs away, because Twolegs are scared of everything, but *we* were brave enough, and we shouldn't let the fire keep us from the best scraps of tasty food."

"There was stuff under there." Cloudpaw pointed at the Twoleg rock, now collapsing into a smoldering heap. "But then the wind shifted, and the Twoleg rock caught fire, and then the branch fell and trapped us. We never should have lis-tened to Duskpaw!" she finished with another miserable wail.

"You should have thought of that sooner," Ebonyclaw snapped. "It's too late to feel sorry, and we need to get Dusk-paw back to camp so Echosong and Frecklewish can help him." She flattened herself on the ground beside Duskpaw. "Hawkpaw, help me to get him onto my back," she directed.

Hawkpaw worked his shoulders under Duskpaw and began to lift him onto the black she-cat's back. Duskpaw revived a little and hooked his claws into Ebonyclaw's fur. When he was settled, Ebonyclaw staggered to her paws and set off slowly back toward camp, with Hawkpaw steadying his brother on one side, and Cloudpaw and Pebblepaw limping behind. As they left the Twoleg greenplace they heard Twoleg monsters screeching in the distance, the sound growing closer as the cats trekked across the stretch of grass and into the bushes at the top of the gorge.

Gazing anxiously at his brother, Hawkpaw could hardly believe what had happened. "Hang in there, Duskpaw . . . ," he whispered.

But now Duskpaw's eyes were completely closed, and he didn't respond at all to Hawkpaw's urging. His legs were hanging limply and he had lost his grip on Ebonyclaw's fur. Hawkpaw could barely manage to steady him and keep him on the black she-cat's back.

Hawkpaw felt as if all his strength had leaked out through his paws, and there was a hard knot in his belly as if he had swallowed crow-food. He was sick with guilt. He couldn't believe he'd wished that Duskpaw would get into trouble. Even worse, he could have saved Duskpaw from the fire, but he hadn't.

Did I make the wrong choice, saving Pebblepaw first? he asked himself. *And what if I lose Duskpaw because of it?*

CHAPTER 2

❧

Helping Ebonyclaw carry Duskpaw down the narrow trail into the
gorge was one of the hardest things Hawkpaw had ever done.
He was terrified that his brother would slip off Ebonyclaw's
back and plummet down onto the rocks below, in spite of the
black she-cat's careful paw steps and his own desperate efforts
to hold Duskpaw still. His heart was pounding and his legs
trembling by the time they reached the bottom.

Already several cats were clustered at the end of the trail,
gazing anxiously upward. The smell of smoke drifted on the
air; Hawkpaw guessed that his Clanmates were already aware
that something was wrong.

Duskpaw was completely unconscious when Ebonyclaw let
him slide from her back. Hawkpaw couldn't stop staring into
his ginger tabby face, desperately searching for some sign of
life. He almost expected his brother to wake up and bounce to
his paws, explaining that it had all been a joke.

Duskpaw is always fooling around. . . .

"What happened?" Waspwhisker thrust his way through
the gathering crowd and gazed down at his motionless apprentice, deep concern in his eyes.

Billystorm, Pebblepaw's mentor, was hard on his paws. "Pebblepaw?" His voice was stern. "Where have you been?"

Pebblepaw's head was bowed in shame, and it was Ebonyclaw who replied. "There's no time to explain now. Some cat fetch Echosong and Frecklewish, quickly."

Billystorm turned and left, as more cats bounded up to see what was happening. Hawkpaw looked around for his mother and father; he spotted Sandynose and Sagenose, followed almost at once by Tinycloud and Firefern, but there was no sign of Cherrytail or Sharpclaw. Every cat was quiet, exchanging dismayed glances.

They know this is bad, Hawkpaw thought. *Really bad.*

Moons seemed to pass before Echosong and Frecklewish slipped through the crowd to reach Duskpaw's side.

"Thank StarClan!" Hawkpaw murmured to himself.

"There's a fire at the Twoleg greenplace," Ebonyclaw meowed, before either medicine cat could ask a question. "There was so much smoke! Duskpaw breathed in most of it, because he was the last to be saved. We almost lost Pebblepaw, too, but Hawkpaw managed to get her out."

Echosong gave a brisk nod. "Frecklewish, go and get some wet moss, and some comfrey and honey to treat the burns," she ordered. As Frecklewish dashed off, she added, "Ebonyclaw, Hawkpaw, lay Duskpaw out on his back."

It took all of Hawkpaw's courage to help his mentor arrange Duskpaw's limp body on the ground. He could barely look at his brother; he seemed so lifeless.

Instead, he forced himself to look at Echosong, as she

pounced on Duskpaw and began to press his chest rhythmically with her forepaws. From time to time she would stop, to breathe into Duskpaw's mouth from her own. Hawkpaw stared at her face, trying to glean information from her expression.

Maybe this was something that *looked* very bad, but was no big deal to an experienced medicine cat.

But all Hawkpaw could tell from gazing at Echosong was that she seemed gravely serious, intent on her task. Duskpaw still wasn't moving.

"What's happening?" Hawkpaw asked at last, unable to stifle the agonized question.

Ebonyclaw touched his shoulder with her tail-tip. "Echosong is trying to restart Duskpaw's breathing and his heart," she explained.

Which means his breathing and his heart have stopped, Hawkpaw realized. He felt again as though a tough piece of crow-food was lodged in his belly, and he was about to vomit it up.

Echosong went on pushing at Duskpaw's chest, while Hawkpaw watched, barely daring to breathe. Finally, after what seemed like moons, the medicine cat stopped and stepped back, shaking her head. Duskpaw still lay motionless.

"You can't give up!" Hawkpaw cried. "What are you doing? You have to *save* him!"

He was aware of all the other cats who were gathered around, staring at him, but no cat spoke. Hawkpaw felt his heart tearing apart as if a badger were ripping it with powerful claws.

He let out a mournful wail, and behind him another cat joined in. Turning, Hawkpaw saw his mother, Cherrytail, along with his father, Sharpclaw, pressing forward into the circle of cats who surrounded him.

Cherrytail rushed forward and flung herself to the ground beside Duskpaw, burying her nose in his fur. A couple of tail-lengths away, Pebblepaw and Cloudpaw were lying on the grass, moaning miserably. Hawkpaw guessed they were beginning to feel the effects of their burns, but they could barely open their eyes. Clearly they weren't aware of what was going on around them.

They don't know yet that Duskpaw is dead!

Sharpclaw stood over his son's body, stony and silent. Then briefly Hawkpaw felt his father's gaze rest on him. But before either cat could speak, Billystorm reappeared with the Clan leader, Leafstar. They joined Sharpclaw and Ebonyclaw, and all four cats conferred quietly together.

Hawkpaw crept up to his mother and pressed himself closely against her side. He couldn't find any words to comfort her, but he wrapped his tail around her shoulders.

Cherrytail didn't respond, her muzzle still buried in her dead son's fur. Hawkpaw didn't blame her for not letting him console her. He couldn't console himself. *I can't tell her it'll be okay. Nothing will ever be okay again.*

By now, Frecklewish had returned with wet moss and the healing honey and comfrey. Echosong joined her, and the two medicine cats began to dress Cloudpaw's and Pebblepaw's injuries. After a few moments, Frecklewish padded over to

Hawkpaw with a bundle of dripping moss in her jaws.

"You have a bad burn on your back," she mewed, setting down the moss. "Keep still and I'll dress it."

Hawkpaw turned to her with the beginnings of a snarl. He hadn't realized that he had been hurt; he still couldn't feel it. All the pain he felt was in his heart.

"I'm okay," he meowed to Frecklewish. "Leave me alone."

"No, you're not okay," Frecklewish persisted. "You need to let me—"

Hawkpaw sprang to his paws. "I said, leave me alone!" he growled with a lash of his tail.

At that, Frecklewish backed off, turning to see to Ebonyclaw's wounds instead. Echosong was still tending to Cloudpaw and Pebblepaw. Pebblepaw's parents, Sparrowpelt and Tinycloud, along with her littermate Parsleypaw, had settled down beside her, and were trying to comfort her.

Hawkpaw turned back to his mother to see that Sharpclaw had joined her, and was gently licking her ears. His green eyes were full of sorrow as he pressed himself against his mate's side.

Hawkpaw stood alone, staring at his brother's lifeless body.

At last Cherrytail rose to her paws and padded over to Hawkpaw, leaning against him. "Ebonyclaw told us what happened," she murmured. "I'm glad that you're okay. I know you did everything you could to save Duskpaw. It's not your fault that he's dead."

"But I—" Hawkpaw tried to interrupt, knowing very well that it *was* his fault.

"You're a hero for saving Pebblepaw," his mother assured

him. "It was very brave of you to rush into that fire."

Hawkpaw couldn't feel any sense of pride at his mother's words. And when he looked up at his father and saw Sharpclaw's face so full of grief, guilt rushed over him again so strongly that he could hardly stay on his paws.

Pain had begun to stab into Hawkpaw from the wound on his back, and he wished that he hadn't told Frecklewish to go away.

But then, maybe I deserve this pain.

"Hawkpaw!" The voice was Echosong's as she padded toward him. "Come back with me to the medicine cat den. You need to rest, and to let me see to that wound on your back."

Hawkpaw opened his jaws, but Echosong gave him no chance to protest. Though she was usually very calm, he knew that she put up with no nonsense from any cat. "You'll do as you're told," she meowed. "You're just an apprentice, and I'm your medicine cat. When I tell you to come with me, you come."

Too exhausted and heartsick to argue, Hawkpaw bowed his head and followed her.

Inside the medicine cat den, Pebblepaw and Cloudpaw were already stretched out asleep in nests of thick moss. Their chests rose and fell rhythmically as they breathed.

"How are they?" Hawkpaw asked, angling his ears toward the two she-cats.

"They're comfortable," Echosong replied. "They'll be okay—their burns aren't as bad as I thought at first. In a few days they'll be up and about again."

Hawkpaw's relief at hearing Echosong's reassurance was mingled with even more guilt. Knowing that Pebblepaw wasn't badly hurt reminded him of what he couldn't stop thinking. *What if I had gone to save Duskpaw first? Maybe Pebblepaw's injuries would have been a bit worse, but Duskpaw would still be alive!*

After a moment, Hawkpaw became aware that Echosong was watching him, her green eyes full of understanding, as if she could read his mind. Then she turned and took a poppy seed from the rock shelf where she stored her herbs.

"Eat this," she mewed, setting it in front of Hawkpaw. "It will calm you down. And you have to let me dress the burn on your back."

Hawkpaw wanted to give in. The wound felt small, but it hurt worse than anything he had felt in his life, a clawing pain that made him feel sick.

No! he decided. *I don't deserve to feel better!*

He began to back away from Echosong, but his body was giving way at last from his injuries and the smoke he had breathed in. He felt his legs buckle and a cloud seemed to swirl around him, blacker than the smoke. As he began to slide into unconsciousness he felt Echosong's gentle paws spread something soothing on his back.

The medicine cat's voice pulsed in his ears, saying something about a prophecy. But Hawkpaw couldn't make out the words, and in a moment the sound was swamped in his own desperate cry.

"I should have saved him first!"

His voice echoed in his own ears as he finally drifted into a painful, fitful sleep.

CHAPTER 3

❧

Hawkpaw scrambled to the top of the gorge and slipped into the long grass. The sun had cleared the tops of the trees, but shadows still lay among the rocks and in the undergrowth, and no cat had noticed him leaving the camp.

Several days had passed since the fire. The scent of smoke had faded from Hawkpaw's fur, and he could hardly feel the pain of his burn anymore. The vigil for Duskpaw was over.

But the tightness in Hawkpaw's chest hadn't eased. He couldn't forget how he had failed to save his brother. *Leafstar will make me a warrior today,* he thought. *I should be excited, but I'm not. I feel as if nothing good will ever happen again.* His heart was so heavy he could barely carry it.

Hawkpaw slid through the bushes until he reached the foot of the tree where Duskpaw had been buried. As he stood over the mound of earth, a wave of guilt and sorrow swept over him.

"You shouldn't be there, beneath the dirt," he mewed aloud. He remembered how lively and mischievous his brother had been, and now he was lying still and silent, with soil clotting in his ginger fur. "You should be here with me . . . about to become a warrior!"

In the days since Duskpaw died, every cat had kept on telling him how brave he had been to rescue Pebblepaw. But Hawkpaw didn't want to hear that, because it only reminded him of how he hadn't rescued his brother. Not in time, anyway.

Hawkpaw stood beside his brother's grave, his head bowed, until he heard Leafstar's voice rising from the gorge, faint with the distance but still ringing out clearly.

"Let all cats old enough to catch their own prey join here beneath the Rockpile for a Clan meeting!"

"Good-bye, Duskpaw," Hawkpaw murmured. "I'll never forget you. And I'll never forget that I could have saved you. I'm so sorry."

Then he turned and headed back to the gorge.

By the time Hawkpaw had clambered down the trail the rest of his Clan had assembled in front of the Rockpile, beside the water that cascaded endlessly out of the black hole beneath the boulders. Leafstar stood on top of the rocks, with her deputy, Sharpclaw, beside her. Blossompaw and Cloudpaw emerged to stand at the front of the crowd of cats, their expressions a mixture of excitement and nervousness. Their mentors, Bouncefire and Plumwillow, followed and halted just behind them, and as Hawkwing padded across the sandy floor of the camp to join them, Ebonyclaw slipped into her place with the others.

"Cats of SkyClan, today we have gathered together for one of the most important events in the life of a Clan," Leafstar began, her head raised proudly. "The making of new warriors. Plumwillow, Bouncefire, Ebonyclaw, have your apprentices learned the skills of a warrior? And do they understand the importance of the warrior code in the life of a Clan?"

"Cloudpaw has worked hard to understand all that," Plumwillow responded.

Bouncefire gave a brisk nod. "So has Blossompaw."

"And Hawkpaw," Ebonyclaw added.

Hawkpaw's heart lurched. *Yes, I worked hard, but what good was that to Duskpaw? I don't deserve this!*

Leafstar dipped her head approvingly and leaped down from the Rockpile to stand in front of the three apprentices. Beckoning with her tail, she summoned Cloudpaw to her.

Cloudpaw stepped forward shakily. Hawkpaw knew that though she was recovering well from her injuries, she still hadn't built up all her strength, and it was hard for her to stand for long. He forced himself to push aside his grief for Duskpaw, knowing that Cloudpaw was grieving for their littermate too, and to focus on what was happening.

This is one of the most important moments of Cloudpaw's life. I don't want to miss it.

Standing over Cloudpaw, Leafstar repeated the words that Clan leaders had used for season upon season, every time an apprentice was made into a warrior, since the first Clans were formed.

"I, Leafstar, leader of SkyClan, call upon my warrior ancestors to look down on this apprentice. She has trained hard to understand the ways of your noble code, and I commend her to you as a warrior in her turn." Turning to Cloudpaw, meeting her gaze directly, she continued, "Cloudpaw, do you promise to uphold the warrior code and to protect and defend this Clan, even at the cost of your life?"

Hawkpaw's heart lurched again as he heard the phrase "at the cost of your life." *Duskpaw never got the chance to take this oath,* he reflected. *He never got the honor of losing his life to protect his Clan. Instead he lost it trying to get a few scraps of Twoleg food. Somehow, that makes it worse . . . and Cloudpaw must be thinking the same thing.*

Cloudpaw looked up at her Clan leader, pausing for a moment. Then she spoke, and her voice was fervent as she replied, "I do."

"Then by the powers of StarClan," Leafstar went on, "I give you your warrior name. Cloudpaw, from this moment you will be known as Cloudmist. StarClan honors your courage and your resilience, and we welcome you as a full warrior of SkyClan."

Leafstar rested her muzzle on the top of Cloudmist's head, and Cloudmist licked her shoulder in response.

"Cloudmist! Cloudmist!" the SkyClan cats yowled, greeting the warrior with her new name.

Leafstar waited for the noise to die down, then touched Cloudmist's shoulder with the tip of her tail. "Because of your injuries," she meowed, "you need not sit vigil tonight. You still belong in the medicine cat den, until you have finished recovering."

As every cat murmured agreement, Cloudmist dipped her head and moved back to sit with her mother, Cherrytail, who gave her ear a proud lick.

Next, Leafstar beckoned Blossompaw to stand in front of

her. Hawkpaw listened as the ceremony was repeated and she was given the name of Blossomheart.

"StarClan honors your courage and fighting skill," Leafstar finished, "and we welcome you as a full warrior of SkyClan."

"Blossomheart! Blossomheart!"

Looking proud and happy, Blossomheart licked her Clan leader's shoulder, and withdrew to stand with her Clanmates.

Nervousness tingled through Hawkpaw, briefly overcoming even his sorrow for Duskpaw, as he realized that now it was his turn. It wasn't only because every cat's gaze would be on him as he went through the ceremony. But he was suddenly aware that a massive change was hovering over his life, like an eagle about to swoop on its prey. He wasn't a kit anymore, and the prospect of taking his place in his Clan as a full warrior was as overwhelming as if the cascade of water from beneath the Rockpile had caught him and swept him away.

I wish Duskpaw could see this, he thought. *He always had a joke to make. I wonder what he would say if he were here now.*

But Hawkpaw couldn't begin to imagine that. Because Duskpaw *wasn't* there, he was under a pile of earth. *He'll never be here again.* Hawkpaw knew that being a warrior wouldn't be any fun without his littermate.

Hawkpaw padded forward to stand in front of Leafstar. She greeted him with a dip of her head, and called on StarClan to look down on him. Then she turned and asked him to take the oath.

"Hawkpaw, do you promise to uphold the warrior code and to protect and defend this Clan, even at the cost of your life?"

Everything that was in Hawkpaw—his guilt and grief for his brother's death, his determination to honor his memory by becoming the best warrior that he could—surged into his voice as he replied, "I do."

"Then by the powers of StarClan," Leafstar continued, "I give you your warrior name. Hawkpaw, from this moment you will be known as Hawkwing. StarClan honors your courage and your bravery, and we welcome you as a full warrior of Sky-Clan."

Courage and bravery? Hawkwing thought. *Aren't they sort of the same thing?* He wondered whether Leafstar thought that there was only one good thing about him. *And am I really even that brave?*

As the Clan acclaimed him by his new name, Hawkwing felt his pelt prickle under some cat's gaze and spotted Sharp-claw staring at him. Ever since Duskpaw's death, Sharpclaw had been cold, and though he had never said as much, Hawk-wing knew that his father blamed him just as he blamed himself. He raised his head to look directly at Sharpclaw, and knew that he was thinking of Duskpaw too: Duskpaw, who would never have another name, who would never be anything but dead.

Cherrytail padded over to the three new warriors, nuzzling each of them in turn. "Congratulations," she meowed. "I'm so proud of you."

But Hawkwing felt a fresh pang of pain to see the sadness in his mother's eyes. And when Sharpclaw leaped down from the Rockpile to join them, he stood by silently, and scarcely looked at Hawkwing.

"Hey, Hawkwing!"

At the sound of his name, Hawkwing felt a tiny flicker of pride. It was the first time any cat had really used the new name. Then he turned, and his heart grew cold as he saw that the cat speaking was Pebblepaw.

Since the fire, Hawkwing had barely spoken to her. He could hardly stand to look at her. *She's always so cocky and arrogant and pleased with herself. . . .*

Then he realized that she seemed different now from how she had been before the fire. *Since then, she hasn't made a single snarky remark to me.*

"I want to thank you for rescuing me," she meowed, a look of genuine gratitude in her eyes. "I was trapped, and you saved my life. What Leafstar said about you is true. You really are brave and courageous. I'm so happy to be alive, and it's all because of you."

Hawkwing stared at her, unsure how to respond. He noticed that she still had a poultice of honey and comfrey on one of her paws, but apart from that she looked as strong and healthy as ever. *She's doing much better than Cloudmist.*

Somehow the realization made anger throb through Hawkwing from ears to tail-tip. He tried to choke out, "You're welcome," because he knew that was what he was supposed to say. But his throat felt as if it was full of ash, and his anger rose until he felt it must burst out of him.

How dare she stand there looking so healthy and happy, when my brother is dead?

Hawkwing didn't feel proud of his warrior name anymore. He didn't even feel sad about Duskpaw. Everything within him had been overwhelmed by his fury.

"I wish I hadn't saved you!" he blurted out. "I wish I'd gone for my brother first. Then maybe he'd still be alive!"

The gratitude in Pebblepaw's face drained away, and her eyes widened in dismay. For a moment she looked crushed. Then her gaze hardened as she stared at Hawkwing, and she shook her head. Without another word she spun around and stalked away.

CHAPTER 4

The dawn patrol had left some time before, and the red glow in the sky told Hawkwing that the sun had risen, though its rays had not yet cleared the top of the gorge. Shivering, he shook out his pelt and rose to his paws to arch his back in a long stretch. The night of his vigil was almost over.

His sister Blossomheart, a few tail-lengths away, had started to groom herself, licking one paw and passing it over her face. After a moment she paused, and parted her jaws in a massive yawn.

"I could sleep for a moon!" she whispered.

New warriors guarding the camp were not supposed to speak to each other, but on the night before, when they started their vigil, Hawkwing had been unable to resist murmuring a few words into his sister's ear.

"I miss Duskpaw so much. I wish he could be keeping vigil with us."

"I miss him too," Blossomheart had responded. "He should be here."

After that, there was nothing to do but keep watch for invaders. And since no invaders appeared, Hawkwing had the whole of the night to sit and think.

Now, as the red sun peeked over the rim of the gorge, he was beginning to feel guilty about the way he had treated Pebblepaw. The thought of her still filled him with despair and anger, but now he began to wonder if it was unfair to blame *her* for the decision he had made and the way he felt now. *It was my choice,* he told himself. *My responsibility.* Even so, his guilt over exploding at her was only one drop in the vast pool of guilt that was his heart.

As the whole circle of the sun appeared above the cliff, warriors began to emerge from their den, stretching before making their slow way down the trails. Leafstar appeared from her den and beckoned some of her cats around her, speaking quickly.

I wonder what all that's about, Hawkwing thought drowsily.

A moment later the group dispersed, the warriors heading more purposefully to the bottom of the gorge. Sandynose broke from the group and walked up to Hawkwing and Blossomheart.

"Your vigil is over," the light brown tom announced. "Come and join the others by the Rockpile. Leafstar is calling a Clan meeting."

Another one? Hawkwing was puzzled. *Why? We all just met yesterday for the warrior ceremony.*

The rest of the Clan began to gather around as Leafstar leaped up to the top of the Rockpile. She was followed by Sharpclaw, and also, Hawkwing noticed with a prickle of curiosity, by Echosong the medicine cat.

"Let all cats old enough to catch their own prey join here beneath the Rockpile for a Clan meeting!" Leafstar yowled.

One or two remaining warriors stuck their heads out of their den, then hurried down the trail to join their Clanmates. Harveymoon, Macgyver, and Ebonyclaw, the daylight warriors, appeared at the top of the cliff and leaped from rock to rock to gather with the others.

"I'm glad we left early!" Macgyver panted as he raced past Hawkwing and Blossomheart. "We might have missed this!"

Birdwing appeared at the entrance to the nursery with Mintfur and Honeytail, all three she-cats looking down at their leader on the Rockpile. Birdwing's kits frisked around her paws, sometimes getting perilously close to the edge of the trail, until their mother gathered them closer with a sweep of her tail.

Pebblepaw and Parsleypaw poked their heads curiously out of the apprentices' den, then bounded down to the bottom of the gorge and found a place to sit close to the edge of the river.

Finally the dawn patrol—Tinycloud, Sparrowpelt, and Bellapaw—returned, appearing at the far side of the gorge and making their way down into the crowd of cats.

When all the Clan was assembled, Leafstar began to speak, her amber gaze traveling over her cats; Hawkwing thought that he could detect trouble in her eyes, and his pads pricked with apprehension.

"Echosong received a prophecy from StarClan a few sunrises ago," the brown-and-cream-colored she-cat meowed. "It will affect the whole future of our Clan. I have thought deeply about this, and I feel that it is time to share her vision with you." She took a step back and waved her tail as a sign for Echosong to speak.

The silver tabby medicine cat hesitated, her gaze seeming fixed on something far away. Then she gave her pelt a brisk shake.

"A few days ago I went to the Whispering Cave, to speak with the spirits of our warrior ancestors," she began. "A pale gray tom appeared to me in a dream. I had never seen him before, but he told me that his name was Skystar, and he was the ancient founder of our Clan."

Hawkwing caught his breath. How many seasons must have passed since SkyClan first came to be, and yet a Clan leader could still appear out of the far past to speak to their medicine cat!

"Skystar told me, 'The fire has burned out, but to dispel the darkness you must find the spark that remains,'" Echosong meowed.

"And what does *that* mean?" Sharpclaw asked with an irritated twitch of his tail.

"I believe that 'the fire that has burned out' must refer to Firestar, the great leader of ThunderClan," Echosong responded.

Firestar, who restored SkyClan after we were scattered and almost destroyed! Hawkwing thought, his wonder growing. *Firestar who was Ravenpaw's friend. Every kit knows that story!*

The concern in Leafstar's expression grew deeper. "I don't want to believe that Firestar is dead . . ." she murmured.

Echosong dipped her head sadly. "I don't see what else Sky-star's words could mean," she continued. "And if that's true, then 'the spark that remains' could well be Firestar's kin in ThunderClan. That must mean that we're being told to seek out ThunderClan, and perhaps the other Clans, too. Perhaps it's time for SkyClan to go home. . . ."

"Really?" Sharpclaw lashed his tail; Hawkwing could see how much he hated Echosong's suggestion. "And just how do you suggest we do that? We know that the Clans have moved away from where they lived when Firestar came to us. How are we supposed to find them now?"

Echosong remained calm in the face of the deputy's objection. "I doubt StarClan would send us on a journey we could not complete," she mewed. "We can seek out Barley, the farm cat who was Ravenpaw's friend, and ask him if he knows where the Clans' camps are now."

"That's exactly what we should do!" Bellapaw called out from where she sat at the foot of the Rockpile.

"Barley will be glad to help," her brother Rileypaw agreed.

They're Barley's kin, Hawkwing thought. *They know him better than any cat. But even if he can help us, is this really what we're being asked to do?*

Silence fell among the Clan, the cats exchanging glances of mingled confusion and dismay. Hawkwing felt as bewildered as his Clanmates. *StarClan can't possibly mean to send us wandering away from here. The gorge is our home. Why would we want to leave it?*

Leafstar had stepped forward again and was about to speak when the silence was broken by Sagenose.

"This is all very well," he declared, "but surely there is a simpler answer. This prophecy must be about the fire that just happened. It can't be a coincidence that the fire broke out at the same time that Echosong had her vision."

"Maybe there's something left over at the Twoleg green-place where the fire happened," Plumwillow suggested. "Maybe Skystar wants us to find it."

Echosong shook her head. "It's true that I had the vision on the same day that the fire happened, but—"

"Was StarClan predicting the fire?" Nettlesplash asked, leaping to his paws.

Hawkwing felt as though a rock had plummeted out of an empty sky and landed on top of him.

Sharpclaw let out a low growl. "Quiet down, all of you, and let Echosong finish."

The Clan obeyed him, though there was still a stir of movement and muttered comments following Nettlesplash's question. Hawkwing felt a tightness in his chest. *Did Echosong know about the fire before it happened? And she kept it to herself?* He tensed every muscle as though he was creeping up on prey as he listened to the medicine cat's reply.

"I believe that 'the fire has burned out' refers to Firestar's death, and not a real fire," Echosong meowed. "I don't think that Skystar—"

This time it was Tinycloud who interrupted. "If this proph-ecy is about some cat with fire in their name, then maybe it refers to Firefern or Bouncefire."

Bouncefire puffed his chest out at the thought of being

mentioned in a prophecy, while Firefern, looking disturbed, opened her jaws to reply.

But Hawkwing couldn't hold himself in any longer. Before Firefern could speak, he sprang to his paws. "If you knew about the prophecy," he cried out to Echosong, "why didn't you warn any cat? You think it's just a coincidence that you received this prophecy on the morning of the great fire, and they're not connected? That doesn't make any sense! StarClan warned you about the fire, and—"

"StarClan has always worked in mysterious ways," Echosong cut in. "By the time I awoke from the dream, it was already too late. When I came out of the Whispering Cave, I could smell smoke, and by the time the smoke reached our camp the fire was already blazing. It was only moments later that you and the others returned with Duskpaw. Hawkwing, believe me, I understand how you feel. But not even a medicine cat can go back in time."

Her words had no more effect on Hawkwing than the cawing of rooks high in the branches of a tree. *That's unfair! Why would StarClan send a prophecy too late for Echosong to do anything? Duskpaw needn't have died!* "What's the point of having prophecies if they can't prevent anything terrible?" he asked bitterly.

Echosong's voice grew gentle, and her beautiful eyes were full of compassion. "Hawkwing, I'm really sorry about what happened to your brother. It is a terrible tragedy. But this prophecy is not about him."

"How *can* it not be about him?" Hawkwing demanded, his heart pounding as if it would break out of his chest. His shoulder fur was bristling and he slid out his claws. He wanted to leap on Echosong as if she were his enemy, and if she had not been standing above him on the Rockpile, he might have done it. "The prophecy spoke of a fire, and Duskpaw died in one!"

"Hawkwing, that's enough!" Sharpclaw stepped forward and gazed down at his son. "Echosong is our medicine cat. She deserves your respect."

His sharp tones made Hawkwing feel embarrassed. He was too old to be scolded like that in front of the entire Clan. He said no more—he could barely speak. His whole body seemed to burn with shame and anger.

"Prophecies can't prevent *every* terrible thing," Echosong explained. "But they can certainly help prevent *some* terrible things. And if StarClan tells us that we must find Firestar's kin, then it's up to SkyClan to listen—or who knows what might happen?" Her words fell into silence; every cat in the Clan had their gaze trained on her.

Finally Leafstar raised her tail, and spoke into the silence. "I will consider sending a few cats on a quest to look for Firestar's kin," she announced. "But before that, a patrol will go to the scene of the fire just in case there's anything in the embers."

"And what if there's nothing to be found?" Sharpclaw asked.

"Then we will be sure that Echosong's prophecy did *not* refer to the real fire," Leafstar responded. "Sandynose, you will lead the patrol. Take Plumwillow and Hawkwing with you."

Hawkwing was startled to be chosen for the patrol. *Surely Leafstar must be furious with me?* Then he realized that his Clan leader must want him of all cats to be certain that there was nothing important at the scene of the fire, and that the prophecy had nothing to do with Duskpaw's death.

Leafstar dismissed the meeting, and the other cats began to disperse. Sandynose and Plumwillow came to join Hawkwing.

"You haven't eaten or slept," Sandynose meowed as he padded up. "We don't have to go right now, if you want some fresh-kill and then take a nap."

"No, I'm fine." Hawkwing's paws were itching to get moving. "If we need to find the spark that remains, who is to say it won't blow away soon? How do we know it hasn't blown away already?"

"Okay." Sandynose gave a brisk nod, and led the way up the trail to the top of the gorge.

As he followed, Hawkwing realized part of the reason why he had been so hostile to Echosong. *I want to believe that the prophecy was about the fire. Then it wouldn't be all my fault that Duskpaw died, because it would have been destined in the stars.* But he realized too that even if that was true, it made no difference. *Duskpaw is still dead.*

"I think the prophecy *must* have something to do with the fire," Plumwillow meowed as the patrol set out across the scrubby grass toward the Twoleg greenplace. "I mean, why would StarClan send us off to find the other Clans, when we're doing well right where we are?"

"True," Sandynose responded. "That would be mouse-brained."

Hawkwing remained quiet, barely listening to his Clanmates' chatter. As they drew closer to the Twoleg greenplace, he began to pick up traces of the terrible smell of burning. He flinched, needing to pause for a moment with his eyes tight shut, as all the memories of that dreadful day came rushing back. He could hear the anguished cries of the trapped cats, and almost see Duskpaw's scared face through the smoke.

Forcing himself into motion again, Hawkwing caught up with his Clanmates. When the Twoleg greenplace came into sight, he could see that most of the debris from the fire had been cleared away, probably by Twolegs. The Twoleg rock was gone, and so was the fallen tree branch. All that remained were a stretch of earth where the grass had burned away, part of the burned tree, and scorch marks on the trash can.

The three cats padded over the site of the fire, carefully examining everything. Sandynose and Plumwillow went on discussing the prophecy, but Hawkwing wasn't interested. He was focused on finding something—anything—that might be "the spark that remains." But the search didn't take long, because there was hardly anything left to search.

"There's nothing here but charred earth and a bad smell," Sandynose declared with a sigh. "Echosong is probably right."

"Yes," Plumwillow agreed. "The prophecy must be about Firestar's kin—the other Clan cats."

Hawkwing remained quiet. He was still unsure about the prophecy, and the image of Duskpaw, trapped and terrified, kept flashing into his head.

"Let's go back," Sandynose meowed.

"Okay. And maybe we can pick up some prey on the way," Plumwillow suggested. "Coming, Hawkwing?"

Hawkwing shook his head. "No, you can go on without me. I'll follow you in a few moments."

As he watched his Clanmates retreating in the direction of the gorge, Hawkwing reflected how strange it felt to be allowed to say that. *I don't have to go back with them, because I'm not an apprentice anymore. It's okay for me to be out here alone.*

Once his companions had vanished, Hawkwing turned to face the stretch of scarred earth.

Even though his brother was buried under the tree at the top of the gorge, Hawkwing felt closer to him here, the last place Duskpaw was alive. *And it's a place he loved—because of all those scraps of Twoleg food.*

"Duskpaw," he mewed aloud, his voice thick with emotion, "I'm so sorry I didn't save you. I'm so sorry that you never got to be a warrior."

As Hawkwing stood there, silently grieving, the scent of another cat drifted into his nose. Startled, he turned to see a strange cat only a tail-length away. His heart pounded, and he twitched his ears, uncomfortable to realize he'd been over-heard. *How did he manage to creep up on me like that?*

The cat scent must have been covered up by the smell from the smoke and fire, he thought, turning his attention to the intruder.

He was a strong, muscular tom, with white fur broken up with black spots, and a long black tail. His expression was friendly as he dipped his head to Hawkwing. But this was a cat Hawkwing had never smelled or seen before.

"Hi," he meowed. "My name is Darktail. I don't mean to interrupt you, but I'm wondering if you're a Clan cat."

A Clan cat? For a moment Hawkwing was silent, not sure how to reply, or what this strange cat wanted. *Why do you want to know?*

"I'm sorry, I wasn't trying to eavesdrop," Darktail continued, glancing down as though embarrassed, "but I heard you talking to your Clanmates. And I couldn't help overhearing that you were talking to some cat who wasn't there. The fire was a terrible tragedy, wasn't it? Did you lose some cat you loved?"

Hawkwing had begun to bristle when Darktail confirmed that he had overheard what he'd said to Duskpaw. *That was private!* But the white tom's voice was so sympathetic that Hawkwing forced his shoulder fur to lie flat again.

"Yes, I lost my brother," he replied.

"I'm so sorry," Darktail meowed. "You know, I was caught in that fire too."

Hawkwing's pads began to prickle with suspicion. *I didn't see you here!* "You don't look injured," he pointed out.

"Well, I wasn't exactly *in* the fire," Darktail explained. "I was resting, in those bushes over there." He gestured with his tail. Hawkwing looked to the bushes, which he knew he had walked past on his way to the Twoleg rock. How had he not seen a sleeping rogue? Then he guessed that he'd been so worried about his Clanmates, he just wasn't paying attention to anything else.

"I breathed in a lot of smoke," Darktail continued. "It made me weak and confused, and I even passed out for a while," he added, letting out a feeble cough. "And I haven't been able to travel on because I can't breathe very well, and I get tired quickly when I move around. I was wondering . . ." He paused, ducking his head in embarrassment.

"What?" Hawkwing asked. *What does this cat want?*

"Well, I know that Clan cats keep herbs for medicine," Darktail replied. "Could you possibly give me something to help with my breathing? I've had trouble hunting, because I'm so weak. If you could, I'd repay you for your kindness."

It was strange, but Hawkwing felt an odd connection to this newcomer. Darktail had been injured in the same fire that killed Duskpaw. He, too, had suffered because of Twoleg foolishness. A sudden compulsion to help pricked every hair on his pelt. Somehow, Hawkwing thought, it would be like fighting the fire all over again, and this time, he could win.

I can't take a strange cat into camp, but maybe I can get Echosong to bring him some herbs to help him. Surely she'll do that, when Darktail was injured in the same fire that killed Duskpaw?

"I'll go and get a medicine cat who might be able to help you," he told Darktail.

"I'll come with you," the white tom responded instantly.

"No, you should stay here," Hawkwing objected. "It's too far for an injured cat." He also didn't want to bring a strange cat onto Clan territory without permission, but Darktail didn't need to know that.

"Please . . . I *must* come with you," Darktail insisted, moving toward Hawkwing with wide, pleading eyes. Hawkwing stepped back, startled.

Darktail dipped his head. "I'm sorry. I don't mean to be

demanding. It's just, I can't bear to stay alone among the charred remains anymore. It's too terrible to be here with the smell and the memory—" He choked and went on, "The memory of the horrible things that happened. I only stayed because I heard there were Clan cats around here, and I hoped to meet one of you. I'm just so relieved to find you! But don't worry, I won't come into your camp unless I'm invited."

Hawkwing took in the strange cat's serious, hopeful expression. "I understand," he murmured finally. *Surely no cat can take issue with my showing him to our border—not after what he's been through.*

Side by side, the two cats headed toward the gorge. Hawkwing set a slow pace because of Darktail's breathing problems, but even so the white tom had to stop two or three times to catch his breath.

I'm glad I found him, Hawkwing thought as they padded into the undergrowth at the top of the gorge. *We went back to the Twoleg greenplace, looking for clues about the prophecy, and I found a cat looking for help.* Excitement tingled through Hawkwing from ears to tail-tip. *Maybe Darktail is a clue . . . Maybe he is "the spark that remains," and I was meant to find him!*

"Stay here," he told Darktail when they reached the edge of the cliff. "I'll go and find our medicine cat." He felt embarrassed at the thought of seeking out Echosong so soon after arguing with her at the Rockpile, but he knew it had to be done.

Echosong was in her den, sorting out herbs while Cloudmist slept curled up in her mossy nest. The medicine cat looked up as Hawkwing paused at the entrance to the den.

"Hi, Hawkwing," she mewed. "Can I help you?"

If she was still upset about their argument, she didn't show it, greeting Hawkwing with the same calm friendliness she showed to every cat. Hawkwing's embarrassment faded.

"I stayed behind at the greenplace after the others left," he told Echosong, "and I met a strange cat there. He was injured in the fire, too, and he doesn't have a Clan to take care of him. I thought he might be somehow connected to the prophecy."

Echosong's green eyes narrowed thoughtfully, but all she said was, "How was he injured?"

"He breathed in too much smoke."

"Coltsfoot for that," Echosong murmured, sorting through her herbs until she found some of the dried flowers. "Come on," she added, picking up two stems in her jaws, "show me where he is."

Darktail was waiting where Hawkwing had left him, under a tree at the top of the gorge. Echosong looked wary as she approached him and set the coltsfoot down in front of him. "Eat one now," she told him with a dip of her head, "and the other one at sunhigh."

"Thank you," Darktail meowed, swallowing the first stem. "It's great how you Clan cats look after each other. It must really make a difference, being part of a Clan."

"How do you know about the Clans?" Echosong asked, her eyes narrowing.

"When I was a young cat, I knew some groups of cats who lived in a forest," Darktail replied. "They all had their own territory, and each cat had its own duties, and they had a special cat who healed them."

"So you've *met* Clan cats?" Echosong asked, her ears perking up with excitement and curiosity. "You've seen them before?"

"Sure I have. All the Clans had different names, and I think one of them was called . . . something like ThunderClan?"

Hawkwing's belly lurched as the white tom named Firestar's Clan. *He really must be part of the prophecy!* He listened as Echosong, intensely interested now, went on questioning the newcomer. Darktail certainly seemed to know a lot about the Clans, as much as any loner would know who had spent some time living near them. Hawkwing could tell that Echosong suspected he might be able to help SkyClan find Firestar's kin. And he realized that perhaps *both* meanings of the prophecy were correct.

Maybe Darktail and ThunderClan are both "the spark that remains." The fire led me to Darktail, and now Darktail is going to lead us to Firestar's kin.

Finally, Echosong turned to Hawkwing. "Go and ask Leafstar to come up here," she ordered him.

As he headed down the trail toward Leafstar's den, Hawkwing's fur fluffed up with importance at the thought that he was fetching the Clan leader to talk to a cat that *he* had brought back from the site of the fire.

When he reached Leafstar's den, his father, Sharpclaw, was there with her. The two cats were talking quietly with their heads close together, and Hawkwing guessed that they were discussing what to do about the prophecy.

He waited quietly by the entrance until Leafstar looked up and noticed him.

"Yes, Hawkwing?" she mewed. "What can I do for you?"

Dipping his head politely, Hawkwing explained how he had met Darktail, and how Echosong was talking to the stranger at the top of the gorge. "He seems to know a lot about the Clans," he finished. "Echosong thinks you should hear what he has to say."

Leafstar nodded. "Of course. This sounds interesting."

"I'll come with you," Sharpclaw added.

Hawkwing was pleased that his father wanted to talk to the newcomer as well. *Maybe he'll finally think that I've done something right!*

Darktail was sitting under the same tree when Hawkwing returned with the Clan leader and deputy. Echosong was pacing to and fro a couple of tail-lengths away, her expression deeply thoughtful. She halted and turned back to Darktail when Leafstar appeared.

"Tell Leafstar what you told me," she directed.

Darktail dipped his head respectfully to the Clan leader, and repeated what he had said earlier about the Clans.

"Thank you, Darktail," Leafstar meowed when he had finished. Her expression was warm. "Please come down into the camp and share our prey. Our hunting patrols have just returned, and there's plenty for every cat. Then you can spend the night in the medicine cat's den and get some rest." She paused, then added, "If what you say is true, then you have given us all a very great gift."

Leafstar would never invite Darktail into camp unless she thought he could be a great help to SkyClan. In spite of his grief about his brother, Hawkwing felt every hair on his pelt tingle with pride that he had brought something useful back from the site of the fire.

As he padded down the trail into the gorge, bringing up the rear behind his father, Hawkwing suddenly felt shaky with exhaustion, and his belly was bawling for food. Until then, the excitement of the morning, of discovering Darktail, had driven his night's vigil and his hunger out of his mind. But now he could feel every moment that he had stayed awake.

I could fall asleep on my paws if I wasn't starving!

Once he reached the camp he split off from Darktail and the others, then bounded over to the fresh-kill pile and picked out a juicy-looking mouse, gulping it down in huge mouthfuls. Then, with a nod at the injured cat, he headed for his new nest in the warriors' den.

As he curled up and closed his eyes he felt a tiny hint of hope for the first time in days, like a light flickering in the depths of a dark forest.

CHAPTER 5

❧

Hawkwing padded over to the foot of the Rockpile to join Billystorm, Waspwhisker, and Pebblepaw. Several days had passed
since he had discovered Darktail near the site of the fire, and
from the information he had given to Leafstar and Echosong,
it seemed as if the other Clans might be only a journey of two
or three sunrises away. The whole Clan had been delighted by
that news, and Leafstar had decided to send a patrol at once.
Hawkwing still couldn't believe that he had been chosen. It
was his first quest away from camp, and it might have been the
most important quest any SkyClan cat had ever undertaken.
He felt a tingling shiver of excitement slip down his spine to
think that they might be only a few sunrises from meeting the
other Clans, and fulfilling StarClan's prophecy.

"Hawkwing!" Billystorm meowed as Hawkwing joined the
group. "It's good to have you along. We're only waiting for
Blossomheart now."

Hawkwing felt his pelt prickle with hostility as he glanced at
Billystorm's apprentice, Pebblepaw, standing beside her mentor. He felt resentful from ears to tail-tip that she was coming
with them, and that Billystorm had specially asked Leafstar to

add her to the patrol. Seeing how Pebblepaw was completely recovered now just made him remember that Duskpaw *wasn't*. He couldn't imagine how he would stand being so close to her for days on end.

She's only an apprentice, he grumbled to himself. *She probably won't be any use at all!*

Blossomheart bounded up to join the patrol just as Leaf-star and Sharpclaw padded up to say good-bye, followed by Cherrytail, Echosong, Parsleypaw, and a few more SkyClan cats. Darktail was with them; he had begged Leafstar to be allowed to join the patrol, but Echosong had pointed out that he still wasn't fit to travel any distance.

"I wish I was coming with you," he meowed. "Billystorm, you remember the directions I gave you?"

"I do," Billystorm replied. "And I hope by the time we get back you'll be well again."

"Thanks." Darktail ducked his head. "I'm so grateful that you've accepted me into your camp."

He deserves it, Hawkwing thought, pride warming his pelt. *He's told us so much that we really need to know. We're so lucky I found him!*

"It's time we were going." Billystorm gestured with his tail for the patrol to gather together. "Is every cat ready?"

Hawkwing touched noses with his mother to say good-bye.

"Be careful," Cherrytail warned him. "And hurry back. I can't wait to hear what you find out about the other Clans."

"Especially ThunderClan," Sharpclaw added, looking down at his son with a gleam of approval in his green eyes. "I find it hard to believe that Firestar is dead."

"We'll find out for you!" Blossomheart assured him.

"Then farewell," Leafstar meowed. "And may StarClan light your path."

Billystorm led the way up the trail to the top of the gorge and through the undergrowth to the stretch of scrubby open ground that separated SkyClan territory from the Twolegplace. The sun shone and the air was still; the only sound was the gentle humming of bees, and the swish of grasses as the cats brushed their way through.

"Darktail says we have to go straight to the Twolegplace and through it," Billystorm meowed. "We—"

"I don't like the idea of traveling through the Twolegplace." Blossomheart sounded as if she was trying hard not to show nervousness. "Twolegs are bad news."

Billystorm flicked her gently over one ear with the tip of his tail. "Some of them are okay, and most of them won't bother us. I can spot a bad Twoleg right away. Plus," he added, "I still know my way through the Twolegplace."

"So where do we go after that?" Hawkwing asked eagerly.

"We cross a Thunderpath, then look for a tree that splits into three," Billystorm went on. "From there we turn and head toward the setting sun. We'll know we're going the right way when we come to a clearing ringed with trees, with a small stream running through it. According to Darktail, there's an abandoned badgers' den there. The Clan cats are two days' journey beyond that."

"That sounds straightforward enough," Waspwhisker commented, then twitched his whiskers. "I can't wait to get there! How exciting to meet the other Clans, after all these seasons apart."

"Yeah, we might get to meet Firestar," Pebblepaw mewed hopefully.

He's dead, mouse-brain, Hawkwing thought, but said nothing aloud; he didn't even want to speak to Pebblepaw.

"Yes, we don't know for sure he's dead," Billystorm responded. "And his kin must still be alive in ThunderClan."

"And Sandstorm," Waspwhisker added. "The she-cat who came to SkyClan along with Firestar. She was brave too."

Blossomheart gave a little bounce. "This is so exciting!"

"Leafstar told me stuff about the Clans that Firestar told her," Billystorm went on. "He said all the other Clans think that ThunderClan is bossy, and its cats always believe they're right."

"If Firestar was their leader, they probably *are* always right," Pebblepaw observed. "Firestar was such a hero!"

"I heard some of those stories too," Waspwhisker mewed. "WindClan cats are fast runners, RiverClan cats swim like fishes, and—"

"And you can't trust ShadowClan cats as far as you could throw them," Billystorm finished. "I wonder if that's true?"

Pebblepaw was silent for a moment, padding alongside her mentor, then meowed, "Do you think it'll be a *good* thing, being around a bunch of other cats who tell us what to do? SkyClan is used to going its own way."

"That's mouse-brained," Hawkwing responded curtly, unable to resist the chance to contradict Pebblepaw. "We'll be stronger if we're all together."

Pebblepaw fluffed up her neck fur and opened her jaws for a retort, but she was interrupted by Blossomheart.

"Ooh, look!" the ginger-and-white she-cat exclaimed. "That cloud up there—it looks just like a cat with a long curly tail!"

Great StarClan, are they all mouse-brained? Hawkwing thought irritably. "I don't see why you're in such high spirits," he snapped at his sister. "Not after everything that's happened."

Blossomheart flinched away from him, her gaze clouding. Hawkwing was immediately sorry that he had hurt her feelings. He knew very well that she was still grieving for Duskpaw.

"I didn't mean—" he began.

He broke off as Pebblepaw thrust herself between him and Blossomheart, with a savage glance at Hawkwing. "*I* think it's a perfectly beautiful cloud," she mewed. "And it looks *just* like a cat!"

The two she-cats padded on side by side, behind the older warriors, and Hawkwing brought up the rear, silently seething. *It's all Pebblepaw's fault! With her around, I can't think straight.*

Before they reached the Twolegplace, Billystorm halted beside a small copse of beech trees, not far from the first of the Twoleg dens.

"We might as well hunt here," he meowed, "before we head into the Twolegplace. There'll be slim pickings there."

Hawkwing's jaws watered at the thought of prey. He had eaten a sparrow at dawn, and Echosong had given traveling herbs to all the questing cats, but he knew better than to turn down a chance to eat. Who knew how much prey they would find when they left their territory. He padded cautiously into the copse, his jaws parted to taste the air.

He dropped into the hunter's crouch as he picked up the scent of a mouse and spotted it nibbling something at the foot of a nearby tree. He began to creep up on it, remembering to set his paws down as light as falling leaves, but as he tensed, ready to pounce, he felt the brush of fur against his pelt and spotted Pebblepaw heading past him toward the same tree.

She's so young and stupid she didn't even scent it! Hawkwing thought as his mouse scuttled off and disappeared among the roots. *It would have to be* her, *ruining my hunt!*

At the same moment that the mouse vanished, Hawkwing heard paw steps scampering through the grass, and spotted a squirrel with Blossomheart in hot pursuit. The squirrel started to swarm up the tree trunk, but Pebblepaw was in the right place. She leaped after it, dug her claws into its back and brought it down, where she killed it with a swift bite to its throat.

"Thank you, StarClan, for this prey," she meowed, her eyes shining with triumph.

Blossomheart ran up to her. "Great catch! That was a brilliant plan, Pebblepaw."

"We make a good team," Pebblepaw purred.

Despite himself, Hawkwing was impressed by Pebblepaw's hunting skills. But he wasn't going to tell *her* that. *Especially when she made me lose* my *prey.*

Billystorm and Waspwhisker came padding through the trees, Waspwhisker carrying a blackbird.

"Wow!" Billystorm exclaimed when he saw the squirrel. "Whose was that?"

"Pebblepaw's," Blossomheart responded.

"We both caught it," Pebblepaw added immediately.

Billystorm gave his apprentice a nod of approval. "Good job. Let's eat."

With a whisk of her tail Pebblepaw invited Hawkwing to share her squirrel. Though he crouched down with the others without a word, every mouthful tasted like crow-food. *She did well,* he admitted to himself grudgingly, *but I wish I'd caught my own prey instead of having to feel grateful to her.*

When the squirrel had been picked to the bones, the patrol set off again. Billystorm took the lead as they headed into the Twolegplace. Hawkwing felt every hair on his pelt rise with apprehension as he padded into the shadows of the tall stone dens. The air grew stale, full of the scents of monsters and unfamiliar food.

"Duskpaw would have loved this," Waspwhisker mewed, dropping back to walk alongside Hawkwing. "He couldn't get enough of Twoleg food. He was always trying to get around the rules and sneak off."

Hawkwing remembered how irritating he had found it when his brother did that. Now all he could think about was how much fun his brother had been; he would have given anything to have Duskpaw back, even if he'd never seemed to take his apprentice training seriously. The memories choked him so that he couldn't reply to Waspwhisker.

"I had to scold him, and punish him sometimes," the gray-and-white tom went on. "That was my job as his mentor, because otherwise he would never learn. He must have shifted more ticks from the elders' fur than any other apprentice in the Clan! But he was never resentful . . . he would always make a joke, so it was hard to be angry with him."

"I know." Hawkwing managed to speak at last. "When we were kits, he thought up the best games . . . and he was really good at sneaking off so we could play."

Amusement glimmered in Waspwhisker's eyes. "I remember Cherrytail saying her paws would fall off, she spent so much time chasing him back into the nursery!"

Gradually, listening to the older warrior, Hawkwing began to feel comforted. This was the first time any cat had spoken to him so openly about Duskpaw. *I guess they thought it would hurt me too much. But it's good to hear Waspwhisker's memories. It makes Duskpaw seem closer, somehow.*

"I'll never stop missing him," Hawkwing managed to mew softly.

Waspwhisker nodded understandingly. "He had so much spirit! You know, I blame myself . . . ," he added.

Hawkwing gazed at him, startled. *But it was my fault. . . .*

"Maybe if I'd been sterner with Duskpaw, about leaving the territory without a warrior, he wouldn't have sneaked off that day to get the Twoleg food. And then he'd still be alive."

"You can't know that," Hawkwing responded, feeling how strange it was to reassure a more experienced warrior. "No cat ever stopped Duskpaw from doing what he wanted."

Waspwhisker let out a little huff of amusement. "No . . ."

"You couldn't be responsible, because *I'm* responsible," Hawkwing continued. "I could have saved him!"

Waspwhisker touched Hawkwing's shoulder with the tip of his tail. "Maybe when some cat dies, part of our grief is feeling guilty and wishing we'd done things differently. Even though there's nothing we could have done." He let out a deep sigh. "You know, I don't think Duskpaw would want either of us to feel guilty. He always wanted every cat to be happy."

"That's true," Hawkwing murmured. "One time, when Ebonyclaw was teaching me to hunt, I was upset because I missed a really easy catch. Duskpaw brought his mouse to share with me, and told me a funny story about how he tripped over his own paws trying to stalk a rabbit."

"We'll grieve for him and miss him," Waspwhisker went on, "but we should remember that it is happiness he would want us to carry in our hearts when we think of him."

Hawkwing's chest swelled at the older warrior's wisdom. But a heartbeat later the sound of high-pitched Twoleg yowling struck his ears and his heart started to pound with the shock.

"Get down!" Billystorm ordered.

Deep in conversation with Waspwhisker, Hawkwing had hardly noticed his surroundings as they followed Billystorm through the Twolegplace. Now he realized that they had left the last of the dens behind them and begun to cross a stretch of grass with a Thunderpath beyond. Crouching close together with the rest of the patrol, he spotted several Twoleg kits ahead of them, running up and down and waving their forepaws around, as if they were having some kind of battle.

"Listen to me," Billystorm hissed. "This could be dangerous. Some Twolegs can be violent and unpredictable, and their kits are even worse. It's usually best to hide and wait for them to go away, but this grass won't give us cover for long. They're bound to spot us soon."

"So what do we do?" Pebblepaw asked.

"We'll have to make a run for it," Billystorm replied. "Once we get across the Thunderpath we should be safe. In my experience, Twoleg kits won't cross it unless they have bigger Twolegs with them. So, when I say run, *run*—and for StarClan's sake, watch out for monsters."

Hawkwing peered out through the stems of grass, his heart thumping harder than ever. The Thunderpath was many foxlengths ahead of them, directly on the other side of the group of battling Twoleg kits. As Hawkwing stared at them, one of the Twoleg kits let out a louder screech and started to run toward the cats, pointing with one forepaw.

"Go!" Billystorm yowled.

Hawkwing sprang forward, wind streaming through his fur as he raced for the Thunderpath. Pebblepaw and Blossomheart pelted along just ahead of him, while Waspwhisker kept pace alongside him and Billystorm brought up the rear. More Twoleg kits were chasing them now, the air filled with their horrible caterwauling.

The Thunderpath drew closer and closer.

We're going to make it! Hawkwing thought.

Then one of Hawkwing's forepaws slid down into a concealed dip in the ground. He lost his balance and rolled over and over, ending up on his side, all the breath driven out of him.

Hawkwing looked up, gasping for air, to see all his Clanmates far ahead of him. Blossomheart and Pebblepaw had already crossed the Thunderpath. Waspwhisker was waiting on the near side while a gleaming blue monster roared past. Only Billystorm skidded to a halt in front of Hawkwing and looked back.

"Go on!" Hawkwing yowled. "I'm okay! I'll catch up!"

As Billystorm raced on, Hawkwing felt a shadow fall over him. He turned his head to see a Twoleg kit stooping over him, one huge forepaw reaching out to grab him. Something strange glittered in its other forepaw and its mouth gaped, letting out a triumphant screech.

Hawkwing sprang up and dodged away, barely avoiding the outstretched paw. But as he streaked away across the grass a blow struck him on his back. He could feel something trickling through his fur.

Oh, StarClan, help me! It must be blood!

Hawkwing wondered if he was somehow so badly injured, he couldn't even feel the pain. But strangely the wound didn't stop him from running. Reaching the edge of the Thunderpath, he hurled himself across it without even looking up. The air was split with a screeching so loud that it drowned out the sounds of the Twoleg kits, and Hawkwing felt wind buffeting his tail and his hindquarters as a massive monster growled past.

As soon as his paws touched the grass on the far side of the Thunderpath, Hawkwing collapsed, panting. His Clanmates gathered around and stared down at him, concerned looks on their faces.

"They got me!" Hawkwing gasped. "The Twoleg kits got me! I'm bleeding!"

Even as he spoke, he felt that something wasn't right. Blood was supposed to be warm, but he realized for the first time that the stuff dripping down his back was cold.

Billystorm bent closer and gave him a long sniff. "That's not blood," he mewed. His eyes were sparkling with amusement, though he was clearly trying to keep it out of his voice. "It's water."

"What?" Hawkwing twisted around, trying to crane his neck so that he could see.

"Water," Billystorm repeated. "The Twoleg kits were shooting it out of weird shiny things they held in their paws."

Relief flooding through him, Hawkwing staggered to his paws. He could see that every cat, like Billystorm, was struggling to keep a serious expression, as if they were all trying to hide how funny they found his misadventure.

I suppose it is pretty funny, he thought. *Duskpaw would be rolling on the ground with laughter if he were here now. . . .*

But then Hawkwing noticed that Pebblepaw had turned away to hide her face, and in spite of her efforts her tail was curling up with amusement. Anger spurted up inside him, stifling his relief. *Duskpaw isn't here to laugh because of her. How* dare *she laugh at me!*

"It's not funny!" he yowled at Pebblepaw. "I could have been killed!"

Pebblepaw spun around to face him again. "With *water?*"

"Well, I could have drowned!"

Blossomheart let out a snort of laughter, and Hawkwing spun around to glare at her.

"Honestly . . ." Pebblepaw rolled her eyes. "Are you a *mouse?* Even a mouse couldn't have drowned in that much water."

Hawkwing slid out his claws, a breath away from leaping on Pebblepaw and scratching her ears. "Well, I know you don't take death very seriously," he snarled.

His gaze met Pebblepaw's, and for a few heartbeats she stared back at him. Hawkwing could see that she understood he was referring to Duskpaw's death. *And I can see that I've hurt her. Well, she deserves it!*

Billystorm's eyes narrowed. He looked ready to step in, then clearly decided to let his apprentice fight her own battles.

"That's totally unfair!" Pebblepaw protested to Hawkwing with a lash of her tail. "We were only having a bit of fun. I *do* take death seriously," she added, clearly trying to calm down. "Never mind—I can see there's no point trying to make you understand." She shrugged, turning away.

Hawkwing didn't want to listen anymore. With a furious hiss he whirled around and stalked off away from the Thunderpath, not waiting to see if any of his Clanmates followed.

The others soon caught up to him. "Take it easy," Billystorm meowed. "Blaming another cat won't lessen our grief. We still have a long way to go before we stop for the night, and we'll only make it more difficult if we start quarreling among ourselves."

Hawkwing simply grunted an acknowledgment of the senior warrior's words. He felt as if no cat would ever understand what he was going through.

Padding forward, ignoring the rest of his Clanmates, Hawkwing decided that the only way to survive this quest was to keep to himself and not talk to any cat. *I don't even know if I'm being fair anymore—and I don't care.* All he could feel was the pain of missing Duskpaw.

He was glad when the sun went down and they could start looking for a place to make camp.

CHAPTER 6

Hawkwing stood staring up into the branches of a massive oak tree, wondering if it might be "the tree that splits into three" that Darktail had told them about. This was the third day since they had left camp, and already the sun was beginning to slide down the sky. Every cat was beginning to wonder whether somehow they had gone wrong and missed Darktail's land-mark.

"This must be it," Billystorm meowed. "Look, the trunk splits into three about five fox-lengths up."

The leaves had still not reached their greenleaf fullness, so it was easy to see how the huge thick trunk divided. And Hawkwing could see that this was clearly the wrong tree. *If we take this as our landmark, then the whole quest is doomed,* he thought. *I have to say something. . . .*

Hawkwing took a breath. This was the first time he had really spoken to his Clanmates since his outburst after the Twolegs' attack.

"See how that branch splits again a tail-length away from the first fork?" He gestured at it with his tail. "So if you're looking closely, the tree splits into four, not three."

"Well, three of the branches are very thick," Waspwhisker pointed out, "and the fourth one is much thinner. So maybe it shouldn't be counted."

Hawkwing felt his neck fur begin to bristle. "Of course it should! Any cat can see it divides into four, not three."

"How great it must be, to be a young cat." Waspwhisker's tail-tip twitched irritably. "They know everything! Hawkwing, if you—"

"That's enough." Billystorm stepped forward. "I suggest we put it to a vote. Is this Darktail's tree, or isn't it?"

"I don't think it is," Hawkwing responded instantly, hurt by Waspwhisker's snarky comment. *We have to follow Echosong's vision and find the other Clans. If we get this wrong, who knows what will happen?* "I vote we carry on until we find a tree that really *does* split into three and not four."

"You know what I think," Waspwhisker huffed. "This is it, no question."

"I agree," Pebblepaw mewed with a glance at Hawkwing. He couldn't read her expression, to know if she was voting against him just to be spiteful. *Could she really be that petty? To risk the whole quest just to get at me?*

"So do I," Blossomheart added.

Hawkwing felt his shoulder fur beginning to bristle. *Even my own sister won't back me up!*

Billystorm nodded. "I have to say, I do too," he responded to Blossomheart. "Hawkwing, maybe Darktail didn't look as closely as you did. At first glance, the tree splits into three."

Hawkwing shrugged. He knew there was no point in arguing anymore, when he was outvoted four to one. *I just hope*

Billystorm is right, otherwise we'll never find the other Clans.

Following Darktail's directions, Billystorm led the way toward the setting sun. It was already low on the horizon, staining the sky red and casting the cats' shadows behind them.

Hawkwing realized that every cat except him was in good spirits, drawing new energy from finding the sign, and believing they were now only a short journey from the cats they had set out to find.

"I wonder what they'll be like," Blossomheart meowed. "The other Clan cats. Won't they be surprised to see us!"

"I wonder . . . ," Pebblepaw murmured awkwardly, concern clouding her gaze. "What will we do if the other Clans don't *want* us to join them? After all, didn't the same Clans drive us out, all those seasons ago? Isn't that why SkyClan lives alone?"

"That was *ages* ago," Hawkwing snapped, adding under his breath, "mouse-brain."

Billystorm let out a sigh, ignoring Hawkwing's comment. "Yes, that's a sad part of SkyClan's history. We had to leave the forest when we lost our territory, and the other Clans didn't help. But Firestar told us that he regretted what happened. As far as we know, the rest of the present-day Clans will feel the same way. They have no reason not to welcome us."

"But—" Pebblepaw began.

"We don't know what will happen when we meet the other Clans." Billystorm cut off his apprentice in a calm but firm voice. "But we have to believe that StarClan would not lead us astray."

The younger cats fell silent, leaving Billystorm and

Waspwhisker to chat casually as the patrol padded on through light woodland.

"I wonder what it will be like, meeting Firestar's kin," Waspwhisker meowed.

"I can't wait." Billystorm's voice was warm. "According to Leafstar, he was such a great cat. Surely we've got a lot to learn from his kin."

Hawkwing wasn't actually sure what he felt about meeting the other Clans. He'd only argued with Pebblepaw because he couldn't stand to agree with her. Privately he wasn't at all sure that the old grudges would have been laid to rest.

He wondered too what it would be like to live close to other cats, when SkyClan had been alone for so long. *Will we have to change the way we do things?*

The forest quickly grew denser, with more fern and bramble thickets between the trees. Soon the cats heard the sound of running water; heading toward it, they came out of a clump of elder bushes and found themselves on the edge of a small stream.

"We should follow this," Billystorm meowed. "Darktail mentioned a stream."

"He also mentioned a clearing," Waspwhisker pointed out. "But I suppose if we follow the stream we might find that before long."

The senior warriors were right. Almost at once the questing cats emerged from the undergrowth into a large clearing surrounded by mossy banks. Hawkwing felt embarrassed to realize that he had argued so vehemently about the tree, and now he had been proved wrong. To his relief, none of his Clanmates mentioned that, not even Pebblepaw.

And at least we are on the right track, so we should find the other Clans soon. If Darktail's directions were correct, they were very close. *Can it really be this easy?*

"This must be Darktail's clearing," Billystorm mewed, glancing around.

"So we're near the end of our quest!" Blossomheart exclaimed, clawing at the ground in excitement. "What did Darktail say—the Clan cats are two sunrises' journey beyond this?"

Billystorm nodded. "That's right. I suggest we make camp here, and—"

"What's that smell?" Pebblepaw interrupted.

Hawkwing tasted the air and picked up a strong, musty scent; he had smelled it before, in the woods at the top of the gorge opposite the camp. "Badger," he murmured. "Darktail said they used to live here."

As the cats advanced farther into the clearing, the scent grew even stronger. Hawkwing noticed several dark holes in the mossy banks, too big to be rabbit burrows. The scent seemed to flow out of them.

All the hairs on the back of Hawkwing's neck began to rise. "This scent is really strong. Do you think the badgers might still be here?" he asked. "Wouldn't it be stale and faint if the badgers really had abandoned the place, like Darktail said?"

Before any cat could reply, Hawkwing spotted movement deep in one of the holes, and a wedge-shaped snout appeared.

Hawkwing stood rigid at the sight of the white stripe down the badger's muzzle and its bright, malignant eyes. As the badger emerged into the open, Blossomheart let out a screech; whirling, Hawkwing saw two more badgers thrust their way out of two different holes on the far side of the clearing.

Panic seized Hawkwing's gut. *Darktail was wrong!* he realized as panic crashed over him. *The badger den isn't abandoned at all!*

For a heartbeat it seemed as if every creature had been frozen into ice. Then the badgers plunged into the attack. The biggest of them headed straight for Blossomheart, its teeth bared. Blossomheart leaped backward, but her paws skidded and she fell. The badger lunged for her neck.

No!

Hawkwing sprang into action, flinging himself between his sister and her attacker. *I'm not going to let another of my littermates get killed!* The badger's teeth sank into his shoulder, but Hawkwing barely felt it; his whole being was filled with terror for Blossomheart, and determination to save her, whatever it took.

"Leave her alone, mange-pelt!" he growled.

The badger began to shake him, lifting his paws off the ground. Then behind him he heard Blossomheart let out another screech. At the same moment she flew over his shoulder and landed on the big badger's back, digging in her claws and raking at its ears as she tried to make it let go of Hawkwing.

The grip of the badger's teeth loosened and Hawkwing tore himself free. He slashed his claws across the badger's flank, then darted back out of range of its blunt, stripy head. The badger reared up on its hind paws, shaking its shoulders in an attempt to dislodge Blossomheart, but she clung on, still swiping at its ears.

In the moment of respite Hawkwing glanced across the clearing to see that the two smaller badgers were attacking Waspwhisker, Pebblepaw, and Billystorm from either side. The three cats had clustered together, back to back, to defend themselves. Hawkwing guessed these badgers were younger and less experienced than the one that had attacked Blossomheart, but their teeth and claws were still powerful and dangerous.

Hawkwing threw himself at the big badger again, springing up to claw at its shoulder, then leaping away. *Maybe we can tire it out. . . .*

The big badger at last managed to throw Blossomheart off. As she hit the ground she rolled over, underneath her attacker, and delivered a raking blow to its belly, then scrambled out on its other side and back to her paws. The badger let out a ferocious cry that echoed around the clearing.

As if in response, another badger emerged from the tunnels and lumbered over to join in the fight. It was even bigger than the first one, a furious glitter in its tiny black eyes as it focused on the cats.

Great StarClan! Hawkwing thought despairingly. *Now we have to take on two of them! How many more are there?*

Even though it was injured, the first badger was still a formidable opponent, and it seemed to draw new energy from the appearance of its denmate. Hawkwing crouched defiantly, ready to leap into battle again. *The odds aren't good, but I'm going to fight my hardest.*

Then a speckled white blur flew across Hawkwing's vision. *Pebblepaw!* The she-cat hurled herself at the first badger, slashed at its eyes, then whirled to swipe at the other one.

Both badgers let out roars of pain and began to back away. The one already injured by Hawkwing and Blossomheart turned and trundled off, back into its hole. The biggest badger remained slumped in the grass, clawing at the blood that trickled from around its eyes and down its nose.

Warm gratitude to Pebblepaw flooded through Hawkwing. *And after I'd been so nasty to her!* Then he realized that he had no idea what had happened to his other Clanmates.

Billystorm! Waspwhisker! Hawkwing thought, whipping around with Pebblepaw and Blossomheart to help them in their battle. Then his heart lurched; he could see now that Waspwhisker was limping on three legs, and blood was pouring from one of his ears. Beside him, Billystorm lay motionless in a pool of blood.

No! Hawkwing felt as if every muscle in his body had been turned to ice. *I can't imagine SkyClan without Billystorm—and he means so much to Leafstar! How will we manage without him?*

Pebblepaw let out a screech and threw herself across the clearing, snapping and clawing as she attacked the badgers. Hawkwing and Blossomheart followed hard on her paws. The biggest badger joined in again, and the clearing seemed full of their reek and their snarling.

The sight of Billystorm's body gave strength to Hawkwing's

fury as he leaped and slashed at the three attackers. But Pebblepaw seemed to be everywhere, a shrieking whirl of teeth and claws, flinging herself into the battle with no thought for her own safety.

She's lost control, Hawkwing thought, anguished. *She's taking too many risks. She must want to avenge Billystorm.*

At last the biggest badger let out a harsh cry. All three badgers began to retreat, and Pebblepaw harried them, biting and clawing at their hind paws as they lumbered across the clearing and vanished down their holes.

"Let them go! It's over!" Hawkwing gasped to Pebblepaw.

Pebblepaw glanced at him, and Hawkwing saw in her eyes the same desperation he had felt when Duskpaw died. She turned back, panting, then raced across the clearing and flung herself down beside Billystorm's body. Hawkwing's heart lurched as he saw the massive wound slashed across the ginger-and-white tom's belly. Blood seeped from it into Pebblepaw's fur.

"Billystorm!" Pebblepaw exclaimed, shaking him by the shoulder. "It's okay. They've gone."

But Billystorm still didn't move. Waspwhisker bent his head to touch the apprentice's ear with his nose. "I'm sorry, Pebblepaw," he murmured. "He's dead."

"No!" Pebblepaw flung her head back and let out a horrible shriek.

Hawkwing felt his heart twist with pain. All his annoyance with Pebblepaw faded in the face of her obvious, inconsolable grief.

"Let's carry him away from here," he suggested. "We'll find

a place to sit vigil for him."

Pebblepaw turned to face him with a blind stare, as if she wasn't sure who he was. Then she bowed her head without speaking.

"What are we going to tell Leafstar?" Blossomheart whispered.

"The truth," Waspwhisker responded, his voice hoarse. "Billystorm died a warrior's death, defending his Clanmates."

Hawkwing supposed that the senior warrior's words should have been comforting.

But he also knew that nothing would comfort Leafstar once she learned that they'd lost Billystorm.

CHAPTER 7

Hawkwing staggered to his paws to give himself a long stretch, then shook dew from his pelt. All night he had crouched under the tree that split into three, keeping vigil beside Billystorm's body. Now milky dawn light was creeping through the trees, banishing the shadows. The air was cool and dry, carrying the fresh scent of growing things.

Hawkwing felt stiff and light-headed, and still stunned by grief. His wounds had started to throb, but he almost welcomed the pain, because it helped to blur his memory of the battle and his uncertainty about the future.

It seemed impossible that the day before, they'd thought they might be mere sunrises away from finding the other Clans. Now, after they'd walked right into a badger attack, no cat could be sure if their directions were even accurate. *If Darktail was wrong about the badger den, what else might he be wrong about?* Hawkwing thought back to their dispute over the "tree that split into three." What if he'd been right? What if it *was* the wrong tree, and they'd been following the wrong path ever since?

Looking at his Clanmates, Hawkwing shook out his pelt

and sighed. Among all these questions, one thing was undeniable: Billystorm was dead, and Hawkwing had no idea what was going to happen next.

Who would have thought our quest would end like this?

Blossomheart and Pebblepaw sat pressed close together at the opposite side of Billystorm's body, both of them still and silent. At first Hawkwing couldn't see Waspwhisker, until he spotted the gray-and-white tom limping out from behind a bramble thicket.

"I've been taking a look around," he murmured as he joined Hawkwing. "We shouldn't stay here, so close to the badgers. But we'll bury Billystorm first."

Pebblepaw raised her head. "No! We should take him back to be buried among his Clanmates. That's what Leafstar would want."

Waspwhisker shook his head. "I understand your concern, Pebblepaw, but it's too far. Besides, his body would attract predators. You don't want that, do you?"

In reply, Pebblepaw let out a small murmur of grief. Then she inspected the ground for a moment, before padding over to a spot near the base of the tree and beginning to scratch at the earth. Hawkwing and Blossomheart joined her, digging out a grave for Billystorm. No cat spoke as they struggled through the task, ignoring their own wounds and their weariness.

Hawkwing couldn't believe how things had gone so wrong. *There's been so much death, in such a short time. First Duskpaw, and now Billystorm . . . Perhaps terrible things will keep happening until we find "the spark that remains."*

Now when Hawkwing looked at Pebblepaw, he could only feel empathy and understanding. It was hard to remember what the old hostility had been like. His heart felt as if it were breaking for her; he could see her paws shaking as she thrust them into the earth, digging the hole for her beloved mentor.

I know exactly how she feels—like I felt when Duskpaw died.

When the grave was deep enough they laid Billystorm's body in it and covered it over, each taking a turn to push earth into the hole. When the task was done, all four cats stood beside the grave for a moment in silent respect, and Hawkwing tried to remember the words that Echosong had spoken over Duskpaw's body.

"May StarClan light your path, Billystorm. May you find good hunting, swift running, and shelter when you sleep."

The cats bowed their heads, and at that moment a shaft of sunlight struck through the branches of the tree and settled on Billystorm's grave.

"Look—that might almost be a message from StarClan," Waspwhisker murmured.

Hawkwing wanted to believe that the senior warrior was right, yet the words brought him very little comfort, and he could see that Pebblepaw wasn't comforted, either.

As the cats stepped away from the mound of earth, Hawkwing turned to Pebblepaw, searching awkwardly for words. He knew as well as any cat how private grief was, and how—sometimes—any cat saying anything, even something nice, could be just another claw snagging at your heart. Yet he couldn't use that as an excuse not to do what was right.

"Thank you, Pebblepaw," he mewed. "You saved my life and Blossomheart's. If it hadn't been for you, I might not be alive right now. I'm very grateful to you."

At first, Pebblepaw didn't answer, just padded away from him. Then she spun around, hurt and anger in her eyes. "I should have stayed to help protect my mentor," she hissed. "If only I hadn't left him to help you and Blossomheart, he might still be alive."

Hawkwing felt his heart sink into his belly. *Pebblepaw isn't just grieving for her mentor; she's blaming herself!*

Until then, it hadn't occurred to Hawkwing that Pebblepaw had done anything she might regret, but now he realized that they shared more than he had ever expected. *I blamed myself for Duskpaw's death because I saved Pebblepaw first. She blames herself for Billystorm because she helped me and Blossomheart defend ourselves when the badgers would have killed us.*

Hawkwing knew that would only make Pebblepaw's grief more painful. But because he'd felt exactly the same way, he also knew that this wasn't the right time to discuss it with her. She needed time to think over what had happened. He kept his jaws clamped shut.

At that moment Waspwhisker called the rest of the patrol together. "What now?" he asked, and Hawkwing stood up at attention, eager to finally discuss what would become of their quest.

"We're here in the open," Waspwhisker continued, "and while there doesn't seem to be any danger threatening us right now, the badgers aren't all that far away. I know I'm injured, and that might make us vulnerable, but I'm willing to carry on. We need to decide if that's what we want to do."

"Do you think we *should* carry on?" Hawkwing asked. While he hadn't been sure, he'd sort of assumed that Billystorm's death would bring an end to their journey. *How can we go on? We've lost our leader.*

Waspwhisker nodded. "While Billystorm's death was tragic, we all know how vital it is for us to complete the quest. We must find 'the spark that remains.' According to Darktail, we're only two days' journey away from the other Clans. We should find the cats we set out to find, in Billystorm's memory, and as StarClan directed us." He paused, and when no cat made a comment, he added, "What do you think?"

The silence stretched out for another few heartbeats. Somehow, after Billystorm's death, Hawkwing was having trouble picturing the other Clans so close. But he supposed it made sense that they must still be.

Blossomheart was the first to speak. "I agree with you, Waspwhisker. We should carry on."

"What?" Pebblepaw whipped her head around to stare at her friend. "It would be disrespectful to Billystorm's memory to continue the quest without him!"

"But finishing the quest is what Billystorm would have wanted," Waspwhisker pointed out.

"There's no way to know what Billystorm would have wanted," Pebblepaw mewed bitterly. "Because he's dead." Her voice shook, but a moment later she was able to continue.

"Besides, it looks like we can't rely on Darktail's directions. He said the badgers' den was abandoned, and it clearly wasn't. Who knows what else he was wrong about?"

"But, I guess the badgers could have moved back in without Darktail knowing," Waspwhisker pointed out. "He might not have been wrong about anything else."

"But we can't take that risk," Pebblepaw argued. "We should go back now, to tell Leafstar that her mate is dead, and to tell the others what happened. Going on isn't safe, and it isn't right," she finished with an emphatic swish of her tail.

"Hawkwing?" Waspwhisker turned to him. "What's your opinion?"

Hawkwing looked for a moment at Pebblepaw, who refused to return his gaze. He understood exactly how she felt. Right after Duskpaw died, he had felt the same. *I missed Duskpaw so much, I couldn't think about anything else. Imagine if I'd been expected to complete a quest right then!*

He couldn't blame Pebblepaw, and in any case her feelings didn't change his decision. "We should go home now. I know one thing Billystorm would have wanted: for us to survive. And now, going home seems the best chance of that. We can worry about finding the Clans when we have a better plan."

Blossomheart nodded. "The plan we had was pretty disastrous," she meowed.

"Yes," Hawkwing continued. "Who can say what else Darktail was wrong about? Who can say what other dangers lie ahead? We might meet more badgers, or something worse." *And we can't afford to lose more cats.*

"I've changed my mind," Blossomheart announced as soon as her brother had finished speaking. "I agree with Hawkwing and Pebblepaw. I still think we should try to find the Clans— but it's clear this quest has failed."

Waspwhisker fluffed out his neck fur, and for a few heart-beats Hawkwing thought he was upset to be challenged by younger warriors. "Maybe you're too young to understand the importance of such a strong message from StarClan," he sug-gested. "Billystorm's death was terrible, but we still *must* find the other Clans. And this seems like the best chance we have."

Then he let out a sigh. "But there are four of us," he mewed, "and if three of you want to go home, there's noth-ing I can do."

He rose to his paws. "Let's go."

The patrol set out on the long trek back to familiar ter-ritory. Heartsick and in pain from his wounds, Hawkwing found it hard to remember the optimism with which they had set out. *We were all so excited about meeting the other Clans, and now they seem farther away than ever. This whole quest has been a disaster. Surely StarClan didn't mean for it to end like this?*

They walked in silence until Waspwhisker called for a halt. "We ought to hunt," he meowed. "I know none of us feel like eating, but we have to keep our strength up."

Hawkwing knew that he was right, though the thought of food made his belly heave.

The cats were standing at the top of a hill; on the far side it sloped down gently into a hollow with a pool at the bottom, edged by bushes and thick vegetation. Hawkwing remembered that they had found good prey there on the way out.

"Let's stop and hunt down there," Blossomheart suggested. "We could rest for a bit, too."

Waspwhisker nodded. "Good idea."

As they padded down the slope, Hawkwing slowed his pace to walk beside his sister. "Let's you and I hunt, once we've found a place to rest," he murmured. "Pebblepaw can't cope yet, and Waspwhisker is still limping."

"Okay," Blossomheart agreed, and added, "We all need Echosong to take a look at us."

The cats found a sheltered spot in the middle of a clump of hazel bushes, the bare earth covered with a thick layer of dead leaves. Once Waspwhisker and Pebblepaw were settled, Hawkwing slipped out and crept closer to the pool, his ears pricked and his jaws parted to pick up the first traces of prey. Blossomheart followed him, then veered off into a bank of ferns.

As Hawkwing neared the pool he heard a plop, and spotted a vole swimming out into the center. Cautiously he crouched at the water's edge and leaned over to spot a second vole poking its head out of a hole in the bank. Reaching down, Hawkwing fastened his claws into the back of the vole's neck and hooked it upward; its high-pitched squeal of terror was cut off abruptly as he bit into its throat.

Easy catch, he thought with satisfaction.

Turning back toward their makeshift den, Hawkwing spotted Blossomheart emerging from the ferns with the body of a mouse dangling from her jaws.

"Good job," Hawkwing mumbled around his own prey. "Let's go eat."

Waspwhisker's eyes gleamed in the dim light beneath the bushes when he saw the fresh-kill, but Pebblepaw merely glanced at it, then turned her head away.

"You have to eat something," Blossomheart urged her.

Pebblepaw shook her head. Hawkwing had noticed that she had hardly touched food since the battle with the badgers. She was starting to look skinny; he could make out her ribs underneath her pelt.

She won't thank me if I try to persuade her, he thought. *Better leave it to Blossomheart.*

His sister took her mouse and set it down in front of Pebblepaw. "Come on, share this with me," she urged her friend. "Look, it's really fat and juicy. I can't possibly eat all of it."

Pebblepaw stretched out her neck, sniffed the mouse, then took a tiny bite. "You can have the rest," she mewed, turning away again.

Hawkwing exchanged a glance with Blossomheart, knowing that there was no point in arguing with Pebblepaw anymore. *We'll get her to Echosong tomorrow; then she'll be better.*

He and Waspwhisker were sharing the vole when Hawkwing heard a sudden rustling outside the hazel clump. He stiffened and his neck fur rose.

There's something out there!

Turning in the direction of the sound, Hawkwing picked up the scent of a cat. *Thank StarClan! At least it's not a badger!* he thought, feeling weak with relief. Their den was flooded with the scent of fresh-kill; that must have been why it had managed to get so close without alerting any of the patrol.

Taking a deeper sniff of the scent, Hawkwing realized that there was a tang of Twolegs about it.

"That's a kittypet," he whispered. "Stay here. I'll deal with it."

What's a kittypet doing here? he wondered as he pushed his way out through the bushes. *I didn't see a Twolegplace when we passed this way before.*

Standing on the grass outside was a fluffy-haired she-cat with pelt of orange, black, and white. She looked almost comical with a black patch over one eye and an orange patch over the other. Her fur was shiny and clean, and she wore a collar; a small gleaming thing dangled from it and made a tinkling sound like water drops as she turned her head to look at Hawkwing.

"Hi," she meowed cheerfully. "My name's Betsy. What's yours?"

Hawkwing found it strange to hear a friendly voice; he and his Clanmates had been traveling in almost total silence. He was surprised too that a kittypet should sound so bold when confronted with a strange cat.

"I'm Hawkwing," he replied warily.

"And I'm Waspwhisker." Hawkwing realized that his Clanmates had followed him out and were standing at his back. "These are Blossomheart and Pebblepaw. What's a kittypet doing so far away from the Twolegplace?"

Betsy looked puzzled for a moment, as if she didn't understand the question. Then she shrugged, and her gaze cleared. "My housefolk live over there." She gestured with her tail, back toward the split tree, but in a different direction from the one the patrol had taken. "Anyway, I could ask you the same thing," she meowed. "What are *you* doing here?"

She's not scared of us at all, Hawkwing thought, feeling a twinge of admiration in spite of himself. *And we must seem a fearsome lot to a kittypet!*

"Oh, we live a long way away," he replied, deliberately not giving Betsy any details. *I don't know who she is, and anyway it's none of her business.* "We're on a journey."

"Have you seen any other groups of cats hanging around here recently?" Waspwhisker asked, taking a pace forward to examine the kittypet more closely.

Waspwhisker means the other Clans. Hawkwing was disappointed when Betsy shook her head. *It would be great if we managed to find them after all . . . but it looks like they're not here.*

"Cats like you, you mean? No, certainly not," Betsy answered. "No wild cats would make a home here, not with all those terrifying beasts around."

"Terrifying beasts?" Hawkwing asked, suppressing a shiver.

"Yes," Betsy continued. "I don't know what they're called, but they're a bit like cats, only bigger, with pointed heads and huge teeth. You look as if you've met them already," she added, her gaze traveling over the Clan cats' wounds. "You look a bit . . . battered."

"Those would be badgers," Waspwhisker growled. "And

yes, we had a difference of opinion with them. Tell us more—
when did they move in?"

"Oh, ages ago. They've been here for seasons and seasons,"
Betsy replied.

Waspwhisker twitched his whiskers in surprise, exchanging a glance with Hawkwing. "Really?"

So why did Darktail think those dens were abandoned? Hawkwing
wondered.

"Oh, yes, this place is known for being *full* of them. There's
one nest in a clearing over there, with a stream running
through it." Betsy pointed with her nose, clearly indicating
the place where the patrol had battled with the badgers. "And
many more nests beyond that. I wouldn't go that way if I were
you."

"No, we're going the other way," Blossomheart put in.
"We've seen quite enough of the badgers, thank you very
much."

"Good. Because those beasts would rip your fur off as soon
as look at you." Betsy's eyes were stretched wide, and Hawkwing sensed that she was getting quite a thrill out of telling
them about these horrors. *Like we don't know about them for ourselves!* "They've killed quite a few pets, so most housefolk don't
allow their cats outside."

"*You're* outside," Hawkwing pointed out to Betsy.

"Oh, I'm a bit reckless," she confessed cheerfully. "No
housefolk are going to keep *me* indoors. I'm good at sneaking,
and I know to keep well clear of those beasts."

"Well, thank you for the warning," Hawkwing meowed.

Even though we didn't need it, it was kind of her to come up to a bunch of strange cats to tell us about them.

"You're welcome." Betsy licked one forepaw and drew it over her ear. "Well, I'd better be going. It's about time for my housefolk to feed me. 'Bye!"

"Good-bye!" Hawkwing called after her as she skirted the hazel bushes with a wave of her plumy tail, then streaked up the slope and was lost to sight over the hill. *She might have made a good daylight warrior,* he thought, surprising himself by feeling a hint of regret.

"So the badgers have been there for seasons and seasons," Waspwhisker muttered. "What was Darktail thinking of?"

"Maybe they were asleep, or out hunting when he passed that way," Blossomheart responded.

Hawkwing flicked his tail-tip at his sister, but said nothing. *She might want to think the best of every cat, but it was still a huge mistake for Darktail to make.* For the first time Hawkwing felt a flicker of uneasiness when he thought about the strange rogue cat. *Did he deliberately lead us into danger?* he asked himself. *Did he get Billystorm killed?* Fury began to bubble up inside Hawkwing. *What do we really know about Darktail? We invited him in so quickly.* He slid out his claws, rustling the leaves beneath his paws. A terrible thought was taking root in his mind.

Were we fools to trust Darktail? Was I a fool to bring him back into our camp?

CHAPTER 8

❧

Sunhigh had just passed when the warriors approached the top of
the gorge above the SkyClan camp. It was the third day since
they had left the split tree where Billystorm was buried. The
sun was shining and the air was warm, but even now that they
were so close to home, their hearts were dark and cold. Once
again they had traveled in almost total silence, and Hawkwing
knew that every cat's grief for Billystorm was growing sharper
as they drew nearer to the moment when they would have to
tell the story to their Clanmates.

I'd almost rather face the badgers again!

Hawkwing felt especially sorry for Pebblepaw, who stumbled along in a daze, as if she was overwhelmed by mourning
and her sense of guilt. Blossomheart padded alongside her,
silently offering her sympathy and support.

Hawkwing's belly clenched at the thought that Leafstar
was to be plunged into the same well of bottomless grief, and
didn't even know it yet. He remembered Cherrytail telling
him how Leafstar had changed SkyClan's warrior code that
said a she-cat leader couldn't have a mate or kits, so that she
could be with Billystorm. *She loves him so much. . . .* Their kits,

Stormheart, Harrybrook, and Firefern, would all be devastated, too.

Billystorm was such an important part of SkyClan. I can't imagine how I'm going to find the words.

He couldn't stop thinking, too, about whether Darktail might have meant to lead them into danger. He had felt so hopeful when he had encountered Darktail at the site of the fire, believing that he was part of the prophecy. Now he saw how wrong he was, how he had unleashed an evil cat upon his Clan.

I hope he's still living with the Clan. I want to talk to him face-to-face— and I'll find the words for him, all right!

The patrol had just crossed the SkyClan border scent markers when Hawkwing heard paw steps ahead of them, and Rabbitleap, Plumwillow, and Nettlesplash emerged into the open, letting out loud caterwauls and hurling themselves at Waspwhisker.

"Calm down, calm down," Waspwhisker gasped, staggering under the force of his kits' welcome. "You're going to lick me to death!"

It's a good thing Billystorm's kits aren't patrolling, Hawkwing thought. *What would we say when they asked where their father is?* All the questing cats had agreed that Leafstar had to be the first to know that her mate was dead.

"It's great that you're safe!" Plumwillow exclaimed, her eyes shining. "Did you find the other Clans?"

Waspwhisker shook his head. "No, we didn't."

"And where's Billystorm?" Nettlesplash added.

To Hawkwing's relief, Waspwhisker avoided the question. "We need to talk to Leafstar right away."

"Yes, you should do that," Rabbitleap meowed.

Hawkwing noticed that once their first delight on seeing their father had ebbed away, all the cats in the patrol seemed somber, and were exchanging uneasy glances with each other.

What's the matter with them? he wondered. *Are they still sad about Duskpaw? Are they worried because Billystorm isn't with us? Or has something else bad happened?*

Apprehension gathered inside Hawkwing like a heavy fog as he wondered whether his last question might be close to the truth. The border patrol continued, and Waspwhisker led the way to the edge of the cliff and down into the camp.

As he descended the trail behind his Clanmates, Hawkwing realized that there were far fewer cats out and about in the camp than he was used to.

"Where is every cat?" Blossomheart asked, echoing his thought.

No cat answered her, and Hawkwing's apprehension deepened.

Waspwhisker headed first to Leafstar's den, but the Clan leader wasn't there, so he and the other questing cats continued down the trail. As they reached the bottom of the gorge, Hawkwing caught a whiff of a scent that was strange and familiar at the same time.

I don't know what animal left that, he thought, pausing to drink in the air and try to identify the scent. *But I've smelled it somewhere before.*

Then Hawkwing remembered. It was the same scent that he and Ebonyclaw had picked up on the border, on the day that Duskpaw died. *Did something happen here? Was that animal somehow involved?*

Dismay swept over Hawkwing as he realized that he had never reported the strange scent to Leafstar. Right after he and Ebonyclaw had noticed it, they had smelled the fire, and then Duskpaw's death had driven everything else out of his mind. *Did Ebonyclaw report it?* Hawkwing guessed not.

With an effort Hawkwing brought himself back to the present, and spotted Patchfoot crouching beside the stream, leaning over to lap the swirling water. Waspwhisker led the way toward him.

"Hi, Patchfoot," the gray-and-white tom meowed. "Have you seen Leafstar?"

Patchfoot looked up, shaking water droplets from his whiskers. "Yes, she's in Echosong's den. It's good to see you back," he added, though Hawkwing felt that he too seemed in a somber mood, not at all like his usual cheerful self.

Something is seriously wrong here.

As he and the rest of the patrol headed toward the medicine cats' den, Hawkwing felt his paw land on something strange. Glancing down, he saw a thing like a leaf wrap, but made of something thin and shiny, in garish colors. He bent his head to sniff it, and picked up the scent of Twoleg food.

For a moment Hawkwing was overwhelmed with memories of Duskpaw. *He loved Twoleg food so much!* But then he began to ask himself questions. *What's a Twoleg food wrap doing here? Have*

Twolegs been in the camp? Or did it blow over here? Maybe the fire dis-lodged some old Twoleg food scraps. . . . But Hawkwing couldn't find any answers to his questions. There was no good reason for the Twoleg food wrap to be in their camp.

Waspwhisker and the others had continued on, and Hawkwing ran to catch up to them as they reached Echo-song's den. On entering, he was shocked to see that Echosong was lying in her nest, injured; there was a fresh notch on one of her ears and cobweb was wrapped around one of her fore-legs. Her apprentice, Frecklewish, was giving her a drink from a bundle of wet moss, while Leafstar bent over her, talking quietly.

"Echosong!" Blossomheart exclaimed. "What happened to you?"

Echosong paused in lapping the moss and feebly lifted her head. "I'll be fine, really."

"Echosong was wounded," Leafstar added, "but she's heal-ing well, and Frecklewish is taking good care of her."

The Clan leader's voice was deeply serious, and Hawk-wing wondered if she already knew the terrible news they had to tell. Maybe because she and Billystorm were so close, she could sense that something had happened to him. *But no, that's not possible . . . is it?*

Hawkwing's heart began to thump harder and harder as he braced himself to tell Leafstar that her mate was dead. It felt even more difficult now that he had to look her in the face. But before he could find words, his Clan leader spoke again.

"Come outside with me," she mewed with a wave of her tail. "There's something I need to tell you."

Hawkwing and the rest of the patrol followed Leafstar into the open and clustered around her to listen. Hawkwing could see from the others' uneasy glances that they shared his apprehension about what had happened in their absence.

"While you were on your quest," Leafstar began, "the camp was attacked by a group of animals."

"Badgers?" Blossomheart asked.

Leafstar shook her head. "Not badgers. None of us had ever seen anything like these creatures."

"What were they like?" Hawkwing asked.

"They were black, white, and gray, with black around their eyes and white around their muzzles," Leafstar replied. "They walk on four legs like we do, but they can stand on their hind paws like a Twoleg. And they can grip things like a Twoleg, with their front and back paws. Their ears are like ours, but they have short, pointed muzzles like a fox." She ended with a shudder. "They're very vicious."

"Is that how Echosong was hurt?" Waspwhisker asked.

"Yes. Harveymoon was injured as well."

Hawkwing felt even worse. "This is awful," he stammered. "It must have been their scent that Ebonyclaw and I smelled on the day of the fire. And I forgot to report it! I'm so sorry."

Leafstar touched her tail to his shoulder reassuringly. "Don't dwell on it," she murmured. "Every cat knows why you didn't remember. Besides, Ebonyclaw *did* report it, and it didn't make any difference. There was no way we could have prevented this attack."

"So where's Harveymoon?" Pebblepaw asked. "Why isn't he in the medicine cat den? Is he okay?"

"Yes, he'll be fine," Leafstar replied. "But he's with his Twolegs now, and we haven't seen him since. In fact, most of our daylight warriors' Twolegs have been keeping them inside their dens since the strange animals moved into the territory."

Just like Betsy said, with the badgers, Hawkwing thought. *And that means we'll have to do without our daylight warriors.*

"And that's not all," Leafstar went on, her voice beginning to shake. "During the attack, Honeytail was killed."

"No!" Blossomheart choked out.

Hawkwing felt a sudden chill, cold creeping over him right down to his pads. Honeytail, the gentle ginger she-cat who loved caring for kits, and lived in the nursery to help with them and the nursing queens. *I can't believe this! First Duskpaw, then Billystorm, and now Honeytail!*

"We held a vigil for her while you were away on your quest," Leafstar continued. "We'll show you where she's buried, so you can pay your last respects." She paused, clearly giving them all a little time to process their grief for Honeytail. "I'll ask you about your quest later," she went on at last, "and then I'll hear all the details. But for now, just tell me this: Did you find the cats you were looking for?"

Hawkwing expected Waspwhisker to speak, as the senior warrior, but the gray-and-white tom was silent, staring down at the ground. When the silence had dragged out for a few heartbeats, Hawkwing took a breath. "There's something we need to tell you," he began, each word forced slowly out of him as his heart began to break for his leader.

Leafstar gazed into his eyes. Then her expression suddenly took on a terrible alertness, as if she was really seeing them for the first time since they arrived. "Where is Billystorm?" she asked, her voice hollow.

The questing cats were all silent except for Pebblepaw, who let out a tiny strangled cry. And Hawkwing could see from Leafstar's eyes, which suddenly became deep and dark with grief, that she already understood. "I'm so sorry, Leafstar," he meowed. "Badgers killed him. He died the death of a brave warrior."

For a moment Leafstar stood still, frozen with shock. Then she drew in a deep, shuddering breath and turned away. "No," she whispered, her voice quiet, sounding almost like a kit. A shiver passed through her, and Hawkwing knew that her heart must be breaking. *She loved Billystorm so much.*

"Why are all these terrible things happening to us all at once?" she demanded. Her voice was raw, and she didn't look at any of her Clanmates, as if she was challenging StarClan for answers. "The strange animals who attacked . . . the failed quest . . . the fire. Is it because we haven't found 'the spark that remains'?"

Leafstar fell silent, then after no more than a couple of heartbeats she turned back. Hawkwing could see that she was pushing everything down, and summoning every scrap of her self-control. He knew that what was most important to her was to be a strong leader for her Clan, in this dark time when death seemed to be all around them.

"We must call a Clan meeting," she mewed, her voice level. "We must decide what to do now. We must work out how to 'dispel the darkness.' It's our only hope."

CHAPTER 9

Hawkwing padded over to the foot of the Rockpile to join the rest of his Clanmates. Leafstar's voice as she called the meeting still rang in his ears, and he marveled at the strength and authority she was showing.

We've just told her that her mate is dead, and that he's been buried far from camp, somewhere she might never find, yet here she is, gathering her warriors around her.

Hawkwing realized that Leafstar must be grieving for Billystorm every bit as much as he grieved for Duskpaw, but she was forcing herself to be strong for the rest of her Clan.

News of the failure of the quest and of Billystorm's death must have traveled, for sadness filled the air like fog as the warriors gathered, and no cat could look up at the Rockpile to meet Leafstar's gaze. Instead, they crouched at the foot of the boulders, their eyes fixed on their paws, or exchanged glances of bewilderment and fear. Firefern, Stormheart, and Harrybrook, the kits of Leafstar and Billystorm, huddled together as if they were trying to find comfort in each other.

"Disaster has fallen upon SkyClan," the Clan leader began, "but we must not allow it to crush us. We must still find 'the spark that remains.' If we give up our quest now, we dishonor the memory of the cats who have died *for* that quest. There is still a prophecy that we must fulfill. And now we know only too well that there is still darkness to be dispelled."

"But how are we going to do that?" Nettlesplash asked.

"Yes," Mintfur, Nettlesplash's mate, agreed, ruffling up her gray tabby fur. "The quest failed, so maybe that's a sign that we mistook the meaning of the prophecy. Maybe we shouldn't be looking for Firestar's kin after all."

"No!" Cherrytail sprang to her paws, glaring at Mintfur. "Echosong has never been that wrong before."

So far Hawkwing had sat in silence, keeping his thoughts to himself, but now he couldn't stop himself from speaking. "Let's not forget that we weren't only following Echosong's advice," he meowed. "She may well have been right, but it was *some other cat* who told us where to go, to find Firestar's kin."

As he spoke, every cat turned to look in the same direction. Following their gaze, Hawkwing spotted Darktail settled comfortably in the shadow of a rock, his paws tucked under him.

So he is still living here! he thought, suppressing a gasp.

"Hawkwing!" Sharpclaw spoke commandingly from his place on the Rockpile at Leafstar's side. "If you want to make an accusation, consider carefully before you speak. Darktail has been living among us since you left, and he was a huge help when the beasts attacked us. He fought valiantly."

Hawkwing rose to his paws and faced his father. In spite of Sharpclaw's words, something encouraging in his voice suggested that the Clan deputy might agree with him—or at least that he wanted Darktail's involvement brought out into the open.

"I have considered carefully," Hawkwing responded. "In fact, I've thought of very little else since Billystorm died. Darktail's directions were all wrong, and they got Billystorm killed."

Fury rising inside him, Hawkwing marched over to Darktail, other cats scrambling to get out of his way. He halted in front of the white tom, thrusting out his neck until they were nose to nose. "Did you know about the badgers?" he hissed. "I'd hate to think you led us deliberately into danger—but it sure *looks* like you did! Why would you do that, to cats you don't even know?"

Behind him, Hawkwing could hear low murmuring from his Clanmates. One or two of them let out angry yowls, echoing his questions.

Darktail was not at all daunted by Hawkwing's attack or the hostility of the other SkyClan cats. Rising to his paws, he dipped his head respectfully to Leafstar. There was an expression of deep sorrow on his face.

"Leafstar, you can't imagine how bad I feel about this," he meowed. "I really thought I had it right, and I can't believe what happened."

Sharpclaw let out a snort. "You really can't tell fresh scent from stale?" he demanded, green eyes flashing with anger. "What were you thinking? You could have gotten *all* the patrol killed."

"I know. It was all a mistake." Darktail's expression was deeply distressed. "It's been a while since I passed through there, and I must have been confused. I was only trying to help."

As he spoke, Hawkwing could sense that the hostility of some of his Clanmates was turning to sympathy in the face of Darktail's obvious regret.

"Hawkwing, don't be too hard on him," Sandynose meowed. "If he made an honest mistake, then we have to put Billystorm's death down to fate."

"Sandynose is right," Mistfeather agreed. "Darktail fought so bravely when the strange creatures attacked our camp. Why would he do that if he wanted to hurt us?"

Hawkwing couldn't believe what he was hearing. *"Fate?"* he sputtered, his shoulder fur bristling. "You think this is fate? How could it be fate for badgers to kill Billystorm? How could it be fate for Duskpaw to die in a fire?"

While he was speaking, Leafstar stepped forward and looked down at him from the Rockpile. Her expression was stern, but not angry, as if she understood the feelings that were flooding through him.

"Hawkwing, I can tell that you're still grieving for your brother. And it's hard to think clearly through the fog of sorrow. I know that as well as any cat."

His leader's words did nothing to calm Hawkwing. Instead, even greater outrage flamed through him, fierce as the fire that had killed his brother. "That is *not* what this is about!" he snarled. "We shouldn't just assume that it's fate when something bad happens. This time, the bad thing happened when Darktail sent our patrol right into the path of a nest of badgers!"

Darktail pressed himself against Hawkwing's flank. "I truly believed the badgers had moved on," he mewed, sounding genuinely remorseful. "I didn't know the beasts could be that sneaky."

As more of his Clanmates murmured their sympathy and agreement, Hawkwing stepped away from Darktail with an angry glare. "We met a kittypet who told us that the badgers had lived there for seasons," he challenged the white tom. "If a *kittypet* knows that, why didn't you? And she told us that there were no Clan cats anywhere near there."

Darktail's eyes widened, his expression innocent and bewildered. "I only told you what I thought was true," he responded. "I don't know this kittypet, and I can't explain her words."

"You can't trust a kittypet to know what she's meowing about," Bouncefire put in. "Why bother, when your food bowl will be filled anyway?"

Hawkwing glared at Bouncefire, his lips drawn back in the beginnings of a snarl. "Even if it was an accident, it was still your stupid fault," he hissed at Darktail.

I wish I'd never brought Darktail to camp, he added silently to himself. *If I'd left him where I found him, Billystorm would still be alive.*

Darktail's head drooped and he cringed as if Hawkwing's words had hurt him. "I'm so sorry . . . ," he whispered.

"I believe Darktail," Bouncefire announced, returning Hawkwing's glare. He raised his voice so all the warriors could hear him. "What cat would be so evil as to lead strange cats into a badger den? We only just met him; it doesn't make sense that he would hold a grudge against us."

Leafstar dipped her head to Bouncefire. "I agree. I have lost more than any cat, and I too believe it was an accident." Raising her head to gaze at the sky, she continued, "What in StarClan is happening? Why is all this misfortune falling on us now? Not just the badgers, but those strange-scented foxlike creatures, too . . . what did you say they were called, Darktail?"

"Raccoons," Darktail replied. Turning to Hawkwing, he added, "I told this to Leafstar and the others after the attack. Twolegs sometimes keep them as pets, but some of them escaped, and now they live in the wild."

"How do you know that?" Hawkwing asked suspiciously.

"I picked up their scent on the way here, and I asked some kittypets about them," Darktail explained.

"Whatever they are called," Leafstar went on, "let's hope we have driven them off for good. We have other problems to deal with. Darktail, I believe you meant no harm, but the sad fact is that we're no nearer to finding 'the spark that remains.' Maybe StarClan will send us a clearer prophecy soon."

Hawkwing's belly churned with anger. *Why aren't we driving this rogue away? We never trust outsiders this easily.* He supposed it must be because Darktail had fought bravely during the raccoon attack. *But I still don't trust him.*

"I understand what you're saying, Leafstar," Sharpclaw meowed when the Clan leader had finished speaking. "Darktail may have had dark motives, or he may not. But it's still a huge risk for the Clan to put our faith in cats we don't know."

Hawkwing was relieved that his father seemed to share his suspicions of Darktail, but a moment later his relief faded away as Leafstar refused to change her opinion.

"I won't turn Darktail out without proof that he meant to harm SkyClan," she insisted. "Besides, he is the only cat among us who might know where 'the spark that remains' might be. StarClan wants us to follow the prophecy, and they don't send us messages that aren't important."

Hawkwing flexed his claws in and out. He knew that he should keep his jaws shut, that it wasn't his place to argue with his Clan leader, but he couldn't stop the words from spilling out.

"Leafstar, this is a bad idea. This cat is not one of SkyClan," he added, staring straight at Darktail. "He doesn't understand what it means to be a Clan cat."

"Come on, that's a bit harsh," Sandynose protested.

"Yes," Bouncefire added. "Not every good cat is *born* to a Clan. Even Firestar used to be a kittypet, for StarClan's sake!"

Hawkwing's fury was rising. He didn't want to listen to any cat. *Are they all too stupid to realize that this rogue could destroy us all?* "I say we drive him out *now*!" he snarled.

A chorus of protest rose from the cats clustering around him and Darktail, but before Leafstar could silence the clamor there was a stir of movement at the back of the crowd, and Frecklewish thrust a path through her Clanmates to the foot of the Rockpile.

"Leafstar—" she began breathlessly.

Leafstar was instantly alert, her ears pricking forward as

she looked down at the young medicine cat. "Has something happened to Echosong?" she asked anxiously.

Frecklewish shook her head. "She's still alive—she's fine. But she just had a vision."

"Another one?" Leafstar's voice was sharp. "What was it?"

"She saw a fire burning out, then blazing up again," Frecklewish explained, managing to catch her breath. "But her voice was strained as she told me about it. She insists that SkyClan must find 'the spark that remains' . . . before it's lost forever."

The angry argument had died away while Frecklewish was speaking, and all the cats looked expectantly toward their leader. Hawkwing was the first to speak.

"Now we know that our destiny is still out there," he meowed. "We should never have listened to Darktail. What does he know about StarClan?"

Leafstar was unimpressed. "Let go of your anger, Hawkwing," she told him. "This is the time to focus on our next move."

"Should we try to find Barley now?" Bellapaw asked. "He might be able to tell us where the Clan cats are. At least we know *he's* trustworthy," she finished with an awkward glance at Darktail.

That's a good suggestion, Hawkwing thought at the mention of Barley, the farm cat who had come with Ravenpaw to bring Bellapaw and her brother Rileypaw to SkyClan. *He would never lead us wrong.*

The white tom dipped his head toward Bellapaw, a thoughtful look in his eyes. "I understand why you might be doubtful," he meowed in response. "Even though I was wrong about the directions, I still believe I know where the Clan cats are, and I can save you a lot of time if you trust me again. I just need to think of a better way to get there."

"Suppose we send out another questing patrol," Firefern suggested, her eyes brightening as she gazed at her mother up on the Rockpile. "They could look for 'the spark that remains,' and bring Darktail along to guide them."

"No! I'm against that," Sharpclaw snorted with a flick of his tail. "What if the vision isn't telling us to *go* anywhere to find sparks to dispel darkness, but rather warning us to be alert? What if a danger is coming *to* SkyClan? If you ask me, we should strengthen our borders as much as we can, before it's too late."

Hawkwing's anger rose again as he listened to his father's cautious advice. Before he could stop himself, he let out a derisive growl.

Sharpclaw's head swiveled to face him. "Show some respect!" he hissed.

"I do respect you!" Hawkwing protested. "But I disagree with you over this. We have to go out and *find* our destiny."

Sharpclaw rolled his eyes. "You make me wonder if we made you a warrior too soon," he snapped. "You're showing all the maturity of a kit."

If Sharpclaw hadn't been standing on the Rockpile, Hawkwing might have leaped at him, claws extended. But his anger had to burst out somehow, even though he knew he should control himself in front of his leader and his Clan. "I'm not a kit!" he yowled. "I survived a quest Billystorm couldn't!"

"That's enough!" Leafstar stepped forward, her amber eyes blazing with fury. "You might be a warrior now," she told Hawkwing, every word forced out through her teeth, "but you should still know your place. You're no good to the Clan if all you do is disrupt our important meetings, and make them all about you."

Hawkwing took a step back, daunted by Leafstar's anger; she was normally so calm and controlled. *I wish I hadn't mentioned Billystorm. That was a cruel thing to say to Leafstar.*

"I'm sorry—" he began.

"'Sorry' catches no prey," Leafstar snapped. "I'm trying to work out how to keep my Clan strong and healthy, and you're getting in the way. You're being disruptive, and I won't put up with that."

Instinctively Hawkwing glanced at Sharpclaw, expecting that his father would back him up, or at least defend him. But Sharpclaw was looking just as stern as their Clan leader.

"You need to hold on to your temper," he told Hawkwing. "It's too short—the kind that can get cats into trouble."

"I know just the thing to calm you down," Leafstar mewed, her eyes glittering. "You can go and tend to Echosong in the medicine cat den. Keep her clear of ticks, and sort through her herbs to throw out any that are shriveled or rotting."

Hawkwing let out a moan, staring at his paws. *That's a job for an apprentice!*

"Well?" Leafstar asked icily. "Why are you still here?"

"What?" Hawkwing asked, briefly confused. "Don't I even

get to stay for the rest of the meeting?"

"The meeting is over, as far as you're concerned." Leaf-star swept her tail in the direction of the medicine cat den. "Leave," she ordered. "Your punishment starts right *now*."

Feeling every cat's gaze upon him, Hawkwing stumbled off after Frecklewish. Every hair on his pelt was burning with shame.

How did that go so wrong?

CHAPTER 10

Hawkwing stood in the medicine cats' den, sorting through Echosong's herb stores. It was the morning after the Clan meeting, and already his punishment seemed to have stretched out for moons.

Sticky juices from the rotting herbs clung to his paws. *They stink!* he thought resentfully. *And they'll taste vile when I try to wash my paws. I'll never get clean!*

The shriveled herbs were no better. They crumbled under Hawkwing's paws, littering the floor of the den with dust and scraps. *And I know which cat will get the "privilege" of cleaning that up!*

"What's wrong, Hawkwing?" Echosong, still resting in her nest, raised her head and gazed at him with compassionate green eyes.

Hawkwing huffed out a breath. *I told Echosong why I'm being punished,* he thought. *So why does she need to ask?*

"I know I shouldn't have challenged Leafstar at the meeting," he admitted. "But I'm annoyed that I'm being punished while that traitor Darktail is still stalking around camp as if he owns the place! It wasn't *my* interpretation of your vision that sent us on a fool's quest and got Billystorm killed. It was that rogue Darktail—*he* should be the one doing the gross duties." He gave a lash of his tail. "In fact, he shouldn't even be in camp at all. He doesn't belong with this Clan—he's not one of us."

As he spoke, Echosong was looking thoughtful. "True, I was not expecting fate's claw to be so treacherous this time," she responded. "But any cat can make a mistake, and I have to believe that StarClan brought Darktail to us for a reason."

"What reason?" Hawkwing challenged her.

"I don't know," she conceded with a nod of her head. "But just because we can't work out what it is yet doesn't mean the reason isn't there. We have to search for it, that's all."

Hawkwing's anger eased a little at the medicine cat's wise words, but a moment later he had to suppress a growl of annoyance as Darktail strode into the medicine cats' den.

"What do *you* want?" Hawkwing demanded. "Have you come to rub it in, that our Clan leader took your side?"

Darktail dipped his head low. "I really didn't mean for any cat to suffer," he mewed. "Not Billystorm, and not you. I understand that you're angry, but I promise you, once you've calmed down, you'll see that I meant no harm. You need the pain in your heart to pass, that's all."

"What do you know about pain?" Hawkwing snarled. *You didn't lose a brother,* he thought. *You don't understand what Billystorm meant to this Clan.*

Darktail heaved a long sigh and sat down beside Hawkwing, wrapping his tail around his paws. "You have no idea . . . ," he murmured. Hawkwing paused, curious. At first,

Hawkwing thought he would say no more, but after a long silence he started to speak again. "I had a friend . . . he was not kin to me, but we were brought up together as kits. We did everything together, for many, many moons. Then, one long, hard leaf-bare, when prey was scarce, he got weaker and weaker. . . ." Darktail's voice quivered; he broke off again, then choked out, "Then he died."

"I'm sorry," Hawkwing mewed, feeling a pang of guilt that he had been so dismissive of Darktail's feelings. *I still don't trust him, but that must have been terrible.*

"If we had lived in a Clan, my friend might still be alive," Darktail continued. "You all take care of each other. That's why I'm so grateful to SkyClan for taking me in. And especially grateful to *you*"—he dipped his head respectfully to Hawkwing—"because you spoke up for me when some of the others weren't too keen on bringing in a rogue. I promise I'll repay the faith you showed me then."

Curiosity stirred inside Hawkwing, so that his anger toward the white rogue began to ebb a little. "How do you plan to do that?" he asked.

"I've volunteered to lead a *new* quest," Darktail replied. "To show that I'm serious about helping SkyClan to find the spark that remains."

"*That's* your plan to fix things?" Hawkwing's anger surged up again, and he put all the derision he could into the words. "You nearly got us killed on the last quest. Why should we trust you?"

"Because this time I'm putting *my* pelt in danger," Darktail replied, an edge to his voice. "If I'm leading the quest, I'll share in any hazards we face. Besides, I've made contact with a friend of mine—a cat named Rain. He'll come on the quest with us, and give us more guidance."

Hawkwing wasn't sure about that. *Another rogue? Another cat we've never heard of, and shouldn't trust!* But before he could voice a protest, he remembered how he had tried to get Darktail driven out at the Clan meeting. *And look where that got me!*

He shrugged. "Fine. So go, then."

Darktail seemed unoffended by Hawkwing's curt response. "I know that I owe you a debt," he meowed. "You were kind enough to bring me into the Clan, and then I put you in danger—even though that was the last thing I wanted. But I'm going to make it up to you."

Yeah, right. Hawkwing flicked his ears. "How?"

"I'm going to go to Leafstar and insist that you're allowed to come along on this next quest. I've talked to Rain," he went on rapidly, before Hawkwing could respond, "and I think I've figured out where my directions went wrong. So now I know where we need to go! And I want you there, Hawkwing, because I think you deserve to be part of the group that finds the spark that remains and dispels the darkness. You should be part of the group that saves SkyClan."

A mixture of emotions rushed over Hawkwing, like a river in spate that threatened to carry him off his paws. He was annoyed that Darktail had been named leader of a quest. *He's only been here for a couple of heartbeats!* But along with that anger came doubt. *Why would Darktail offer to lead us himself if he meant to do us harm?*

Even stronger than both these feelings was pride that

Darktail would honor him in this way, and vouch for him to his Clan leader, especially after all Hawkwing had said to him at the meeting.

Unsure how to respond, Hawkwing looked toward Echosong for guidance, but the medicine cat was curled up in her nest, letting out gentle snores with her tail over her nose.

"Well, I don't think you'll be able to persuade Leafstar," Hawkwing told Darktail as the deflating thought came to him. *I'm sure she is still upset with me.* "I've been too quick to lose my temper lately. That's what put me in here," he added, gesturing toward the pile of herbs with his tail. "When I'm angry, I get hot-headed and make rash decisions. That wouldn't be good on a quest."

Darktail huffed out a breath, half contemptuous, half amused. "I don't agree. The cat with a temper, the cat who's the quickest to swipe a claw, is often the cat most likely to survive. Being a bit hot-headed, a bit impulsive, makes you a great asset to your Clan. You should never forget that, Hawkwing."

As the white tom spoke, Hawkwing found his feelings, still bruised from his father's scolding the day before, gradually soothed. *Maybe Darktail has a point. And maybe, if I'm allowed to go on this quest, I can prove that I am an asset to my Clan, hot temper and all!*

Sunhigh had almost arrived by the time Hawkwing had finished his tasks in the medicine cats' den. Leaving Echosong still sleeping, he padded out into the camp and headed toward the fresh-kill pile. He noticed that the hunting patrols had returned, and most of his Clanmates were clustered around the prey.

Hmm . . . it's not a massive pile, but it looks as if we'll all get fed.

Hawkwing had joined the others, and chosen a blackbird for himself, before he spotted a stranger in the camp, a handsome gray tom who was standing beside Darktail.

"This is Rain," Darktail meowed, dipping his head with the deepest respect to Leafstar and Sharpclaw, who stood in front of him, eyeing the newcomer warily. "He's been living close by, but he hasn't tried to cross your borders until now."

"Just as well," Sharpclaw growled, sliding out his claws and inspecting Rain through narrowed green eyes.

"He would never do that," Darktail assured the Clan leader and her deputy. "And I would never even think of bringing a new rogue to stay in SkyClan's camp. It's not my place to do that, not without permission."

"So why is he here?" Leafstar asked, her even tone giving nothing away of how she felt.

"Rain thinks he knows where the Clan cats are living," Darktail explained. "And he's willing to come on the quest to help find them."

"I'm happy to do what I can," Rain added with a polite nod.

"Then thank you, Rain," Leafstar mewed, warmth creeping into her voice. "You're welcome to our camp."

Hawkwing paused in gulping down his blackbird, wondering whether Darktail had really meant what he had said earlier in the medicine cats' den. His belly started to churn with anxiety.

"There's one more thing, Leafstar," Darktail continued. "I wondered if you would allow Hawkwing to come on this next quest with us."

"Hawkwing?" Leafstar sounded doubtful. "He's still being punished for the way he behaved at the meeting."

"I know." Darktail twitched his whiskers. "But he's a good, strong cat, and very brave. There are so many dangers out there, beyond the borders of your territory, that I think it would be a good idea to have a cat with us who doesn't hesitate to fight."

"He has a point." Leafstar leaned across to murmur into Sharpclaw's ear.

"It will be for the good of the Clan to let him come," Darktail went on, obviously encouraged by Leafstar's comment. "What better way for him to make up for losing his temper at the meeting, than to help his Clan find the spark that remains and dispel the darkness?"

Leafstar glanced around until she spotted Hawkwing, who tried to look as if he hadn't been listening the whole time. By now he was so excited that his belly was churning even harder, and he was afraid that he might throw up the prey he had just eaten.

Leafstar gazed thoughtfully at Hawkwing for so long that he had to clamp his jaws firmly together to stop himself from telling her to hurry up and decide.

"Very well," she mewed at last. "I guess Hawkwing can go."

"Really?" Hawkwing's father Sharpclaw turned an incredulous look on his Clan leader. "You're going to *reward* that hot-headed young mouse-brain for arguing with you in front of the whole Clan? Is it really the best idea to send a cat who can't control himself?"

Despite himself, Hawkwing felt a hot blaze of anger, and had to clamp his jaws shut to bite back a sharp protest. He had to turn away to hide from every cat how furious he was. *I don't want to react to being called hot-headed by acting even more hot-headed . . . but it isn't fair! Why does Sharpclaw have to ruin everything?*

"I've made my decision, Sharpclaw," Leafstar meowed firmly.

Hawkwing glanced up, too nervous to hope. *I know she won't let me go—not after Sharpclaw's rant.*

Leafstar looked down at him, her even gaze revealing nothing. "Hawkwing will go on this quest."

Hawkwing's anger ebbed away like rain sinking into parched earth. *I can go! I can go on the quest, and help find the spark that remains!* He thought again of the other Clans—how exciting it would be to meet other cats who lived like SkyClan. It was all he could do not to break into a happy, self-satisfied purr.

The sun had set, and shadows stretched across the gorge. As Hawkwing headed toward his den, thinking longingly of his comfortable nest, he spotted Sharpclaw padding determinedly toward him.

What does he want? Hawkwing wondered nervously.

He halted to wait for his father. "Don't start complaining or arguing!" he burst out, before Sharpclaw had the chance to say a word. He knew it wasn't advisable to speak to his father this way, but he just couldn't stomach another lecture. Not while he was still glowing from their leader's announcement. "Leafstar has decided, and I'm going, whether you're happy about it or not."

"I'm *not* happy about it," Sharpclaw admitted, his eyes narrowing, "but maybe not for the reason you think. One day, Hawkwing, when you have kits of your own, you'll know what it feels like to almost lose them."

What does that mean? "Don't you think I can look after myself?" Hawkwing retorted, a growl in his voice. "You're talking like a queen in the nursery—but I'm not a kit anymore. I'm a warrior!"

Sharpclaw nodded, unexpectedly serious. "I know that. But I can still be worried about you, Hawkwing. I've been talking to Cherrytail about this," he mewed. "Do you think you might have become too reckless since Duskpaw died?"

Hawkwing was already on edge, and the mention of his brother made his self-control snap. *Just when I finally feel like I don't have to feel guilty every moment . . .* "I don't want to hear about Duskpaw anymore!" he spat.

Sharpclaw's green eyes widened in a mixture of shock and dismay. He stared at Hawkwing in silence for several heartbeats before he spoke again. "How can you want to forget your own brother?" he asked incredulously.

"That's not what I meant—" Hawkwing began, horrified that Sharpclaw believed he could ever feel that way, but his father had already spun around and begun to walk away.

Watching his father's retreating back, Hawkwing felt claws

of guilt grip around his heart. *Of course I'm not trying to forget Duskpaw. I didn't mean it like that! Did I?*

He searched his heart, and realized no, he didn't. He never wanted to forget Duskpaw, his silliest littermate, who had always been able to make him smile. All he had wanted was to push away the painful memories, and not always think about how much he was missing his brother. But Sharpclaw hadn't given him a chance to explain.

Hawkwing hung his head, despair clouding out the happy glow he'd felt at Leafstar's decision.

Whatever the rest of the Clan sees in me, Sharpclaw doesn't. Will my father ever understand?

Clouds covered the sky and a thin drizzle was falling, soaking through Hawkwing's fur and making him shiver. The dawn light was strengthening, but there was no sign of the sun.

Sagenose, Firefern, and Harrybrook had been chosen to go on the new quest with Hawkwing, Darktail, and Rain. All of them were crouching around the fresh-kill pile, bolting down prey before setting out on their search.

Hawkwing swallowed the last bite of mouse and stretched out his forelegs to loosen up for the long journey. Beside him, Darktail was doing the same.

"How long do you think we'll be away?" Hawkwing asked him.

The white tom paused before replying, a thoughtful look in his eyes. "As long as it takes," he replied at last. "Until we find the spark and dispel the darkness."

His words awoke a glow of determination in Hawkwing's heart. *Yes! This time we won't stop until we find Firestar's kin!*

Rising to his paws, Darktail gathered his patrol around him with a sweep of his tail. At the same moment Leafstar appeared through the drizzle, with Echosong limping at her side, and a group of the SkyClan cats straggling behind.

"We're ready to go," Darktail announced, sharing a solemn look with the Clan leader. "I promise you, I'll succeed this time."

Leafstar dipped her head, while Echosong padded around and gave traveling herbs to each of the questing cats. Hawkwing licked them up, grimacing at the bitter taste on his tongue.

"May StarClan light your path," Leafstar meowed, "and bring you home safe."

Calling their good-byes, the patrol followed Darktail as he headed for the trail that led to the top of the cliff. As he brought up the rear, Hawkwing noticed the apprentice Pebblepaw staring at him, a worried look in her eyes.

Is she anxious about me, or the whole group? Hawkwing asked himself.

He had barely spoken to Pebblepaw since their return from the first quest. Not out of hostility—that was all in the past—but because he knew she was grieving for Billystorm, and that he was maybe the last cat she would want to comfort her.

Now he realized that Pebblepaw could just be thinking about the good of the Clan, but he couldn't stifle the feeling that she was especially fearful for him.

But I'm not sure she cares anything about me, he told himself. *I can't even begin to imagine it.*

All Hawkwing could do was tear his gaze away and bound over to the foot of the cliff, scrambling to catch up with his Clanmates. He had no idea anymore of how he felt about the young she-cat.

With Darktail in the lead, the patrol headed across a wide stretch of grass, bounded by lines of bushes on all four sides. Several fox-lengths away a group of huge black-and-white animals were standing, tearing at the grass and grinding it slowly between teeth like jutting stones. Hawkwing cast sidelong glances at them, trying hard not to look nervous in front of the two rogues.

"What are those?" Harrybrook asked, the fur on his shoulders beginning to bristle. "I didn't think animals could be that big!"

"They're called cows," Rain informed him with a wave of his bushy gray tail. "They're not dangerous, but it's best to stay away from them. They never look where they're going."

Two days had passed since the questing cats had left the SkyClan camp. After the first rainy morning the weather had cleared and now a stiff breeze was blowing, sending fluffy white clouds scudding across the sky. Hawkwing was enjoying the warmth of sunlight on his pelt, and the enticing scent of prey from the bushes up ahead.

I hope Darktail lets us stop to hunt soon.

Beyond the line of bushes Hawkwing could see a copse of taller trees, and beyond that the walls of a Twoleg den, looming up vast even at that distance. Darktail seemed to be heading straight for it.

"We're not going there, are we?" Hawkwing asked. "We don't want to get mixed up with Twolegs."

"That's exactly where we're going," Darktail replied. "It's a Twoleg barn, sure, but the Twolegs abandoned it long ago."

Like the badgers abandoned the dens in that clearing? Hawkwing thought, instantly wary. But he kept his suspicions to himself, only resolving to be very careful as he and the rest of the patrol approached the den.

"Why are we going there?" Firefern asked, putting on speed to pad beside Darktail and Hawkwing.

"Because I think it might be one of the places where Firestar and his kin took refuge," Darktail replied. "They might even still be there, but if they have moved on, we might be able to find traces of them."

"Cool!" Firefern meowed.

Hawkwing's pads prickled with excitement. He hadn't realized that they could be so near to meeting with the other Clans. *What will they think of us? What will we say to them?*

Darktail led the way through the bushes, the thorny branches scraping the cats' sides as they wriggled through the gaps. The copse lay a few tail-lengths ahead, in a tangle of ferns and bramble. The air was still full of prey-scent, but Hawkwing wasn't thinking about hunting anymore, when they might be so close to the end of their quest.

Then as they drew nearer to the trees, Hawkwing caught a flicker of movement in the branches. Instantly he froze.

"Darktail!" he called out in a hoarse voice. "Up ahead—"

Then he broke off as Darktail bounded forward, obviously relaxed, and called out, "Toad? Toad, is that you?"

At the sound of Darktail's voice a skinny, mottled brown tom jumped down from one of the trees and trotted forward to meet Darktail. "Hi," he mewed, stretching out his neck so that the two cats could touch noses. Darktail mewed a happy greeting, his whiskers twitching with excitement.

"It looks like they're old friends," Hawkwing murmured to Firefern.

"Yes, we are," Darktail responded, glancing over his shoulder as the rest of the patrol caught up with him. "I'm sorry, friends, let me introduce you—this is Toad. We've known each other for ages! Toad and Rain and I have often hunted together in the past—isn't that right, Rain?"

Rain nodded. "Right. Hi, Toad. It's good to see you again."

Toad nodded. "So what are you doing in these parts?" he asked. His glance raked over the SkyClan cats. "And who are these?"

"More friends of ours," Darktail replied, settling down comfortably in the shelter of a clump of ferns and wrapping his tail around his paws. Rain sat beside him, and beckoned with his tail for the other questing cats to join them.

"We're looking for even more cats," Darktail continued to Toad. "A big group of them. Have you seen any unfamiliar cats around here?"

"Funny you should say that." Toad raised one hind paw to give his ear a vigorous scratch. "I did see a whole crowd of them—strong cats, well fed, with glossy fur. It was weird . . . I've never seen so many traveling together in a group."

Excitement blazed through Hawkwing like fire licking through dry bracken. *The spark that remains!* His earlier apprehension at the sudden appearance of another rogue was swallowed up and forgotten. "They sound like Clan cats!" he exclaimed. "Could they have been Firestar's kin?"

Toad twitched his whiskers dismissively. "I've never heard of any cat called Firestar," he replied. "But I kept my distance. I just know that they camped for a while, here in this barn, and they weren't rogues."

Hawkwing's paws itched to sprint straight to the barn. *We were right all along!*

"Come on!" he urged Darktail, springing to his paws and kneading the ground in his eagerness to get going. "Let's hurry!"

"Hang on a moment." Sagenose flicked out his tail to stop Hawkwing from bounding toward the barn.

Irritated, Hawkwing opened his jaws to protest, then saw the doubt in his Clanmate's eyes. He sat down again, saying nothing.

"As I understand it," Sagenose went on, "the other Clans have an awful lot of cats between them. Would they all fit in that barn?"

"Good question," Harrybrook put in. "And how long have they lived there? According to Ravenpaw, they left the forest many, many moons ago."

"Well, it's a big barn," Toad responded. "And it would take many moons for that many cats to find a suitable place to live."

"Of course, we don't have all the answers now," Darktail replied with an unconcerned flick of his ears. "Perhaps some Clans have splintered off. Perhaps their numbers have dwindled . . . but surely we should check out the barn, at least?"

The SkyClan cats glanced at each other, Hawkwing struggling to conceal his impatience.

"Do you know if the Clan cats are still there?" Sagenose asked Toad.

The skinny rogue shrugged. "They may be," he replied. "I noticed them when they first moved in, but I haven't been back there in a while."

"Why don't we just go and *look*?" Hawkwing demanded. "What do we have to lose?"

Sagenose gave a grunt of agreement. "Okay, but let's all stay alert. We need to be ready if there's any trouble."

"It'll be fine," Darktail mewed easily. "Toad, come along with us. Perhaps we can introduce you."

Toad padded alongside as Darktail led the questing cats toward the barn. As he drew closer, Hawkwing couldn't work out what he thought of the place. His fur began to bristle as he spotted a monster crouching beside a wall of reddish rock, only to lie flat again as he realized it must be dead: Its insides were blackened and shriveled as if fire had roared through it.

Hawkwing shivered. *Even for a monster, that's a cruel way to die!*

There were no sounds coming from the barn, which made

Hawkwing think Darktail must be right, and that the Twolegs who built it had abandoned it long ago. But when he opened his jaws to taste the air and pick up the traces of the Clan cats, strong Twoleg scents flowed in.

Would Firestar's kin really hide out here, so close to Twolegs?

Hawkwing glanced at his Clanmates, who were all creeping around the barn, sniffing eagerly for the cat scent they hoped to find. Warily he padded over to join them, but the scent of Twolegs was swamping everything else. And there was another scent, cutting through it; alarm jolted through Hawkwing as he identified it.

"Dogs!" he yowled.

At the same moment the doors of the barn burst open. Two huge dogs sprang out, then skidded to a halt. Their jaws were parted and their tongues lolled as they let out bone-chilling howls. Two vicious-looking Twolegs were holding them back by long tendrils fastened around their necks.

For a heartbeat Hawkwing and the other cats froze with terror. One of the Twolegs growled something, and to Hawkwing's horror both Twolegs let go of their tendrils. The dogs were free!

"Run!" Darktail screeched.

Hawkwing spun around and raced away, his Clanmates pelting alongside him, with Darktail and the other rogues just ahead.

"Follow me—make for the trees!" Darktail yowled. "Dogs can't climb!"

Hawkwing's paws barely touched the ground as he hurled

himself toward the copse. He could hear the dogs barking behind him, and imagined he could feel their hot breath on his hindquarters. His heart pounded at the thought of their vicious teeth meeting on his tail.

Toad was the first cat to reach the nearest tree. At once he swarmed up the trunk and balanced on a low branch. Darktail clambered up beside him. Hawkwing leaped up into another tree next to them. Digging his claws into the fork where he crouched, he looked around and gasped with relief as he saw Firefern, Harrybrook, and Sagenose safe among the branches of a third tree on the other side of Darktail.

Last of all, the dogs only a mouse-length behind him, Rain made an enormous leap and dug his foreclaws into a branch of Darktail's tree. Hoisting himself up, he crouched there, hissing defiance at the dogs below.

Hawkwing gazed down at the ferocious creatures, his chest heaving as he fought for breath. The dogs were running in wild circles at the base of the trees, barking fiercely as they looked up, their jaws slavering. Their Twolegs stood at a distance, pointing their forepaws and letting out huffs of laughter.

How are we going to get out of this? Hawkwing wondered, trying to stop himself from trembling with fear.

His gaze was still fixed on the dogs when he heard a sudden shriek, and whipped his head around to see Toad falling from his branch in a frantic tangle of paws and tail. His claws scraped on another branch as he plummeted past it, but he couldn't get a grip; he hit the ground right between the two dogs.

Toad was obviously half stunned by the impact. He struggled to his paws and tried to run, but he was far too slow. Before he had staggered more than a couple of steps, the nearest dog was upon him, grabbing his hind leg in its jaws.

Toad let out a terrified screech. "Help me!"

Hawkwing couldn't see what he or any of the others could do. *If we jump down and fight, the dogs will kill us . . . they're fiercer even than the badgers.*

Howls of anguish came from the other SkyClan cats. Hawkwing opened his jaws and let out his own terror and despair. *This is too horrible! It's happening right in front of us, but there's nothing we can do!* He couldn't go on looking any longer, as Toad's shrieks were abruptly cut off.

"Listen, all of you!" Darktail hissed. "This is our chance. While the dogs are distracted, we can escape."

"But what about Toad?" Hawkwing asked, even though he knew how useless the question was.

The rogue's gaze turned dark. "There's nothing we can do for Toad now."

CHAPTER 11

Turning, Darktail began to scramble from branch to branch, heading toward the far side of the copse. Hawkwing followed him, thankful that his Clan had trained him to hunt in trees, so he could be sure-pawed so far above the ground. With every paw step he struggled not to listen to the dreadful snarling and tearing that came from the dogs. His Clanmates clambered after him, and Rain brought up the rear.

When they reached the edge of the trees, Darktail leaped down. "Run!" he yowled.

The rest of the patrol pelted after him, their belly fur brushing the grass and their tails streaming out behind them. Darktail led them to the hedge, where they thrust their way through again, ignoring the thorns that tore at their fur, until they could halt, panting, on the other side.

Hawkwing's belly was cramping so hard he thought he would have to vomit. He wanted to shut out the memory of Toad being ripped apart by the dogs, but he thought the sound and the reek of blood would stay with him for the rest of his life.

Crouching down, he peered through a gap in the hedge,

ready to warn his Clanmates if the dogs pursued them. But he saw nothing; all he heard was some distant barking and the yowls of Twolegs, which quickly faded away.

"Now what do we do?" Sagenose asked, when all the cats had managed to catch their breath.

Darktail sat with his head bowed; the light had gone out of his eyes, and he looked smaller, hunched in on himself. "I'm sorry," he mewed. "It looks like there aren't any cats here—at least, not anymore."

"I can't believe that!" Hawkwing protested. "Toad said he saw them! We can't have traveled so far from camp, only to fail again. We must try to pick up their scent."

Darktail made no reply. He wouldn't look at any cat, and his fur bristled as if he was still in shock. *He's too overcome with grief to think clearly,* Hawkwing thought. But Sagenose gave Hawkwing a brisk nod.

"You're right," he told Hawkwing. "We'll search, but we have to stay well away from that barn. Harrybrook, you keep watch, and warn us if you see any sign of those dogs, or the Twolegs, coming back."

Encouraged by the older warrior, Hawkwing led his friends in a wide circle around the barn, noses to the ground as they desperately searched for some trace of the Clan cats.

If Toad was right, Firestar's kin must be close, he thought. *We can't give up now!*

But eventually even Hawkwing had to admit that they had failed. The sun was much lower in the sky, and they still hadn't picked up even the faintest trace of cat scent. Apart from themselves, there were no cats here, and no evidence that cats had ever been there: no scraps of fur, no scratched-up ground where they might have buried their dirt, no feathers or other remains of prey.

Finally, tail drooping dispiritedly, Hawkwing led the way back to where Darktail still crouched in the shelter of the hedge with Rain beside him. He looked up as the SkyClan cats approached.

"No luck?" he asked.

Hawkwing shook his head. "Nothing. I can't understand it."

"Maybe the Twolegs and their dogs chased the missing Clan cats away," Rain suggested. "They might even have killed them."

"All of them?" Hawkwing couldn't believe that, even though he had just seen those dogs kill a cat. "Even if they did, surely we would have found traces—blood, or fur, or *something*."

"And you led us into this mess," Firefern hissed, her ginger fur bristling as she padded up to Darktail and thrust her muzzle close to his. "Is this a game to you? Watching cats get hurt?"

Darktail looked up at her, his eyes wide and tragic. His ears were flattened to his head and his whiskers quivered. Hawkwing couldn't remember ever seeing a cat so distressed. *Except maybe me, after Duskpaw died.*

"Okay! I messed up!" Darktail confessed, flattening himself onto his belly. "I promised to lead you to the Clan cats, and I failed. I failed horribly! *Again*. And I'll never, ever forgive myself for the death of Toad. He was my friend. There's nothing I can do to make up for my stupidity. *I deserve to be fed to the dogs—not poor Toad!*"

Firefern backed off, looking ashamed of her outburst. "Sorry," she muttered. "You just lost your friend. I know you must be feeling bad."

"I'll go and search the barn!" Darktail staggered to his paws. "I don't care if the dogs are still there. I'll find out if the Clan cats stayed there, or die trying!"

"You'll do no such thing," Sagenose growled, while Rain pressed Darktail down again with a paw on his shoulder. "It's not worth another life."

Sympathy for Darktail flooded over Hawkwing, swamping his frustration and sense of failure. The rogue looked not just grief-stricken, but confused—as if he'd just woken up from a dark, terrifying dream . . . that was actually real. He clearly couldn't believe what had happened.

Hawkwing settled down beside the rogue cat, so close that their pelts brushed.

"Don't be too hard on yourself," he meowed. "Toad just fell off the branch. There was nothing you could've done."

Darktail nodded. "Yes. I . . . I tried to grab him, but he was too heavy for me to hold."

"My brother Duskpaw died in a fire," Hawkwing went on, pressing his muzzle briefly into Darktail's shoulder. "And I keep telling myself I should have saved him. So I know what it's like to feel responsible for a cat's death. It's like a vicious claw underneath your fur, snagging and tearing at you. I don't want you to go through that, too."

Darktail gave Hawkwing a brief glance before going back to studying his own paws. "Thanks," he whispered.

Hawkwing drew away slightly, leaving Darktail with Rain, and gestured with his tail for his Clanmates to gather around. "We have to decide what to do now," he meowed.

Sagenose shrugged. "What can we do? We've no proof that the Clan cats were ever here."

"Even if they were," Firefern agreed with a frustrated twitch of her tail, "there's nothing to tell us where they've gone now."

"You mean we should just turn around and go home?" Harrybrook asked, blinking unhappily.

Hawkwing opened his jaws to protest. "But we—"

"What else do you suggest?" Sagenose interrupted. "Should we just wander around, trying to pick up scent that might never have been there in the first place? That's a good way to get ourselves killed."

Firefern and Harrybrook both let out approving murmurs as Sagenose spoke. Hawkwing could tell there was no arguing with them, and deep down he had to admit they were right. *There's no way we can find Firestar's kin now.*

"Okay," he mewed, reluctant to believe this was his second failed quest. *I was so sure we would succeed this time! And now we're no closer to finding the spark that remains.* "I guess we go home."

As he was speaking, Darktail rose to his paws and padded over with Rain at his shoulder. Hawkwing could see that he was beginning to recover, though he still looked shaken.

"We should move away from here," he meowed. "Those dogs could still be around."

Hawkwing cast an uneasy glance back at the barn. There

was no sign of the dogs or Twolegs—he was almost certain they had gone away—but he couldn't rid himself of the fear that they could come bursting out at a heartbeat's notice and hunt him and his Clanmates down.

Their paws trailing despondently, their tails dragging on the ground, the patrol followed Sagenose, who took the lead back across the stretch of grass toward a holly thicket at the far side. "I think we should make camp for the night," he suggested, "and then head back to the gorge at sunrise."

Within the thicket was a small clearing sheltered by ferns, where water seeped from a crack in a rocky outcrop and trickled into a small pool. Darktail let himself flop down at the water's edge with a drawn-out groan. Hawkwing could see that though he had roused himself to follow the others away from danger, he was still devastated by the death of Toad.

"Why don't you rest," he urged, "and some of us will hunt."

"I'll go," Sagenose offered immediately. "Harrybrook, will you come with me?"

"Sure," the young gray tom replied.

"I'll come too," mewed Rain.

The hunters moved off into the bushes, leaving Hawkwing and Firefern beside Darktail. While Firefern coaxed the rogue to lap some of the water, Hawkwing drew into himself, unable to think anymore of what he could say to Darktail. He was too busy imagining all too clearly what it would be like when they returned to the SkyClan camp.

Sharpclaw doesn't think I can do anything right. And now I'll have to explain to him that we've failed again.

By the time the hunting party returned the sun was going down, filling the thicket with shadows. A chilly breeze had sprung up, rustling the fern fronds and piercing Hawkwing's fur with cold claws.

Rain strode into the clearing dangling two mice by their tails, while Sagenose followed with a thrush and Firefern dragged a rabbit between her forelegs.

"At least the hunting was good," Sagenose mewed, dropping his prey beside the pool. "Come and eat."

Hawkwing forced himself to move forward and take his share of the prey, but he felt every mouthful was going to choke him. Darktail hardly touched a morsel, and none of the others had much appetite either, except for Rain, who devoured his mouse and swiped his tongue around his jaws with satisfaction.

As full darkness gathered, Hawkwing curled up and closed his eyes, but it took a long time for sleep to come, and when it did, his dreams were full of Toad's desperate shrieks as the dogs tore him apart.

Hawkwing opened his eyes and stretched his jaws into a wide yawn. Pale dawn light was filtering through the branches of the holly thicket. Blinking, Hawkwing sat up and saw that the rest of the patrol were rousing too. For a moment he found it hard to remember where they were and what they should be doing. When his memory flowed back, he felt as if a huge rock had dropped into his belly.

This is the day we have to head back and admit we failed—again.

A few scraps of prey were left from the night before. No cat felt like hunting for more, so when they had shared the meager remains they set out again, with Darktail in the lead. The rogue tom seemed to be looking inward, scarcely speaking; Hawkwing guessed that he was still reliving Toad's terrible death.

The sun was just coming up, shedding a golden light across their path. Every blade of grass glittered with dew. But Hawkwing's thoughts were still dark as he thought of their return to their waiting Clan. *How am I going to explain all this to Leafstar and my father?*

After a while, Darktail dropped back a few paw steps to pad alongside Hawkwing. "You look worried," he meowed. "Are you okay?"

Hawkwing was touched that Darktail should think about his feelings in the midst of his own grieving. "Yes, I am worried," he confessed. "I'm nervous about going home and telling every cat that we're no nearer to finding Firestar's kin. I really hoped I would impress Sharpclaw on this quest, but now he's going to despise me as much as ever."

Darktail gave him a sympathetic glance. "Sharpclaw doesn't sound like much of a father," he observed, "if he blames you for something that isn't your fault."

Hawkwing felt a tinge of defensiveness at the white tom's words. *After all, Darktail doesn't really know Sharpclaw.*

"He's a great cat," he responded. "But . . . well, things haven't been the same between us since Duskpaw died."

"Then maybe you'll both get over it," Darktail mewed with

an understanding nod. "But remember—it's all well and good being kin to a cat, but in the wild you have to take your kin where you find it."

His somber tone convinced Hawkwing that he was speaking from personal experience. He felt a sharp prick of curiosity, wondering if this had anything to do with Darktail's friend who had starved to death in a harsh leaf-bare, but Darktail said no more, and Hawkwing didn't feel that he could ask him about it.

Hawkwing and the rest of the patrol approached the Sky-Clan camp as their second day of travel drew to a close. The sinking sun cast red light over the stretch of grass that separated the gorge from the Twolegplace, and a few warriors of StarClan already glimmered in the sky.

As the cats headed toward the gorge, Hawkwing picked up the scent of the border markers, and halted abruptly, his pads prickling with apprehension. "That's odd," he muttered.

"What's the matter?" Harrybrook asked.

"The scent markings are stale," Hawkwing replied. "They haven't been renewed since dawn at least."

His Clanmates tasted the air, and after a moment Sage-nose nodded. "You're right," he mewed. "Maybe they're just late with the evening patrol. . . ."

"Do you really think so?" Hawkwing challenged him. "Or has there been more trouble? Let's get down there!"

The patrol picked up speed as they wound their way among the shrubs at the top of the gorge, and the shadows of the trees lay dark across their path. Hawkwing imagined they were ominous paws reaching out to grab him, then gave his pelt a shake, telling himself not to be so mouse-brained.

Twilight lay thick in the gorge as Hawkwing and the others reached the head of the trail that led down into the camp. It was impossible to see exactly what was going on down below, except that there seemed to be a crowd of cats clustering around the entrance to Echosong's den.

Hawkwing took the lead as the patrol headed into the gorge. He was scarcely aware of the cliff dropping away below him as his paws skimmed over the rocks. His heart was pounding and he could hardly catch his breath.

"What happened?" he demanded, thrusting his way into the group of cats around Echosong's den. "Is something wrong?"

His sister Blossomheart turned to face him. In the dim light he saw that she had an angry wound on one shoulder, with a clump of fur missing, as if some creature had bitten her.

"Those animals came back," she told Hawkwing. "Those . . . raccoons. It was terrible. Leafstar lost a life!"

Hawkwing felt as though he had been clawed in his belly. Now he understood why the scent markings hadn't been renewed, and why his Clanmates were waiting anxiously outside the medicine cats' den. And now that he had a moment to catch his breath, he could pick up the reek of the raccoons, fading now but still clear enough to reveal the creatures' recent presence in the camp. The scent of blood was mingled with it, and as Hawkwing looked around he saw that more of his

Clanmates bore the marks of the raccoons' teeth and claws. Most of them were already patched with cobweb and poultices of marigold; both medicine cats must have been working tirelessly.

"There were more of them this time," Rabbitleap added from where he stood beside Blossomheart. "What are we going to do?"

Before any cat could reply, Sharpclaw appeared at the mouth of the den. His green eyes glinted in the twilight as his gaze swept across the cluster of cats.

"Leafstar will be fine," he announced. "There's no need to worry about her, or to hang around here like a bunch of sick rabbits. Tinycloud . . ." He angled his ears toward the white she-cat. "You're okay, aren't you? Round up some of the other uninjured warriors and take them to renew the scent markers."

Tinycloud gave a brisk nod. "Right, Sharpclaw." She headed off, waving her tail to collect more of her Clanmates around her.

As the crowd thinned out, Sharpclaw spotted Hawkwing and the other questing cats, who had hurried up behind him. "You're back!" he exclaimed, his tail curling up in surprise. "Come in here and report—no, not all of you, just Hawkwing and . . . yes, Darktail."

Hawkwing's belly cramped; this was the moment he had been dreading. *StarClan, help me. It wasn't our fault! No cat could have tracked Firestar's kin from that barn.* But Hawkwing knew that Sharpclaw wouldn't see it like that.

He padded into the medicine cats' den, with Darktail hard on his paws. Inside he saw Leafstar lying in a nest of moss; she was stretched out on one side with her belly exposed, and Echosong was patting marigold pulp onto a scar on her chest between her forelegs. Hawkwing felt sick as he realized that must be the wound that had taken one of his Clan leader's lives.

On the other side of the den, Frecklewish was patching Mistfeather's shoulder with a thick wad of cobweb. The gray tom flinched as her paws pressed the web down firmly to stop his wound from bleeding.

Leafstar raised her head as Hawkwing and Darktail entered the den. She looked exhausted, but her voice was steady as she meowed, "So you're back! Are all of you safe?"

Hawkwing nodded. "We're all fine."

"And did you find Firestar's kin?"

Hawkwing felt as if the one word was going to choke him, it was so hard to get it out. "No."

"No?" It was Sharpclaw who spoke, his voice edged with irritation. "Why not?"

Glancing at Darktail, Hawkwing saw that the rogue tom was standing at his shoulder, his head bent dejectedly as he stared at his paws. Obviously there was no use expecting him to explain anything.

"We traveled for two days," Hawkwing began, speaking to Leafstar. It was easier to face his leader than the icy green stare of his father. "Then we met a cat called Toad, a friend of Darktail's." He went on to describe how Toad had told them of a group of cats who had stayed for a while in the abandoned Twoleg barn, and how Twolegs and dogs had sprung out on the patrol when they tried to investigate. His voice shook and cold shivers ran through him as he related the story of Toad's death. In his mind he could still hear the rogue cat's shrieks and the terrible snarling of the dogs. "And when we tried to pick up a scent trail," he finished, "we couldn't find anything. Not a single trace that Clan cats had ever been there."

Sharpclaw turned a hostile gaze on Darktail. "You told us you knew how to find Firestar's kin."

Darktail didn't look up. "I was wrong," he mewed humbly. "I'm sorry."

"'Sorry' doesn't help us," Mistfeather put in with a snort of contempt. "We're no nearer to finding out what StarClan's prophecy means."

"And yet more darkness seems to be gathering, with all these attacks," Sharpclaw added. "We need to follow StarClan's advice as soon as we can."

"As far as I can see," Mistfeather growled, still glaring at Darktail, "we'd have been far better off if you and your rogue friend had never set paw in our camp."

Darktail cringed away from him. "I tried my best—" he began.

"And your best wasn't good enough," Sharpclaw told him curtly. "Hawkwing, did this Toad tell you anything about where the Clan cats might have gone?"

"No," Hawkwing replied, beginning to feel annoyed. "If he had, don't you think we would have tried to follow them?"

"I don't know what you would have done," Sharpclaw retorted. "I only know that you've gone out twice now, and we're still no nearer to fulfilling the prophecy."

"*And* we've lost Billystorm," Mistfeather added.

Hawkwing's belly churned and he twitched the tip of his tail to and fro, doing his best to hold on to his temper. *Like you would have done any better if you'd been there,* he thought, but he had the sense not to say the words out loud.

"That's enough." Leafstar's voice was weary, and Hawkwing realized that Mistfeather's mention of Billystorm was more than she could cope with just then. "We need to think more deeply about this before we decide what to do next."

"And you need to rest." Echosong spoke for the first time, her voice firm. "Out, all of you! Frecklewish, go and see if any cat still has untreated wounds. Otherwise, no cat sets paw in here until morning."

As he left the den in obedience to the medicine cat's orders, Hawkwing felt as if his heart had sunk right down into his paws. *We have enough trouble with these new creatures attacking our camp,* he thought. *How can StarClan expect us to follow their prophecy as well? And what's going to happen to us if we don't?*

CHAPTER 12

❧

Hawkwing was roused from his sleep in the warriors' den by the sound of his father's voice yowling through the camp. "Let all cats gather here beneath the Rockpile for a Clan meeting!"

Around Hawkwing, his Clanmates were already leaping up and heading out of the cave. He staggered to his paws and shook scraps of bedding out of his pelt. Exhausted from the journey and the shock of learning about the fresh attack, he felt as if he had hardly rested at all, even though the sun was already well above the trees.

Hawkwing was the last to leave the den, following Rileypaw and Stormheart down the trail to where Sharpclaw waited at the foot of the Rockpile. There was no sign of Leafstar—Hawkwing guessed she was still resting—but he spotted the two rogues, Darktail and Rain, off to the side of the gathering crowd.

Hawkwing joined the others and flopped down beside his sister, Cloudmist. "What now?" he muttered into her ear.

Cloudmist shook her head. "Just listen," she whispered back.

"SkyClan has suffered a second attack," Sharpclaw

announced when all the cats had settled down. "It's time to change our strategy. To begin with, patrols will be larger from now on. The raccoons may have been driven off for the time being, but if they think we are weak, or that there aren't many of us, they'll try to attack again for sure."

"That makes sense," Hawkwing murmured to his sister.

"It means every cat will have to patrol more often," she agreed, giving a quick lick to a scratch on her shoulder, "but if it keeps the raccoons away, it'll be worth it."

Hawkwing noticed that some of his Clanmates were casting mistrustful glances at Darktail and Rain, and he remembered the hostility of Sharpclaw and Mistfeather when the questing patrol had returned the night before with news of their failure.

He thought too about his own hostility toward Darktail before they had left on the second quest. *Every cat blamed me for feeling that way—but now they seem to agree that Darktail is a menace.*

But Hawkwing didn't feel the same way anymore. After the events of the quest, and especially after seeing Darktail's grief at the death of his friend Toad, he couldn't help but trust the white tom.

The same suspicion his other Clanmates had begun to show appeared in the eyes of Waspwhisker as he rose to his paws with a sidelong glance at the two rogue cats. "What if the threat is actually *inside* the camp?" he asked.

Every cat knew what he meant, and heads turned to stare at Darktail and Rain. Hawkwing heard one or two hisses, and some cat called out, "Yes! What about that?"

Darktail remained calm in the face of Waspwhisker's accusation. He stood up and dipped his head politely toward Sharpclaw, as if he was asking permission to speak.

"I never meant to hurt the Clan," he meowed. "But I admit I made some mistakes. Surely it's a measure of my honor that I want to do everything I can to make up for it? Surely the fact that I'm still around, trying my best to put things right, has to count for something?"

Waspwhisker gave a dismissive flick of his tail. "Rogue cats just don't belong with a Clan. They will never understand Clan cats' ways," he growled. "It's impossible!"

"This is true," Sharpclaw agreed. "Clan cats have rules; rogues have none. Clan cats are taught to care for each other; rogue cats think only of their own survival. Darktail is not one of us, and he never will be."

"That's not fair!" Hawkwing blurted out, leaping to his paws. "Sharpclaw, you know that Darktail fought bravely for the Clan when the raccoons attacked. And you should have seen the grief on his face when his friend Toad fell out of that tree. He *has* lost friends, just like we have. He doesn't need us throwing accusations at him."

Even while he was speaking, Hawkwing was torn about contradicting his father, especially for a cat he hadn't known for very long. He wasn't keen, either, on repeating his earlier argument with Sharpclaw in front of the whole Clan. But he couldn't stifle the conviction that this time Sharpclaw was being unreasonable and harsh.

Sharpclaw whipped his head around to glare at his son, a

look of outrage in his green eyes. "Why do you always have to argue with me?" he demanded. "Darktail isn't your replacement brother, and he doesn't deserve more loyalty than kin!"

"Wait . . . I'm sure that's not what Hawkwing thinks," Cherrytail put in, but Sharpclaw ignored her, still fixing Hawkwing with a hard stare.

Hawkwing's fur began to bristle. He felt like a scrap of twig being whirled around in a fierce gale of emotion. Grief and anger filled him at his father's words, along with confusion about why he would say such a thing. And every hair on his pelt burned with embarrassment as he realized that all his Clanmates were looking at him.

The conflicting pressures were too much to bear. Unable to stop himself, even though he knew that it made him seem as immature as a day-old kit, Hawkwing whipped around with a contemptuous flick of his tail and stormed away, back up the trail to his den.

I know it looks like I'm sulking, but I don't care what any cat thinks. If their father had been so unfair to them, they'd be as angry as I am now.

Back in the warriors' den, Hawkwing flung himself down into his nest, letting his anger surge over him. But after a few moments, guilt and renewed embarrassment began to prick him like a thorn in his belly.

If my Clanmates are patrolling, I want to be there with them, he realized. *I want to help them, and keep them safe. Oh, fox dung . . . I know I'm behaving like a petulant kit!*

Taking a deep breath, Hawkwing rose to his paws, ready to head back out of the den. Just then, a shadow fell over the den floor, and he saw that Pebblepaw was poking her head through the entrance. She was the last cat Hawkwing had expected to see. *This feels totally weird. I've hardly spoken to her since we went on the first quest together.*

"Are you okay?" Pebblepaw asked. "That must have been awful, having your father be harsh to you like that. In front of the whole Clan, too."

For a moment Hawkwing didn't know how to reply. He didn't want to seem weak or immature in front of Pebblepaw. At the same time, he couldn't help asking himself what it meant that she'd left a Clan meeting just to come check on him.

I can't cope with this right now.

"I'm fine!" he snapped at last. "I don't need any cat's pity."

Pebblepaw's eyes widened with hurt. Without another word she withdrew from the den; Hawkwing followed her out and saw her stalking down the trail.

That went well, he thought, annoyed with himself. *Why can't I think before I speak?*

"Pebblepaw, wait!" he called out.

The speckled white she-cat halted, then after a heartbeat turned her head to look up at him. "What?"

"I'm sorry," Hawkwing meowed. Even though he knew he had been wrong, it was hard to force the words out. "I shouldn't have snapped at you."

For a moment more Pebblepaw hesitated. "It's okay," she responded at last, ducking her head. Then she bounded off to the bottom of the cliff where her brother Parsleypaw was waiting.

Hawkwing watched her go, an unexpectedly warm feeling creeping through him from ears to tail-tip. *I'm glad I said that. I don't want to fight with her anymore.*

Glancing farther out across the camp, Hawkwing could see cats still gathered around Sharpclaw at the foot of the Rockpile. By the look of their bushed-up fur and twitching tails, they were still bickering. On the opposite side of the gorge, Darktail and Rain were heading up the cliff, leading a patrol with Bellapaw, Sandynose, and Mistfeather.

Hawkwing bunched his muscles, preparing to bound down the trail and across the camp to catch up with the departing cats. Then he relaxed again with a sigh. *It's no good. I want to protect the camp, but if I go haring after Darktail, it'll only make things worse with Sharpclaw.*

He waited until the patrol was gone. Then he turned and walked back to his den.

Hawkwing slipped through the undergrowth at the top of the gorge, following Bouncefire, Nettlesplash, Pebblepaw, and Sandynose, who had taken over Pebblepaw's training after Billystorm's death. As part of one of the new, larger patrols, Hawkwing kept all his senses alert for any sign that the raccoons were back on SkyClan territory. To his relief, everything seemed peaceful.

The camp had become more peaceful, too, in the few days since the questing patrol had returned. Hawkwing's Clanmates had stopped interrogating him about what had happened, and why they hadn't managed to track down Firestar's kin.

Leafstar, seeming recovered from the loss of her life, had spoken from the Rockpile, proclaiming that SkyClan would wait until Echosong received another vision from StarClan. "Maybe," she had meowed, "the next prophecy will be clearer."

Hawkwing wasn't sure that his leader was right. *StarClan's advice hasn't exactly been helpful so far,* he mused. *What if they don't actually want to help us?* He couldn't imagine why the spirits of their warrior ancestors would turn against them. *But our luck could not have been worse, and there has to be a reason for that. . . .*

Bouncefire, leading the patrol, brought them out of the undergrowth and across the stretch of grass that separated SkyClan territory from the Twolegplace. As they approached, Hawkwing saw that a new Twoleg rock made from freshly cut flat sticks had replaced the one that was burned. Thicker foliage had covered most of the scorch marks on the tree. Renewed grief swept over Hawkwing.

It's like my brother was never even here. . . .

He was careful not to look at Pebblepaw as they and their Clanmates padded past the Twoleg greenplace. He didn't want to be reminded of how he had saved her instead of Duskpaw, and also, he was surprised to realize, he didn't want Pebblepaw to feel any trace of guilt about that terrible day.

Reaching the farthest stretch of SkyClan territory, the patrol turned back. "Nothing to report, thank StarClan," Bouncefire commented.

But as they drew nearer to the wooded area above the gorge, Hawkwing spotted Darktail, alone, skirting the edge of the trees as if he was heading for the camp from the direction of the Twolegplace.

He's not with a patrol, so what is he doing? Hawkwing wondered.

His pelt prickled with anxiety as he saw Darktail crouch down, his head jerking as if he was being sick. But after a moment the rogue tom rose to his paws again and padded calmly away, making for the Twolegplace again.

That's really weird. . . .

"Hey, Bouncefire, I need to make dirt," Hawkwing called out. "I'll catch up to you."

Bouncefire waved his tail in acknowledgment as he and Nettlesplash, Sandynose, and Pebblepaw vanished into the undergrowth. Hawkwing bounded over to where Darktail had stopped. On the ground, he saw a few scraps of what looked and smelled like Twoleg food.

Hawkwing stood for several heartbeats, gazing down at the scraps. In one way, he wasn't surprised, assuming that rogue cats would eat anything, but what was really strange was that the food hadn't been eaten. Darktail hadn't been sick. He must have been carrying the food in his mouth, and then dropped it.

Maybe he didn't like the taste, Hawkwing thought, with a pang of pain as he remembered how much Duskpaw would have loved it. *But then, why did he go back toward the Twolegplace?*

Darktail was still in sight, a distant figure across the grass. Hawkwing decided to follow him, keeping his distance, and making sure that the breeze was blowing toward him, and wouldn't carry his scent to the rogue tom.

Unaware he was being followed, Darktail headed onward, until he slipped down a narrow Thunderpath between the first dens of the Twolegplace. Hawkwing felt his pelt prickle with apprehension. *I don't want to go in there.* Then he took a deep breath, bracing himself. *If Darktail can do it, so can I!*

Hawkwing kept glancing around warily, alert for the appearance of Twolegs or monsters, as he crept along in Darktail's paw steps. To his relief, not much time had passed before Darktail halted, then wriggled underneath a shiny barrier that blocked a gap between two lines of bushes.

Giving Darktail enough time to get ahead, Hawkwing squeezed through after him, and found himself standing at the edge of a stretch of smooth grass, surrounded by bushes covered with strange, brilliantly colored flowers. At the far side of the grass the walls of a Twoleg den, built of reddish rock, loomed over him. His head spun at the mixture of unfamiliar sights and scents.

There was no sign of Darktail, but Hawkwing could hear odd clanging noises coming from somewhere beyond the den. A moment later the rogue tom reappeared, whisking around the corner of the rock wall.

Terrified of being spotted, Hawkwing dived under the nearest bush. He crouched there, panting, as Darktail passed within a tail-length of him. *I only hope these weird flowers are masking my scent.* Then he tensed, digging his claws hard into the ground. Darktail had another piece of Twoleg food gripped in his jaws.

What does Darktail need Twoleg food for? He wasn't eating it.

No—he's taking it somewhere. But what other possible use could he have for the Twoleg scraps?

The white tom was too intent on his peculiar mission to notice Hawkwing in his hiding place. He wriggled under the shiny barrier again and headed back the way he had come.

Still tracking him, Hawkwing saw Darktail drop this new mouthful about halfway between the Twolegplace and the spot where he had dropped the first scraps of food. Then he bounded off, making for the camp.

Hawkwing followed more slowly, not sure what to make of any of this. He felt like he'd gotten to know Darktail better on their last quest, and he now believed that the rogue cat was good at heart. *But what is this about?*

I could ask him. But Hawkwing felt a shiver of dread at the thought of admitting to his friend that he'd spied on him. *He already thinks the whole Clan doesn't trust him. I'm the one friend he has.*

Glancing back at the Twoleg scraps, Hawkwing felt uneasy. *I have to think about how to handle this,* he thought. *I'm not really sure he's doing anything wrong.*

As Hawkwing slowly made his way back to camp, his heart was heavy. *I want to trust Darktail,* he thought. *I just hope we really can.*

CHAPTER 13

Dew still gleamed on the grass and soaked into Hawkwing's pelt as he brushed through it, following Waspwhisker on the dawn patrol. Pale light seeped between the branches, though the forest floor still lay in shadow, with ragged scraps of mist floating among the trees.

Though Leafstar had still not appeared from Echosong's den, she had given orders to Sharpclaw that the boundaries of SkyClan's territory should be extended. Hawkwing assumed she thought that a new barrier might deter the raccoons; he wished that he could feel confident that she was right.

Waspwhisker was leading the patrol, with Hawkwing, Darktail, Bellapaw, and Sparrowpelt. They had hardly left the camp when Hawkwing realized that Waspwhisker was in a bad mood, and he seemed to be taking most of it out on Darktail.

"For StarClan's sake!" the gray-and-white tom hissed. "Can't you walk a bit more quietly? You sound like you've got rocks instead of paws."

"Sorry," Darktail muttered, casting his eyes downward and clearly making an effort to set his paws down more lightly.

Waspwhisker gave the white tom a cold look from narrowed eyes, but said no more until Darktail sneezed.

"Good job, Darktail," Waspwhisker snapped. "You might as well just call out to all the prey, 'Watch out for cats!'"

Darktail's head swung up, and for a moment Hawkwing thought that he would snap back at Waspwhisker. Then he simply nodded, and mewed that he really would try to be quiet.

Bellapaw exchanged a glance with Hawkwing. "What's wrong with Waspwhisker?" she murmured. "He's being way too hard on Darktail."

Hawkwing shrugged. "I don't know. Maybe he doesn't want Darktail here anymore."

For his own part, Hawkwing was impressed that Darktail was managing to keep his temper. *I don't think I could, if Waspwhisker spoke to me like that.*

His feelings of sympathy brought him back to the problem he had been struggling with ever since he had seen Darktail carrying food from the Twolegplace the day before. *Should I report him or not?*

So far he had said nothing, partly because he couldn't be sure that Darktail was up to no good, and partly because Leafstar and Sharpclaw had too much on their minds after the raccoon attack to worry about something that might be completely unimportant.

For now, I'll just keep a close eye on Darktail, Hawkwing decided, *and see what he does next.*

So far, the rogue tom had done nothing else suspicious, and

he was doing his best on this patrol, in spite of Waspwhisker's hostility.

Along with his uneasiness about Darktail, Hawkwing's mind was full of memories of his brother. Seeing the evidence of the fire wiped away from the Twoleg greenplace had brought all his grief flooding back. In a way, it was like wiping Duskpaw away too.

Is it true, what Sharpclaw said about Darktail? Hawkwing wondered. *That I'm trying to make him into my replacement brother?* His first instinct was to deny it, but then he asked himself whether it would be such a bad thing if it was true.

Duskpaw is gone, and isn't ever coming back, he told himself, claws of pain gripping his heart again as he put the thought into words. *But cats need other cats in the wild. Surely it's good that I've made new bonds with other cats like Darktail, and . . . and Pebblepaw.*

Fresh confusion surged into Hawkwing's mind as he thought about the young she-cat. He felt as though he was trying to find a path through fog. *I hated her not long ago . . . so why am I thinking about her so much now? I blamed her for Duskpaw's death. Why do I hope she missed me when I was away on the second quest?*

"Stop!" Waspwhisker's urgent hiss broke into Hawkwing's thoughts. "Lie flat!"

Instantly obeying, Hawkwing flopped to the ground, his Clanmates doing the same around him, and peered out through the long grass. Every hair on his pelt began to bristle as he braced himself for trouble.

Are the raccoons back?

But when Hawkwing tasted the air, the only scent that he

could pick up came from cats. Unfamiliar cats. Just ahead he spotted a bank of ferns, their fronds waving as unseen animals pushed their way through.

A heartbeat later the fern fronds parted and a powerful silver-gray tom strode into the opening. A long-furred black she-cat followed him, and behind her was a ginger tom, and two tabby she-cats. Their pelts were ragged, but muscles rippled beneath their ungroomed fur; apprehension fluttered in Hawkwing's belly as he saw how dangerous they looked.

What are they doing on our territory? he asked himself.

All Hawkwing's instincts told him to leap out of hiding and challenge the approaching rogues. Instead, he glanced at Waspwhisker. "We should fight them off!" he whispered.

"Wait," Waspwhisker ordered curtly. Turning to Darktail, he added, "Are these more friends of yours?"

Darktail shook his head, looking mystified. "I've never seen any of them before."

By this time the leading silver-gray tom had drawn level with the clump of long grass where the SkyClan cats were hiding. He halted to sniff the air, and Hawkwing realized he had picked up the Clan cats' scent.

Before the tom could react, Waspwhisker rose to his paws and faced him. "Who are you, and what are you doing here?" he demanded.

The silver-gray tom looked Waspwhisker over with insolent green eyes. "Who wants to know?" he asked.

"We do." Hawkwing rose to stand beside Waspwhisker, while Bellapaw, Darktail, and Sparrowpelt took up positions just behind them.

"And who are you, mange-pelt?" the silver-gray tom sneered, as the rest of the rogues spread out threateningly on either side of him.

"We are cats of SkyClan," Waspwhisker replied, "and you're on our territory. It's time for you to leave. Now."

"Oh, we're on their territory!" the black she-cat exclaimed, stretching her eyes wide. "I'm *so* scared!"

"Are you going to leave or not?" Waspwhisker's shoulder fur bristled up aggressively.

The silver-gray tom slid out his claws and raised one fore-paw to examine them. "I guess . . . not," he mewed.

"So get out of our way," one of the tabby she-cats ordered.

Anger flashed in Waspwhisker's eyes, and he let out a ferocious yowl. "Attack!"

Hawkwing hurled himself at the ginger tom, who was closest to him. His paws splayed out, he landed on the tom's shoulders and dug his claws in hard. Screeching in fury, the ginger tom let himself drop to the ground and rolled over, crushing Hawkwing beneath him. For a few heartbeats Hawkwing's nose and mouth were muffled in his enemy's pelt, so he could hardly breathe. Bringing up his hind legs, he thrust at the ginger tom and managed to throw him off.

"Ugh!" he gasped, spitting out fur. "I've got a mouthful of your fleas!"

The ginger tom crouched in front of him, green eyes glaring, his hindquarters waggling, while his tail lashed from side to side. Hawkwing was bracing himself to meet his pounce when he spotted Sparrowpelt behind the ginger tom, struggling with the long-furred black she-cat. The she-cat had

Sparrowpelt pinned down, her teeth aiming for his throat.

Bunching his muscles, Hawkwing sprang right over the ginger tom and barreled into the black she-cat, thrusting her away from Sparrowpelt.

The older warrior staggered to his paws. "Thanks!" he panted, and flung himself back into combat, driving the black she-cat backward, paw step by paw step.

Hawkwing glanced around, and spotted Bellapaw chasing one of the tabby she-cats back into the bank of ferns. Wasp-whisker and the other tabby she-cat were rolling around on the ground in a snarling tangle of tails and paws.

Then Hawkwing's eyes widened in amazement as he saw Darktail whirling around the silver-gray tom, darting in to slash at him and immediately leaping back out of range. The tom kept trying to face him and attack, but Darktail was moving so fast that by the time the gray tom managed to strike at him, he had moved on. The tom's claws barely touched him.

"Flea-pelt! Trespasser!" Darktail yowled. "Get out of here!"

A hard blow caught Hawkwing on the side of the head, driving him off his paws. As he hit the ground a surging darkness covered his vision, and as it cleared he glimpsed green eyes close to his own. A paw clamped down on his neck.

To Hawkwing's horror he realized that, distracted by Darktail's skillful battle technique, he had forgotten about the ginger tom. He writhed furiously, desperate to throw off the weight that was holding him down. Twisting his neck, he tried to sink his teeth into the ginger tom's leg.

Just then, a loud caterwaul sounded in Hawkwing's ears. "Back off! Run!"

The weight on top of him abruptly vanished. Hauling himself up, Hawkwing saw the two remaining she-cats fleeing for the ferns, with the ginger tom hard on their paws. The silver-gray leader, still yowling his orders to retreat, brought up the rear. Darktail, charging after him, managed to get in a couple of blows on the tom's hindquarters before he vanished into the undergrowth.

Waspwhisker huffed out a long breath. "Cowards!"

Hawkwing was surprised that the fight had ended so quickly. He had thought that the two groups were well matched, and he had never imagined that the rogues would give up so easily.

But Darktail showed their leader a thing or two, he reflected. *That mange-pelt couldn't stand up to him!*

Hawkwing watched the final quivers of the ferns as the rogues beat a retreat, then turned to Waspwhisker. "Are you still doubtful about Darktail?" he asked. "Look how bravely he fought!"

Waspwhisker let out a grunt. "That was well fought," he mewed, with a nod to Darktail. "But if the rogue had moved a bit faster, what would you have done then? He'd have had you at his mercy."

Darktail looked up from grooming his shoulder, where a tuft of fur had been torn away. "I'd worry about that if it happened," he replied calmly.

Waspwhisker turned away with a single twitch of his tail,

showing he was still unconvinced. Hawkwing let out a growl of annoyance at the older warrior's grudging praise of the cat who had probably won them the battle, then instantly regretted it.

Waspwhisker was a good mentor to Duskpaw, he told himself. *I don't want to fight with him. I just wish some of my Clanmates would give Darktail a break.*

Meanwhile, Waspwhisker was looking over the rest of the patrol, checking them for injuries. Every cat was carrying a few scratches, but none of them was badly injured.

"Right, let's finish marking the border," he growled. "And then we'll get back to camp and report this."

Padding along the new border with his Clanmates, Hawkwing's mind went back to his earlier decision not to mention that he had seen Darktail leaving Twoleg food on SkyClan territory.

He fought so well against the rogues, he thought. *He can't mean any harm to SkyClan. Maybe I should just ask him what it was all about.*

"Darktail," he began, falling in beside the white tom, "I saw you yesterday near the Twolegplace." *No need to let him know I followed him there.* "It looked like you had some Twoleg food. . . ."

Darktail gave him a sidelong glance, half guilty and half amused. "I've been around a few kittypets in my time," he admitted. "And I kind of got a taste for Twoleg scraps. Don't tell any cat, will you? I think Waspwhisker would claw my ears off!"

"Uh . . . no. But that doesn't explain why you left—"

"You know, I've been thinking about those rogues,"

Darktail interrupted, as if he had dismissed the whole question of the Twoleg food. "I wonder if there are any more of them around. Maybe Leafstar should set a watch."

As Darktail moved on with the patrol, Hawkwing stopped and raised his head to sniff the air, catching a sweetish, rotting smell coming from the edge of a nearby bramble thicket. He bounded over to take a look, and spotted more Twoleg food there, crumbling away into pieces as if the flesh it was made of had been clawed into tiny scraps and then somehow mashed back together. It was beginning to rot; Hawkwing guessed that it had been there for two or three days.

"Hey, Darktail, have you seen—" Hawkwing began, but as he turned he realized that while he was investigating the Twoleg food the rest of the patrol had moved on.

Hawkwing picked up the pace to catch them up, and found Darktail chatting amiably to Bellapaw. Pleased that for once Darktail was having a friendly conversation with a SkyClan cat, Hawkwing didn't interrupt.

There's no point, he told himself. *What's a bit of Twoleg food? Every cat would think I had bees in my brain if I made a fuss about it.*

CHAPTER 14

As soon as Waspwhisker led the patrolling cats back into camp, he bounded over to Leafstar, who was sharing fresh-kill with Sharpclaw at the foot of the Rockpile. Hawkwing and the others followed; Hawkwing noticed that several of his Clanmates, sunning themselves on the rocks nearby, sat up with ears pricked at the patrol's rapid approach.

Pebblepaw was among them, licking one paw and drawing it over her ears to give them a thorough wash.

She looks so cute when she does that! Hawkwing thought, then instantly felt ashamed of himself. *I shouldn't be thinking like that when the Clan is in danger!*

"Leafstar," Waspwhisker announced breathlessly as he halted in front of the Clan leader, "rogues attacked us in the forest!"

Instantly Leafstar sprang to her paws. "What? Where? Tell me everything!"

"Just where we were setting the new border markers," Waspwhisker explained, while more of the SkyClan cats gathered around to listen. "There were five of them, led by a huge silver-gray brute."

"We told them to get off our territory," Hawkwing added. "But they wouldn't go, so we had to fight them. We—"

He was interrupted by a storm of questions and protests from his Clanmates, who pressed closer around the patrol, their fur bristling at the news of the attack.

"First raccoons, now rogues! What next?"

"How dare they? This is our place!"

"Are we still safe here?"

Drawn by the clamor, more SkyClan warriors appeared from their dens, scrambling down the trail or leaping from rock to rock until the stretch of ground beside the Rockpile was a heaving mass of cats.

Hawkwing found that Pebblepaw was by his side, gazing at him with anxious eyes.

"Are you okay?" she asked.

Hawkwing felt a hint of warmth deep in his belly that Pebblepaw was concerned for him. "I'm fine," he replied. "Just a bit bruised."

Pebblepaw still held him with her gaze, making Hawkwing feel awkward and yet strangely excited. "That's good," she murmured at last.

Before Hawkwing could respond, Leafstar fought her way through the crowd of cats and jumped up the mass of boulders until she stood at the top, with Sharpclaw close behind her.

"Cats of SkyClan!" she yowled, flourishing her tail for silence. "Listen to me!"

But several moments passed until the caterwauling died down enough for the Clan leader to make herself heard.

"It's vital that we don't panic," she began. "Waspwhisker, did you drive the rogues away?"

"We did," Waspwhisker replied with a lash of his tail.

"But they'll be back!" Sagenose called out from the crowd.

"Yes, how long can we keep fighting?" Nettlesplash asked.

"And what about the kits?" Birdwing added.

The Clan erupted again into renewed clamor, until Cherrytail leaped onto a boulder beside the stream and managed to raise her voice above her Clanmates'.

"Leafstar, the whole of the Clan should hunt down these rogues immediately," she meowed. "We have to teach them that they can't mess with SkyClan!"

His mother's words woke a fire of determination inside Hawkwing. "Yes!" he yowled, kneading the ground eagerly with his forepaws. "Let's do it!"

He was even more encouraged to see that his father, Sharpclaw, was nodding in agreement. "I'll lead a patrol—" he began.

"That's crazy," Plumwillow interrupted.

"Yes," Firefern agreed. "Since the raccoons first attacked, we've lost the daylight warriors, and StarClan knows when their Twolegs will let them out again. We're not as strong as we used to be."

"And so many of our warriors are new," Plumwillow pointed out. "They're good, strong cats, but not exactly experienced fighters."

Hawkwing began to bristle at the gray she-cat's words. *How many badgers have you fought off, flea-brain?* But he managed not to speak his thought out loud.

"I agree with Plumwillow," Bouncefire mewed, a hint of fear in his voice. "We're more vulnerable than we've ever been. If we can't protect our territory, then is this the end of SkyClan?"

"Who says we can't protect our territory?" Mistfeather snarled.

"But the rogues . . . ," Firefern protested.

"Silence!" Leafstar hissed, lashing her tail. "I will not hear such talk. Have you forgotten our history?" she went on when the outcry had died down into something approaching quiet. "SkyClan has endured so much. When Twolegs invaded our old territory and drove us out, when the other Clans refused to share with us—not even that could end SkyClan. And this new attack won't, either!"

Sharpclaw let out a discontented snort. "I know my history as well as any cat," he grumbled. "And I've been wondering why we're so keen to find the spark that remains—if that really does mean the kin of Firestar—when the other Clans are at least part of the reason why we were driven to settle here in the gorge in the first place."

"Yes, the other Clans have failed us in the past," Leafstar admitted. "But if StarClan says that we must find Thunder-Clan, their will is not to be questioned."

"But so far," Tinycloud put in, "trying to follow the will of StarClan has only led us into trouble."

At her words, true silence fell over all the SkyClan cats, and the gaze of every cat turned to Echosong. The medicine cat was sitting on a rock at the edge of the crowd, with

Frecklewish at her side. Hawkwing realized that so far she hadn't added anything to the discussion.

"I confess that I'm confused," Echosong mewed after a moment's pause. "I don't believe that I've misinterpreted my visions, but there must be something that I'm not seeing."

"Can't you seek out StarClan?" Darktail, who had sat silent all this while at the foot of the Rockpile, rose to his paws and turned to Echosong. "Can't you ask them for more details?"

Hawkwing twitched his whiskers in annoyance at the rogue tom's tone, which was close to disrespectful. Then he shrugged, reflecting that Darktail wasn't a Clan cat, and didn't know Clan ways, especially how a medicine cat should be treated by her Clanmates. *He doesn't mean to insult Echosong.*

"It doesn't work like that," Echosong told Darktail, her tail drooping. "I should have expected that StarClan would have given me some kind of new sign by now—but they haven't. If StarClan had wanted to warn us about this new attack, they would have done so."

"So does that mean this StarClan has no interest in saving SkyClan?" Rain protested, rising to stand beside Darktail. His tone was even more brusque. "Is that what you're getting at?"

Echosong hesitated before replying. A thrill of pure dread tingled through Hawkwing as he realized that even the medicine cat might not be totally sure of what their Clan's destiny was meant to be.

"Maybe . . . maybe this is our chance to prove ourselves to

StarClan," Echosong suggested at last, though her voice and her flustered look drained all the conviction out of her words. "But how or why . . ." The medicine cat shook her head. "I don't know."

A horrible silence fell over the Clan as the cats exchanged dismayed glances. *What will happen to us now,* Hawkwing wondered, *if our medicine cat can't advise us anymore?*

"Cats of SkyClan!" Leafstar meowed after a few heartbeats. Clearly she was trying to force energy and certainty into her voice. "We will not do anything rash. We will protect our camp and our borders, as we always do. These rogues won't drive us out—we'll never let that happen. And we will wait for the next message from StarClan. I'm sure it will be coming soon. Now go to your duties."

As the Clan began to disperse, the cats muttering uneasily to each other, Hawkwing wished that he could believe what Leafstar had said. Even more, he wished that he was sure Leafstar believed it herself.

Hawkwing joined a hunting patrol and returned just after sunhigh with a squirrel for the fresh-kill pile. All through the hunt he had been distracted, remembering the battle against the rogues and worrying about the troubles that were gathering like thick shadows around his Clan.

When he had dropped his prey on the pile, Hawkwing spotted Sharpclaw grooming himself beside the river. Longing flooded over him to ask his father's advice, and whether there was anything he could do to help in this crisis.

But as he padded toward Sharpclaw, Hawkwing felt tension cramping his muscles, and his belly fluttered with nervousness. *Sharpclaw has been angry with me for so long, he's not going to want to advise me now.*

Hawkwing paused for a moment, his gaze fixed on Sharpclaw, who was vigorously washing his belly, quite unaware that his son was hovering nearby. Then, letting his tail droop, Hawkwing turned and began trudging back to his own den.

But as he reached the bottom of the trail, his mother, Cherrytail, bounded up to him and intercepted him before he could begin to climb.

"What's the matter, Hawkwing?" she asked. "Don't you want to talk to your father?"

"He won't want to talk to me," Hawkwing muttered.

Cherrytail gave an irritated twitch of her whiskers. "Oh, get over yourself!" she exclaimed. Then, more gently, she added, "Sharpclaw will forgive you if you apologize to him. You might even get an apology in return."

Anger spurted up inside Hawkwing. "Why do I need to apologize? Why is it still all *my* fault?" he demanded, his shoulder fur beginning to bristle. "Anyway, that wasn't what I wanted to talk about."

"Then what was it?" his mother asked.

Her quiet voice, and her eyes full of sympathy, quenched Hawkwing's anger.

"I'm worried about what happens now," he confessed reluctantly, feeling as weak and fearful as a lost kit. "Is this what life is going to be like from now on? Always struggling, always looking out for attacks? Raccoons, rogues, or badgers—they're all as vicious as each other. How bad are things going to get for SkyClan?"

"I don't know," Cherrytail admitted, heaving a sigh from the depths of her chest. "And there's one thing I won't say to the rest of the Clan. I'm afraid of what will happen if SkyClan is driven out of this territory as we were driven out of our old home."

"Do you think that will happen?" Hawkwing asked, alarmed. *That's worse than I ever imagined!*

Cherrytail's eyes were thoughtful. "Surviving our exile from our first territory is what made SkyClan who we are," she murmured. "Of course, I don't know for sure, but I suspect that the other four Clans, wherever they are, don't have anything close to our spirit, because they've never been through the same troubles."

"But that should make us stronger, right?" Hawkwing suggested.

Cherrytail nodded. "True, but it took a long time—and a visit from Firestar and Sandstorm—before we could find a way to put ourselves right. I'm afraid that if we are driven into exile again, SkyClan may be lost forever."

Too troubled to sleep, Hawkwing crouched at the entrance to the warriors' den and gazed out across the gorge. The moon was barely a claw-scratch, making the stars blaze out more brightly than ever.

"Oh, StarClan," Hawkwing breathed out. "What are you doing to us?"

Behind him, he could hear his Clanmates shifting in their nests; he didn't think any of them were sleeping, either. *We're all so afraid that the rogues will come and attack us in the camp.* He angled his ears forward, trying to pick up any strange sounds beyond the gorge, but all he could hear was the wind rustling in the trees.

Ever since he had spoken to his mother, her ominous words had repeated themselves in Hawkwing's mind. *SkyClan may be lost forever.*

He didn't want to believe that could be true.

Hawkwing knew he was young; he hadn't lived through SkyClan's most trying days. Still, the Clan meant more to him than he could possibly say. Even though he'd gone searching for the other Clans, it was difficult for him to imagine a life outside the gorge he loved so fiercely, or away from these cats who were all like kin to him. Spending time with Darktail, a former rogue, had only emphasized the value of his Clan to Hawkwing. *We look out for each other,* he thought now. *We put the Clan first, and ourselves second. That's important.* He paused, looking up at the narrow moon and his ancestors twinkling in the sky. *And what would it say to StarClan if we let SkyClan fall?* he wondered. *So many cats have fought so valiantly to preserve SkyClan, through the seasons.* Those cats dated all the way back to Skystar—the great founder of SkyClan.

We have to save our Clan.

Every hair on Hawkwing's pelt began to tingle, but this

time it was not with fear. He felt a fierceness run through his body, powerful as flame, a determination to make sure that the worst would never happen.

As long as I'm alive, SkyClan will never be exiled. We will always survive!

CHAPTER 15

The dawn patrol had just returned, reporting no sign or scent of the rogues on SkyClan territory. Even so, Hawkwing was still aware of deep uneasiness within the Clan. Echosong had still received no further visits from StarClan, and every cat knew that their future was desperately uncertain.

At the foot of the Rockpile, Sharpclaw was organizing the hunting patrols. "Sparrowpelt, you lead one," he instructed, "and Waspwhisker, you take another. I'll lead the third. Leafstar wants senior warriors to go out more, just in case we run into any of the rogues."

"Right, Sharpclaw," Sparrowpelt meowed, sliding out his claws. "I'd be *delighted* to run into them. I could use some extra fur to line my nest."

"Hawkwing, you're with me," Sharpclaw continued, as the cats began to divide into three groups. "You too, Darktail. We know you can fight, but I haven't seen your hunting technique yet."

"Gladly, Sharpclaw," Darktail responded with a brisk nod.

Hawkwing was pleased, too, that his father had chosen him for his patrol. *Maybe he's not so angry with me anymore.*

While Sharpclaw was supervising the departure of the other patrols, Darktail sidled up to Hawkwing and stood so close that their pelts were brushing.

"Have you seen your friend this morning?" he asked Hawkwing, angling his ears toward Pebblepaw, who was chatting with Rain over their fresh-kill a few tail-lengths away.

Immediately Hawkwing's pelt grew hot with embarrassment. "My friend?" he muttered.

"Pebblepaw. I've seen you staring at her," Darktail meowed, a gleam of amusement in his eyes. "Don't try to tell me you don't like her."

"Uh . . ." Hawkwing scrabbled on the ground with his forepaws.

"You need to talk to her more and figure out what your feelings are," Darktail continued. "You won't get any closer to doing that by avoiding her!"

"I'm not avoiding her," Hawkwing mewed defensively.

"And hedgehogs fly!" Darktail scoffed. "Besides, from the way Pebblepaw looks at you, she needs to sort out her feelings, too."

Hawkwing blinked with a mixture of hope that Darktail might be right, and awkwardness that the rogue was forcing him to discuss it. "I don't think so . . . ," he murmured.

Darktail flicked Hawkwing's ear with the tip of his tail. "Either Pebblepaw likes you back, or she doesn't, but you need to know the truth, so you can make a decision before it's too late."

With a massive effort, Hawkwing let out a huff of laughter.

"I'm still a young cat," he mewed, "and Pebblepaw is still an apprentice. It's way too early to start thinking about time running out."

I'd never admit it to Darktail, he added to himself, *but I have started to think about the future. It feels really weird.*

Darktail shook his head, still amused. "That's not what I meant."

Hawkwing realized there was something odd about Darktail's tone of voice. "Whether I'm with Pebblepaw or not can't be that serious, can it?" he asked.

"Of course it can," the rogue tom replied, his voice still dark and ominous. "It is the most serious choice. You can't afford to make a mistake when choosing which cats to have by your side."

To Hawkwing's relief, before he could say more, Sharpclaw called to them to head out on patrol. As the other two groups had climbed the trails to hunt in the forest above the gorge, Sharpclaw led his cats downstream toward the stretch of shrubs and spindly trees that grew on either side of the river where the gorge widened out.

Hawkwing hoped that this would be a good opportunity to straighten things out with his father, but his belly churned with anxiety at the thought that Sharpclaw might snap at him again. Besides, he didn't want to talk about anything important with Sharpclaw where Darktail might overhear.

Instead, Hawkwing concentrated on picking up the traces of prey, hoping that he might impress his father with a good catch. As they slid into the scrubby undergrowth Sharpclaw halted, then plunged into the shadow of an elder bush and emerged with a mouse dangling from his jaws.

"Good job!" Darktail mewed admiringly. "I never even smelled it."

Sharpclaw twitched his whiskers. "Figures."

Hawkwing could see that his father was still not impressed with Darktail. He wished that the white rogue could catch something, if only to dispel the frosty atmosphere that had spread through the patrol.

When Sharpclaw had scratched earth over the mouse so it could be collected later, the patrol moved on. Padding alongside the river, Hawkwing came to a spot where the bank had crumbled away into a sandy spit of land stretching out into the current. A vole was scrabbling around among the pebbles.

Hawkwing dropped into the hunter's crouch and began to creep up on his prey, when something white flashed past him and he saw Darktail hurl himself off the bank and land on top of the vole, crushing it between his forepaws.

"I smelled that one," he announced as he picked up his fresh-kill and leaped back onto the bank.

Hawkwing tried not to be annoyed that Darktail had stolen what had clearly been his prey. *What matters is that the Clan is fed.* But it was still irritating, especially when he had hoped to show off his hunting skills to his father.

The patrol padded on, getting farther and farther from the camp. Hawkwing became more alert still, his pelt prickling with apprehension as he wondered if they might meet the rogues again. A flicker of movement in the bushes drew his attention, but it was only a rabbit, hopping into the open with no idea of the danger it was in. But clearly if any cat startled it, it would head straight back into the safety of the undergrowth.

"Hawkwing," Sharpclaw whispered.

When Hawkwing glanced at his father, Sharpclaw waved his tail in a wide sweep, while he angled his ears toward the rabbit.

He wants me to circle around and come up behind it.

Hawkwing set off, careful to keep his distance from the rabbit, and made sure that the breeze wouldn't carry his scent toward his prey. He noticed that Sharpclaw had gestured with his tail for Darktail to keep back.

Reaching the bushes, Hawkwing burrowed into them, creeping along cautiously until he could peer out from underneath a branch and spot the rabbit still peacefully nibbling at the grass. He risked raising his tail above the foliage to tell Sharpclaw that he was in position.

At once Sharpclaw let out a ferocious growl and sprang at the rabbit. It let out a squeal of terror and dashed for the bushes with Sharpclaw racing after it. Hawkwing tensed his muscles. *I mustn't lose this one!*

The rabbit fled into the bushes, almost flinging itself into Hawkwing's paws. Hawkwing gripped it with his forepaws and killed it with a rapid bite to its neck. Warm triumph flooded through him as he emerged from cover with his prey in his jaws.

"Well done, both of you," Darktail meowed, though his

voice was cool, and Hawkwing wondered if the rogue wasn't too thrilled to see him and his father working together as a team.

But why would that bother him?

As Hawkwing padded up, Sharpclaw gave him an approving nod. Though he said nothing, Hawkwing felt that perhaps the tension between him and his father was beginning to ease a little.

But Sharpclaw still seemed distant as the three cats made their way back to camp.

I wish I could talk to him, Hawkwing thought, thinking back to his conversation with Cherrytail. *But I don't know what to say anymore.*

When they had deposited their prey on the fresh-kill pile, Sharpclaw bounded away toward Leafstar's den, while Darktail headed off to talk to Rain.

Hawkwing couldn't help feeling disappointed that Sharpclaw hadn't been warmer after they had hunted so well together. He remembered what Darktail had said to him before they set out, about cats needing to choose who they wanted by their side.

Maybe my father has chosen not to be by my side, Hawkwing thought miserably. *Could that be true?* Then he gave his pelt a shake, determined to be more cheerful. *It can't be true—Sharpclaw and I are kin. Whatever has happened between us, that loyalty must always be there.* His mood lightening, Hawkwing told himself that eventually he and his father would be okay together.

Neither of us is going anywhere. We have our whole lives to work this out.

Darktail's words had made Hawkwing aware of something else, too. He decided it was time to go looking for Pebblepaw, and found her crouching beside the river where it had scoured out the bank into a shallow pool. She kept dabbing her paw into the water, sending up a shower of glittering drops.

I never noticed how her fur shines, he thought. *And the way she moves her paw is so graceful!*

Pebblepaw looked up as Hawkwing padded up to her. "Hi," she greeted him. "Did you know there are fish in here? But they won't let me catch them."

Hawkwing looked into the pool and saw minnows, tiny silver flashes darting here and there near the sandy bottom. He watched them, not looking at Pebblepaw, as he mewed, "I wanted to tell you something."

"Okay . . ." Pebblepaw sounded puzzled, but still friendly.

Hawkwing dug his claws nervously into the ground. "I . . . I wanted to say how sorry I am, about the way I treated you after Duskpaw died. I want you to know that I never actually blamed you."

He risked a glance at Pebblepaw and saw that she was blinking at him happily. "I kind of figured that out," she responded.

"You did?" Hawkwing was relieved to hear this.

Pebblepaw half turned away, obviously embarrassed, which made Hawkwing feel embarrassed in his turn. Yet at the same time excitement was tingling through him.

"Well . . . uh . . . that's it, really," he went on. "I guess we can be friends now."

Pebblepaw gave him a flickering glance. "I guess."

Hawkwing dipped his head to her and retreated, feeling Pebblepaw's gaze following him as he headed for his den. He felt better now that he had told her he was sorry, but he was still confused when he thought about her.

I wonder if she feels just as confused when she thinks about me.

That night, Hawkwing was still feeling a prickle of excitement about his talk with Pebblepaw when he settled down into his nest to sleep. He wanted to stay awake and think about her, but he was exhausted, his limbs aching, after the hunt.

His Clanmates were curled up around him too, the fear and tension of the night before beginning to ease. The Clan had fed well, and the patrols had found no traces of rogues or raccoons.

Maybe everything will be okay after all. . . .

Hawkwing jerked awake. He sat up in his nest, not sure at first what had roused him. Then he heard it again: the creak and rustle of bushes, coming from overhead, as if some creature was pushing its way through the undergrowth.

Hawkwing's first instinct was to rouse his Clan. But then he realized that every cat was asleep, and wouldn't thank him for disturbing the whole Clan if the sound meant nothing.

Rising to his paws, Hawkwing picked his way across the den, slipping silently between Sandynose and a gently snoring Rabbitleap, and emerged onto the trail outside. There was a little more moonlight than on the night before, but the frosty shimmer revealed nothing moving as far as Hawkwing could see.

A gentle breeze was blowing from the far side of the gorge, bearing nothing except the familiar scents of the forest. Hawkwing was about to give up and go back inside when he heard the rustling sound again, coming from the top of the trail.

Could it be raccoons? he asked himself, tensing. *Or rogues, or dogs—or even Twolegs?*

He tasted the air, but he could still pick up nothing unusual, nothing alarming.

Then the breeze shifted, blowing now from the top of the gorge. Now scent flooded over Hawkwing, so strong that it was unmistakable.

Cats!

As Hawkwing stared in horror, dark shapes appeared at the top of the cliff, flowing like water as they swarmed down the trails. More and more of them appeared, more cats than he had imagined in his worst fears. He caught a glimpse of moonlight shining on the pelt of the silver-gray tom.

Rogues, he realized. *The rogues who attacked us on patrol—but there are more of them now. So many more! They may outnumber us. . . .*

His heart pounded as he realized what was happening.

Rogue cats were attacking the SkyClan camp!

CHAPTER 16

❧

"Rogues!" Hawkwing yowled. "Rogues in the camp!"

He shot back inside the warriors' den, stumbling over the sleeping bodies of his Clanmates as he poked and prodded them into wakefulness.

"Get up!" he urged them. "Rogues are attacking! They're here in the camp! Lots of them!"

The SkyClan cats struggled to their paws, so confused by sleep that they were hardly able to take in Hawkwing's panicked yowls.

"Take it easy," Sparrowpelt yawned. "You've had a bad dream, that's all. No need to wake the whole Clan." He yawned again and added, "Stormheart's on watch. She would warn us if—"

A screech coming from the bottom of the gorge interrupted what Sparrowpelt was saying. Hawkwing reached out a paw and roughly shook the senior warrior's shoulder.

"That was Stormheart," he meowed. "And this is no dream. We have to fight."

Hawkwing rapidly checked that his mother and sisters were rousing. Then, knowing that Stormheart was alone beside the

Rockpile, he darted outside again and bounded down the trail behind the wave of attacking cats. As he hurtled downward he let out more warning yowls.

Leafstar was already awake, emerging from her den and stretching her jaws in a long caterwaul before racing down the trail just ahead of Hawkwing.

A quick glance over his shoulder showed Hawkwing that his Clanmates were following, fully roused now and shrieking defiance. Sharpclaw was in the lead, his paws hardly touching the rocks as he hurled himself toward his Clan's enemies.

Yes! Hawkwing thought with a touch of pride. *My father will fight them off!*

He couldn't spot Darktail, and briefly wondered where the rogue tom was, but there was no time to think about that now.

Pebblepaw and Parsleypaw bundled out of the apprentices' den, their eyes wide and their fur bushing up. Bellapaw and Rileypaw followed.

"Stay back!" Hawkwing snapped. "This is no place for apprentices."

"Fox dung to that!" Pebblepaw hissed through clenched teeth, as the four young cats fell in behind Hawkwing.

They're all so brave! Hawkwing couldn't help but be impressed, even while he felt that the apprentices would have been safer in their den.

A shriek sounded from the bottom of the gorge, abruptly cut off. Every drop of Hawkwing's blood seemed to freeze. *Stormheart!*

With a final massive leap, Hawkwing slammed into the

rear of the rogue attack. For a few moments he struggled with fur pressing in on him from every side, unable to get any strength behind his blows. He thrust at the bodies surrounding him, finally managing to win a little space for himself. At last he could attack, his paws splayed out, his claws slashing in a hot surge of fury, as he struck out at random, not knowing or caring who his enemies were.

Then a face loomed up in front of him, and he recognized the ginger tom he had fought when Waspwhisker's patrol were setting the border markers.

"Oh, you again!" the ginger tom snarled. "You want to finish what we started?"

"Mange-pelt!" Hawkwing snarled, raking his claws across the ginger tom's muzzle. "Get out of our camp!"

The tom staggered back, clearly startled at Hawkwing's swift response. Hawkwing felt a grim satisfaction as he saw dark drops welling out of the wound he had made, and the reek of blood hit him in the throat.

He ducked as the ginger tom swept his forepaw around in a blow aimed at his shoulder; the rogue cat's claws passed harmlessly through his fur, and Hawkwing managed to butt his head into the tom's belly, unbalancing him.

Another rogue—a black-and-white tom—pressed forward into the gap between Hawkwing and his opponent, his claws reaching for Pebblepaw, who was still fighting at Hawkwing's side. Instinctively Hawkwing slipped in front of the apprentice, shielding her as he dug his claws into the black-and-white tom's shoulder.

"Get out of here!" he gasped to Pebblepaw.

The young she-cat didn't even bother to reply. Instead, she leaped at the rogue tom on the other side and raked her claws along his flank. The tom let out a screech and backed off, disappearing into the fray.

Hawkwing felt furious with Pebblepaw, terrified and proud all at once. They exchanged a glance, Hawkwing gave her a nod of acknowledgment, then both cats sprang back into the battle.

The first heaving bundle of fighting cats had begun to split up into separate skirmishes straggling alongside the river. In a brief respite, Hawkwing saw that his Clanmates were holding their own, even though they were outnumbered by the band of rogues.

If only we had our daylight warriors! he thought. Then a sudden realization hit him. *The rogues must have been watching us. They must have* known *that the Twolegs were keeping our Clanmates inside because of the raccoons!*

He noticed too that clouds were building up overhead, blotting out the stars. The moon gleamed fitfully through the gaps. The air was heavy and damp, and Hawkwing felt the first fat drops of rain spatter onto his pelt.

He had lost sight of Pebblepaw, and as he glanced around, desperately trying to spot her, he saw Sandynose near the foot of the cliff, pinned down by an enormous tabby rogue, who slashed his claws again and again over the Clan cat's shoulders. Sandynose was writhing furiously in an effort to throw him off.

Hawkwing hurled himself across the ground and barreled into the side of the tabby tom, flinging him against the rock face. The tabby let out a yelp of pain, all the breath driven out of him. Before he could recover, Hawkwing scored his claws down his hindquarters, and drove him off, yowling, into the night.

"Thanks!" Sandynose gasped, staggering to his paws, then bounding off to where Waspwhisker was tussling with a skinny tortoiseshell rogue.

In the darkness and the rain—growing heavier with every heartbeat—it was becoming harder to distinguish the Clan cats from the rogues. Hawkwing spotted a ginger tom racing toward him and whirled around, one forepaw raised to strike.

"Hey, it's me!"

Hawkwing recognized Bouncefire's voice, and lowered his paw. "Sorry."

Beyond Bouncefire, Hawkwing made out the pale pelt of Darktail. "This way," the white tom meowed, angling his ears toward a cluster of the invading rogues who were battling Tinycloud, Rabbitleap, and Harrybrook at the very edge of the river.

Hawkwing sprang forward with Bouncefire next to him, and Darktail on the ginger tom's other side. A rogue cat leaped into their path to stop them, but Hawkwing pushed him aside with one swipe of his claws.

With Bouncefire and Darktail beside him, Hawkwing suddenly felt more optimistic. *We can win this battle!*

Another rogue hurtled toward them, closest to Darktail;

Hawkwing held off, expecting that the white tom would throw himself into the attack. Instead, Darktail whipped around, letting the rogue race past unscathed.

"Darktail . . . what—?" Hawkwing began.

Darktail ignored him. With a snarl of mingled fury and triumph, he sank his claws into Bouncefire's neck.

Sheer shock kept Hawkwing frozen for a moment. Bouncefire too was so astonished that for a couple of heartbeats he was unable to defend himself. In that moment Darktail threw himself on top of the ginger tom, pinning him to the ground and tearing at his throat. Blood gushed out; Bouncefire's legs jerked spasmodically and then he went limp.

"Darktail!" Hawkwing choked out. "What are you doing?"

Darktail didn't reply. For a moment he stood motionless over Bouncefire's body, his jaws still red with the ginger tom's blood.

He looks like a killer, Hawkwing thought in a whirl of confusion and grief. *Who is this cat?*

Darktail spun around again and flung himself into the tussle beside the river, aligning himself to fight on the side of the rogues. Hawkwing forced his paralyzed limbs into motion and bounded after him as a horrible realization washed over him.

"*Traitor!*" he yowled. "Traitor! I trusted you!"

Was it all lies? If Darktail was fighting on the side of the rogues, then clearly he'd never been a true friend to SkyClan. What else had he lied about? *Knowing the other Clans? The quests?* Hawkwing's blood ran cold when it suddenly occurred to him that Darktail must have been *planning* this attack—manipulating SkyClan as he and his rogue friends prepared for it. *Was every moment he spent here part of some twisted plan?*

He thought again of the Twoleg food and thought he might be sick. *He was up to something. . . .*

Spotting Hawkwing, the white tom stepped aside from the combat and waited calmly as Hawkwing drew closer and closer. He seemed as confident as if he was about to slam his paws down on a mouse.

I'll claw that smug look off his face!

But just as Hawkwing's claws were reaching for Darktail, a heavy body slammed into him from one side. His paws skidded and he fell, to find himself looking up into the face of the silver-gray tom who had led the trespassing patrol the day before.

How long has Darktail known these rogues? Hawkwing wondered. *How long has he been planning this? From the moment he first showed up?*

The gray tom swooped down on him, aiming for his throat. Hawkwing's foreleg flashed upward and he planted his paw in the tom's face, digging his claws into his muzzle as he pushed his head back.

The rogue cat let out a screech, batting Hawkwing's paw away and thumping down on top of him, almost smothering him. He tried to bring up his hind paws to batter at his enemy, but the tom was too heavy for him to shift.

Twisting from side to side in his struggle to escape, Hawkwing spotted his father, Sharpclaw, battling fiercely with two rogue cats: the long-furred black she-cat from the previous day's patrol, and a mottled black-and-gray tom. In spite of his own peril Hawkwing had to admire his father as Sharpclaw whirled from one rogue to the other, beating both of them back toward the water's edge.

As Hawkwing watched, Leafstar appeared out of the darkness and slashed her claws at the she-cat, who whipped around and fled. Sharpclaw gave the mottled tom a shove; the rogue tottered for a heartbeat on the very edge of the river, then fell into the torrent with a shriek and disappeared.

Hawkwing wanted to let out a yowl of triumph for his father, but the gray tom had clamped a paw down on his neck, and he could hardly breathe.

Then to his horror he saw Darktail sneaking up behind Sharpclaw, his belly pressed to the ground as if he was stalking prey. Hawkwing made a massive effort to call out a warning, but the feeble choking sound was all he could manage, and it was lost in the clamor of the battle. He felt a hot stickiness in his throat, as if this were a nightmare where he could only watch the terrible combat unfold, and not do anything to stop it. *Sharpclaw, look out!*

Darktail sprang, aiming to land on Sharpclaw's back, but at the last instant Sharpclaw seemed to become aware of him, and slipped to one side so that Darktail landed hard on the rock. He was briefly winded; Sharpclaw stood over him, one paw raised, but clearly puzzled.

"What's gotten into you?" he demanded. "How could you betray SkyClan?"

Kill him—now! Hawkwing wanted to cry out, but the gray

tom was still pressing down on his throat. Hawkwing's vision began to spin away in a dark spiral, but he kept on struggling to stay conscious and throw off his attacker.

He saw Darktail recover and spring at Sharpclaw again. "I was never part of SkyClan!" the rogue tom snarled.

Sharpclaw's confusion was replaced by shock, but now he was no longer in doubt. He retaliated with a familiar battle move, leaping up and twisting in the air to land behind Darktail and lash his claws across the rogue's hindquarters. Darktail spun around and reared up, bringing his forepaws down hard on Sharpclaw's shoulders. Sharpclaw rolled away and jumped to his paws again, leaping out of range.

Hawkwing tensed his muscles and tried to get free, but the gray tom held him down. Hawkwing kicked and thrashed, but it was no good.

When he looked back, he saw that blood was dripping down Darktail's face as he stalked after Sharpclaw, who was crouched and ready to pounce. Then Hawkwing noticed that Darktail was holding his tail high, waving it to and fro like a branch in the wind.

He spotted a flicker of gray from the corner of his eye. Painfully twisting his head around, he saw that Darktail's friend Rain was creeping up on Sharpclaw from behind. *The waving tail was a signal!*

Hawkwing made another desperate effort to cry out and warn his father, but the paw pressing on his throat still stifled his voice. Despair filled him as he watched, helpless. *This* must *be a nightmare. My father is in danger, and there's nothing I can do!*

Rain let out a hiss; distracted by the sound, Sharpclaw glanced over his shoulder. In the same heartbeat, Darktail leaped. He landed on Sharpclaw's shoulders and slashed a paw over his throat and down his belly. Rain leaped on Sharpclaw from behind and held him down while Darktail slashed at him again. Blood streamed out of Sharpclaw's body.

Shock and anger surged through Hawkwing, giving him a last burst of energy. He threw off the silver-gray tom and rushed forward to his father's side. "Get off him!" he croaked out, his voice still hoarse.

Darktail jumped up, and Rain withdrew a pace, as if they were obeying Hawkwing's order. But Hawkwing knew that wasn't the reason. The rogues had finished their deadly work, and Hawkwing was too late. He saw his father's limbs spasm in a final convulsion and then lie still. The last flicker of light died from his green eyes.

"No . . . no . . . ," Hawkwing gasped. *This can't be happening. This can't be real!*

Darktail stepped forward, putting himself between Hawkwing and his dead father. Hatred surged up in Hawkwing as he bunched his muscles to leap on the white tom, but Darktail simply gave him a push with one paw. Exhausted from his battle with the silver-gray rogue, Hawkwing staggered back.

"Why?" he choked out, stunned by the depths of the rogue cat's cruelty. "Why have you turned on us? We never did you any harm."

"I never *turned* on you," Darktail sneered. "My plan was to destroy SkyClan all along."

Destroy SkyClan? Hawkwing remembered his conversation with Cherrytail, and her fear that being driven from the gorge would end SkyClan. *Was that what Darktail wanted this whole time? But why would he hate SkyClan so much? He hadn't even met us until a couple of moons ago.*

Hawkwing didn't know what to say. He could only repeat his desperate question. "Why?"

"Listen," Darktail meowed, his tone softening. "I like you, Hawkwing. You're different from the other SkyClan cats. You're more like me. Surely you realize your best chance of survival will be with me and my rogues? We're going to take the gorge for ourselves. Join us! We're so good together, Hawkwing. We understand each other. I'll make you my deputy."

Hawkwing could hardly believe what he was hearing. *We're going to take the gorge for ourselves.* And Darktail's claim of affection made him want to vomit. "Even if I believed you," he spat, "do you think I would join you? After you and Rain *murdered* my father? Never!"

To Hawkwing's amazement, something flickered in Darktail's eyes and he angled his head aside, as if he were honestly disappointed by Hawkwing's response. But when he looked up again he wore a savage glare, his whiskers bristling. "If that's what you want," he snarled, "you can die along with the rest of your mange-ridden Clan!"

Full of grief and rage, Hawkwing leaped at him. But Darktail slipped aside, and was lost to sight in the rain and the darkness.

CHAPTER 17

❧

Hawkwing's heart was beating hard, pounding loud in his ears in spite of the rain that thrummed against the ground with relentless strength. Everything seemed unreal, and as he flung himself back into the battle he felt as if each move was taking place in slow motion.

The powerful long-furred she-cat leaped toward him, and he felt as if he had all the time in the world to extend his claws and slice them through her black pelt into her shoulder. Another rogue attacked him from the side; Hawkwing automatically dodged his swipes and drove him off with two swift blows around his ears.

Hawkwing fought on with the battle moves ingrained in him through moons of SkyClan training, but he was barely aware of the strikes he delivered or the ones he received. All he could think of was the look of utter surprise on Sharp-claw's face at the moment that Darktail struck him down. And Darktail had looked so cold and calculating.

I can't believe I felt so close to that vile cat! I even thought he might help to make up for losing Duskpaw! But Darktail was never anything like my brother!

The storm raged on, matching the storm in Hawkwing's heart. Raindrops bounced off the ground, gathering in puddles that spread and flowed into one another. The ground was slippery, and it was hard to see through the sheets of driving rain.

Through the chaos, Hawkwing spotted Patchfoot close to the cliff wall, locked in combat with a skinny ginger rogue. He began splashing over there to help the elder. Patchfoot had reared on his hind paws, pinning the rogue against the rock face, but just as he was poised to strike, his hind paws slipped in the mud and he fell. With a yowl of triumph the ginger rogue fell on him, biting and scratching. Patchfoot let out a choking gasp of pain.

Putting on a burst of speed, Hawkwing flung himself at the rogue and drove him back, landing a couple of blows on his hindquarters as the rogue turned and fled. Then he turned toward Patchfoot, only to realize with a fresh shock of grief that the old cat was dead, his limbs stretched out as rain flowed through his pelt.

Hawkwing let out a growl of pure fury. Close by he spotted Clovertail and Fallowfern fighting with two more of the rogues, and began to rush toward them. But before he reached them, he was distracted by a panic-stricken screech from the cliff above his head.

"Help us!"

Looking up through the rain, Hawkwing managed to make out a knot of cats fighting outside the nursery. He recognized Mintfur and Birdwing, bravely holding their own but outnumbered by three rogues who were steadily driving them away from the nursery entrance.

They want to hurt the kits! Hawkwing realized. *They're striking at the heart of our Clan!*

"I'm coming!" he yowled, launching himself up the trail.

As he drew closer, Hawkwing could hear the thin wails of Mintfur's four terrified young kits, and the stronger voices of Birdwing's three, who were almost old enough to be apprenticed.

"We can fight!" Curlykit called out. "We'll protect the young ones!"

"We'll claw any rogue who comes in here!" Fidgetkit agreed, while Snipkit simply let out a threatening growl.

Hawkwing raced upward and realized after a few paces that another cat was following hard on his paws. Afraid that a rogue was chasing him, he paused to look back and saw that it was Pebblepaw. Her speckled fur was plastered to her body by the rain, but thankfulness surged through Hawkwing as he realized she was unhurt.

There was no time to talk. Hawkwing sped up the trail with Pebblepaw behind him, until they reached the ledge outside the nursery and fell on the rogues from behind.

Hawkwing swatted at the nearest attacker, a black-and-white tom, with both forepaws, pushing him off the ledge to fall shrieking into the gorge. Pebblepaw dug her claws into the hindquarters of a huge ginger tom and clung there as he twisted around, trying to get at her. Hawkwing slashed at his ears, and with a wail of fear the rogue tore himself away and fled up the trail to disappear over the cliff top. The third rogue was a gray she-cat; Hawkwing faced her, his lips drawn back from his teeth in a threatening snarl. He was aware of Pebblepaw at his side; faced with the two of them, the rogue backed away slowly, then suddenly turned tail and headed back down into the gorge.

"So much for them!" Pebblepaw panted, a note of triumph in her voice.

Hawkwing gave her an admiring glance. *She's so brave,* he thought, reflecting on how well they fought together.

"Thank you!" Birdwing exclaimed. "We were so afraid for the kits."

"We wouldn't have let them in here." Curlykit's voice came from the mouth of the den. All three of Birdwing's kits were crouched there, claws extended from their tiny paws, their eyes gleaming in the darkness.

"Well done; you're very brave," Hawkwing meowed. Turning to Pebblepaw, he added, "Stay here and help protect the nursery."

He half expected Pebblepaw to argue, but she responded with a brisk nod. "You can count on me, Hawkwing."

Satisfied that he had done the best he could for the two queens and their litters, Hawkwing headed down the trail again. At the foot he spotted Rileypaw and Bellapaw, struggling with two much bigger rogues. One of them had Rileypaw pinned down, and was about to sink his claws into the young tom's throat.

Hawkwing leaped to the top of a boulder, just above

Rileypaw and his attacker, and hurled himself onto the rogue's shoulders, thrusting him away from his Clanmate. As soon as he was freed, Rileypaw scrambled to his paws and went to help Bellapaw.

Hawkwing cuffed the rogue around the ears until he stumbled away, squealing, then turned to see the two littermates driving off the second attacker.

"Thanks, Hawkwing," Rileypaw gasped. "I thought I was dead for sure."

"Are you both okay?" Hawkwing asked.

Though Bellapaw and Rileypaw both bore the marks of the rogues' claws, they simply nodded. "Fine," Bellapaw mewed.

"Then go and help the elders." Hawkwing angled his ears toward Clovertail and Fallowfern, still locked in their struggle with the massive rogues. Clovertail looked to be at the end of her strength, but she was still striking out bravely.

The two young cats bounded off, and Hawkwing spotted Sandynose limping toward the foot of the cliff with Plumwillow, who was leaning on him heavily. Blood streamed from the gray she-cat's shoulder.

"She's hurt!" Sandynose gasped. "And she's expecting kits."

"I'm so slow," Plumwillow confessed, breathing hard. "I'm off-balance somehow."

For the first time Hawkwing noticed Plumwillow's rounded belly. "Take her up to the nursery," he meowed to Sandynose. "You can help protect the kits."

Sandynose nodded, looking relieved, and began guiding his mate up the trail.

Hawkwing's whole body tensed with horror as he looked

around the camp and realized how badly the battle was going for SkyClan. The bodies of his Clanmates were strewn on the ground between the cliff and the river; he couldn't tell whether they were dead or only injured. Between the darkness and the storm, with every cat plastered in mud, it was becoming harder still to tell friend from foe.

"Retreat! SkyClan, retreat!"

Leafstar's voice yowled out into the night; Hawkwing turned and saw her standing on top of the Rockpile. Her voice rang out once more; then she leaped down and vanished into the darkness.

We've lost, Hawkwing thought, a dark mist of sadness and disbelief swirling around him. *Our leader is giving up the gorge.*

At Leafstar's order the SkyClan cats began to stream out of their camp. Hawkwing froze for a moment as he watched them scatter in all directions, disappearing into the night and the pouring rain.

He thought again of his mother's words: *I'm afraid that if we are driven into exile again, SkyClan may be lost forever.* And here they were, about to be driven out of their home. *Can it really be over so quickly?*

Still, Hawkwing didn't question his leader's decision. He would follow her order. Forcing his limbs into motion, Hawkwing fled with his Clanmates, heading downstream, but after a few paces he halted and looked back.

Darktail stood on top of a boulder in the middle of the camp, a terrible expression of triumph on his face. His white pelt was clotted with blood.

Sharpclaw's blood . . . the blood of my Clanmates.

With horror, Hawkwing realized that Darktail was staring straight at him. He froze, panting and full of rage. He thought of how Darktail had asked him to stay with him in the gorge—right after he'd delivered the killing blow to Sharpclaw! *I'm nothing like you!* he thought fiercely. He desperately wanted to fling himself on Darktail and claw that look of triumph from his face, but he knew this wasn't the time. Instead, he tore his gaze away and raced out of the camp, his heart ready to break from anger and pain.

He remembered now how proud he'd felt to bring Darktail back to camp from the ashes of the fire. He'd truly believed he might be the "spark that remains," or might have helped SkyClan find it. *I brought Darktail here. I trusted him, and all the time he was deceiving us. He wanted to take away everything we cared about . . . and he has. But I was the cat who started it all. It's my fault we've lost the gorge. Darktail might have been his killer, but still, it's my fault that Sharpclaw is dead.*

Hawkwing fled blindly, not stopping until he came to the riverbank and realized that he had reached the patch of scrub and small trees where he had hunted with Sharpclaw and Darktail in what felt like another life. At first he thought he was alone, unsure where the rest of his Clan had gone.

Are we all scattered? Is this the end?

Rain was still driving down, and the river was running high and strong, sweeping twigs and debris down with it as it rolled between the banks. Hawkwing had to strain to see anything in the darkness.

Then Hawkwing heard voices coming from farther

downstream. Heading in that direction, he spotted Birdwing's three kits trying to cross the river over a set of stepping-stones. Curlykit was urging them on; there were no adult cats in sight.

"Stop! It's too dangerous!" Hawkwing yowled.

But the kits seemed not to hear him through the rain and the roar of the river, launching themselves on the perilous crossing.

Hawkwing bounded toward them, and realized as he drew closer that there were other cats on the far bank. He could just make out their shadowy shapes and hear their meows, though he couldn't distinguish what they were saying. From their voices, Hawkwing thought they might be Echosong and Pebblepaw, but there was no sign of Birdwing or the kits' father, Sagenose. He understood now why the kits wanted to cross the river, but they were still in terrible danger.

By the time Hawkwing reached the stepping-stones, all three kits were well on the way across; Curlykit, in the lead, was more than halfway. Hawkwing began to follow. He was more frightened still for the kits when he felt the slick surface of the stones with the river water lapping over them. *Oh, StarClan! Don't let them slip!*

Curlykit reached the far bank and was hauled to safety by a cat who Hawkwing could now see was Pebblepaw. Fidgetkit followed, leaping up the bank by himself and turning, ready to help his remaining littermate.

Hawkwing thought that Snipkit looked exhausted. She was moving slowly, hesitating before she leaped from one stone to the next. Her legs were wobbling. Hawkwing speeded up, not bothering to check his balance as he sprang from rock to rock. At each landing he felt his paws shift under him, and only pushing off for his next leap saved him from falling.

Before Hawkwing could reach Snipkit, her paws slipped as she tried to jump. She fell short, letting out a terrified wail; her forepaws scrabbled at the next stone, but she couldn't get a grip. She fell with a splash, her eyes wide with disbelief as the current quickly swept her away.

Instantly Hawkwing plunged into the river. "Snipkit! Snipkit!" he yowled, desperately peering into the darkness in the hope of spotting the drowning kit.

The fierce current dragged at Hawkwing, and soon he was struggling desperately simply to stay afloat. "Don't swim after her!" he gasped to the frantic cats on the bank. "It's too—"

Water flowed into Hawkwing's mouth, cutting off his warning. His head went under and he lost all sense of direction; surging black water was all around him.

I'm going to die, he thought, and then his next thought surprised him: *Maybe that's best. If I survive, I'll have to face Cherrytail and the others, and live with the guilt of knowing that I brought Darktail into the Clan.*

In his mind, Hawkwing once again saw his father's terrible death, murdered while he had looked on, powerless to help him. *If I drown, I'll never have to remember that again.*

Then, as Hawkwing felt himself begin to spiral away into darkness, he imagined his father's brilliant green gaze fixed on him. "My son is *not* a coward!" Sharpclaw meowed.

The memory of his father's faith in him filled Hawkwing

with new energy and determination. He began to fight again, his legs churning the water, until abruptly his head broke the surface. Coughing, he forced himself to keep paddling until he felt the gravelly bottom of the river under his paws and managed to stand. With water streaming from his pelt, he staggered ashore, as Pebblepaw came bounding over to him, followed by Echosong, Curlykit, and Fidgetkit.

"This way!" he choked out, pointing downstream with his tail.

He forced his aching legs into motion to race downstream, scanning the rolling current for any sign of Snipkit. Pebblepaw ran beside him, the others less than a tail-length behind.

"Snipkit! Snipkit!" Every cat was calling for her, but there was no reply, and nothing to see in the night and the rain.

Eventually Hawkwing staggered to a halt, and Pebblepaw collapsed to the ground beside him.

"It's no use," Pebblepaw gasped. "We have to stop."

The two remaining kits came limping up with Echosong.

"We can't just leave her!" Curlykit protested. "We have to find her!"

"It's too dark," Echosong mewed gently. "We could easily miss her if we carry on. We'll look for her in the morning, I promise."

Curlykit and Fidgetkit exchanged a glance; Hawkwing could tell that they wanted to be reassured, but they were still doubtful. Their wide eyes glimmered in the gloom and their flanks were heaving as they fought against their grief. Hawkwing could see how desperately they were trying to be brave.

He knew how they felt. Little as he wanted to admit it, even to himself, he thought that probably Snipkit was already dead.

A wave of anger surged through Hawkwing, so hot that he stopped shivering and dug his claws fiercely into the ground.

Another death because of Darktail! If he hadn't attacked, Snipkit would be tucked up safely in the nursery. She wouldn't have had to try to cross this angry river in a rainstorm late at night.

Exhausted, the five cats headed into the undergrowth and trampled down a clear space among ferns for a makeshift den. Echosong and Pebblepaw settled the kits, licking their fur the wrong way to dry them off and make them warm. Hawkwing thought about keeping watch, in case any of Darktail's rogues should come marauding down the riverbank, but his exhaustion was too strong. Letting himself relax, he fell into a bottomless pit of sleep.

It was still dark when Hawkwing awoke. At first he couldn't work out what had changed; then he realized that he couldn't hear the rain drumming on the leaves above his head. There was only the distant roar of the river, and close by a steady drip of raindrops falling from the bushes.

His Clanmates were still asleep, Echosong and Pebblepaw curled around the two kits. Careful not to wake them, Hawkwing rose to his paws and slid out into the open.

I need to think. Somehow we have to find the rest of our Clanmates, and make a plan to take the gorge back.

Sadness overwhelmed Hawkwing as he realized how much had changed. This damp refuge on the riverbank was so different from his nest in the warriors' den. He couldn't even begin to imagine where the rest of the Clan might be, or even whether they were still alive.

The faces of his dead Clanmates passed in front of him. His father, Sharpclaw, who had died a hero's death at the claws of a traitor. Bouncefire, the traitor's first victim. The elder Patchfoot, always cheerful, always ready with a story for the kits and apprentices. Stormheart, who had almost certainly been killed at the very beginning of the attack.

Probably Snipkit, Hawkwing thought sadly, *and probably more, too. I saw cats fall, but I couldn't tell if they were wounded or dead. And now every cat is scattered.*

He whipped around at a faint sound of movement behind him, then relaxed as he saw Pebblepaw sliding between the ferns to sit at his side. She leaned against him, and Hawkwing was grateful for the warmth she gave.

"I feel so responsible for this," Hawkwing told her, putting words to his terrible burden of guilt for the first time. "If I hadn't trusted Darktail, if I hadn't brought him into Sky-Clan—"

"You couldn't have known," Pebblepaw interrupted, resting her tail-tip on his shoulder.

"But I *should* have! Sharpclaw had his doubts about him, and I should have listened to him! Great StarClan, I had my *own* doubts. If I hadn't ignored them, none of this would have happened. It's all my fault."

"No, it's not." Pebblepaw's warm tongue rasped comfortingly around Hawkwing's ear. "You're a very young warrior,

Hawkwing. If Leafstar and the senior warriors hadn't agreed, Darktail and Rain would never have been allowed in the camp. *Every* cat made the mistake of trusting them."

Hawkwing wanted to believe Pebblepaw, but he was finding it hard. The sharp pang of his guilt was too painful.

"There's something that frightens me," he confided to her. "Darktail wanted me to join him and stay in the camp. He thinks we're *alike*. What if that's true?"

Pebblepaw let out a snort of disgust. "How can you believe such a pile of mouse droppings? You're brave and loyal, Hawkwing, a true SkyClan warrior. Did you fight for your Clan back there?"

"Well . . . yes," Hawkwing murmured reluctantly.

"And did it even occur to you to betray them?"

"No!"

"Then what makes you think you're anything like Darktail?" Pebblepaw challenged him. "You would never plot against cats who had been kind to you."

As she spoke, Hawkwing began to feel his burden grow a little lighter. *She's right. Yes, I made mistakes, but I will make up for them. I will be as brave and loyal as Pebblepaw thinks I am, and I'll protect my Clanmates' lives with my own.*

Nestling closer to Pebblepaw, Hawkwing felt a wave of gratitude to her. *Terrible things have happened, but at least she is by my side. I'd like her by my side for always.* Looking into her eyes, shining in the darkness, he couldn't help feeling a tiny sliver of warmth.

CHAPTER 18

❧

Hawkwing and Pebblepaw drowsed outside the den until the sky began to grow pale with dawn, and Echosong pushed her way into the open.

"We ought to look for the others," she meowed.

Hawkwing nodded, anxiety for Cherrytail and his sisters pricking at his pads. "And first we have to look for Snipkit."

Rousing the kits, Hawkwing led the way along the riverbank, heading farther downstream. As the dawn light strengthened, it dazzled off puddles and water droplets hanging from every branch. The river had grown quieter, winding among the rocks like a glittering snake. The dawn air was fresh and clear; once or twice Hawkwing's heart beat faster with hope as he thought that he had picked up a trace of the missing kit's scent. But each time, the trail petered out, and he realized that he had been wrong. The brilliant morning didn't reveal any sign of Snipkit.

Curlykit and Fidgetkit grew more and more frantic with every paw step they took.

"We *have* to find her!" Curlykit meowed. "What are we going to tell our mother and father?"

Hawkwing couldn't escape a heavy feeling of despair. He was certain in his own mind that they weren't going to find the little black she-cat. *Even if she didn't drown, she'd be a defenseless kit all on her own. She could have been snatched up by a hawk, or killed by a fox.* Firmly he shook off these dark thoughts to focus on the remaining kits.

"When did you last see your parents?" he asked them.

"We were with Birdwing when Leafstar called the retreat," Fidgetkit explained. "But we lost her in the crowd. We don't know where she went, or where Sagenose is."

"We don't know where *any* cat is!" Curlykit wailed.

"Well, we're here," Pebblepaw mewed comfortingly. "We'll look after you, and I guess we'll find your family soon."

I hope she's right, Hawkwing thought.

He led the cats farther along the bank, his hope dwindling with every heartbeat. As he was wondering whether to give up and turn back, he heard the rustling of some creature pushing its way toward them through the undergrowth.

"Snipkit?" Fidgetkit mewed eagerly, beginning to hurry toward the sound.

"Wait!" Hawkwing warned him.

The sound suggested a much bigger animal than Snipkit, and a low growl coming from the bushes convinced Hawkwing that whatever was in there, it wasn't the missing kit. Opening his jaws, he picked up a musky, unpleasant scent.

Hawkwing and Echosong sprang forward, pushing Fidgetkit behind them as the branches parted and a strange black-and-white animal burst into the open, glaring at them from malignant eyes.

"A raccoon!" Pebblepaw exclaimed.

Hawkwing froze, amazed at his first sight of one of the vicious creatures that had attacked his Clanmates while he was away. It was black, white, and gray, with white around its short, pointed muzzle and black rings around its eyes. Its claws were long and flexible, reminding Hawkwing of a Two-leg's forepaws. He had no doubt about how dangerous it was.

As he and Echosong gazed at it, for a moment too startled to move, the raccoon darted forward toward Echosong. The medicine cat started back, but she didn't move fast enough. She let out a screech of shock and pain as the raccoon sank its teeth into her shoulder.

At first Hawkwing wasn't sure what to do. He had never seen a raccoon before. *What can these creatures do? How do I fight it?*

In his moment's hesitation, Pebblepaw leaped at the raccoon, slashing her claws through its thick fur. With a hideous tearing sound the raccoon let Echosong go, and the medicine cat slumped to the ground with a dull thud. Then the creature turned on Pebblepaw, hissing ferociously.

Terrified for her, Hawkwing barreled into its side, thrusting it away, and lashed at its muzzle with one forepaw. With a grunt of pain the raccoon spun around, scattering drops of blood from its injured muzzle, and vanished once more into the undergrowth.

"Thank StarClan!" Pebblepaw exclaimed. "They were much fiercer than that when they attacked us in the gorge."

"Maybe they're not so brave when they're alone," Hawkwing responded, grateful that the encounter had been no worse. "It seemed just as surprised as we were when we came across each other. I don't think it was looking for a fight."

Though he and Pebblepaw were both bruised and exhausted, the raccoon hadn't injured them. The kits were fine, too, crouching under a bush with bristling fur and eyes stretched wide with a mixture of fear and excitement.

So all we need to worry about is the bite on Echosong's shoulder, Hawkwing thought, relieved.

"Echosong, are you badly hurt?" Pebblepaw asked.

The medicine cat shook her head. "It's not too bad," she replied. "It just needs cleaning out, and cobweb to stop the bleeding."

"I'll clean it up," Pebblepaw offered at once. "Echosong, come and lie down here in the shelter of this bush."

Echosong padded over into the shade of a hazel bush and sank down with a sigh of relief. Pebblepaw crouched beside her and began to clean the wound with strong, rapid rasps of her tongue.

"Come on, kits," Hawkwing directed. "We'll go and look for cobwebs."

The kits sprang up instantly, obviously pleased to be able to help. "We'll find lots!" Curlykit boasted.

Hawkwing kept an eye on the kits as they all headed into the bushes, and tried to imagine how they felt. *They've lost their home and a littermate, all at once. I'm scared, so they must be terrified.*

"You're doing really well," he told them as they peered under branches to find the cobwebs Echosong needed.

By the time Hawkwing and the kits returned with pawfuls of cobweb, Pebblepaw had finished cleaning Echosong's wound. Already the bleeding had almost stopped, but she still showed Hawkwing how to plaster the cobweb over the bite. Fidgetkit patted it carefully all around to seal the edges.

"You should rest now," Hawkwing told Echosong when the cobweb was in place. "Keep the kits with you, and Pebblepaw and I will hunt."

"But shouldn't we go on looking for Snipkit?" Curlykit objected.

"No," Echosong replied, curling her tail around to draw the little gray she-cat closer to her. "We need to eat to keep up our strength. We can't help Snipkit by making ourselves ill."

Fidgetkit nodded seriously. "We'll look after you, Echosong," he mewed. "Are you comfortable there? If you stretch out more it should be better. And can we find you any herbs to help with the pain?"

"Not right now," Echosong replied, blinking affectionately at the little tom. "It's more important for us to stay together."

When Hawkwing was satisfied that Echosong and the two kits would be safe for a while, he headed farther downstream with Pebblepaw at his side. Though they still kept a lookout for Snipkit, their main purpose was to find some prey. Hawkwing hadn't realized until then how hungry he was.

"We'd better watch out for raccoons, too," Pebblepaw murmured, tasting the air. "It's weird that they started coming onto our territory so often, when we'd never seen them before."

Hawkwing nodded agreement, then halted as a sudden realization struck him. "You know," he began slowly, thinking aloud, "I saw Darktail scattering Twoleg food scraps near the camp. Suppose he was trying to lure other animals—foxes, maybe, and these raccoons—onto our territory to cause trouble for us and put us in danger. How long have Darktail and Rain been working against us? From the very beginning?"

Pebblepaw listened in silence, her eyes widening as Hawkwing explained his suspicions. "I saw Darktail leaving half-eaten pieces of prey outside camp once," she meowed when he had finished. "But that was a long time ago. I didn't know what to think about it, and I didn't want to confront Darktail." Her head drooped in regret. "I should have shared my suspicions with some cat."

Hawkwing shook his head. "It's not your fault. I could have spoken up too, but I thought of Darktail as a friend. I still can't really believe what he did. I felt so close to him. The cat I thought he was just wasn't the same as the cat who did these dreadful things and spent so much time planning how to destroy us. The quests, too," he added. "I don't think he ever knew where we could find Firestar's kin. He just wanted to distract us and weaken us."

"Then he succeeded," Pebblepaw mewed solemnly. "We followed his directions and we lost Billystorm."

"It's my fault," Hawkwing continued, fighting with a renewed onset of guilt. "I *saw* him leave the food scraps, and I should have reported it. If I'd told Leafstar or Sharpclaw, the attack last night might never have happened."

Pebblepaw huffed out a breath. "Don't deceive yourself. Darktail is clever and sneaky. He would have thought up some excuse. And you couldn't possibly have known just how evil he is."

"Maybe you're right," Hawkwing sighed. Pebblepaw's words comforted him, even though he couldn't entirely get rid of his guilty feelings. "At any rate, once we find our Clanmates I'll protect them from now on—even with my last breath!"

Pebblepaw pressed her muzzle against his shoulder. "We'll make things better," she purred. "We'll work together, and save SkyClan any way we can. And now let's hunt," she added. "My belly thinks my throat's been clawed out!"

Sunhigh was approaching by the time Hawkwing and Pebblepaw returned with a mouse and a couple of voles. Echosong was asleep, with the two kits nestling against her flank, but all three of them roused as Hawkwing and Pebblepaw padded up and dropped their prey beside them.

Curlykit and Fidgetkit blinked sleepily, then sprang to their paws and looked around hopefully. Only for a heartbeat; then their tails drooped in disappointment.

"You didn't find Snipkit," Curlykit mewed.

"No, but we found fresh-kill," Pebblepaw told her, pushing the plumpest vole toward her. "Come and eat."

"So can we go and look for Snipkit now?" Fidgetkit asked when every cat had gulped down the last mouthfuls of prey.

Hawkwing glanced at Echosong. *We know that Snipkit is dead,* he thought. *Maybe this is the time to tell the kits.*

Echosong shook her head sadly. "No," she responded to Fidgetkit's question. "If Snipkit had made it to shore, we would have found her by now."

Curlykit and Fidgetkit gazed at each other in dismay, and Curlykit let out a miserable wail.

"That doesn't mean she's dead," Fidgetkit meowed. "She could be on the opposite bank."

Hawkwing exchanged a doubtful look with Echosong, while Pebblepaw studied her paws and wouldn't meet the kits' gaze.

"You could be right," Echosong agreed at last. "I think if Snipkit did swim to shore, she would try to find the rest of the Clan. And so should we. Hawkwing, where do you think the others would have gone?"

Hawkwing wasn't sure. "Maybe near the gorge?" he suggested. "Watching the rogues and getting ready to attack?"

"I doubt it," Pebblepaw meowed. "They'll be injured and exhausted—in no fit state to fight. Not yet, at least. I think they'd try to find a place where they're sure to find other Clanmates."

"And there's only one place like that," Echosong stated. "In the Twolegplace, with the daylight warriors."

Hawkwing's pelt began to bristle with nervousness as he and his Clanmates approached the Twolegplace. This was only the fourth time he had been there: once with Ebonyclaw, who was a daylight warrior and thoroughly familiar with the hard Thunderpaths separating the huge stone dens; once with Billystorm and the rest of the patrol on the first quest; and once when he followed Darktail. He had hoped that he would never have to go there again, and when the first of the dens loomed over them he felt lost and uncertain.

The two kits had never been there before, and were staring around in wonder.

"It's so big!" Curlykit exclaimed.

"Will we see Twolegs?" Fidgetkit asked. "What will they do to us?"

"Probably nothing bad," Echosong mewed briskly. "Follow me."

Hawkwing stared at the medicine cat as she took the lead so confidently. "Have you been here before?" he asked.

Echosong glanced at him over her shoulder. "Of course," she replied. "Didn't you know that I was once a kittypet?"

Hawkwing exchanged a surprised glance with Pebblepaw. "No," he meowed, shocked that a kittypet could become a medicine cat with such a strong connection to StarClan. "You really lived with Twolegs in one of these dens?"

"I really did," Echosong told him. "Firestar found me, and explained why I was dreaming of cats with stars in their fur. But that was a long time ago," she added dismissively. "I hardly think about it anymore."

Echosong led her Clanmates along the edge of Thunderpaths, down alleyways, and past so many Twoleg dens that Hawkwing became quite bewildered. "If I was on my own, I'd never find my way out of here," he murmured to Pebblepaw.

At last Echosong squeezed under a Twoleg fence and beckoned with her tail for the others to follow. Hawkwing brought up the rear, and heard the two kits squeaking with excitement as he pressed his belly to the ground and crawled through the gap with the bottom of the fence scraping his spine.

Rising to his paws on the other side, Hawkwing found himself in a Twoleg garden. The powerful scent of cats caught him in the throat. Looking around eagerly, he saw that a long stretch of grass led up to a Twoleg den at the far side. Close by, crouching in the shelter of some bushes with glossy dark leaves, was Leafstar, surrounded by several of their Clanmates.

Relief filled Hawkwing like rain filling an upturned leaf. *Some of us have survived! There's hope after all!*

But within a couple of heartbeats Hawkwing's feelings of relief began to give way to dismay as he realized how many of his Clanmates were missing. Something cold gathered heavily inside him as he looked in vain for his mother, Cherrytail, and his sisters, Cloudmist and Blossomheart.

Have I lost all my kin?

Ebonyclaw was with the others; when she spotted the newcomers she bounded over to them and dipped her head. "You're alive!" she exclaimed. "Oh, it's so good to see you. Welcome to my nest."

In spite of his anxiety about his family, Hawkwing couldn't wait to rejoin his Clanmates. They looked exhausted and their pelts were ragged, but their eyes were bright as they clustered around, eagerly welcoming.

"There's Parsleypaw!" Pebblepaw exclaimed, running to touch noses with her brother. "Oh, I'm so glad you're safe!"

Sparrowpelt and Tinycloud were there, too, hurrying up

to greet their daughter and brushing their pelts against hers.

Birdwing sprang up and bounded up to Curlykit and Fidgetkit, closely followed by their father, Sagenose. "Thank StarClan you're safe!" she mewed, relief shining in her eyes. Then she paused, her gaze traveling over the newcomers. "But where's Snipkit?"

"She's not with you?" Fidgetkit asked anxiously.

Sagenose shook his head. "We haven't seen her since last night."

The two kits launched into their story, of how Snipkit had fallen into the river. Hawkwing could see growing dismay in Birdwing's and Sagenose's eyes, and Birdwing let out a wail of pain when Curlykit told how their search had failed. She drew her two remaining kits close to her, and Sagenose buried his muzzle in her shoulder fur.

Giving them space to grieve, Hawkwing looked around to see who else was there. He spotted Mintfur with all four of her kits, as well as her mate, Nettlesplash. Plumwillow and Waspwhisker had made it, too. But his relief at seeing they had survived couldn't wipe out his desolation that his mother and sisters were missing.

Then after a moment Pebblepaw left her family and came to sit beside him, offering silent support with understanding in her eyes. Hawkwing leaned toward her, grateful for her warmth.

"It's been a while since any kittypets were attacked by raccoons," Ebonyclaw was explaining to Leafstar. "So my Twolegs have started letting me out again, though only in the daytime."

"What about the others?" Leafstar asked.

"I haven't seen them," the black she-cat replied. "But I reckon they'll be free again soon. Twolegs like to do things at the same time as each other. If only Darktail hadn't made his move while all of us daylight warriors were shut up," she added. "Maybe we would have been able to turn the tide in the battle. I'll never forgive myself for not being there!"

"Don't blame yourself. I'm sure Darktail took all that into account when he was making his plans," Leafstar meowed grimly.

No cat looked angrily at Hawkwing when the evil rogue was mentioned, but he felt another painful pang of guilt. *I never want to hear Darktail's name again!*

"Well," Sparrowpelt began, sounding determinedly cheerful, "now that we have the daylight warriors again, we can gather up the rest of the Clan, attack the rogues, and take back our territory."

An enthusiastic murmur rose from the group of cats. "We'll teach those rogues!" Tinycloud called out.

"Yes, rip their pelts off!" Nettlesplash growled.

Hawkwing flexed his claws eagerly, relieved that he could put the past behind him and prove himself anew.

But Leafstar raised her tail for silence. "You're right that we need to find our missing Clanmates," she meowed. "But simply attacking the rogues might not be the smartest course of action right now."

Hawkwing's jaws gaped in shock. *How could we not fight back? How could we not avenge my father's death, and so many others?*

Several of his Clanmates leaped to their paws, their fur bristling in outrage.

"You can't mean that!" Waspwhisker protested. "They're in *our* home!"

"But we're not the Clan we used to be," Sparrowpelt pointed out. "We've suffered so much. It might be moons before we can take on those rogues."

"Could . . . ?" Pebblepaw's voice was a soft mew, but somehow it caught the attention of every cat. Hawkwing could tell from the way she looked at the ground that she was uncomfortable asking her question. "Could this be StarClan's plan? Could they be punishing us for something?"

The gathered warriors passed uneasy glances back and forth, no cat sure how to respond. Some of them looked worried.

"I don't know." Leafstar's sigh was weary. "The important thing now is to follow the prophecy. Our Clan is on the verge of being destroyed. If we want to save SkyClan, we must find the spark that remains. Then we will see what the future holds for us."

Hawkwing's belly lurched and he felt as if he would vomit. *We've already tried twice to find ThunderClan, and both times it ended in disaster.* He reflected that it was Darktail who had led them into trouble on the previous quests, but even so, SkyClan knew no more now than they had then. *How can we possibly succeed?*

"It's clear that StarClan is testing us in many ways," Leafstar continued. "We lost our deputy, Sharpclaw."

As he heard some cats gasp, others sigh, Hawkwing felt as

though clouds had gathered to cover the sun. He knew that SkyClan now needed a new deputy, but everything in him refused to accept it. *Sharpclaw is our deputy.* Replacing him just made it clear that Sharpclaw was truly dead.

In his mind's eye Hawkwing could see Rain creeping up on his father, and Darktail's murderous blow that had ended Sharpclaw's life. Repressing a shudder, he met Pebblepaw's steady gaze, and immediately felt a little stronger. She stretched her tail across his shoulders, wordlessly comforting him.

"Cats of SkyClan," Leafstar began, her gaze traveling over the remnants of her Clan. "Yesterday Sharpclaw died honorably in battle, killed by the most treacherous cat I have ever known. We will never forget him. But the Clan must go on, and I must appoint a new deputy."

Hawkwing's grief eased just a little as Leafstar praised his father. *She's right; we'll never forget you,* he thought. *I'm proud to be your son.*

"I say these words before StarClan," Leafstar continued, "that the spirits of our ancestors may hear and approve my choice. Waspwhisker will be the new deputy of SkyClan."

A murmur of appreciation rose from the cats clustered around their leader, while Waspwhisker's eyes widened in surprise, and a pleased expression spread over his face.

"Leafstar, I never expected this honor," he meowed. "I can never be as noble a cat as Sharpclaw was, but I swear by StarClan that I will be a loyal and faithful deputy."

"Waspwhisker! Waspwhisker!" the SkyClan cats chanted.

Hawkwing joined in; a mixture of pride, happiness, and

grief warmed his pelt at the words Waspwhisker had spoken about his father. Though he was still troubled that Sharpclaw would no longer be deputy, he knew what a good choice Leaf-star had made. Waspwhisker was a strong, brave warrior, but he was wise as well, and he would support his leader and his Clan through the dark days that were to come.

Every cat respects him, Hawkwing thought. *If any cat can help lead us out of these dark times, it's Waspwhisker.*

CHAPTER 19

"Can you see any cat?" Hawkwing called, craning his neck to make out Pebblepaw's speckled pelt among the leaves of the beech tree.

"Not a whisker!" Pebblepaw replied.

She reappeared, carefully sliding down from branch to branch, then leaped to the ground and landed with a thump at Hawkwing's side.

Two sunrises had passed since the remains of SkyClan had gathered at Ebonyclaw's nest. Since then, many more cats had made their way there, but some were still missing.

Blossomheart is back, but there's been no sign of Cherrytail or Cloudmist, Hawkwing thought, his heart aching. *Plumwillow's mate, Sandynose, isn't back yet, and neither are Frecklewish and Fallowfern.* He knew that every cat was beginning to lose hope of ever seeing them again.

And there had been more sad news to add to the survivors' grief. Rileypaw had seen Stormheart struck down at the foot of the Rockpile when the battle had barely begun. Tinycloud had found Snipkit washed up on the riverbank, and carried the tiny limp body back to her Clan for burial.

Laying the tiny body in the earth, seeing Snipkit's life cut off when she was so young, was one of the most painful experiences of Hawkwing's life. Her littermates, Curlykit and Fidgetkit, had whimpered all through it, and ever since, Hawkwing had noticed that they wandered around in a daze, all their high spirits gone.

I wonder if they'll ever get over losing her.

Every time another cat found their way to Ebonyclaw's nest, Hawkwing hardly dared speak to them, in case they brought news of Cherrytail's or Cloudmist's death. It was harder still to go out on patrol.

I'm almost afraid to go on looking, Hawkwing thought, *in case I find something else terrible.*

Now he and Pebblepaw were searching the forest on the opposite side of the gorge from the camp. Pebblepaw had suggested climbing the tree to see if she could spot any cat, but she had seen nothing.

"This is hopeless," Hawkwing muttered. "Our missing Clanmates must be dead by now."

"You don't know that," Pebblepaw insisted, twining her tail affectionately with Hawkwing's. "Good things do happen, remember? Blossomheart made it back to camp soon after we did, and you heard from Harveymoon how he found Firefern trapped in a Twoleg den. He had to brave the Twolegs' dog, but he got Firefern out."

"That's true," Hawkwing responded, "but . . ."

"And Darktail's rogues haven't bothered us," Pebblepaw added. "That has to be good."

Hawkwing twitched his whiskers. *I wonder what Darktail is up to, now that he has what he wanted. Will we ever see the gorge again?* "Since we haven't tried to take back the gorge," he mewed dryly, "Darktail probably thinks we aren't a threat."

But though his words were somber, Hawkwing rubbed his cheek against Pebblepaw's, grateful for her hopeful spirit. *We're both young, and she's still an apprentice—but I know she'll be my mate someday. And I know she feels the same.*

The two cats continued through the forest, stopping every few fox-lengths to yowl for their missing Clanmates. Hawkwing was ready to give up, convinced that their efforts were pointless, when they heard an answering, distant yowl.

Delight sprang into Pebblepaw's eyes. "This way!" she exclaimed.

Hawkwing followed her as she raced around a bramble thicket and up a fern-covered slope on the other side. At the top of the rise a steeper slope fell away into a clearing covered with low-growing bushes.

Hawkwing let out another yowl as he and Pebblepaw scrambled down. To his amazement the undergrowth parted and his sister Cloudmist emerged.

"Hawkwing!" she called. "Oh, it's so good to see you!"

Hawkwing skidded to a halt in front of his sister, touching noses with her and drinking in her sweet, familiar scent. "I'd given up hope of finding you," he choked out.

"And I'm not alone," Cloudmist purred, her eyes shining. "Cherrytail is here too. Come and see."

Turning, she led the way into a clear space among the

bushes, where Hawkwing found his mother lying stretched out on a bed of ferns. Cobweb was plastered over her tortoise-shell fur all along one side.

"You're hurt!" Hawkwing meowed.

Cherrytail's eyes were shining as she stretched upward to press her muzzle against Hawkwing's shoulder. "I'll be fine," she murmured.

"She was wounded in the battle," Cloudmist explained. "We managed to hide here, but I was afraid to leave her to get help. Darktail and his rogues might have found her."

Hawkwing's chest swelled, and he couldn't help give a sigh of relief.

Cherrytail cocked her head. "What's wrong?"

Hawkwing hesitated. He was relieved to find his kin, but he had just lost his father—something his mother and sister didn't know.

When he told them, Cherrytail sent an anguished yowl to the sky. "What about Blossomheart?" she asked anxiously. "Have you seen her?"

"Yes, she's safe," Hawkwing reassured her.

"We've made a temporary camp in the garden of Ebonyclaw's Twoleg den," Pebblepaw mewed, as Cherrytail relaxed with a sigh of relief. "We'll help you to get there now."

It was a long way; eventually the cats had to cross the river by the stepping-stones where Snipkit had slipped.

"We need to be very careful," Hawkwing warned his mother and sister. "Birdwing's kits tried crossing here just after the battle, and . . ." His voice quivered and he had to start again. "Snipkit slipped into the water and drowned."

"No!" Cherrytail's eyes stretched wide with horror. "Poor little one!"

"I'd like to drown Darktail!" Cloudmist declared, sliding out her claws as if the vicious rogue was standing in front of her.

"One day he'll get what's coming to him," Pebblepaw meowed. "But for now we have to keep going. The river's quieter now, so it shouldn't be too hard."

With the younger cats' help Cherrytail was able to limp across and hobble up one of the trails leading to the top of the gorge and across open ground to the Twolegplace. Hawkwing kept a wary eye out for rogue patrols, but he saw nothing of Darktail or his cats.

"Just as well . . . for them," he growled to himself, flexing his claws.

The rest of the SkyClan cats gathered around Cherrytail and Cloudmist when they arrived at Ebonyclaw's Twoleg nest, enthusiastically welcoming them. Hawkwing supported his mother as far as a sheltered spot under a holly bush where Echosong had made herself a den, with a collection of whatever herbs the Clan cats had been able to find. Cloudmist followed and a moment later Blossomheart joined them.

The medicine cat sniffed Cherrytail's wound carefully as she peeled away the covering of cobweb. Hawkwing winced when he saw the wound, a long gash down his mother's side, the edges looking red and inflamed.

"There's some infection there," Echosong murmured, "but

don't worry. It doesn't look too bad. Fidgetkit, can you clean that up for me, please."

The little black-and-white tom crouched down and began lapping gently at Cherrytail's wound. Ever since he had arrived in the camp with Echosong he had stayed by her side, working tirelessly to help the medicine cat while she patched up her Clanmates' injuries.

Maybe he has the makings of a medicine cat, Hawkwing thought as he watched. *It would be good for Echosong to take another apprentice, especially if we never find Frecklewish.*

When Echosong had treated the wound with a poultice of marigold, she and Fidgetkit slipped away, leaving Cherrytail to rest with her kits around her.

"I'm so glad we're all together again," Blossomheart mewed, covering her mother's ears with gentle licks. "Hawkwing and I have been so worried."

But we're not all together, Hawkwing thought. *We never will be again, because Sharpclaw is dead.* He felt as though he had an uncomfortable piece of fresh-kill lodged in his throat.

"What's the matter?" Cherrytail asked gently.

Swallowing hard, Hawkwing meowed, "I'm so sorry. I should never have trusted Darktail. If I'd known what kind of cat he is . . . I never imagined he would do something like killing Sharpclaw." His voice broke and he couldn't go on.

"I know, I know," Cherrytail breathed out. Her green eyes were full of sorrow, but there was love and understanding there too.

"We all know," Cloudmist added reassuringly. "It's not

your fault, Hawkwing. There's nothing to forgive."

Blossomheart merely blinked at him affectionately, and Hawkwing felt the pangs in his heart ease a little.

At least they don't blame me, but I'll never stop blaming myself. From now on, I'm going to make Sharpclaw proud, and never let my kin or my Clan down like that again.

When Hawkwing emerged into the camp again, leaving his mother to sleep, he found Leafstar standing on the edge of the bushes, with Pebblepaw, Harveymoon, and Firefern beside her. She beckoned Hawkwing to join them with a whisk of her tail.

"I'm going to lead a patrol back to the gorge," Leafstar announced. "I must be certain of the will of StarClan, and I intend to review every option. If the rogues look weak, or if some of them have left, then maybe that's a sign that StarClan wants us to stay. Do you want to come with us?"

Hawkwing was torn. There was some sense in his leader's decision, but they could also be walking right into more trouble. And the thought of seeing Darktail again, and revisiting the place where his father was killed, made his belly cramp with nausea.

I've been homesick for the gorge—but for the gorge as it used to be. I don't want to see what Darktail has made it now.

"There's no need, if you don't want to," Pebblepaw put in, clearly understanding how he felt. "I don't mind going, Leafstar."

The Clan leader dipped her head. "That's fine, then.

Hawkwing, stay alert and guard the camp while we're away."

She and the rest of the patrol headed off, squeezing under the Twoleg fence. As soon as they had disappeared, Hawkwing began to wish he had gone with them. *What if the rogues attack them and Pebblepaw is injured?* He imagined her, cornered by Darktail, hurt and afraid. *I might never see her again!*

He spent his time prowling restlessly around the borders of the camp, while the sun rose to sunhigh and began to slip down the sky. He tensed, afraid that he and his Clanmates had been discovered, when a Twoleg appeared from the den and brought out a small, growling monster. But all the Twoleg did was to push the monster up and down across the stretch of grass. Neither the Twoleg nor the monster seemed aware that there were cats hiding in the bushes.

Waspwhisker had gone out with a hunting patrol, and the rest of the Clan was gathering around to share the fresh-kill when Leafstar and her Clanmates returned.

Hawkwing bounded over to meet them, touching noses with Pebblepaw. "What happened?" he asked, overwhelmed by relief to see that none of the patrol were injured.

Leafstar's expression was grim, but she didn't reply until she had padded over to address every cat beside the fresh-kill pile. "I'm sorry to tell you," she announced, "that the gorge is lost to us. Darktail has moved in so many rogues that the place is crawling with them. We're badly outnumbered." Her voice shook on the last few words, but after a brief pause she went on firmly, "Our best chance of survival now is to forget the gorge. It is not the home we made there, not anymore. We must find new territory. We must find ThunderClan."

Hawkwing glanced nervously at his mother. Cherrytail had slept well, and emerged from Echosong's den to eat, but her eyes looked glazed and her body gave off a dry heat, as if her infection was worsening in spite of the medicine cat's treatment. Hawkwing worried that she might be too weak to travel.

As the SkyClan cats exchanged anxious looks at Leafstar's decision, Echosong slipped out of her den and dipped her head to her Clan leader. "I heard what you said," she meowed. "While you were away, I slept, and StarClan sent me another vision."

At her words Hawkwing felt his heart begin to beat faster. *This is what we've been waiting for!* He could see that the rest of his Clanmates felt the same, their ears flicking up and their whiskers quivering.

"Leafstar, you're right," the medicine cat went on. "StarClan has told me that our future does not lie in the gorge. I dreamed of SkyClan happy and safe together, in a place beside a large body of water."

"The river?" Rabbitleap asked. "But—"

"Not the river," Echosong interrupted. "This was much wider and calmer. It is a place I've never seen before, not even in dreams."

Leafstar had listened to the medicine cat with a look of deep seriousness. "This confirms my plan," she meowed. "StarClan wants us to leave this place. When we find ThunderClan, somewhere near this wide stretch of water, we will find our new home."

"But we don't know where to look!" Blossomheart protested.

"We know where to start. Bellapaw and Rileypaw will lead us back to where they used to live," Leafstar told her. "We leave in two sunrises."

As the Clan leader announced her decision, the whole of SkyClan erupted into debate, a chorus of protests and questions swirling around her.

"We can't leave!" Plumwillow exclaimed. "Not without knowing what happened to our other Clanmates."

"Yes!" Rabbitleap jumped to his paws. "What about Frecklewish, or Mistfeather? Where are they?"

"And my kits are too young to travel so far," Mintfur added, gathering the four tiny cats closer to her with a sweep of her tail.

Hawkwing noticed that Harveymoon and Ebonyclaw, at the edge of the group of cats, were exchanging a few quiet words with each other. Then Harveymoon spoke up.

"I can't leave here," he mewed, his voice soft but decisive. "I'm loyal to SkyClan, but I'm loyal to my Twolegs, too. I'm not going to leave them behind."

"That goes for me, too," Ebonyclaw added.

Hawkwing's pelt bristled with shock at the black she-cat's words. *Ebonyclaw was my mentor—and no cat could have had a better one. She's one of our best warriors. How can she give all that up to stay with Twolegs?*

He noticed that most of the cats who had not added their voices to the debate were looking just like he felt: hesitant and confused. But Pebblepaw was watching Leafstar closely, her eyes shining. Hawkwing realized that she was excited. *She wants to go with Leafstar!*

Moving closer to Pebblepaw, Hawkwing brushed his pelt against hers. *I can't imagine being without her,* he thought. *If she goes, I'm going too.*

Leafstar's voice rang out again, silencing the tumult. "This is not up for discussion," she meowed. "I am leaving. I will follow the vision StarClan has sent us."

"And I'm going too," Echosong added.

"Any cat who feels they can't leave here may stay behind," the Clan leader continued. "No cat will blame you. But first, before we go, we need to become a Clan again."

That's true, Hawkwing thought. *But how does Leafstar mean to do it?*

CHAPTER 20

❧

At sunrise on the following day, Leafstar called the Clan together. A gentle breeze was blowing, carrying the scents of the forest even into the heart of the Twolegplace. Hawkwing's pelt itched with restlessness, and he had the sense that something momentous was about to happen.

When her Clan was gathered around her, Leafstar beckoned with her tail to Bellapaw, Rileypaw, Pebblepaw, and Parsleypaw. The four young cats stepped out of the crowd, exchanging glances that were half excited, half bewildered.

"We must become a Clan again," Leafstar announced, repeating her words from the day before. "Our journey will be hard, and there are dark times ahead. We will need every one of our warriors. And so this is the right time to make some new ones."

"What, us? Now?" Pebblepaw squeaked, then slapped her tail over her mouth in embarrassment.

"Yes, you, now," Leafstar confirmed, amusement glimmering in her amber eyes. "Come closer."

The four apprentices padded up to their leader, their eyes shining as they gazed at her. Hawkwing thought that his heart would burst with pride and affection as he watched Pebblepaw take her place.

She's going to be such a fine warrior!

"Rabbitleap," Leafstar began, addressing Parsleypaw's mentor, "has your apprentice trained well, and does he understand what it means to be a warrior?"

"He has, and he does," Rabbitleap replied solemnly.

"Pebblepaw," Leafstar went on, "your first mentor, Billystorm, was killed by the badgers on your first quest. And no cat knows what happened to his replacement, Sandynose."

At her words, Hawkwing saw Sandynose's mate, Plumwillow, close her eyes in pain. *It must be so hard for her,* he reflected. *She's expecting kits, and she has no idea where their father is.*

"But I have watched you, Pebblepaw," Leafstar continued, "and I know that you have earned your warrior name."

Pebblepaw glowed at her Clan leader's praise, and Hawkwing kneaded the ground in front of him, purring. *If any cat deserves this, it's Pebblepaw!*

"Tinycloud." Leafstar turned to Bellapaw's mentor. "Are you satisfied that your apprentice has earned her warrior name?"

"Without a doubt," Tinycloud responded, while Bellapaw shivered in excitement.

"And so has Rileypaw," Nettlesplash added, without waiting to be asked.

The Clan leader dipped her head in acknowledgment. "I, Leafstar, leader of SkyClan," she continued, "call upon my warrior ancestors to look down on these apprentices. They have trained hard to understand the ways of your noble code, and I commend them to you as warriors in their turn."

Leafstar's gaze rested on Parsleypaw, who straightened up, his whiskers quivering. "Parsleypaw," Leafstar meowed, "do you promise to uphold the warrior code and to protect and defend this Clan, even at the cost of your life?"

"I do," Parsleypaw replied firmly.

"Then by the powers of StarClan," Leafstar declared, "I give you your warrior name. Parsleypaw, from this moment you will be known as Parsleyseed. StarClan honors your loyalty and your courage, and we welcome you as a full warrior of SkyClan."

Taking a pace forward, Leafstar rested her muzzle on Parsleyseed's head, and he licked her shoulder in response, before stepping back to stand beside his mother and father.

"Parsleyseed! Parsleyseed!" the Clan acclaimed him.

As soon as the noise had died down, Leafstar turned to Pebblepaw, and asked her the same question. "Do you promise to uphold the warrior code and to protect and defend this Clan, even at the cost of your life?"

Pebblepaw held her head and tail high and her voice rang out clearly across the Twoleg garden. "I do."

"Then by the powers of StarClan," Leafstar continued, "I give you your warrior name. Pebblepaw, from this moment you will be known as Pebbleshine. StarClan honors your determination and your intelligence, and we welcome you as a full warrior of SkyClan."

She rested her muzzle on Pebbleshine's head, while Pebbleshine responded with a lick to her leader's shoulder.

"Pebbleshine! Pebbleshine!"

That's the perfect name! Hawkwing let his voice rise in a joyous yowl as Pebbleshine too retreated to her parents and touched noses with them. *Pebbleshine shines like the brightest moon!* Then she ran across to Hawkwing and twined her tail with his, her purrs almost as loud as a Twoleg monster.

"I like your new name," Hawkwing mewed as he gave her ear a lick. "It suits you."

He was so pleased that he barely paid any attention as Bellapaw and Rileypaw were made warriors, though he joined with the rest of his Clan in chanting their new names.

"Bellaleaf! Rileypool! Bellaleaf! Rileypool!"

The ceremony over, the Clan was beginning to disperse when Leafstar halted them with a commanding wave of her tail.

"Wait," she meowed. "We still have more to do." When the Clan had settled again, she continued, "The youngest cats—kits and apprentices—are the future of any Clan. It's time now for some kits to be apprenticed, and these strong young warriors-to-be should give us *all* hope. Fidgetkit, Curlykit, come here."

The two kits scampered up to their leader, their eyes brighter than they had been since Snipkit's death. Birdwing and Sagenose watched them proudly, though Birdwing let out an exasperated sigh. "I'd have groomed them if I'd known. Look, Curlykit has a leaf in her fur!"

"Fidgetkit," Leafstar began, "Echosong tells me you have shown a real interest in caring for your Clanmates since the battle, and she thinks you would make a wonderful medicine cat."

Fidgetkit let out a gasp. "Really?"

Leafstar dipped her head. "With Frecklewish missing, and new adventures ahead of us, SkyClan badly needs a medicine cat apprentice. It's a difficult and important job, and a medicine cat stands apart from the rest of the Clan. If you take this step, you won't find a mate or have kits, and you'll be responsible for caring for your Clanmates and, eventually, passing along the will of StarClan. Fidgetkit, are you willing to take on this responsibility?"

Solemn and with shining eyes, Fidgetkit nodded fervently. With a purr of approval, Leafstar turned to Echosong and beckoned her forward with a sweep of her tail.

Echosong padded up to Fidgetkit and looked down at him, her green eyes full of wisdom. "Fidgetkit," she mewed, "is it your wish to share the deepest knowledge of StarClan as a SkyClan medicine cat?"

"It is," Fidgetkit replied. He suddenly sounded much older, and completely certain that he was making the right choice.

Echosong has chosen the right cat, Hawkwing thought. *That must mean things are going to get better for SkyClan.*

"Warriors of StarClan," Echosong continued, looking up at the sky, "I present to you this apprentice, who has chosen the path of a medicine cat. From this moment his name will be Fidgetpaw. Grant him your wisdom and insight so that he may understand your ways and heal his Clan in accordance with your will."

Fidgetpaw stood blinking in front of her, overcome with awe, scarcely reacting even when his Clanmates began to call his new name. Hawkwing could share some of his wonder.

That's a huge step for a kit to take.

"Before the rogues came," Echosong meowed when the Clan was quiet again, "I would have performed this ceremony in the Whispering Cave, where StarClan would have greeted you as a new medicine cat. I can't do that now. But don't worry, Fidgetpaw. Wherever we may be at the next half moon, you will meet with StarClan."

Fidgetpaw dipped his head. "Thank you, Echosong," he whispered.

The Clan was hushed and serious as Echosong drew Fidgetpaw to one side. Hawkwing knew that every cat shared his feelings: pride in their new medicine cat apprentice, but sadness too that Frecklewish was missing.

Meanwhile, Leafstar turned to Curlykit, who had waited patiently while her brother was apprenticed. "From this day forward," the Clan leader announced, "this apprentice will be known as Curlypaw. Hawkwing, you will be her mentor. I trust you will pass on to her your loyalty to your Clan, your generous heart, and your courage in battle."

What, me? Hawkwing thought, shocked to the very depths of his pelt. His heart was pounding hard as he stepped out of the crowd of cats to meet Curlypaw. *Am I really ready to be a mentor?* Even though no cat had blamed him, he knew that he should have been a better judge of character, to know what kind of cat Darktail really was. And he could never forget the last words Darktail had said to him: that they were alike. He wasn't sure he deserved the faith that Leafstar was putting in him by making him a mentor. *Will I really be able to guide*

Curlypaw? She was so brave when the rogues attacked the nursery, and so determined to cross the river. . . . She has so much to offer her Clan.

The little gray she-cat bounced up to him and stretched upward to touch noses with him. "I'll work really hard," she assured him.

Then so will I, Hawkwing thought, his heart filling with warmth. "I know you will," Hawkwing responded. "And I'll do my best to make sure you become a great warrior."

The next day dawned bright and warm, with a brisk wind that sent white puffs of cloud scudding across the sky. Hawkwing hoped that the fine weather was a good omen for the journey he and his Clan were about to make.

The remaining cats of SkyClan gathered together under the bushes at the end of Ebonyclaw's Twoleg garden. Hawkwing's pads prickled with excitement, but there was a hollow feeling in his belly, because he knew that not all his Clanmates would be setting out on this new journey.

"We've thought a lot about this, and decided we won't be coming with you," Nettlesplash meowed, standing protectively over Mintfur and their litter. "The kits are too small to travel."

"They'll be safer here, on familiar territory," Mintfur added. "But we'll miss you all terribly. And who knows what StarClan has in store for us? Maybe one day we'll all be together again," she finished with a sigh.

"I'm afraid we have to stay with our Twolegs." Ebonyclaw was standing beside Harveymoon, who murmured agreement.

"We'll miss you all," he told his Clanmates. "And we'll always be SkyClan warriors at heart. But this decision is right for us."

Listening to them, Hawkwing felt as if his life was splitting into two parts. There was Before, where he had lived in the gorge, played with Duskpaw and grieved over his death, trusted Darktail and then been betrayed by him. Now, from this point forward, his life would be After. After Darktail and his rogues took the gorge, and SkyClan was forced out. Hawkwing had no idea what After would hold, but he knew that he was unlikely to see the gorge or these cats again.

Am I being selfish to want to leave with Pebbleshine? he asked himself, glancing over at Blossomheart, Cloudmist, and Cherrytail. *Do I owe it to my father to attack Darktail and avenge his murder?* A hot, sick feeling gathered in Hawkwing's chest and throat, and he slid out his claws as if Darktail were right in front of him.

While he hesitated, Curlypaw scampered up to his side. "This is so exciting!" she mewed. "Hawkwing, will you teach me to hunt while we travel?"

Hawkwing dipped his head, his feelings of rage dissipating like fog when the sun broke through. "Of course."

My duty is to my Clan now. And if I'm going to be loyal to my Clan and to Leafstar, I have to follow where she leads. I have to be the best mentor to Curlypaw that I can be.

Then his gaze met Pebbleshine's. Her eyes were bright with excitement and hope at the thought of setting out into new territory. He realized, staring at her, that there had never been any real question of what his decision would be. *Wherever Pebbleshine goes, I go.*

Leafstar nodded understandingly to the cats who were staying behind, though Hawkwing could see sadness in her amber eyes. "We will miss you," she mewed. "But wherever your paws lead you, may StarClan light your path."

The Clan cats called out their good-byes as Leafstar led the way toward the Twoleg fence. But before any cat reached it there was a sudden scurry of paws from outside the garden. Macgyver appeared, leaping up to the top of the fence and tottering there for a heartbeat before he half fell, half jumped down beside his Clanmates.

He's a bit of a show-off, Hawkwing thought, amused.

"I thought I'd never find you!" Macgyver exclaimed. "My stupid Twolegs wouldn't let me out. What's happening?"

"We're leaving," Waspwhisker replied, and explained to the daylight warrior everything that had happened since the battle in the gorge.

"Then I'm coming with you," Macgyver stated without hesitation. "I'll miss my Twolegs, but, well . . . I'm a SkyClan cat!" He paused, and his Clanmates let out yowls of approval. Hawkwing joined in, glad that at least one of the daylight warriors had decided to stay with SkyClan as they searched for a new home.

Twitching his whiskers happily, Macgyver turned to Leafstar. "So . . . ," he began, "where are we going?"

"Rileypool and Bellaleaf are going to lead us back to where they came from," Leafstar told Macgyver when she could make herself heard. "Barley may be able to point us in the right direction to find ThunderClan. He's our best hope, since Ravenpaw died."

Hawkwing's fur tingled with excitement. This was a good idea. The old farm cat who had visited SkyClan territory with Ravenpaw had seemed kind and sensible—if any cat knew where the other Clans had gone, he would.

The SkyClan cats followed Leafstar out of the Twoleg garden and began their careful journey through the Twolegplace. Pebbleshine and Blossomheart padded alongside Hawkwing, with Curlypaw hard on his paws.

As they set out, Hawkwing felt his heart lift a little. Gazing at Pebbleshine and Curlypaw, he knew that these cats were giving him real purpose. *Moving into life After isn't all bad.* It was as though he was making a fresh start, as if he was leaving behind all the mistakes and sorrow of the past. *I will be a different cat,* he decided. *I will think before I speak or act, and I will put my Clan before anything else.*

But then, as they approached the corner where two Thunderpaths met, Hawkwing glanced over his shoulder and saw his former mentor, Ebonyclaw, sitting on the garden fence, with the other cats Hawkwing had known all his life, watching their Clanmates go.

Hawkwing let out a long sigh. *I'm leaving such a huge part of my life behind here.*

But he knew that the cats beside him were his kin, and his future.

CHAPTER 21

❧

Hawkwing stood on the edge of a shallow stream, gazing at the walls of the Twolegplace on the opposite side. All around him spindly hazel trees rustled in the wind. The ground underpaw was damp, and Hawkwing shivered as the chill struck upward through his pads.

Two sunrises had passed since SkyClan had set out, and so far their journey had been easy. Though Hawkwing still felt the bitter loss of his way of life in the gorge, excitement was tugging his paws onward to find the new home by the water where they would meet the other Clans.

But I guess we still have a long way to go, he thought. *And I think our journey is about to get a whole lot harder.*

"This is the Twolegplace where we fought the battle against Dodge," Leafstar meowed. "We must travel through it quickly, and hope we don't meet any of the cats who live here."

Hawkwing's ears pricked alertly at his leader's words. The huge battle had been fought before he was born, but he had heard the story many times while he was still in the nursery. Some of the cats from the Twolegplace had traveled upriver to the gorge, and lived with SkyClan as warriors until they revealed they had come to ask for help.

A vicious tom named Dodge was terrorizing them and their friends, and they weren't strong enough to fight him off. Leafstar had led some of her warriors into battle in the Twolegplace, defeated Dodge, and forced him to agree to share the territory.

Almost like they were two neighboring Clans, Hawkwing thought.

"We don't have to avoid all the cats," Rabbitleap objected in response to Leafstar's order. "Some of them were our friends. I was only a kit then, but I remember when they lived with us. They were friendly!"

Leafstar gave a doubtful snort. "It wasn't as simple as that," she replied. "I don't want any more to do with those cats. So let's go, before they spot us."

A few fox-lengths downstream a fallen tree stretched across the water. Leafstar led the way to it and padded confidently across, then turned to wait for the rest of her Clan.

As Hawkwing followed he shuddered at the gurgling sound of the current just below his paws, recalling the stepping-stones where Snipkit had fallen to her death. He kept a careful eye on Curlypaw and Fidgetpaw, wondering if their memories would make it harder for them to cross safely.

This stream is too shallow to drown in, he reassured himself. *If some cat did slip, they would just end up damp.*

After a moment's hesitation, both the apprentices padded over without any trouble, and Leafstar set out at the head of her Clan, farther into the Twolegplace.

A narrow alley led directly ahead, the walls on either side so high that they let in little daylight. Every hair on Hawkwing's pelt rose in apprehension as the shadows swallowed him up.

Before he had gone many paw steps Hawkwing realized that this was nothing like the Twolegplace where the daylight warriors lived. The stone path felt slimy underpaw, and weird Twoleg rubbish lay scattered in all directions. The reek of Twolegs, monsters, and crow-food—and other things Hawkwing preferred not to think about—filled the air and almost choked him.

Hawkwing's pelt prickled more strongly still once he became aware of cats watching him and his Clanmates as they penetrated deeper among the Twoleg dens. He could scent the cats, but he never saw them; the air crackled with hostility.

Curlypaw came to pad alongside him, so close that their pelts brushed. "I don't like this," she murmured. "Is it far to the other side, do you think?"

"I don't know," Hawkwing replied. "Just stick close to me, and you'll be fine."

He let out a trill of welcome as Pebbleshine bounded up to pad along on Curlypaw's other side.

"We're a whole Clan," the mottled she-cat meowed reassuringly. "These Twolegplace cats had better not mess with us."

Hawkwing hoped that she was right. *We still haven't recovered from the battle in the gorge,* he thought. *The last thing we want is another fight.*

More alleyways branched off on either side, and sometimes the cats had to cross a Thunderpath. Leafstar seemed less confident as she continued, as if she wasn't sure of the way any longer. Hawkwing recalled that she had only visited this Twolegplace once before.

It's so big and confusing here, I wouldn't be surprised if Leafstar couldn't remember.

Waspwhisker and Cherrytail, two of the cats who had accompanied Leafstar on that first expedition, walked beside her at the front of the group. At every corner or place where the path divided they would pause to discuss their route, before heading onward.

Hawkwing began to feel even more uneasy. The sun was going down, and he realized that they would be stuck in this horrible place overnight. *I won't be able to sleep a wink, that's for sure!*

Finally Leafstar led the way across a Thunderpath and down another alley which soon led out into a wide open space with a couple of monsters crouching at one side. Hawkwing examined them with narrowed eyes, and decided with a grunt of relief that they were sleeping.

"I don't remember this place at all," Waspwhisker mewed, gazing around in confusion.

"Nor do I," Cherrytail agreed. "We've never been here before."

Leafstar lashed her tail a couple of times in frustration. "We've been following the sun so far," she pointed out after a moment's thought. "If we keep on doing that, then we should be okay."

"And when the sun is gone?" Waspwhisker asked sharply.

Already the sun had almost disappeared behind the roof-tops of the Twolegplace, though red streaks in the sky showed where it was going down. Hawkwing could see that it wouldn't be there to guide them for much longer.

"We'd better get a move on," Leafstar meowed. "This way."

But as the Clan leader headed for the entrance to another alley that led directly toward the sun, a dark shape appeared on top of the wall, outlined against the scarlet light. It leaped down into the mouth of the alley, and Hawkwing could see it was a brown tom with a short tail. He braced himself, ready if the newcomer should attack, and glanced around sharply to check for any other approaching enemies.

The tom blinked, a friendly look in his amber eyes as he faced Leafstar and the SkyClan cats. "Hi," he meowed.

"Shorty!" Leafstar exclaimed. Hawkwing relaxed when he heard relief in his leader's voice. "Greetings! How are you?"

"Fine," the brown tom, Shorty, replied. "Hey, I see some familiar faces here!"

The older SkyClan warriors crowded around him, echoing Leafstar's greeting. Hawkwing exchanged a glance with Pebbleshine. "This must be one of the cats who came to live in the gorge," he murmured.

"Sparrowpelt! Cherrytail . . . and Waspwhisker!" Shorty's voice was warm, as if he was meeting again with old friends. "And this hulking great creature is little Rabbitkit?"

"Rabbit*leap* now," the warrior mewed proudly. "And this is Plumwillow."

"But what are you all doing here?" Shorty asked, when the excitement had died down. "Leafstar, this must be almost all of your Clan."

"This is *all* my Clan," Leafstar responded, her tone bleak once more. "Rogues attacked us in the gorge and drove us out. Many cats were killed or scattered, and the rest of us have been forced to look for a new place to live."

For a moment, Shorty was silent in shock. "That's terrible news," he murmured at last. "You must let us help you."

"How can you do that?" Leafstar asked.

"Well, at least we can offer you somewhere to spend the night," Shorty replied. "It's getting dark, and this is no place to be wandering around, not if you don't know where you are."

While they had been talking the last traces of sunlight had vanished from the sky, and the alleyway ahead was plunged in gloom. Hawkwing didn't like the idea of setting one paw step into those ominous shadows.

"I wanted to move on quickly," Leafstar meowed. "But perhaps you're right, Shorty."

"But only for one night," Echosong put in, stepping up to her Clan leader's side. "This is not where StarClan wants us to be."

Leafstar dipped her head. "Of course. Lead on, Shorty."

The brown tom's amber eyes gleamed in the gathering darkness. "Great!" he exclaimed. "I'll show you the best way out in the morning. And you'll meet some more old friends," he added, giving his chest fur a couple of embarrassed licks. "I'm with Cora now. We have kits."

"That's wonderful news," Leafstar purred. "I'd love to see Cora again."

Shorty gave a wave of his stumpy tail. "Follow me, then."

He led the SkyClan cats across the open space and down a

narrow Thunderpath at the far side.

"Do you think Leafstar is right to trust this cat?" Pebble-shine murmured to Hawkwing as they followed. "He might be leading us into a trap."

"He sounds friendly enough," Hawkwing responded.

"It's easy to *sound* friendly. But there were cats watching us on the way in, and they didn't feel friendly at all."

"They could have been the other group," Hawkwing pointed out. "Dodge's cats."

Pebbleshine's tail-tip twitched uneasily. "Maybe."

Shorty led the way along the Thunderpath until it came to an end and the cats emerged into another open space. Here the ground was covered in coarse grass with a few scrubby bushes here and there, and even one or two stunted trees. Hawkwing had stopped expecting to see anything green and growing, but the open ground was still washed with the acrid scents of Twolegs and monsters.

"Do you think this is their camp?" he whispered to Pebbleshine.

Shorty raised his voice in a loud yowl. "Stick! Coal! Look who's here!"

Hawkwing stiffened, forcing his shoulder fur to lie flat as more cats emerged from the shelter of the bushes, fluid shadows in the twilight. As they drew closer he made out a skinny brown tom with a torn ear, and a more powerful black tom.

Leafstar nodded to the newcomers. "Stick. Coal."

"Greetings," the skinny tom, Stick, responded. "What brings you here, Leafstar?"

Hawkwing had just enough time to notice the chilly

nature of the exchange before Shorty burst in with a reply. "This is *all* of SkyClan, Stick! Rogues have driven them out of the gorge."

Stick's whiskers twitched in surprise. "Really?"

"That's just terrible!" A new voice broke in, a graceful white she-cat who came bounding up with a plump tabby tom just behind her. "You remember me, don't you—Snowy? And this is Percy."

"I remember you both." Now there was more warmth in Leafstar's tone. "It's good to see you again."

The plump tabby dipped his head. Scars around one of his eyes gave him a fearsome look, but his voice was friendly as he meowed, "Welcome."

While they were talking, Shorty had dashed off, and now he returned with a slender black she-cat. Three kits—two tabby toms and a black-and-white she-cat—frisked around their paws.

"Cora!" Leafstar exclaimed. "How are you?"

"Fine, thank you." Cora stretched forward to touch noses with the Clan leader. "Shorty says that you've been driven out of your territory. That's terrible!"

Leafstar let out a sigh. "Yes, but StarClan is guiding us to a new home." Hawkwing guessed that she didn't want to talk about her Clan's troubles with these Twolegplace cats. "So these are your kits?"

"Yes." Cora's eyes shone proudly. "The two tabbies are Branch and Stone, and the she-cat is Night. Kits, come and meet Leafstar."

The three kits, who had been happily play-fighting, straightened up and dipped their heads to Leafstar, gazing at her with wide eyes.

"Shorty and I have told them all about you and your Clan," Cora meowed. "But we never expected to see you here. Are you planning to stay?"

"Just for the night, with your permission," Leafstar replied. "I know there are a lot of us, but we can help you hunt."

"Good idea." Stick waved his tail, beckoning more cats forward until they stood in a ragged half-circle behind him. To Hawkwing they looked younger—more like his own age and Pebbleshine's—and he guessed they hadn't yet been born when Leafstar and the others had visited the Twolegplace to fight against Dodge.

Stick moved among them, rapidly giving orders and splitting the cats into patrols, mixing his own cats with SkyClan. Hawkwing found himself with Pebbleshine and a couple of strangers.

"Where's Curlypaw?" he asked, glancing around as the patrols began to move off.

"I saw her going with Fidgetpaw and Bellaleaf," Pebbleshine replied.

"Mouse dung! I wanted her with me." Hawkwing's pads prickled with anxiety at the thought of his apprentice wandering off by herself in this dark and unfamiliar place. Then he reminded himself that she wasn't alone; she had two Clanmates with her, and Twolegplace cats who knew their way around.

She'll be fine, he told himself, though he wasn't entirely convinced.

"Hi, I'm Foggy," one of the strange cats mewed. He was a long-furred gray tom; jerking his head toward the other, a small tortoiseshell, he added, "This is Suzy."

"Hi," Pebbleshine responded.

"Are you ready?" Suzy asked briskly. "We'll show you some good places to hunt."

Hawkwing realized for the first time how hungry he was. "That sounds good to me," he replied. "Lead the way."

"I've never hunted in a Twolegplace before," Hawkwing mumbled around the rat that he was carrying by the scruff. "It's so weird."

Pebbleshine was dangling two mice by their tails. "We did all right, I suppose," she meowed. "I never thought we'd find any prey. But it's still not as good as hunting in a forest."

Hawkwing yearned for the feeling of grass underneath his paws and the rustle of wind in the trees above his head. "At least this is only for one night," he pointed out. "We'll manage . . . Just as long as no cat expects me to eat this rat. It tastes foul."

"I'll take it off your paws," Foggy put in, glancing over his shoulder from where he and Suzy were padding ahead. He had caught a mouse, and Suzy had a blackbird. "There's good eating on one of those."

Yuck! Hawkwing thought.

When he and his patrol returned to the stretch of empty ground where the Twolegplace cats had their camp, more of the cats were gathering around one of the twisted trees in the center. Hawkwing spotted Leafstar and Stick with Sparrow-pelt, Shorty, and the black tom called Coal. He padded over to join them, depositing his prey on a nearby heap for the cats to share.

"How are things here with you?" Leafstar was asking Stick as Hawkwing came into earshot.

Stick shrugged. "Dodge kept to his side of the border at first, but we've had a few skirmishes lately. I'm afraid he's up to his old tricks."

"Things are getting really bad, just like before," Shorty agreed. "Cora and I are scared for our kits."

"You need to scent-mark the border," Leafstar told him. "And make sure that cats who cross it learn not to do it again."

"We're not a Clan!" Stick's eyes flashed at her.

Hawkwing blinked in surprise at Stick's hostile tone, then turned away as Pebbleshine offered him one of her mice. The two cats settled down close to Sparrowpelt to eat.

"Why don't Leafstar and Stick like each other?" Hawkwing asked the senior warrior in a low voice.

Sparrowpelt swallowed a mouthful of thrush. "When we defeated Dodge, Stick wanted Leafstar to kill him. Leafstar wouldn't do that. Stick was furious, and she was angry with him because he didn't know how to treat a defeated enemy. She warned Dodge to stay on his own side of the border, and we left."

"It doesn't sound as if Dodge is doing that anymore," Pebbleshine commented.

Sparrowpelt shrugged. "That's Stick's problem."

Finishing his mouse, Hawkwing glanced around to see that most of the hunting patrols had returned. But he didn't see Curlypaw.

"I'm getting worried," he murmured to Pebbleshine. "Where is she?"

His mate rose to her paws and gave the assembled cats a careful scrutiny. "Well, Bellaleaf and Fidgetpaw aren't here either," she meowed. "Maybe they—"

She broke off as a screech split the night. Bellaleaf raced out of an alleyway on the far side of the barren ground. Her fur was bushed up, and her eyes were wild; blood was trickling from a scratch above her eye. Fidgetpaw followed her more slowly, limping on three legs.

"Leafstar! Leafstar!" Bellaleaf yowled.

The Clan leader sprang up and wove her way rapidly out of the group of cats to meet Bellaleaf. "What's happened?" she demanded.

"Oh, Leafstar, it's terrible!" Bellaleaf gasped. "They took Curlypaw!"

CHAPTER 22

❧

"Who? Where?" Leafstar's voice was urgent.

"Other cats . . . They jumped down on us from the top of a wall," Bellaleaf replied. "There were so many of them! I managed to get Fidgetpaw away, but I couldn't help Curlypaw."

"What about Stick's cats?" Leafstar asked. "Where are they?"

"They ran away." Bellaleaf's mew was bitter. "Cowards!"

By now Hawkwing and the others had leaped to their paws and were crowding around Leafstar and Bellaleaf. Echosong hurried up to Fidgetpaw and began examining his injured paw with careful sniffs.

"We have to do something!" Hawkwing exclaimed. "If they've hurt Curlypaw, I'll—"

"We must stay calm," Leafstar interrupted sharply. "Bellaleaf, can you take us back to where this ambush happened? We can try to follow the scent trail and find out where these cats took Curlypaw."

"I wouldn't bother." Stick padded up to join the Clan leader. "They must have been Dodge's cats, and if Dodge has your friend there's nothing you can do to help her."

Leafstar whirled around to face Stick, a blaze of fury in her amber eyes. "*We* don't abandon our friends," she hissed. "*We're* Clan cats!"

Stick shrugged. "Suit yourself."

"Stick, you should be ashamed of yourself!" Shorty exclaimed, bounding up to the group with more of Stick's cats behind him. "Have you forgotten how SkyClan helped us? I'll come with you, Leafstar."

"So will I," Snowy added.

"Thank you," Leafstar meowed. "Let's go. I'll take Bellaleaf, of course, and Rabbitleap, Harrybrook, Sagenose, and Tinycloud. Waspwhisker, you're in charge here."

"What about me?" Hawkwing asked, his fur beginning to bristle in anger at being left out. "Curlypaw is *my* apprentice."

Leafstar fixed him with a hard gaze. "Can I trust you to follow orders and not lose your temper?"

Hawkwing swallowed. "Yes, Leafstar." Underneath his anger was fear, fear that Curlypaw might be in real danger.

"Then you can come. But . . ."

Leafstar's voice trailed off as she gazed past the twisted trees, toward the alley where Bellaleaf had appeared. Another cat had emerged, and was pacing slowly toward them. As he drew closer, Hawkwing could see that he was a powerful grayand-brown tabby tom. Muscles rippled under his pelt as he padded up to the group and halted a tail-length away.

Stick was glaring at him, his shoulder fur bristling and his eyes narrowed. "Harley!" he snarled. "You're not welcome here!"

Hawkwing thought that Harley looked no happier to be there than Stick was to have him, but his voice was even as he responded. "I've brought a message from Dodge. Not for you, Stick, but for Leafstar."

This must be another one of the cats Leafstar met when SkyClan was here before, Hawkwing thought.

"What message?" Leafstar asked calmly.

"Dodge has your cat," Harley replied. "He wants you to meet him and discuss the situation. *All* of you," he added, sweeping his tail around to include the whole Clan.

"You must think they're all flea-brained," Stick sneered. "Walk into Dodge's territory, just like that? No way!"

Harley ignored him. Dipping his head respectfully to Leafstar, he meowed, "I give you my word that none of you will be harmed until the meeting is over."

"And what is your word worth?" Stick challenged him.

"That's not your affair," Harley replied. "I'm not offering it to you. If you or any of your cats set paw in Dodge's territory, you can expect trouble."

"Like I don't know that!" Stick snorted.

Leafstar gave Stick a sidelong glance. "I have to trust Harley," she stated. "We cannot abandon Curlypaw."

"But what if you're wrong?" Waspwhisker asked, in the midst of uneasy murmuring from the rest of the Clan.

"Then I'm wrong," Leafstar replied. "But I believe StarClan will be with us if we do what is right." To Harley she added, "Show us the way."

As the Clan moved off, Hawkwing heard a low mutter

from some cat behind him. "Why can't StarClan ever just *say* what they want us to do?"

Harley headed back toward the alley, with the whole of SkyClan hard on his paws. Hawkwing padded at Leafstar's shoulder, with Pebbleshine next to him. Apprehension swelled inside him with every paw step. Part of him would have liked to run and run until he left this terrible place behind him, but first he and his Clanmates had to rescue Curlypaw. So he kept padding steadily onward, grateful for the touch of Pebbleshine's pelt against his own.

Complete darkness had fallen. As Harley led the Clan deeper into the Twolegplace, the only light was pale and fitful as the moon appeared now and again through gaps in the clouds that surged across the sky. They followed a twisting path down alleys, over walls, and once through a tunnel beneath a Thunderpath, and Hawkwing thought that the only way they would be able to find their way back to Stick's camp would be by following their own scent trail.

That's if any of us come back at all.

Finally Harley drew to a halt outside a tumbledown Twoleg den. Two of the walls had almost completely crumbled away, the red square-cut stones lying scattered on the ground. The other two walls met at an angle across a stretch of muddy, broken ground where the uncertain moonlight reflected from puddles covered with rainbow-colored scum. In the center of the ruined den the ground fell away into a pit.

Everywhere Hawkwing looked, cats were sitting on top of the tottering walls, or perched in the gaps where stones had fallen away. He almost felt as though their unblinking gazes were scorching his pelt.

At the edge of the pit a dark brown tabby tom was sitting with his paws tucked under him. He rose as Leafstar padded forward across the broken ground, and took a pace forward to face her.

Hawkwing drew in a sharp breath at the size of him and the powerful muscles of his shoulders and hindquarters. Slitted yellow eyes stared out from a flat face seamed with scars. One of his ears was shredded and there was another deep scar running from his neck to halfway down his flank.

"That's Dodge?" Pebbleshine whispered into Hawkwing's ear. "Great StarClan, he looks dangerous!"

As Leafstar halted in front of him with her Clan clustering around her, the tabby tom dipped his head, mockingly polite. "Welcome to my camp," he meowed.

Leafstar gave him a curt nod. "Where is our apprentice?" she asked.

Before Dodge could reply, a desperate wail came up from the depths of the pit. "Leafstar, is that you?"

At the sound of Curlypaw's voice, Hawkwing thrust his way through his Clanmates to stand at the edge of the pit. Its sides were lined with more of the red Twoleg stone, and a jagged slope led downward from one corner. Curlypaw crouched at the bottom, with two hulking toms keeping guard over her.

"I'm here, Curlypaw!" Hawkwing called. "Don't be scared!"

"Hawkwing! Thank StarClan!" Curlypaw yowled. She leaped to her paws, but one of the toms guarding her gave her a hard cuff over one ear, and she sank back down to the ground.

"Stay there!" Hawkwing told her. To his relief she didn't look badly hurt. "We'll get you out!"

Turning away from the edge of the pit, he padded back to where Leafstar and Dodge still stood facing each other.

"I was expecting a visit from you," Dodge meowed.

Leafstar's whiskers twitched suspiciously. "What do you mean?"

"Last time we met," Dodge replied, "you told me to keep to my own side of the border, or you would come back and fight me again."

"And now you've broken that agreement," Waspwhisker broke in. "But we didn't know that. That's not why we're here."

Dodge licked one paw and drew it slowly over his uninjured ear. "Oh, I *know* why you're here," he purred.

"What do you mean?" Leafstar repeated sharply.

"I expect that you've had a few visitors of your own," Dodge responded.

Leafstar and Waspwhisker exchanged a sudden, startled glance, and shocked exclamations rose from the Clan cats clustered around them.

Hawkwing felt as though a wave of hot rage was surging through him. He shouldered his way forward until he stood nose to nose with Dodge. "You mean Darktail?" he choked out. "You *know* him?"

Dodge raised one paw and thrust him back contemptuously. Hawkwing braced his muscles to spring, only to feel Leafstar's tail laid warningly on his shoulder.

"Hawkwing, *no*," she snapped with a shake of her head. Turning back to Dodge, she asked, "Did you send Darktail and his rogues to our camp?"

"Not exactly," Dodge replied. "They passed through here a while back, looking for Clan cats. They would have found you anyway, but I might have helped them on their way a little."

Now Hawkwing's rage was burning deep within his belly. "Why?" he demanded. "A decent cat would have warned us."

Dodge's yellow stare suddenly grew hard and malignant. "Do you think I've forgiven you for what you did to us?" he asked Leafstar. "No. I've often thought of gathering my cats together and traveling upstream to give you another taste of our claws. But then . . . well, wasn't it lucky that Darktail and his rogues turned up to do the job for me?"

Leafstar's eyes were sparkling with anger, but Hawkwing could see the massive effort she was making to keep it under control. "So you've had your revenge." Every word was spat out. "You have helped to wound my Clan—but we are not destroyed. SkyClan still lives!"

A chorus of voices erupted from behind her. "SkyClan lives!"

Leafstar waved her tail for silence and waited until the clamor of support from her Clanmates had died down. "So why are we here?" she asked Dodge. "Why have you taken one of my cats?"

Dodge blinked slowly. "I told you I expected you to come through here," he rasped. "So I made a plan. Now one of your cats is my prisoner. You can have her back unharmed if you fight on my side this time, and help me drive Stick and his cats out of this Twolegplace for good."

Hawkwing felt his jaws drop open in astonishment. Leaf-star was gazing at Dodge as if she couldn't believe what she had just heard. For a moment she didn't reply.

"Well?" Dodge slid out the claws of one paw and examined them nonchalantly. "Do we have a deal?"

"We do *not*!" Leafstar snarled. "Stick and the others were our friends. Clan cats do not betray their friends."

Dodge shrugged. "Okay. If that's the way you want it." He turned aside and took a pace back toward the pit, his jaws opening to call out to Curlypaw's guards.

"Wait!" Leafstar followed him. "You can't do this."

"Oh, I think you'll find I can," Dodge drawled. "Of course, you could always try fighting your way out, but that young cat of yours will still be the first to die."

From where he was standing Hawkwing couldn't see Curlypaw, but he guessed she could hear what Dodge and Leafstar were saying.

She must be so scared! he thought. *She's such a young apprentice—hardly more than a kit. Oh, StarClan, help us!*

"Please . . ." The plaintive mew came from Birdwing, Curlypaw's mother. Her eyes were full of fear and grief, and Hawkwing guessed she hardly knew what she was asking for. Whatever Leafstar decided, all their lives were in danger.

Glancing around, Hawkwing realized that all the cats sitting around on the crumbling walls of the camp were suddenly more alert. Their eyes gleamed in the fitful light, and many of them had risen to their paws, the fur on their shoulders rising. Here and there he caught the glitter of extended claws.

They're only waiting for Dodge's order before they tear us apart!

In contrast, the cluster of SkyClan cats were hopelessly outnumbered, and not in any fit state to fight. Bellaleaf and Fidgetpaw had fresh wounds, while other cats, like Cherry-tail, were still weakened from injuries they took in the gorge battle against Darktail.

If we fight Dodge's cats, we're bound to lose. But if we fight against Stick, we lose the honor of our Clan, and some of us will still die. What are we going to do?

Then to Hawkwing's surprise, the tabby tom Harley—who had escorted them from Stick's camp—sprang up onto a pile of tumbled stones near the edge of the pit.

"Dodge, this is wrong," he protested. "I gave these cats my word that they would be unharmed until the meeting was over."

"It *is* over," Dodge growled. "But I'll give their so-called leader one more chance. What is it to be?" he asked Leafstar. "Fight for us, or against us? There's no other choice."

Dead silence fell over the whole camp. Dodge's cats waited with scarcely concealed excitement, while the cats of SkyClan were silent with horror. Beside Hawkwing, Pebbleshine stood rigid, her eyes closed.

I wish I could tear that cat apart! Hawkwing glared at Dodge, trying to pour all the hatred he felt into his gaze. *He helped Darktail, and now he's taken Curlypaw. But they would never let me get at him.*

"You're just a coward," Hawkwing snapped. "You keep your claws sheathed until you think you have the upper paw. But a *real* leader of cats steps up and leads even in the face of uncertainty. That is *real* bravery!"

Dodge cocked his head, eyes narrowing in a contemptuous sneer. "Your 'bravery' won't save you in a *real* fight. . . ." Dodge flexed his claws, hissing: "And we can prove that to you right now!"

CHAPTER 23

❧

Hawkwing gave an amused mrrow, enjoying the way Dodge's eyes flared in fury. "Cat for cat, we're much better fighters than any of you. I'll bet there's not a single cat in your group that could stand a chance against one of our warriors."

Dodge let out an incredulous snort, while at the same time Leafstar exclaimed, "Hawkwing, don't be reckless!"

"It's not reckless," Hawkwing retorted steadily. He turned back to Dodge. "You and me. If we fight and I win, then you let us go unharmed—including Curlypaw down there."

"And if I win?" Dodge rumbled, looking amused.

"Then the SkyClan cats will fight for you, as you wish. You will have backup in your attack on Stick. But either way, you will release Curlypaw."

"Doesn't sound like much of a deal," Dodge meowed. "I've already got what I want."

"But have you?" Leafstar asked him. "If we decide to fight against you, then some of us will die. But so will some of your cats. Maybe even you."

"Unless you really are too much of a coward?" Hawkwing sneered.

A flame of fury lit in Dodge's yellow eyes. His tabby fur bristled until he looked almost twice his size. He slid out his claws. "Stop calling me a coward!" he snarled, and leaped straight for Hawkwing. "I accept your pathetic challenge!"

Caught off guard by the unexpected onrush, Hawkwing was bowled off his paws. Dodge's weight was pinning him down; he was half smothered by tabby fur. Dodge's eyes gleamed close to his own.

"Are you ready to die, mouse-breath?" Dodge hissed.

"Not yet!"

With a massive effort Hawkwing brought up his hind paws and thrust Dodge upward, enough for him to roll free and spring to his paws. In a brief glance he saw his Clanmates standing around them in a wide circle, ready to intercept any of Dodge's cats who might try to interfere.

As Dodge rushed at him again, Hawkwing stepped neatly aside and raked a pawful of claws across Dodge's good ear and the side of his head. Dodge let out a screech, more of fury than pain. He spun around faster than Hawkwing would have thought possible and reared up on his hind paws. Hawkwing tried to dive in and slash at his belly, but Dodge dropped down on top of him, claws digging deep into his shoulders. For a moment Hawkwing staggered as a red wave of pain surged through him. He knew that if he fell to the ground now, the fight would be over.

Letting himself go limp, he slid downward, bracing his legs underneath him. As Dodge let out a triumphant yowl, Hawkwing powered upward again, heaving Dodge's massive weight off him. Briefly unbalanced, Dodge spat a curse, and Hawk-wing leaped at the muscular tom in a storm of teeth and claws. The two cats wrestled in a screeching knot of fur, their legs and tails tangled together.

Head spinning, Hawkwing fought free and sprang back, taking in huge gulps of air. Dodge faced him, lips drawn back in a snarl. Blood was trickling from his shoulder and a clump of fur was missing from his chest; Hawkwing didn't even remember striking the blows.

A confused roaring sound was coming from all around him, and as his head cleared Hawkwing realized that his Clan-mates were chanting his name. "Hawkwing! Hawkwing!" He caught a glimpse of Pebbleshine, her eyes glowing with pride.

The support from his Clan poured new energy into Hawk-wing. He sprang at Dodge, darting past him while he slashed his claws down Dodge's side. Dodge followed him up with lumbering paw steps.

He's slowing down! Hawkwing thought with a spark of hope. *He's a big cat, but big cats like him don't have much energy. He's tiring. Maybe I can win this battle!*

But Dodge wasn't finished yet. He hurled himself at Hawk-wing, carrying him off his paws again and using his greater weight to hold him down. Blinded by his fur, Hawkwing felt teeth meet in his shoulder. With Dodge pressing down on him, he could hardly breathe. He struggled to free himself, but he could feel his strength beginning to ebb away.

But in the darkness of Hawkwing's mind a vision appeared. He remembered the last time a strong cat had him pinned to the ground; remembered Sharpclaw in combat, unaware of the rogue cat, Rain, sneaking up on him. . . .

The memory fell away, and Hawkwing thought of Darktail triumphant in the gorge, while SkyClan scattered. *Dodge could have warned us, and then none of us would have trusted Darktail. But he didn't . . . I will not die at the claws of this vile cat!*

Hawkwing gathered all his remaining strength. Freeing a paw, he lashed out at random. He felt his claws slice through fur and flesh, and warmth gushed over his paw. The grip of Dodge's teeth slackened and his body convulsed; one flailing paw caught Hawkwing in the belly.

Pulling away, Hawkwing tottered to his paws and saw Dodge lying in front of him, a twitching heap of tabby fur. Blood still pumped from a gash in his throat. As Hawkwing gazed at him the last twitches faded and his eyes began to glaze over.

He's dead! Hawkwing could hardly believe what he was seeing. *I killed him without even knowing it.*

As he stood there, breathing hard, stunned at finding himself still alive, Hawkwing's Clanmates surged around him.

"You won!"

"Well fought!"

"Hawkwing! Hawkwing!"

Pebbleshine ran up to him and rubbed her cheek against his. "You're so brave!" she whispered. "And so *stupid*!"

Gradually triumph began to swell in Hawkwing's chest. He could feel the pain from Dodge's teeth and claws in his shoulders, and the stinging of innumerable scratches he hadn't felt before, but none of that mattered.

SkyClan is safe!

A moment later he wasn't so sure. Furious screeches came from Dodge's cats; some of them leaped down from their positions on the walls and came bounding toward Hawkwing and his Clanmates.

At a swift order from Leafstar, the SkyClan cats gathered in a tight circle, facing outward, with Hawkwing and the other wounded cats in the center. Despite his injuries, Hawkwing wriggled through to the outside, ready to take part in what might be SkyClan's last battle.

"Stop!"

Before any of Dodge's cats could reach SkyClan's defensive circle, Harley let out a yowl from where he still stood on top of the pile of stones. The attacking cats halted, giving each other uncertain glances.

"Dodge made a bargain, and he lost," Harley continued. "Now we must honor it. SkyClan must be allowed to leave, unharmed."

"Just like that?" One of the cats, a ginger-and-white tom, looked up at Harley with disbelief in his eyes.

"Exactly like that, Skipper," Harley retorted. Raising his head to address all the cats, he continued, "Do you *want* to live like this, always fighting and killing? There's enough prey in this Twolegplace for every cat. We should stay on our side of the border and let Stick and his cats stay on theirs."

To Hawkwing's surprise, yowls of agreement came from all around on the ruined walls. He could see that not all the cats were happy about what Harley had said, but none of them argued any further, and none of them moved forward to attack.

"I hope Harley can establish himself as leader," Sparrow-pelt murmured into Hawkwing's ear. "He would do a better job of it than Dodge, that's for sure."

"Bring up the prisoner," Harley ordered.

Soon Hawkwing saw the two guards escorting Curlypaw up the jagged slope to ground level. She rushed over to Sage-nose and Birdwing; they pressed closely against her and covered her ears with licks.

"Thank you," Leafstar meowed to Harley. "Now will some cat show us the way out of here?"

"I can do that." A small, dark shape darted out of the shadows behind the ruined wall; Hawkwing recognized Shorty.

"What are you doing here?" Harley challenged him.

Shorty dipped his head. "I followed my friends," he replied, angling his ears toward the SkyClan cats. "I needed to know what was going on. Wouldn't you have done the same?" he challenged Harley.

A glimmer of amusement appeared in Harley's eyes. "I suppose I would," he admitted. "Now get out of here. All of you."

CHAPTER 24

❧

"Tuck your hind paws in a bit further," Hawkwing told Curlypaw. "That way, you get more strength in your pounce."

"Like this?" Curlypaw asked, shifting her paws farther forward.

"Very good. But if you stick your tail up in the air like that, the mouse will see you coming."

The cats of SkyClan were sprawled out on the riverbank, taking a rest in the warmth of sunhigh. The river was wider here, winding along more slowly than in the gorge, and the edge was thickly fringed with reeds. On the landward side, a grassy slope stretched upward to where trees were outlined against the sky.

Several days had passed since the SkyClan cats had left the Twolegplace. Hawkwing's wounds from his fight with Dodge were healing well, and he no longer needed Pebbleshine to hunt for him. But it was still pleasant to relax and feel his strength returning as the sun soaked into his pelt.

"She's doing well," Blossomheart meowed as she watched Curlypaw practicing the hunter's crouch.

"I think she is," Hawkwing agreed. "Curlypaw," he went

on, "you need to understand that hunting on the move, like we are, is very different from hunting in familiar territory."

Curlypaw sat up, her eyes wide as she drank in every word her mentor was saying.

"On the move," Hawkwing continued, "you have to be continually scouting for good spots where prey might be hiding. But in a familiar place, you already know the likely spots."

"Yes," Blossomheart put in. "Do you remember that rotting tree stump near the gorge? It was almost always full of mice."

"Of course I remember it," Hawkwing responded with a happy sigh. "The prey practically leaped into our paws."

Curlypaw's eyes gleamed. "Do you think there'll be lots of good hunting spots in our new home by the water, when we find it?" she asked.

"I'm sure there will be," Hawkwing replied. "And you remember Leafstar telling us about the friendly Thunder-Clan cats, Firestar and Sandstorm? They'll probably tell us the best places to hunt. Now," he added, "can you see a likely hunting spot around here?"

Curlypaw sprang to her paws and looked around. "What about up the slope?" she suggested, pointing with her tail toward a big oak tree with lots of twisting roots. "Prey could be hiding in there!"

"Very good," Hawkwing purred. "Why don't you go and check it out?"

While Curlypaw sped off up the slope toward the tree, Hawkwing followed more slowly. Blossomheart fell into step beside him.

"Do you think we'll ever find Barley?" she meowed quietly after a moment. "We've been traveling for days and days. I didn't get the impression that it took Barley that long to get to us when he and Ravenpaw brought Bellaleaf and Rileypool to SkyClan."

"You may be right," Hawkwing responded. "Rileypool and Bellaleaf were very young when they made the journey. I wonder if they really remember the way."

"Well, they know to follow the river," Blossomheart mewed. "That's easy enough. But I don't think Barley lives on the riverbank. So at some point we have to leave it, and maybe Bellaleaf and Rileypool don't remember where. We could already have come too far."

A yowl interrupted their conversation. "Cats of SkyClan! It's time to move on!" Leafstar ordered.

Hawkwing turned back with Blossomheart and called to Curlypaw, who was crouched among the oak roots. He headed toward Cherrytail and Cloudmist, who had been resting in the shade of the reeds by the water's edge.

Anxiety bit at Hawkwing when he looked at his mother. She still seemed tired and she stumbled a little as she rose to her paws in response to Leafstar's summons.

"Are you okay?" he asked, padding up to her.

"I'm a bit weak still," Cherrytail admitted, "but I'll be fine. I don't want to slow any cat down. We have to find the other Clans!"

Then I hope we find them quickly, Hawkwing thought. *I'm not sure Cherrytail is up to a long journey.*

"We'll be heading off in a different direction," Leafstar

announced, when all the Clan was gathered. "Bellaleaf thinks she's recognized a landmark."

"Over there!" Bellaleaf meowed excitedly, flourishing her tail at a tall pointed hill outlined on the horizon. "You can see that from where Barley lives."

Hawkwing and Blossomheart exchanged a glance, relieved that they seemed to be getting somewhere. "Maybe we're not far away from the other Clans!" Blossomheart exclaimed.

At that moment Curlypaw dashed up. Her eyes were sparkling with triumph and the limp body of a mouse dangled from her jaws. "Look!" she exclaimed, dropping her prey at Hawkwing's paws. "I caught one!"

"Your very first! Well done," Hawkwing praised her, almost as pleased as Curlypaw herself. "Now you can take it to Clovertail. Warriors take care of Clan elders. And after that you can walk with Fidgetpaw for a while. I'm sure you want to hear all about his medicine cat training."

Curlypaw padded off importantly with her prey, her tail straight up in the air.

While they rested, Pebbleshine had sat down to groom herself and talk to Plumwillow, whose belly was swelling with her unborn kits. Hawkwing knew that all the Clan shared his compassion for the pregnant she-cat. *It must be so hard, expecting kits when she has no idea what happened to her mate.*

Now, as the Clan turned away from the river, Pebbleshine bounded up to Hawkwing to walk alongside him. There was a gleam of excitement in her eyes, and a spring in her step that Hawkwing hadn't noticed before.

"What's going on?" he asked.

"Nothing." Pebbleshine turned toward him, blinking inno-cently. "Nothing at all."

And hedgehogs fly, Hawkwing thought. Pebbleshine was hid-ing something, he was sure. *Well, she'll tell me about it in her own good time.*

"How is Plumwillow doing?" Blossomheart asked.

At once Pebbleshine looked more serious. "She's coping well," she replied, "but she misses Sandynose a lot. It must be so hard to lose her mate," she added with a sigh. "Especially when she's expecting their kits."

Hawkwing exchanged a glance with her, and saw all the love she felt for him shining in her eyes. "I can't imagine losing you," he murmured.

"Well, excuse *me!*" Blossomheart snorted, half amused, half exasperated. "I'm going to walk with Tinycloud." She bounded off and joined the small white warrior.

As the cats continued, the grassland became broken up by lines of bushes or Twoleg fences made of shiny tendrils, reminding Hawkwing of the terrain he had crossed with Darktail and Rain on the second quest. His pelt prickled with uneasiness, though he told himself that he had no reason to suspect danger here.

"This is so weird!" Pebbleshine exclaimed as they slipped along the edge of one of the fences. "Look at those huge white animals! I've never seen anything so big."

"Those are cows," Hawkwing told her.

"They look like they could swallow a cat with one gulp,"

Curlypaw meowed, keeping close to Hawkwing as they padded past.

"No, they're not dangerous," Hawkwing reassured her, watching the cows rhythmically champing the grass beyond the fence. "They don't have any claws, and as far as I know they only eat plants. Besides, they can't move as fast as we can."

They had not left the cows far behind when Hawkwing heard a screech of triumph from the front of the Clan, where Rileypool and Bellaleaf were walking with Leafstar.

"That's it!" Bellaleaf exclaimed. "That's our kin Barley's barn!"

Every cat clustered around to look where Bellaleaf's tail was pointing. Hawkwing spotted a huddle of Twoleg dens in the distance, and another, larger den a little way away from them.

Bellaleaf and Rileypool were purring with excitement. "I *knew* we'd find it!" Rileypool mewed, though Hawkwing thought he could detect relief in his Clanmates' faces, as if they hadn't been quite sure they could find the barn until they actually set eyes on it.

Hawkwing's optimism was rising as he and his Clanmates veered toward the barn. He could see from their bright eyes and brisk paw steps that the others felt the same, now that the first stage of their journey was coming to an end. *Maybe we're not far from finding ThunderClan and our new home by the water.*

As they drew closer to the barn, they could hear the distant barking of a dog, which sounded like it was coming from the cluster of Twoleg dens. Hawkwing's pelt began to bristle, and Leafstar called for a halt.

"Stay closer together," she ordered. "Stronger warriors on the outside. Cherrytail, Clovertail, Plumwillow, keep in the middle of the group. And every cat, stay alert!"

Bunched together more tightly, the cats moved off again, using bushes for cover. The barking continued, but grew no nearer, and there had been no sign of the dog by the time they approached the barn.

Rileypool and Bellaleaf broke away from the rest of the Clan and bounded up to the barn door. "Barley! Barley!" they yowled excitedly.

Hawkwing spotted a flicker of movement at the bottom of the door, and recognized the broad, black-and-white face of the old farm cat peering out through a gap.

"Rileypaw? Bellapaw?" Barley sounded astonished. "What are you doing here?"

"We're Rileypool and Bellaleaf now," Rileypool told the farm cat proudly.

"Congratulations!" Barley meowed. He squeezed his plump body out through the gap and only realized as he straightened up how many cats were standing in front of him. His eyes widened. "What are you *all* doing here?"

Leafstar stepped forward and dipped her head to the farm cat. "It's a long story," she meowed. "May we come in?"

"Of course."

Barley stood aside and Leafstar led the remains of her Clan through the gap and into the barn.

Hawkwing was one of the last cats to enter, and stood motionless for a few heartbeats as he took in his surroundings. Dim light filtered in through holes in the roof. Dried grasses were heaped up everywhere in huge piles, and the air was filled with their sweet scent. There was another scent too: Hawkwing's mouth watered as he picked up the unmistakable traces of mice and heard the rustle of their tiny bodies.

While most of the cats settled down comfortably in the dried grass, Leafstar told Barley the story of how Darktail's rogues had driven SkyClan out of the gorge. Echosong added the prophecy StarClan had sent to her, and how they were sure that "the spark that remains" must refer to Firestar's kin.

"I'm so sorry to hear what happened to you," Barley meowed when they had finished. "And sorry too that your vision must mean that Firestar is dead. I can point you in the direction Ravenpaw told me the Clans went, but I don't know anything beyond that." He sighed. "The days when Ravenpaw and I lived alongside the Clans seem such a long time ago now."

For a moment the old cat remained lost in thought, his eyes seeming fixed on something in the distance; Hawkwing realized he must still be grieving for his friend.

Then Barley gave his pelt a shake. "You're all welcome here," he mewed. "Feel free to hunt; there's plenty for every cat."

His words made Hawkwing aware of the yawning emptiness in his belly. What he had told Curlypaw earlier was true: It was harder to find prey when the Clan was on the move. Along with every other cat, Hawkwing had become used to feeling hungry.

"Let's go," he meowed to Curlypaw. "You can show me your hunting technique."

His apprentice sprang up, bright-eyed, and began prowling among the heaps of grass. Tiny sounds of scuttling and squeaking came from all directions.

Hawkwing watched his apprentice with approval, noticing how she remembered to set her paws down lightly. When she had pinpointed her prey her hunter's crouch was perfect; waggling her hindquarters, she sprang into a vigorous pounce. Hawkwing heard a shrill squeal cut off in the middle, and Curlypaw stood up with a mouse dangling from her jaws by its tail.

"Great catch!" Hawkwing purred. "You've got a real talent for pouncing."

Curlypaw's eyes shone at his praise, and she carried her prey over to where Cherrytail, Plumwillow, and Clovertail lay stretched out in the dried grass; Echosong was checking Cherrytail's wound.

Hawkwing caught a couple more mice for the exhausted she-cats, marveling at how easy it was. *It's no wonder Barley looks so plump!*

"Thank you," Cherrytail murmured, giving her mouse a sniff. "This is a good place. I'm so glad we came here."

"Yes, it's great," Hawkwing responded, wondering with a prickle of concern if his mother really thought this was the end of their journey. "And Barley should be able to help us find the other Clans."

Cherrytail gave him a puzzled look, her eyes clouded by weariness. "Oh, yes, of course," she mewed at last.

Hawkwing still wasn't sure that Cherrytail was fully aware

of what was going on. *She'll be better after a good night's sleep,* he reassured himself.

Finally Hawkwing and Curlypaw were able to hunt for themselves. As Hawkwing was stalking a mouse, he came close to where Leafstar and Waspwhisker were talking to Barley.

"I don't know how you're going to find ThunderClan," he heard the old tom meow. "It's a big world out there, and you don't know where you're going."

"StarClan will guide us," Leafstar told him. "They'll send Echosong a vision."

Barley let out a grunt, as if he wasn't convinced, and Hawkwing found that he shared the farm cat's doubts. *I hope that Leafstar is right, and StarClan is watching over us,* he thought. *But Barley is right, too. It's a big world out there, and full of dangers. Besides, there aren't so many of us now. How many more fights do we have left in us?*

Clouds were building up, covering the sun, as the SkyClan cats ventured out of the barn on the following morning. Hawkwing fluffed out his pelt against the damp air, guessing that it would rain before long. Cold seeped into his pads from the dew that still remained on the grass.

"That's the way you need to go," Barley meowed, pointing with his tail to the hill Rileypool and Bellaleaf had spotted from the riverbank. "After that, I can't help you."

"It's a start," Leafstar responded. "We're all grateful to you, Barley."

"It's been good to see you again," Waspwhisker added.

Leafstar gestured with her tail to gather her Clan around

her, but before they could move off, Cherrytail spoke up.

"There's something I have to say," she began hesitantly, looking down at her paws. "I've been talking to Barley, and I've decided to stay here in his barn until I've recovered from my injury."

Surprised exclamations rose from every cat. "You can't!" Hawkwing exclaimed.

Cherrytail raised her head, gazing at him with eyes filled with love and sorrow. "I have to," she insisted. "I haven't felt *right* since we left the gorge. It's not just this infected wound. It's leaving the place where Sharpclaw was killed." Her voice shook as she continued. "He was my mentor when Firestar first restored SkyClan. All my life in the gorge was with him. Now I feel as though I'm leaving him behind."

"But we need you!" Blossomheart protested, staring at her mother with consternation.

Cherrytail's gaze traveled over Hawkwing, Blossomheart, and Cloudmist; she blinked rapidly as she struggled to control her emotion. "I love you all dearly," she whispered. "But I'm not sure I'm up for this journey. My body is too weak, and my heart is tugging me home."

"But it's *not* our home anymore," Cloudmist pointed out. "You can't go back to the gorge, not when Darktail and his rogues are there."

"I don't know where I'll go," Cherrytail mewed. "But for now, I want to stay here."

Hawkwing shook his head, desperate to find some way of making his mother change her mind. "We've just lost our father," he meowed. "Now you say you're going to leave us too?"

Cherrytail glanced from Hawkwing to Pebbleshine and back again. "Your future lies ahead of you, where the Clans are. I'm not sure where my future lies, and I need time to work it out. Oh, my dear kits, you are all so brave and loyal. I shall miss you dreadfully, but I can't follow you into a future I know is not the right one for me."

"Then I'm staying with you." Cloudmist took a pace forward to stand at her mother's side. "I can't lose you, so soon after losing Sharpclaw."

Cherrytail turned to look at her daughter, all the love she felt shining in her eyes. "I can't ask you to do that," she whispered. "You belong with your Clan."

"And so do you," Cloudmist responded determinedly. "And we'll both find our Clan again one day. I know it."

She brushed her pelt against Cherrytail's, and her mother didn't protest again.

Hawkwing stared at them both, unable to believe that this was happening. He couldn't share Cloudmist's certainty. *My family is breaking up like ice in newleaf!* Shock almost overwhelmed him; his legs felt weak and his head as light as if it would drift away like a cloud. His heart clenched in dread that he would have to go on without his mother and sister and never see them again. A dark mist swirled before his eyes.

Then Pebbleshine drew close to him, nuzzling his flank, and Hawkwing felt the darkness retreat.

"Then, good-bye," he murmured, dipping his head to his

mother and sister in acceptance. "I hope we'll meet again one day." *But I'm not sure we will, and I can hardly bear it.*

"That's in the paws of StarClan," Cherrytail responded. "But I hope so, too. I'm so proud of you, Hawkwing. I know you will go on to achieve great things."

Hawkwing touched his nose to hers and stepped back, while Blossomheart said good-bye too. *Is this really the last time we'll see our mother?* Hawkwing asked himself, his legs shaking with renewed shock.

Then Leafstar turned away, and the whole Clan began to move off. Hawkwing followed, with Pebbleshine by his side, but before they lost sight of the barn he looked back, to see his mother and sister, tiny at that distance, sitting with Barley outside the barn door.

"May StarClan light your path," he murmured.

SkyClan had begun the day with full bellies, for they had hunted in Barley's barn before they set out. But as the day wore on, Hawkwing began to feel hungry again.

"Are we going to hunt soon?" Curlypaw asked. "I feel like I haven't eaten for moons!"

"Soon," Hawkwing promised. "You can show off the moves I've been teaching you, and maybe you'll catch a nice shrew!"

Glancing around, he realized that all the cats were looking thinner than when they left the gorge, especially the two young apprentices. Thinking back to the conversation he had overheard between Barley and Leafstar, Hawkwing wondered what would happen if StarClan didn't guide them to their new territory before Plumwillow's kits were born.

I'd better sharpen my own hunting skills, he reflected. *I'm going to need them!*

Skirting the foot of the hill Barley had pointed out, the cats came upon a stretch of woodland where a stream ran through banks of fern and bramble. Leafstar announced that they would stop to rest.

"See if you can find any mice or shrews in the under-growth," Hawkwing suggested to Curlypaw.

Though Curlypaw's tail had been drooping in weariness, she straightened up as soon as Hawkwing spoke, a determined look on her face. Hawkwing watched as she padded off, proud of her willingness to help her Clan. *She's going to be a great warrior.*

When his apprentice had vanished into the bracken, Hawk-wing gazed up into the trees and spotted a squirrel leaping from branch to branch.

That looks good and fat, he thought. *One or two of those would fill our bellies nicely.*

When he spotted a second squirrel higher in the branches, Hawkwing couldn't resist the temptation any longer. *I'm a Sky-Clan cat; I can handle trees.*

Without thinking, Hawkwing sprang into the nearest tree, swarming up the trunk and out onto a branch near where he had seen the squirrel. Pausing to taste the air, he spotted Fidg-etpaw staring up at him, and Curlypaw, emerging from the undergrowth with a mouse in her jaws, dropped her prey, and let out a yowl of excitement.

Pebbleshine had spotted him too. "Be careful!" she called out.

Hawkwing didn't understand why his mate sounded so nervous. *She's not usually like that,* he thought. *It's like she's never seen me climb a tree before.*

Determined to prove that Pebbleshine had no reason to fuss over him, Hawkwing leaped farther and faster, showing off his strength and skill. The squirrel was just ahead of him, its bushy tail streaming out behind it as it jumped from branch to branch, farther up the tree.

Hawkwing ignored the way the branches at this height were much thinner, hardly able to bear his weight. He was stretching out his forepaws to grab the squirrel with his claws when he felt his hind paws slipping. He let out a yelp of alarm as he tried to regain his balance, but the branch sagged under him and a moment later he was falling. Legs and tail flailing, he bounced from branch to branch, twigs raking through his fur, until he landed hard on his paws, staggered, and collapsed on one side.

At once his Clanmates clustered around him.

"Hawkwing, you stupid furball!" Blossomheart exclaimed.

"Are you all right?" Pebbleshine asked anxiously, the question echoed by almost every cat.

"That was *amazing!*" Fidgetpaw sounded awestruck, gazing at Hawkwing with his eyes stretched wide. "But scary," he added.

"And quite unnecessary," Echosong mewed sharply, padding up to Hawkwing and beginning to prod him all over. "Does that hurt?" she asked with each prod.

Hawkwing took a deep breath, ready to snap at her, then calmed down as Pebbleshine crouched beside him and gently licked his cheek.

"I'm bruised and scraped from hitting the branches on the way down," he complained.

"And you're lucky you did," Sparrowpelt told him crisply. "At least they broke your fall."

Hawkwing nodded. "I suppose . . . I don't think I'm badly hurt," he added to Echosong.

But as soon as he tried to rise to his paws, Hawkwing felt a sharp pain shooting up one of his hind legs; gasping, he almost fell down again.

"You've sprained it," Echosong told him, giving the injured leg a good sniff. "Fidgetpaw, go dip some moss in the stream to wrap around it. I wish I had my herb stores with me," she continued. "I can't do much without them." She looked up at Leafstar, who had stood by to watch without commenting. "We'd better stay here for a few days," she mewed.

Leafstar nodded agreement. "Accidents happen," she murmured. "StarClan grant you're better soon, Hawkwing."

Even though his leader was understanding, Hawkwing felt hot with embarrassment, and furious with himself. *That was stupid, and now I'm holding my Clan back. Maybe they'd be better off if I'd stayed in the barn with Cherrytail.*

Hawkwing let himself down into a nest of moss and dead leaves among the roots of an oak tree, wincing as pain clawed again at his injured leg.

"Thanks, Curlypaw," he meowed to his apprentice, who had collected the bedding. "Go and get some rest now."

Curlypaw ducked her head and scampered off to where Fidgetpaw was making another nest beneath arching fronds of fern. Twilight had fallen and all the SkyClan cats were settling down for the night in the sheltered hollow that had become their temporary camp. Hawkwing still felt guilty about keeping his Clanmates there when they should have been well on their way to finding ThunderClan.

He was shifting in an attempt to find a comfortable position when Pebbleshine's pale pelt appeared in the gathering darkness and she slid into the nest beside him. Hawkwing drew in a breath, drinking in her scent, and relaxed a little at the warmth of her fur.

"Are you okay?" Pebbleshine asked him.

"Oh, sure," Hawkwing grunted. "I've sprained my leg, I lost my prey, and now the Clan is stuck here because of me. Other than that, I'm fine."

"Hey, that's enough of that!" Pebbleshine swept her tail around to flick Hawkwing on the nose. "You're as grouchy as a fox in a fit!"

Instantly Hawkwing regretted snapping at Pebbleshine. "I'm sorry," he meowed. "It's my own stupid fault, and it's not fair to take it out on you."

His gaze met Pebbleshine's, and he saw her eyes soften into warm affection. "I've something to tell you," she murmured. "Just to prove that things aren't all bad."

"Well, what is it?" Hawkwing asked when Pebbleshine said

no more. "Has Echosong had another vision?"

Pebbleshine shook her head. "No, nothing like that." She hesitated for another heartbeat, then added, "I'm expecting kits."

Delight and terror thrilled through Hawkwing from ears to tail-tip. At the same time he realized how selfish he was being, preoccupied with himself even though Pebbleshine had been looking more tired than usual for the last few days.

And I never even asked her why! he scolded himself. *Well, that stops now! From now on, I'm going to put my family first.*

"So that's what you were being so secretive about the other day!" he meowed.

Pebbleshine nodded. "I wasn't certain then, but I am now. Are you pleased?"

"Pleased?" Hawkwing could hardly find words. "I'm . . . Oh, Pebbleshine, this is wonderful!"

Pebbleshine leaned closer to him, rhythmic purrs coming from deep within her chest. Hawkwing rasped his tongue gently over her ears.

This is truly a new start for me, he thought. *Back in the gorge, I failed Duskpaw and my father, but I will never again fail my kin.*

"I'm going to be the best father I can be to these kits," he vowed.

"You won't be raising them all by yourself, you know!" Pebbleshine responded with a small *mrrow* of laughter.

"I know. And you're going to be a wonderful mother."

Hawkwing rested his chin on his mate's back, resolving that he would protect her to the last drop of his blood. He would take care of her, and their kits, and the whole Clan.

I know now we made the right decision to leave the gorge, he reflected. *Our kits won't be born with the sounds of battle ringing in their ears and the reek of blood in their noses. These kits will live in a new territory, surrounded by other Clans, and supported by them. They will be safe. Maybe, hopefully, they will never know danger.*

Oh, StarClan, it will make all our struggles worth it!

CHAPTER 25

Hawkwing limped along at the rear of his Clan. His leg ached terribly, but he forced himself to keep going. Almost a moon had passed since he had injured himself falling from the tree, and his leg was mostly better, but they had been walking since dawn, and now it was past sunhigh.

Leafstar would call for a rest break if I asked her to, Hawkwing thought. *But I can keep going for now. If Plumwillow can do it . . .* He was ready to suffer through his pain if it would get them to their new home faster. *I hope we find it before Plumwillow kits, or failing that, before Pebbleshine does.*

Plumwillow's belly was huge now; she was close to the time of her kitting, but she kept up with her Clanmates and never complained. Pebbleshine often walked beside her, encouraging her, and Curlypaw did her best to make sure that both she-cats had prey. Hawkwing was prouder of his apprentice with every day that passed: her energy, her commitment to her Clan, and the way she made sure every cat was fed before she took fresh-kill for herself.

But fresh-kill was hard to come by on their journey. Every cat was tired, sore-pawed, and thinner than they had been when they lived in the gorge. Life had become an endless round of sleeping, traveling, and hunting.

Though Leafstar still took the lead, encouraging her Clan onward, she looked wearier with very day that passed, and Hawkwing sometimes detected doubt in her eyes. *Surely our leader can't be losing her faith that StarClan will guide us?*

On the worst days, Hawkwing struggled to keep his own hope alive that soon they would find ThunderClan, and sensed that his Clanmates were struggling too. StarClan hadn't sent Echosong any more visions, so there was nothing to do but trek onward and trust that they were heading in the right direction. But when each nightfall found SkyClan still wandering in the wilderness, it became harder to hold on to that trust.

Sometimes, at night, Hawkwing had heard Leafstar and Waspwhisker talking together in low, anxious tones. A hollowness opened up inside Hawkwing as he listened. *If the Clan leader and the deputy don't know what to do, what hope is there for the rest of us? And why is StarClan putting us through all this?*

Still, Hawkwing reflected, SkyClan had become even closer, more tightly bound together as they traveled, each cat depending on the others. Now he could see Macgyver letting a tired Clovertail lean against his shoulder as they walked, and everywhere cats were meowing quietly and peacefully to each other.

Maybe that's why StarClan is letting our journey take so long, Hawkwing thought. *So that we learn how much we need each other.*

Pebbleshine dropped back to pad alongside Hawkwing,

brushing her tail along his pelt. Hawkwing blinked at her affectionately.

"I'm so glad our kits will be born in this Clan," he mewed.

"So am I," Pebbleshine purred. "There can't be a better Clan anywhere."

Coming to the top of a rise, the cats looked out across a wide valley, with the dens of a small Twolegplace near the bottom.

"We'll take a break here," Leafstar announced. "We need to be fed and rested before we tackle that Twolegplace down there."

She led the way a few fox-lengths down the slope to where a stretch of gorse and bramble gave shelter from the wind and some hope of prey. Plumwillow and Clovertail flopped down there with sighs of relief.

"We'll hunt for you," Bellaleaf meowed, bounding up to the two she-cats with her brother Rileypool at her shoulder.

"And I'll catch something for you!" Curlypaw promised Pebbleshine.

The speckled she-cat flicked Curlypaw's ear with the tip of her tail. "Thank you," she responded. "But I'm not so big yet that I can't hunt for myself. Come on, Hawkwing, let's all go together."

"And me!" Blossomheart added.

Waspwhisker joined them as well, and Hawkwing's spirits lifted as he and his friends crept into the undergrowth, jaws parted to taste the air for prey. *This is almost like a hunting patrol in the forest above the gorge!*

Venturing deeper into the bushes, Hawkwing and the others spread out in their search. Hawkwing picked up the strong scent of a rabbit and followed it along a narrow path between brambles. Finally he spotted the creature lolloping ahead of him, its white tail bobbing up and down. Hawkwing kept pace with it, two or three fox-lengths behind, until it halted, sniffing at something on the ground.

Glancing back, Hawkwing saw that Blossomheart and Curlypaw were both within sight. He beckoned to them, signing to them for silence. "Circle around," he whispered, gesturing with his tail. "Come at it from the other side, and I'll drive it toward you."

Curlypaw nodded, her eyes gleaming with excitement, and slid through the undergrowth in one direction, while Blossomheart veered off in the other. While Hawkwing waited for them to get into position, he was painfully reminded of his last hunt with his father, when he and Sharpclaw had cooperated just like this. With an effort he pushed the memory away, forcing himself to concentrate on *this* rabbit, and his Clanmates' need for fresh-kill.

Finally Hawkwing spotted movement in the undergrowth on the other side of the rabbit, which told him Curlypaw and Blossomheart were ready. Letting out a fearsome yowl, Hawkwing pelted forward, heading for his prey.

The rabbit sat erect, terror in its bulging eyes. Then it took off, but instead of making for Blossomheart and Curlypaw, it doubled back until Hawkwing thought it was going to run right onto his own claws.

As Hawkwing reached for it, the rabbit veered aside, and Hawkwing spotted the entrance to a burrow among the roots of a nearby gorse bush.

"No!" he screeched.

He made a frantic pounce, landing awkwardly and jarring his injured leg so the pain jolted right up into his ribs. But he was too late. With a last flash of its white tail, the rabbit plunged into the hole and vanished.

"Fox dung!" Hawkwing snarled, lashing his tail in frustration.

This is what happens when we hunt in strange territory, he thought, clawing furiously at the ground. *The prey knows the terrain, but we don't.*

Blossomheart and Curlypaw reappeared, both of them looking disappointed.

"Never mind." Blossomheart was clearly trying to sound cheerful. "We'll find something else."

But no more prey showed itself as they made their way through the undergrowth, until they emerged onto the hillside again, where they came upon Waspwhisker and Pebbleshine.

"I caught this shrew," Pebbleshine mewed, giving her prey a disdainful prod. "But it's a scrawny little thing. It's hardly a mouthful."

"Better than nothing," Hawkwing responded, brushing his pelt against hers. "Bury it, and we'll pick it up on the way back."

While Pebbleshine scraped earth over the shrew, Hawkwing glanced around, realizing that they had come out of the thicket much closer to the Twolegplace. Farther down the hill a line of bushes separated them from the first of the dens.

"We might try down there," Waspwhisker suggested.

Hawkwing wasn't too keen on going so close to the Twolegplace, but he realized that there was a lot of sense in the Clan deputy's suggestion. *I probably scared off all the prey up here, screeching at that rabbit!*

Waspwhisker led the way down the slope to the bushes, but when they reached them there were too many competing scents: the acrid tang of monsters and a Thunderpath, traces of dogs and Twolegs, and more that Hawkwing couldn't even identify.

"This is hopeless," Blossomheart mewed. "Let's go back."

Pebbleshine had slipped farther into the bushes, and now she glanced over her shoulder, her eyes gleaming. "Come look at this!"

Hawkwing slid through the branches to her side, and saw a wide stretch of ground in front of him, covered with the same hard black surface as a Thunderpath. Several monsters crouched there, and at one side a Thunderpath led away. Beyond the monsters loomed the gray walls of a Twoleg den.

"It's a kind of monster camp!" Pebbleshine whispered.

Waspwhisker poked his head through the branches just behind them. "What are you playing at?" he demanded. "Get away from there."

"It's okay," Pebbleshine responded. "All the monsters are asleep. And there's a really interesting smell coming from that one."

She angled her ears toward a monster at the edge of the camp. It had a big platform jutting out of its back, with low sides, and something shiny resting inside it.

Hawkwing drew air over his scent glands and realized what Pebbleshine meant. The smell coming from the monster was rich and appetizing. *It smells like prey . . . but how can it be, on the back of a monster?*

Waspwhisker had scented it, too. "Okay, let's take a look," he meowed. "But keep watch for Twolegs. And if the monsters start to wake up, get out of here, fast."

He took the lead as the three cats ventured into the open. Blossomheart and Curlypaw followed a few paces behind them. Curlypaw's eyes stretched wide, half excited and half afraid; Hawkwing realized that she had never been so close to monsters before.

As he drew nearer, Hawkwing could hear clucking noises coming from the back of the monster. The shiny things he had seen from the bushes were some kind of weird nests.

"There are birds in there!" he gasped.

"And they're trapped," Pebbleshine added. "They must be some kind of Twoleg prey."

"That's just what they are," Waspwhisker told the younger cats. "They're called chickens. Some Twolegs near the gorge used to keep them."

"Are they good to eat?" Curlypaw asked.

Waspwhisker swiped his tongue around his jaws. "Oh, yes," he mewed.

For a few heartbeats the cats stood still, staring at the

clucking, feathery mass of chickens. Hawkwing felt even hungrier as the succulent smell flowed over him.

"You know," Pebbleshine meowed, glancing warily around, "the monster is asleep, and there aren't any Twolegs around. Why don't we—"

"You're not suggesting we climb onto a monster's back?" Blossomheart interrupted, half intrigued and half scared.

"Why not?" Hawkwing asked, with an admiring glance at Pebbleshine. *She's so brave!* "We could get enough fresh-kill to feed the whole Clan."

Curlypaw gave an excited little bounce. "Just think of their faces when we get back!"

"We could do it." Hawkwing turned to the Clan deputy. "What do you think, Waspwhisker?"

For a moment Waspwhisker still gazed thoughtfully at the monster. Then he nodded slowly. "Let's go for it. Hawkwing, you and Curlypaw keep watch. The rest of you, follow me."

"I can climb up, too," Hawkwing mewed before any cat could move.

"No, I can tell your leg is hurting," Waspwhisker responded. "You're more use here on the ground."

"Then Pebbleshine should stay here, too," Hawkwing meowed.

"Yes, Pebbleshine, you have to be careful," Blossomheart agreed, while Waspwhisker nodded.

Pebbleshine twitched the tip of her tail. "I'm not big enough yet for it to make any difference," she protested. "I can still run just as fast as the rest of you. And it was *my* idea."

"Okay," Waspwhisker sighed. "Let's just get on with it before we all die of starvation."

Hawkwing and Curlypaw watched anxiously as their three Clanmates clambered onto the back of the monster. The harsh sound of their claws scraping against the monster's pelt made Hawkwing's neck fur rise with the strangeness of it. The gentle clucking of the chickens rose to an alarmed squawking, but to Hawkwing's relief the monster didn't wake up.

"It's amazing up here!" Pebbleshine yowled. "There are so many of these fat birds, and they're all just trapped here. If we can work out how to open the nests, we can feed the whole Clan!"

Hawkwing crouched on the ground beside his apprentice, his heart pounding as the moments slid past. *What's taking so long?* he wondered, expecting at any moment to see his Clanmates' heads pop back up. He tried to make sense of the sounds that were coming from the monster; the chickens' squawks had risen to a terrified clamor, but he couldn't hear the cats at all.

Then Hawkwing heard another noise, coming from the Twoleg den beyond the monster camp. A moment later a Twoleg came into view, heading toward the monsters.

"Don't move!" Hawkwing called out. "A Twoleg!"

"Maybe the Twoleg will go to one of the other monsters, and he won't notice us," Curlypaw whispered.

"Let's hope so."

But Hawkwing realized his hope was in vain as the Twoleg strode purposefully toward the monster with the chickens.

"He's coming right toward us!" he yowled. "Get out of there now!"

At first there was no response from the cats inside the monster. *The Twoleg will wake it up,* Hawkwing thought, agonized. *Then they'll know we were trying to steal their prey!* "Hurry!" he urged.

Waspwhisker's head popped up from behind the low barrier at the back of the monster, and Blossomheart appeared a heartbeat later. "Fox dung!" Waspwhisker exclaimed, looking furiously disappointed as he and Blossomheart scrambled over the barrier and leaped down to join Hawkwing and Curlypaw.

"Where's Pebbleshine?" Hawkwing asked as they landed beside him.

"I'm still here!" Pebbleshine replied from inside the monster, her words almost drowned out by louder squawking. "I've managed to open one of the nests. I've got a chicken!"

"Then get down here, fast!" Hawkwing responded.

His gaze was fixed on the Twoleg, who tramped across the hard surface of the monster camp, opened up the monster, and climbed into its belly. He didn't seem to have noticed the cats crouching a few tail-lengths away from the monster's round black paws.

"Pebbleshine, *now!*" Waspwhisker screeched.

"I'm coming!" Pebbleshine sounded frustrated. "But this stupid bird is fighting!"

"Then let it go!" Hawkwing yowled.

"But the Clan needs it!" Pebbleshine protested.

More loud squawking followed, then Pebbleshine's fore-paws appeared on the side of the monster. Hawkwing could see her face. At the same moment the monster woke up with a deep-throated growl.

"Jump! Pebbleshine, jump!" Blossomheart shrieked as she and Waspwhisker backed away.

Hawkwing shoved Curlypaw after them, then ran toward the monster. But just then the monster lurched into motion. Shock jolted through Hawkwing as its huge black paws rolled backward, threatening to crush him. The others scattered. Trembling, Hawkwing stood his ground.

I won't run away while Pebbleshine is in danger!

When the monster was a tail-length away from Hawkwing, it halted. He crouched, ready to leap up beside Pebbleshine. With a louder roar and the belch of a stinking cloud from its hindquarters, the monster began to move forward, heading for the Thunderpath.

Hawkwing was too late.

"Pebbleshine!" he screeched.

He pushed off in an enormous leap, but he fell short, landing with a thump on the hard ground. His last sight of his mate was her scrabbling at the side of the monster, only for the big brute to stumble and lurch, making Pebbleshine lose her grip and fall back down. She stared, wide-eyed, at Hawkwing, her mouth moving as if she was yowling something to him.

But Hawkwing couldn't hear it over the roar of the monster.

Putting out every scrap of his strength, Hawkwing hurled

himself foward in pursuit, but as the monster sped up he realized it was hopeless. The gap between him and Pebbleshine grew wider and wider, and the monster roared down the Thunderpath until it disappeared into the distance.

CHAPTER 26

Hawkwing lay on the cold ground in the shelter of a gorse bush. Three sunrises had passed since the monster had carried Pebbleshine away, and the cats of SkyClan remained in their camp on the hillside above the Twolegplace, hoping that she would find her way back to them.

But Hawkwing's hope was dwindling. He felt as though a heavy weight was crushing his ribs, pressing him into the earth. Hearing movement close by, he blinked his eyes open and saw his sister Blossomheart leaning over him.

"Look, Hawkwing," she mewed. "I brought you this shrew." She patted the small creature toward him.

Hawkwing gave the prey a perfunctory sniff, then closed his eyes again. His belly churned; he had no appetite at all.

"Hawkwing!" Blossomheart pleaded. "You haven't eaten for days. You can't go on like this. Please . . ."

Hawkwing ignored her, and after a couple of heartbeats he heard her paw steps receding. He didn't want to eat, or talk, or do anything except lie here and grieve for Pebbleshine. He hadn't thought it possible to feel such pain and still go on living, as if a cat's claws were snagged in his heart and he would never get free of them.

The whole Clan was grieving too, ever since the terrible day when Hawkwing had limped back with the hunting patrol and told them how the monster had carried Pebbleshine away.

But she'll find her way back, Hawkwing had at first told himself. *I'm sure of it. She's clever and brave . . . she'll come back. Won't she?*

But it had always been a struggle for Hawkwing to convince himself of that, and as the days slipped by it became harder still. There were so many dangers out there for a cat on her own. Twolegs, dogs, monsters . . .

She has to *come back,* Hawkwing insisted to himself. *Our kits have to be born. I have to be a father to them.*

Ever since Pebbleshine had told him her news, Hawkwing had pictured the kits in his mind, and thought about the things he would teach them. *I'd show them the hunter's crouch, and how to stay downwind of prey, and I'd tell them the noble history of their Clan. . . .*

Hawkwing's body contorted in a sudden spasm of rage. *This is all Darktail's fault!* If the rogue tom hadn't turned on the Clan that had taken him in, Hawkwing knew, none of this would have happened. Pebbleshine would still be safely in the gorge, waiting in the nursery for their kits to be born. *And I was the cat who made friends with Darktail!* The claw in his heart sank deeper still. *I spoke up for him, even against my own father. . . .*

Sighing, Hawkwing pressed his face into the cold grass. He was too grief-stricken even to sustain his anger for more than a few heartbeats.

A little while later, Hawkwing heard cats approaching him again.

"Hawkwing." It was his Clan leader's voice.

Hawkwing opened his eyes to see Leafstar and Echosong sitting beside him. Wearily he waited to find out what they wanted.

"We've stayed here for several days," Leafstar began, her voice gentle and compassionate.

Hawkwing understood at once what his Clan leader was about to say. *No!* he yowled inwardly, digging his claws into the ground. *I won't leave until Pebbleshine comes back!*

"If Pebbleshine had been able to escape from the monster anywhere nearby," Leafstar continued, "she would have come back to us by now. It's time for us to move on."

"No!" Hawkwing protested aloud this time, half sitting up. "We can't leave her. I *won't* leave her!"

"This is my decision." The Clan leader's tone was firm, though sympathy glowed in her amber eyes. "We're too exposed here, too near Twolegs, and the hunting is poor. We can't stay any longer."

"Pebbleshine is strong and smart," Echosong added. "She knows which direction we're headed, and what we're looking for. She'll try to find us."

Hawkwing knew that the medicine cat was right, but that didn't ease the hard knot of grief in his belly, or shake his conviction that he needed to stay near the place he had last seen his mate.

"I don't believe this is the end of Pebbleshine's story,"

Echosong continued. "You won't lose her forever."

Hope struck through Hawkwing like the sun shining through storm clouds. "Have you had a vision?" he asked eagerly.

The medicine cat shook her head, and Hawkwing sank back, crushed.

"No, StarClan hasn't told me anything," Echosong mewed sadly. "It's just what I believe."

A few tail-lengths away, the other cats were rising to their paws, casting doubtful glances at Hawkwing. Curlypaw padded nervously up to him, carrying a mouse in her jaws.

"I caught this for you myself," she told Hawkwing, dropping her prey at his paws.

"Thanks, Curlypaw." Hawkwing pushed the mouse away. "But *you* should eat it. I won't be traveling with you. I'm going to wait here for Pebbleshine, in case she comes back."

Leafstar fixed her amber gaze on Hawkwing, deep concern in her eyes. "Hawkwing, you have to come with us," she meowed. "Please. SkyClan needs you."

"You don't," Hawkwing argued. "I'm just one cat. When Pebbleshine comes back, we'll both catch up to you."

"No, we need you now," Echosong agreed with the Clan leader. "Do you remember how you and Pebbleshine drove off the raccoon when it attacked me and the kits after the gorge battle? And how you saved us when you killed Dodge in the Twolegplace. What would we have done without you then?"

Leafstar nodded. "You've always been so loyal and strong—both of you."

Curlypaw ventured closer to Hawkwing, leaning into his shoulder so that he felt the warmth of her long-furred pelt. "You're such a great mentor, Hawkwing," she mewed. "I can't imagine learning so much from any other cat. I need you."

Hawkwing dipped his head. *My duty is to my Clan now.* Wasn't that what he'd decided when they left the gorge? And he could see that Leafstar had a point: The Clan *did* need him. Something inside Hawkwing wanted to give way, but he didn't know how he could force his paws to carry him away from the last place he and Pebbleshine had been together.

"We don't even know we're heading in the right direction," he pointed out. "What if we're not? What if I leave with you, and miss Pebbleshine, only to end up wandering for moons?"

"Our faith is being tested," Echosong admitted with a sigh, "but we must believe StarClan wouldn't lead us astray. There are so few of us now that our only chance of surviving is to stick together."

"Pebbleshine would want you to stay with us," Leafstar pointed out.

Hawkwing realized that his medicine cat and his Clan leader were right. *Pebbleshine has always been loyal to SkyClan. She never even considered leaving it to stay on our old territory. She understood that the Clan is more important than one cat.* Looking into Leafstar's eyes, he saw that she truly believed his mate wasn't coming back. *At least, she won't be coming back* here.

He wondered if he could bear to give up hope. Realistically, he knew, it was unlikely—perhaps one chance in a whole field of chances. *Is that tiny chance worth the cost to the Clan?*

No, he accepted at last. *It isn't.*

Heaving a huge sigh, Hawkwing bent his head to sniff Curlypaw's mouse. Although the very thought of food made him sick, he forced himself to eat. He knew that he would need his strength for the long journey that lay ahead. Leafstar, Echosong, and Curlypaw all nodded encouragingly.

"You're making the right decision, Hawkwing," Leafstar said solemnly. "I'm grateful. The whole Clan is grateful."

Maybe my Clanmates are right, he thought. *We still need to find the spark that remains, and make our new lives with the rest of the Clans. Pebbleshine and our kits will find SkyClan again one day. We will all be together again in the new territory beside the water, the home that Echosong dreamed of.*

But as he swallowed the last of his prey and joined his Clanmates to set out again, Hawkwing still felt as if he was leaving Pebbleshine behind. *What chance will she have of finding us now?* he wondered.

Padding along at the rear of the Clan, his head down, Hawkwing tried to shake off the thought. But it clung in his mind like a burr in his pelt.

Will I ever see Pebbleshine again?

❧

CHAPTER 27

"Do you want to lean on my shoulder?" Hawkwing asked Plumwillow.

The SkyClan cats were still trying to go in the direction
Barley had shown them, trudging up a long slope covered with
tough moorland grass. The ridge ahead of them never seemed
to get any closer. A wide blue sky arched above them, where
one or two birds were circling, and a stiff breeze buffeted
their fur.

"Thanks, Hawkwing." Plumwillow shifted a pace sideways
so that she could lean against him.

Her belly is absolutely enormous! Hawkwing thought. *It won't be
long before her kits are here.*

A pang of sadness clawed through him as he wondered
whether Pebbleshine would get as big as this before the end.
Wherever she was—and Hawkwing had to believe that she
was alive, somewhere—their kits would still be growing inside
her.

A half moon had passed since Pebbleshine had been carried
away by the monster with the chickens. Since then there had
been no sign or scent of her, but Echosong had dreamed the

same dream several times: a pleasant place near water where SkyClan would belong.

"Have you seen Pebbleshine in your dreams?" Hawkwing had asked.

The medicine cat had paused for a long time before replying. "No," she mewed with a sad shake of her head. "But that doesn't necessarily mean that she won't find her way there."

Hawkwing was left to struggle with his grief. Even though he had decided to stay with his Clan, he still wondered what the future could possibly hold for him. Everything he did: hunting, seeking for safe places to rest, even his mentoring of Curlypaw, was completely meaningless now. Only Plumwillow, who had lost her mate, Sandynose, seemed to understand his pain.

Now Plumwillow huffed out a gasping breath, and Hawkwing felt something move against his side. *That must be the kits!* he realized, shivering as wonder and a terrible sadness threatened to tear him apart.

"I understand," Plumwillow murmured. "It's really hard for me to go on without Sandynose, but I have to believe he's out there somewhere—just like Pebbleshine. I have to believe that we and our kits will be reunited someday."

Hawkwing gazed deeply into the gray she-cat's eyes, and saw that she really did understand what he felt. *Maybe she's the only one who can.*

After what felt like a moon of toiling upward, the SkyClan cats reached the top of the hill.

"Look at that!" Waspwhisker exclaimed.

Hawkwing looked down to see a shallow valley in front of him. The ground was covered with grass and stretches of woodland, dotted with outcrops of rock. At the bottom lay a reed-fringed lake, its shimmering surface reflecting the blue of the sky. In the distance, on the far side of the lake, was a small cluster of Twoleg dens.

"This must be it!" Tinycloud exclaimed. "Our new home!"

Parsleyseed's eyes were sparkling: It was the first time, Hawkwing realized, that he had looked happy since his sister disappeared. "This must be the place that Echosong dreamed about!"

Anticipation stirred inside Hawkwing and his pads prickled with excitement. The valley looked just right for a Clan's territory, with its grassy open spaces and wooded areas full of undergrowth for shelter and hunting grounds.

But I don't see any other cats, Hawkwing thought. *Where is ThunderClan?*

Glancing to the side, he spotted Echosong; she was gazing down into the valley with interest, but he didn't think she looked convinced just yet that this was the place of her visions.

Leafstar tilted her head toward Waspwhisker, gesturing him out of earshot of the other cats. For a few moments they conferred quietly together; then they both returned to join the other cats.

"Okay, listen up," he meowed. "This could be the place from Echosong's visions, but we have to be cautious. We're going to split into patrols to explore. Look out for places we might camp, and good places to hunt. And keep your eyes open for other cats."

"Yes," Leafstar added. "For all we know, this is the territory of one of the other Clans. The last thing we want is to walk into another conflict."

"We'll meet up again beside the lake," Waspwhisker finished.

Waspwhisker led one patrol and Sparrowpelt another. Hawkwing was surprised when the deputy chose him to lead the third. Meanwhile Leafstar led the way to a nearby copse where Plumwillow and Clovertail could rest. Echosong and Fidgetpaw joined them, and the remaining warriors stayed with them, on guard.

Hawkwing set out with Macgyver, Parsleyseed, Birdwing, and Curlypaw. Together they headed down into the valley, pausing to investigate clumps of trees, thickets of fern and bramble, and the crevices in rocks where prey might hide.

"Can we hunt, Hawkwing?" Macgyver asked. "My jaws are watering, there's so much prey-scent around!"

"Sure," Hawkwing replied. "We need to know that the Clan can feed itself here."

Macgyver's eyes gleamed. "Then it would be pretty irresponsible *not* to hunt!"

"Don't get carried away," Hawkwing warned his patrol while they padded toward a stretch of deeper woodland. "Remember this is strange territory, and we don't know what might be lurking. Foxes . . . maybe badgers," he finished with a shudder. "And if this is another Clan's territory, we don't want them to think we're stealing their prey. Curlypaw, stay close to me."

Hawkwing looked around warily as he ventured into the woodland with his apprentice by his side. The trees were old and twisted here, many of them covered with ivy, and interspersed with banks of fern and bramble thickets. Sunlight filtered down through the foliage, dappling the ground with green-gold light.

"It's great here!" Curlypaw sighed. "I hope we can stay."

"Let's find out a bit more about the place first," Hawkwing meowed. "What can you scent?"

Curlypaw stood still, her jaws parted to drink in the air. Watching her, Hawkwing reflected that since he had lost Pebbleshine, his heart hadn't been in Curlypaw's training. *Am I teaching her anything?* he wondered. *I've got to start making more of an effort.*

"Mouse," Curlypaw murmured after a few heartbeats. "And squirrel . . . oh, and rabbit. And . . . I think there's fox, Hawkwing, but I'm not sure." She glanced around as if she expected to see the red-pelted creature slinking toward her with its fangs bared.

"Very good," Hawkwing told her with an approving nod. "You're right, a fox has been through here, but two or three days ago. The scent is faint, so I don't think it stayed long."

As he finished speaking he heard a yowl of triumph from farther into the woods, and Parsleyseed appeared, dragging the body of a plump rabbit. "Look what I caught!" he announced, obviously pleased with himself. "We can all share."

"Great catch!" Hawkwing praised him.

Macgyver and Birdwing reappeared a moment later, Birdwing carrying a mouse, and the patrol settled down to eat.

"I've got something to show you," Macgyver mewed between mouthfuls. "Something good. But it can wait."

With the rabbit picked clean, Macgyver led the way farther into the trees, around a bramble thicket and up a steep bank to a flat shelf of rock. "Look down there," he meowed, pointing with his tail.

Hawkwing looked out over a deep hollow, the sides formed from rocks and the tangled roots of trees. Long grass and ferns covered the ground at the bottom. Just below Hawkwing's paws a small spring bubbled out between two boulders and trickled out across the hollow in the direction of the lake.

"What about that?" Macgyver asked proudly. "Isn't it a perfect place to camp?"

Hawkwing nodded slowly. There were plenty of sheltered spots for dens, with room enough for every cat, and the steep sides would provide some protection. There was even a source of water.

"It's a bit like the gorge," Curlypaw murmured. There was a hint of wistfulness in her voice, telling Hawkwing how homesick she must feel.

"Let's go find Leafstar," Hawkwing suggested. "We'll get her to come and see it."

Heading out of the wood again, Hawkwing reflected that this could be the perfect place for SkyClan to settle, except for one thing.

There were no other cats here.

If this is where StarClan intends us to be, where are the other warrior Clans?

Hawkwing tasted the air once more, wondering if somehow they could have missed picking up the traces of a large number of cats. This time he did smell cat, but only one, and there was something not quite right about the scent.

Emerging from the undergrowth, Hawkwing spotted the cat: a plump dark tabby tom, sitting on a tree stump at the edge of the wood, grooming his long glossy pelt. Hawkwing didn't need to see the collar around his neck to recognize a kittypet.

I should have known, he thought. *Is this territory so unfamiliar that I can't even tell when I'm smelling kittypet scent?*

"Greetings," he meowed, approaching the kittypet and dipping his head politely. "Do you live around here?"

The kittypet looked up, mildly surprised. "You're the second group I've seen today," he mewed. "There are plenty of you, aren't there?"

The second group? Hawkwing was briefly excited, until he realized that the kittypet must mean he'd seen one of the other patrols. Trying to keep irritation out of his voice, he repeated his question.

"Oh, no, my nest is a long way away, with my housefolk," the kittypet replied with a vague wave of his tail. "My name's Max. Who are you?"

"We are SkyClan," Hawkwing replied proudly, introducing himself and the rest of his patrol.

"You're a scruffy-looking bunch, if you ask me," Max commented, looking the patrol up and down, then licking one forepaw and drawing it over his ear.

No cat did ask you, Hawkwing thought, beginning to feel annoyed.

"You would look scruffy too if you'd had to fight for your life and then traveled for days and days looking for a new home," Macgyver snapped.

"Keep your fur on," Max responded, not at all offended. "I know all about traveling. I stay out away from my housefolk all the time." He riffled his whiskers. "It drives them crazy. But I always get a really good meal when I come home," he finished, swiping his tongue around his jaws.

Macgyver flashed Hawkwing a glance, as if he was asking, *Do we have to put up with this idiot?*

"We're looking for more cats," Hawkwing began, determined to get as much information from Max as he could.

"Aren't there enough of you already?"

The heat of anger roiled in Hawkwing's belly, but he pushed it down. *No, I will not claw his ears off. But oh, it's tempting. . . .*

"A specific group of cats," Birdwing explained patiently, as if she guessed that Hawkwing was close to losing his temper. "They're called ThunderClan. Their leader is—was, I suppose—a tom called Firestar, with a flame-colored pelt."

Max yawned. "Never heard of them. In fact, there aren't many cats around here. And none living by the lake."

Hawkwing acknowledged his words with a brief nod. "Thank you for your help."

"Any time." Max went back to his grooming.

By now, Hawkwing could see that some of his Clanmates were gathering by the lake, and led his patrol to join them. They arrived at the same time as Leafstar and her group; the other patrols were already waiting.

"What do you think?" Blossomheart asked, bounding up to Hawkwing as soon as he reached the rest of the Clan. "Isn't it great?"

"It seems okay." Hawkwing still had his reservations, especially now that he was sure there were no other Clans here.

Leafstar called a Clan meeting, speaking from a rock at the water's edge while her Clan sat around her. "This is the first place we've found where it seems possible to settle," she began. "But we need to decide if it's the right place. Let's start by hearing from the patrols."

Waspwhisker, Sparrowpelt, and Hawkwing all made their reports.

"There's good hunting here," Waspwhisker meowed. "And we didn't spot many signs of predators. A fox here and there, maybe, but no trace of badgers."

"And there are plenty of places we might make our camp," Sparrowpelt added.

"We could do worse," Waspwhisker summed up at last. "There doesn't seem to be much danger, and the Twoleg nests are far enough away that the Twolegs won't bother us."

"But there aren't any other cats," Hawkwing objected. "If this is the place StarClan wanted us to find, then where is ThunderClan?"

"Well, maybe they—" Waspwhisker began.

He broke off as Echosong rose to her paws and came to stand beside the rock where Leafstar sat. "This is *not* the place where we're supposed to be," she announced.

Gasps of shock and protest came from the cats gathered around her.

"You mean we have to do *more* traveling?" Rabbitleap asked. "My paws are worn away already!"

"What's wrong with it here?" Firefern mewed. "I don't want to go on."

"I *can't* go on," Plumwillow added. "Not until my kits are born—and that won't be long now."

"Plumwillow has a point," Sparrowpelt agreed with a nod to the gray she-cat. "We should stay here, at least until she gives birth and her kits are old enough to travel. We have to stop *somewhere* for that, and this is a good place, near water, with plenty of prey. Echosong, we need a home!"

The medicine cat's green eyes were full of distress, but she never wavered. "This is not the place StarClan showed me in my dreams," she insisted. "If it was, ThunderClan and maybe the other Clans too would be here to greet us. Believe me, if we stay here, no good will come of it. It doesn't feel right. I *know* Plumwillow would be better off having her kits while we're traveling."

Plumwillow gave a disdainful sniff. "*You* don't have to carry them every paw step of the way," she snapped, loud enough for Echosong to hear her.

"And we're all exhausted," Rabbitleap added, exchanging a

doubtful look with Birdwing. "We'd have to have bees in our brains to leave a place as good as this."

Hawkwing felt his irritation rising. *Can't they see that's not the point? We're not just looking for a new home, we're trying to follow the will of StarClan. What about the prophecy?*

In the midst of more rebellious muttering from his Clanmates, he rose to his paws. "I agree with Echosong," he meowed. "This place feels wrong. It's good, but ThunderClan isn't here, so it can't be what we've been looking for."

"And what about my kits?" Plumwillow demanded.

Hawkwing gave her a warm glance. "You're strong, Plumwillow. You'll take good care of them, whatever happens." Turning back to the rest of the Clan, he added, "We've followed StarClan this far. How can we start ignoring them now?"

And if we find the place where StarClan has been leading us, then maybe Pebbleshine and our kits will be there, too. They'll find us there, somehow. . . .

Every cat looked at Leafstar, who paused for a long moment before speaking. "Plumwillow, what do you think?" she asked. "You're the cat with the most to lose right now if we make the wrong decision."

Plumwillow dipped her head. "I *am* tired," she confessed. "And I think this is a good place to have my kits."

Leafstar nodded, remaining silent for a moment more. "I think we should stay here, Echosong," she mewed, "at least for a little while. Sparrowpelt and Plumwillow are right: This is a good place. I'm too tired and heartsick to go any further, and so are all of us. The entire Clan needs a rest."

"But that isn't right!" Echosong protested. "StarClan—"

"StarClan isn't sending us any *clear* guidance," Leafstar interrupted. "And we can't keep chasing hunches, hoping that fortune will favor us. We have traveled so far, and we are weary—we must get some strength back, if we are to complete this quest."

Murmurs of relief and approval followed the Clan leader's words. Hawkwing couldn't share his Clanmates' feelings. He had hoped that when they reached the destination StarClan had in mind for them, he would be reunited with Pebbleshine—and now those hopes were dashed.

This is wrong . . . she'll never find us here, I know it. Oh, StarClan, I'm trying to trust you that our destiny is still in front of us, that we haven't made a terrible choice that will see the end of SkyClan.

But why must you test us this way?

CHAPTER 28

Hawkwing crouched beside Pebbleshine in the milky warmth of the nursery. He was so full of joy that he thought it must burst out of him like a stream in greenleaf overflowing its banks.

His mate looked exhausted, but her eyes shone with love for the three new kits who lay snuggled against her belly, protected in the curve of her tail.

"They're so beautiful . . . ," Hawkwing whispered.

"The little gray tom looks just like you," Pebbleshine murmured.

Hawkwing gazed down wonderingly at the fluffy gray fur of his son. "And the speckled white she-cat is just like you," he added. "And the speckled gray tom . . . well, he's like you *and* me." He touched his nose to the tiny kit's head. "It's like seeing the best of us both combined into one cat."

Pebbleshine let out a small *mrrow* of laughter.

A shadow fell across the entrance to the nursery and Cherrytail padded in, a mouse dangling from her jaws. "I thought you could do with some fresh-kill," she meowed, dropping her prey beside Pebbleshine.

"And I brought some wet moss," Cloudmist added, creeping

softly in beside her mother, with Blossomheart just behind her. She blinked in wonder as she looked down at the kits. "They're just perfect!"

Hawkwing spotted more movement at the nursery entrance and looked up to see his father, Sharpclaw, poking his head inside. "Is everything okay?" he asked.

"We're all fine, thanks," Hawkwing replied.

"Let me know if you need anything," Sharpclaw continued. "Hawkwing, you can take a day or two off from patrolling to be with Pebbleshine."

"Thanks," Hawkwing meowed.

"Just wait until their eyes open," Sharpclaw gave a snort of amusement. "You'll have your paws full then!" More seriously, he added, "I know you'll be a good father, Hawkwing."

Their visitors withdrew, leaving Hawkwing to curl up beside Pebbleshine, matching his rhythmic purr to hers. *This is perfect . . .* , he thought drowsily.

From somewhere outside the nursery, Hawkwing heard a harsh, repetitive sound. *What can that be?* he wondered, turning to look through the nursery entrance. Pebbleshine's head was still bent over her kits. *And why doesn't she hear it?*

SQUAAAAAAWWWWK!

Hawkwing jolted awake to the sound of a raucous screech coming from outside the warriors' den. Normally the sound would have alarmed him, but he was so furious at being awoken from such a happy dream that he charged recklessly out into the open, searching for the source of the noise.

The screech came again from the direction of the lake. Hawkwing pounded through the trees until he reached the edge of the forest. In the pale light of dawn he spotted a brown-and-white bird swooping across the lake. *A big, stupid water-bird.*

Hawkwing watched as the bird dived down, dipped its talons under the surface, then rose into the sky again, gripping a wriggling silver fish.

A small part of Hawkwing's mind was interested to watch a bird he had never seen before, but that was overwhelmed by the hatred he felt because it had broken into his dream.

Hawkwing let out a deep sigh. *Stupid bird. Stupid lake. Stupid life. I know this isn't the right place for us to stay.*

SkyClan had been living beside the lake for a quarter moon, making their camp in the hollow Macgyver had discovered on the first day. Every cat had been busy, arranging the dens, exploring their new territory, and collecting herb stores, but none of the activity had lightened Hawkwing's grim mood.

Now that he and his Clanmates were no longer traveling, he had time to confront the fact that he was still alive, even after losing his mate and everything they'd planned for their future. Misery engulfed him like a dark fog, and he had no idea how to find his way out of it.

I have my whole life ahead of me—but what can the future possibly hold that would ever make up for what I've lost?

Blossomheart appeared at Hawkwing's side, looking still ruffled from sleep. "What on earth was that noise?" she asked with a yawn.

Hawkwing only grunted in reply, waving his tail at the stupid bird.

Blossomheart shrugged. "We never had to deal with that in the gorge," she mewed.

Her words stung Hawkwing like a thorn in his pad. He knew that his sister wasn't scolding him, but he could never forget that in a way *he* was responsible for SkyClan being driven from the gorge. *If I'd never trusted Darktail . . . Or what would have happened if I'd stayed and tried to take revenge? I might have done that if I'd known that I'd lose Pebbleshine on this journey.*

Hawkwing dragged himself away from his dark thoughts to realize that Blossomheart was speaking to him. "I'm sorry . . . what?"

His sister heaved a sigh. "I *said*, why don't we take Bellaleaf and Curlypaw and go exploring on the other side of the lake? We haven't hunted over there yet."

"Yes, good idea," Hawkwing responded, making an effort to be more positive. He wanted to be a good mentor to Curlypaw, but he knew he hadn't spent enough time with her since he lost Pebbleshine, and even less since they arrived at the lake. "I'll check with Waspwhisker, and if he doesn't want us for a dawn patrol, we'll go."

There were fewer trees on the far side of the lake; the ground was covered with smooth grass that stretched as far as the row of small Twoleg dens.

"I don't like it as much over here," Blossomheart mewed, with a wary look at the dens. "The Twolegs are too close for comfort, and there's not as much cover. I'm glad we settled on the other side."

"Waspwhisker led a patrol over here yesterday," Bellaleaf responded. "Rileypool went with him, and he told me all the Twoleg dens are abandoned. There's not even the scent of Twolegs there."

"Weird . . . ," Hawkwing murmured. *Why would Twolegs build dens here and then just go off and leave them?* Then he shrugged. "It's not as good for prey over here, either," he added. "There aren't as many places for them to hide. Still, we can get in some practice. Come on, Curlypaw, let's see your stalking. Pretend Bellaleaf is a mouse."

Bellaleaf crouched down in the grass. "Oh, I'm only a tiny little mouse," she mewed in a squeaky voice. "Please don't eat me!"

Curlypaw flattened herself against the ground and began to creep forward, one paw at a time.

"Oh, no—no," Hawkwing interrupted before she had gone many paw steps. "You're putting your paws down far too hard."

His apprentice looked dejected, her head and tail drooping. "Sorry."

"You have to remember that a mouse will feel your paw steps through the ground before it hears you," Hawkwing told her. He couldn't remember whether he had actually told her that before. *It's one of the first things an apprentice learns. . . . I'm not being a good mentor at all. Everything's gone wrong since Pebbleshine disappeared.*

"Try it again," he told her.

Curlypaw gave him a nervous glance before flattening herself to the ground again. Hawkwing took a deep breath. He knew his frustration was coming out in his tone. *But it's not you I'm frustrated with, Curlypaw; it's me.*

This time, his apprentice's stalking was perfect. She seemed to glide over the ground as if her paws were hardly touching it. "That's much better," Hawkwing meowed, trying to put some warmth into his voice. "Bellaleaf, you're doomed!"

During the lesson, Blossomheart had been poking around among the reeds that fringed the lakeshore. Now she beckoned Hawkwing over with her tail.

"There are voles here," she murmured when her brother padded up to her. "Shall we take some fresh-kill back for the Clan?"

Hawkwing peered into the reeds and spotted movement among the stems. "Good idea," he responded, gesturing with his tail for Curlypaw and Bellaleaf to join them.

Spotting a vole, Hawkwing began to creep up on it, remembering what he had told Curlypaw about setting her paws down lightly. His prey was nibbling something, seeming quite unaware of danger.

Completely focused on the vole, Hawkwing was bunching his muscles for the final pounce when Curlypaw suddenly let out a loud caterwaul. The vole gave a start of terror, then scrambled to the water's edge, jumped in, and swam away.

Furious, Hawkwing swung around. "Curlypaw, what—?"

He broke off as he heard the same raucous screech that had woken him from his dream. Looking up, he saw the brown water-bird above his head, diving straight down at Blossom-heart. His belly lurched and his shoulder fur bristled at the sight of the creature's powerful beak and claws.

With a challenging yowl, Hawkwing raced over to his sis-ter. As the bird swooped over her, Blossomheart reared up on her hind legs and managed to swipe her claws over its eye. The bird let out another screech, raking its talons over Blossom-heart's shoulder.

Hawkwing leaped up and sank his claws into the bird's shoulder, catching it off guard. As the huge head swung around toward him, glaring with a malignant yellow eye, Blossomheart got in a harder blow, digging her claws into the eye she had scratched.

At the same moment Bellaleaf leaped up from the other side, only to be swatted away by a flap of the bird's wing. She hit the ground with a thump and lay there half stunned.

Screaming again, the bird began fighting valiantly to free itself from Hawkwing and Blossomheart, flailing with wings and claws and stabbing with its hooked beak. As they fell back, it rose unsteadily into the air and circled around a few tail-lengths above the ground.

At first Hawkwing thought that they had scared it off. Then with belly-churning dread he realized that it was swooping in for another attack, and this time its target was Curlypaw.

"No!" Hawkwing yowled.

He lunged toward Curlypaw, reaching her just as the bird gripped her with its talons and began flapping its wings to take off again. "Help!" she wailed, digging in her claws in an effort to cling to the ground. "Hawkwing, help me!"

Using all his strength, Hawkwing hurled himself upward and managed to snag his claws on the bird's leg. The extra weight unbalanced it, so that it flopped back to the ground, and Hawkwing was able to sink his teeth into its back.

With another screech the bird loosened its grip on Curlypaw, who twisted around and slashed her claws at its underbelly, even though the bird still had her hind legs pinned. Blossomheart came charging up, blood from her wound spattering the grass, but before she reached them Hawkwing dug his teeth deeper into the bird's back and wrenched his head around, tearing out a chunk of the bird's flesh.

Shrieking furiously, the bird let go of Curlypaw and awkwardly flapped its way back into the air. Blood dripped from its wound onto the grass as it flew slowly away.

Hawkwing turned to his sister. "Blossomheart, are you okay?"

Blossomheart twisted her head to get a good look at the wound on her shoulder. "I've been better," she panted. "But I'll be fine. Hawkwing, that was amazing! You really lived up to your name."

Glancing around to check on his Clanmates, Hawkwing saw Bellaleaf stagger to her paws and pad shakily over to join the others.

"Are you hurt?" Hawkwing asked.

Bellaleaf gave her head a shake as if to clear it. "No, I'm okay. Just a bit stunned. That bird was really strong!"

Reassured, Hawkwing turned to Curlypaw and gave her

scratches a good sniff. He was thankful that they all seemed to be shallow, hardly bleeding at all. But the apprentice was still shivering, her eyes wide with the memory of fear.

"Hawkwing, you saved my life!" she exclaimed, her voice shaking. "Just like you did in the Twolegplace. If you hadn't been here . . ." Her eyes grew dark, as if she could see herself being carried away in the grip of the enormous bird.

Feeling her terror as if it was his own, Hawkwing bent his head and began to lick Curlypaw's wounds. "Don't think about it anymore," he mewed between strokes of his tongue. "You were very brave, and you're safe. That's what matters. You've got your whole life ahead of you."

Curlypaw nodded and gave her pelt a shake. "I'll try."

As he comforted his apprentice, Hawkwing remembered the kits in his dream—his kits. *They'll have meaningful lives, too,* he thought, *even if I never get to see them. I wouldn't want them to give up because they don't have a father.*

"And now we'd better go home and get Echosong to check us out," Bellaleaf meowed.

The cats skirted the edge of the lake as they made their way back to their new camp. Hawkwing kept a watchful eye on the sky, in case the fierce bird returned.

"Hawkwing, that was good advice you gave Curlypaw," Blossomheart murmured. "I've noticed you've not been yourself lately. Of course, you have good reasons, but you can't live your whole life like that. You have to believe what you told Curlypaw, too. You've got your whole life ahead of you, you know?"

For a moment Hawkwing considered how he should respond. *I wouldn't want my kits to give up, so maybe I shouldn't, either.* "I'm trying to believe," he replied at last, even though it was a struggle to get the words out.

Blossomheart touched her nose to his. "All of SkyClan needs to believe that we have a future. If this isn't the right lake, then we have to believe we *will* find the right one, where the other Clans live. If we don't find it soon, surely StarClan will send us a sign. . . ."

Hawkwing dipped his head, almost overcome. "I hope so," he managed to mew.

He watched Bellaleaf and Curlypaw padding ahead of him; now that the danger was over, they were excitedly discussing the encounter with the water-bird. *They're so young and brave!* Hawkwing knew that they were the future of SkyClan—the SkyClan that must live on, for seasons beyond counting, and prosper.

Blossomheart is right.

CHAPTER 29

❧

The sun was going down, casting red light over the forest. Shadows were already gathering in the camp, but there was still a sunny spot near the fresh-kill pile, where Hawkwing and several of his Clanmates were eating.

"We've been here a moon now," Waspwhisker remarked, pausing as he devoured his vole. "It's starting to feel like home."

Hawkwing murmured agreement. He watched Curlypaw and Fidgetpaw playing with Rileypool at the other side of the camp. Rileypool was pretending to be a badger, and the air was filled with the apprentices' joyful squeals of terror.

As newleaf melted into greenleaf, the weather had grown warmer and the land around the lake had become lush and green. Somehow Hawkwing felt that his cold grief was melting, too. He still missed Pebbleshine desperately, and feared for her and their kits, but he was able to look forward to a better time.

Someday I'll find them all again.

Curlypaw was also doing much better. She had begun to thrive once he started really paying attention to her again, trusting that he could be a good mentor to her instead of always questioning himself.

She's finally living up to her potential. She just needed patience and understanding. She's going to be an incredible warrior!

A few heartbeats later the peace of the camp was shattered by raised voices coming from the medicine cats' den. As Hawkwing turned toward it in surprise, Leafstar stormed into the open, followed by Echosong.

"It's not just a hunch!" the medicine cat protested. "It's a message from StarClan."

Leafstar whipped around to face her. "You just told me you had no vision," she retorted furiously. "This is just a 'feeling' you have."

Hawkwing exchanged a glance with Waspwhisker. It was almost unheard of for the Clan leader and their medicine cat to have a serious disagreement, and just as unusual for Leafstar to show so much anger. *Something is really wrong here.*

"But the feeling is so strong," Echosong meowed, "that I believe that StarClan *is* telling me something. There's no other explanation! I've known this since we arrived here. We can't stay here!"

Hawkwing pricked his ears. Echosong was putting into words the feeling he himself had experienced ever since Sky-Clan had made camp here. *Something is simply wrong with this place.*

He had made the best of it, trying to concentrate on teaching Curlypaw and doing everything he could for his Clan. He had made a huge effort to rein in his runaway temper and behave *sensibly* for once. And now he had to push down his instinct to join in the argument and agree with the medicine cat.

But what does Echosong think we should do?

"Remember how long it took us to find *this* place?" Leafstar continued, clearly making an effort to speak more calmly. "And how hard it was, traipsing through strange territory with no home. A Clan *needs* a home to be truly strong!"

"Yes, I know that," Echosong responded with a sigh. "But this *isn't* meant to be our home! You can't deny that we haven't found the other Clans here."

Leafstar grunted a reluctant agreement. "There's no sign that any other cats have ever lived here."

"Then wouldn't we be stronger if we were surrounded by equally strong Clans?" Echosong asked.

Leafstar paced to and fro, the tip of her tail twitching, before she replied. "I've heard your argument," she meowed at last, "but I am not convinced that we should uproot yet again. We're surviving here—and we should remember, SkyClan has survived on its own for many seasons, with no help from other Clans. If StarClan wants us to move on," she added after a heartbeat's pause, "then they need to send us more guidance. We can't go on chasing 'the spark that remains' forever—not when we don't know where we're supposed to go."

"But that's not how StarClan works," Echosong protested. "You know that as well as I do, Leafstar."

"But that's what SkyClan *needs*, after all we've been through."

"I understand." Hawkwing thought Echosong sounded desperately unhappy to be in conflict with her Clan leader.

"But you have to understand too. I have deep concerns about this place. It doesn't *feel* right."

Leafstar's shoulders drooped in exhaustion. "I hear you, Echosong. But I am not convinced that leaving is the right decision for SkyClan."

"I will respect your leadership, Leafstar," the medicine cat mewed, dipping her head resignedly. "But I feel we are going against the advice of StarClan. And as long as we do that, we're at risk."

Hawkwing watched as the Clan leader and the medicine cat separated, stalking off in opposite directions. He was deeply disturbed by what he had overheard. *Whether we stay here or not,* he thought, *it can't be good for Leafstar and Echosong to disagree so wildly. Clan cats need certainty from their leader and their medicine cat.*

Not having that certainty made Hawkwing feel as if icy claws were raking through his pelt.

A painful yowl broke into Hawkwing's dream of the big bird attacking his Clanmates. At first he thought the noise was part of the dream, but then he realized it was coming from outside the den. Picking his way around his Clanmates, who were beginning to stir, Hawkwing blundered into the open.

The morning was damp and misty, but the sun was already breaking through the foliage above the camp, and every drop of dew glittered with light. At first everything seemed peaceful; then the yowling came again and Hawkwing spotted Curlypaw standing outside the entrance to the nursery, her eyes wide with distress.

"What's happening?" Hawkwing asked, bounding over to her.

"It's Plumwillow," Curlypaw replied. "Her kits are coming, but something is going wrong!"

For a moment Hawkwing felt as though his fur was tightening around his flanks. He could barely breathe, imagining all too clearly what Plumwillow must be suffering, to go through her kitting without a mate. A pang of renewed pain passed through him as he wondered whether Pebbleshine would have any cat to help her when the time came for their kits to be born.

It's not really my place to help Plumwillow, he thought, *but I can't let her face it alone.*

Slipping into the nursery, he found Echosong there with Fidgetpaw, both of them bending over the motionless body of Plumwillow. The tense argument with Leafstar the day before might as well never have happened; Echosong was back to normal again, the calm, efficient medicine cat.

"What's the matter?" Hawkwing asked.

"The first kit is coming out feetfirst," Echosong replied with a brief glance over her shoulder. "Plumwillow can make it through if she has the energy for it, but she's weak. Plumwillow, you've got to *try.*"

"I can't," Plumwillow murmured. Her eyes were glazed and her voice was blurred, as if she had withdrawn far into herself.

Hawkwing's instincts told him what was wrong. "Plumwillow," he mewed, moving to stand beside the gray she-cat's head, "I know you *can* do this."

Plumwillow looked up at him, startled and almost hostile.

"What are you doing in here?" she asked. "You have no—"

"I'm the perfect cat to help you through this," Hawkwing interrupted, resting his tail-tip on Plumwillow's shoulder. "I know what it feels like to lose your mate. How it feels like there's no reason to go on . . ."

Slowly Plumwillow nodded. "All this time, I've been going on for the sake of the kits. But if there's something wrong with them, there *is* no reason."

"You're wrong!" Hawkwing tried to put all the strength into his voice that he wanted to give to Plumwillow. "You have a big reason coming. Sandynose's lovely kits! They can still be born healthy if you stay strong. And every time you look at them, you'll see the best of both you *and* your mate."

Hawkwing had to struggle to keep his voice steady on the last few words, remembering the kits from his dream. *I'll never see my own kits, never sit with Pebbleshine while she gives birth.*

"You look so sad," Plumwillow whispered.

"That's why you have to pull it together," Hawkwing told her. "You have to be strong, because you're lucky enough to have something I will never have."

Understanding began to dawn in Plumwillow's eyes. "Why do you care about what happens to me?" she asked.

"Because I know what it feels like to be alone." *Trapped in a dark cave, with no light and no way out.*

Plumwillow gritted her teeth and Hawkwing realized that another powerful pain was rippling through her belly. This time she didn't cry out, but flexed her muscles to push her kits into the world.

"Yes!" Echosong meowed. "That's right—it's coming!"

Within heartbeats, as Hawkwing watched in wonder, a tiny gray kit slid out onto the mossy bedding of the nursery. Its pelt was wet, plastered to its body, and Echosong nudged it toward Plumwillow, who began licking it vigorously.

"A little tom—and very strong and healthy," Echosong meowed.

Plumwillow's belly spasmed again, and almost before Hawkwing realized it, a second and then a third kit were born: another tom, light brown with ginger legs, just like his father, Sandynose, and a pale tabby she-kit.

Plumwillow couldn't stop purring as she nuzzled and licked them, and guided them toward her belly so that they could suckle. "They're so beautiful!" she whispered, her eyes shining with joy.

Hawkwing gazed down at the happy family, an ache in his heart so deep that he almost cried out with the pain of it. *I'm not really part of this. . . .* "You're okay now, so I'll just go . . . ," he began.

Plumwillow raised her head to look at him. "No, don't," she mewed. "I could never have managed this without you. Losing Sandynose still feels so raw, and I could never take another mate, but I'll need help with these kits—if I'm not presuming too much, would you want to help me?"

Gazing down at the kits, Hawkwing felt the empty places in his heart begin to fill again. *They're not mine, and they never will be,* he thought, *but they're so tiny, so perfect. . . .*

"Of course I'll help you, Plumwillow," he promised.

* * *

Hawkwing padded into the camp with a rabbit dangling from his jaws. At once excited squealing came from the nursery and Plumwillow's three kits came tumbling out, tripping over each other in their eagerness to greet him first.

"Uh-oh!" Firefern mewed around her vole as she followed Hawkwing into camp, her eyes glinting with amusement. "It looks like you're wanted."

The three kits were a moon old now, and already developing into healthy, energetic cats. Dewkit, the sturdy gray tom; Finkit, who looked exactly like his father, with the same brown pelt and ginger legs, and Reedkit, the little tabby she-kit. Hawkwing loved them all, and loved every moment that he spent with them.

Firefern carried her prey to the fresh-kill pile, along with Harrybrook and Birdwing, the other members of the patrol. Hawkwing glanced sharply around until his gaze fell on his apprentice, Curlypaw, who was grooming herself outside her den.

"Curlypaw!" he called, beckoning with his tail.

His apprentice sprang up and padded over to him, stumbling over Finkit, who was bouncing around Hawkwing, along with his littermates. "Yes, Hawkwing?" she mewed.

"Don't 'yes, Hawkwing' me," he snapped. "Where were you this morning? I wanted to take you for battle practice, and you were nowhere to be found."

Curlypaw blinked innocently. "Oh, sorry, Hawkwing," she responded. "I was awake early, so I thought I'd go hunting on my own for a while. I caught two mice," she finished proudly.

"That's all very well, but—" Hawkwing began, then broke off as all three kits jumped on him, digging their tiny claws into his pelt. "Okay, Curlypaw," he meowed, struggling to make himself heard over the joyful squealing of the kits. "Just ask first, next time. And take this rabbit to the fresh-kill pile."

As Curlypaw snatched up the prey and carried it off, Hawkwing flopped over on his side with the three kits swarming all over him. "Dewkit, take your paw out of my ear," he protested. "And Finkit, that's my tail you're biting!"

"You're a rabbit, and we're hunting you," Reedkit informed him.

"Oh, no!" Hawkwing let out a pretend wail of terror. "You're such good hunters! I can't escape!"

As the kits pummeled him with their soft paws, Hawkwing glanced across at the nursery to see Plumwillow sitting outside, watching their game with a happy expression. He rose to his paws and staggered across to her, with the kits still hanging on to him.

"You've got your paws full there," Plumwillow observed with a small *mrrow* of laughter.

"I certainly have!" Hawkwing agreed. "But they—"

He broke off at the distant sound: the bark of a Twoleg monster. His contented mood faded and he let out a huff of annoyance. "Twolegs again!"

Through the long days of greenleaf the sun had shone brightly. Prey had been running well, and every cat was well fed.

There's only been one problem with the warm weather: Twolegs!

Every cat had thought it was odd that the Twolegs had made nests beside the lake and then left them behind. But as soon as the days got warmer, they had come back. The lake, which should have been peaceful under the brilliant blue sky, was suddenly surrounded by Twolegs, playing and shouting and sometimes even throwing themselves into the water to splash about.

All of them with monsters full of Twoleg-stuff, Hawkwing thought irritably. *And they run around as if they own the place!*

"I wish they'd all just go away," he complained.

"Some of them even bring dogs," Plumwillow responded. With an anxious glance at the kits, she added, "They come far too close to our camp for my liking."

"But the dogs look pretty stupid." Hawkwing tried to reassure her. "They mostly lie around on the grass and chase sticks the Twolegs throw."

"Maybe . . ." Plumwillow still looked uneasy. "But do you know what I saw the other day? A Twoleg got into a water monster! It tore around the lake, churning up the water and scaring the ducks! What next, that's what I want to know."

Hawkwing had no idea. He only knew that the territory seemed to get noisier every day, and it felt more dangerous. He hadn't told Plumwillow, because he didn't want to upset her, but sometimes when he and Curlypaw had been out hunting, Twolegs had spotted them and tried to coax them closer. But he and his apprentice knew the tricks Twolegs liked to play; they had always managed to run off before the Twolegs could grab them.

Why do Twolegs always think you want to go to them, anyway? Like they're so fascinating!

The roar of another monster filled the air, growing rapidly louder and then stopping abruptly. Leafstar, who was chatting with Firefern a couple of tail-lengths away, glanced up and caught Hawkwing's gaze.

"It sounds like we have more Twoleg company," Hawkwing remarked.

Leafstar let out an exasperated noise. "We just need to keep our distance," she mewed.

That's been Leafstar's solution ever since the Twolegs appeared, Hawkwing thought. *But is that even possible? There are so many of them now, swarming all over.*

As the sun sank lower in the sky, the cats of SkyClan gathered around the fresh-kill pile to eat. Hawkwing basked in the scarlet light, thinking of how much he loved greenleaf. *The long days and nights, the beautiful sunsets . . .*

But then his thoughts flew back to Pebbleshine, and the pain of loss gripped his heart again as if powerful claws were sinking into it. The prey in his belly felt heavy as he remembered how Pebbleshine's fur shone in sunlight. *She must be close to kitting by now,* he thought. *Or maybe our kits are already born.*

To distract himself from these dark thoughts, he turned to Plumwillow's kits.

"Look, kits," he meowed, scratching up some moss from the floor of the camp and patting it into a ball. "Which of you can throw this moss-ball farthest?"

"I can!"

"Can *not*!"

"Watch me!"

As his gaze followed the three kits, scrambling and falling over each other's paws, shredding the moss-ball in their eagerness, Hawkwing found the ache in his heart eased.

Then a different sound reached Hawkwing's ears, drowning the happy squeaking of the kits. *That's a dog barking—and another, and another!*

Hawkwing's belly lurched in surprise as he realized how close the dogs were. *They're normally so lazy they stay by the lake, well away from our camp.* He had only a moment, just enough time to glance across at Leafstar, before four dogs burst into the camp. Their huge paws slammed against the ground, their jaws drooling as they growled. Hawkwing gagged as their scent flooded over him.

These weren't like the dogs Hawkwing had seen with their Twolegs, lounging on the grass beside the Twoleg dens. One of those had been even smaller than a cat, wearing some weird kind of Twoleg pelt. All four of these dogs were big and fast, lean and long-legged with sleek brindled pelts. Their jaws gaped to show rows of huge, sharp teeth. Hawkwing almost thought they were some kind of wild creature, until he noticed their Twoleg collars.

As the dogs spotted the group of cats their eyes rolled in excitement. Their barking grew even louder. Without taking the time to think, Hawkwing grabbed Dewkit by the scruff and shoved Reedkit onto his back. "Run!" he mumbled to Plumwillow through his mouthful of fur as he pushed Finkit toward her.

Plumwillow grabbed Finkit but stumbled in her haste as

she picked him up. One of the dogs spotted her and raced toward her. After one terrified glance Plumwillow whipped around and kept pace with Hawkwing as he scrambled up the steep slope at the far side of the camp and took off into the woods. Behind him he heard more barking, and the panic-stricken screeching of his Clanmates, but he had no time to look back.

The dogs were on their trail.

CHAPTER 30

❧

Hawkwing fled into the trees with Plumwillow at his side, racing along until his lungs burned. He risked a glance over his shoulder and realized that only one dog was following them. But it was much bigger than they were, and Hawkwing knew they would be outmatched if it came to a fight.

The dog's disgusting scent was all around them, and Hawkwing could hear its panting breath. It ran with its jaws open, its tongue lolling out, and it seemed tireless.

We're not going to make it. . . . Hawkwing remembered how Echosong had prophesied that bad things would happen if they stayed beside the lake. *Was I wrong not to speak up and support her?* he asked himself. *After all we've been through, is this how SkyClan will end?*

Then Hawkwing spotted a gorse thicket at the bottom of a rocky slope. "Down there!" he gasped.

Together he and Plumwillow scrambled down the slope, the kits letting out shrill wails of terror. When they reached the thicket they shoved the kits deep within the thorns, followed them as far as they could, then turned to face the dog.

"It might be too big to get at us in here," Plumwillow panted.

At first the dog whined and scrabbled around at the edge of the thicket, and Hawkwing began to hope that it would get bored and go away. But then its whines changed to snarls of frustration and it began to push its way into the gorse, ignoring the thorns that tore at its pelt.

Hawkwing slid out his claws. "Back off, mange-pelt!" he growled.

He could feel the dog's hot breath on his face. "If it comes in, go for its eyes," he whispered to Plumwillow.

But before the dog could attack, distant barking sounded from the direction of the camp. The dog halted, its head raised to listen, and Hawkwing caught his breath, suddenly hopeful. The barking came again; the dog swung its head around, then with a last snarl it backed out of the gorse thicket and ran off.

Thank StarClan! Hawkwing thought as he poked his head out of the bushes to watch it go.

Hawkwing's heart was pounding and he was shaking with relief as he turned to Plumwillow. "It looks like we're safe—for now," he meowed.

Plumwillow was quivering with fear and tension. "Thank you, Hawkwing," she whispered, pressing herself against his side. "You saved the kits."

"We both did."

The kits crept to their mother's side, eyes still wide with shock. Plumwillow encircled them with her tail, and held them close to her and Hawkwing.

They are not my family, Hawkwing told himself. *But oh, StarClan, I wish they were!*

* * *

Night had fallen by the time Hawkwing limped back into the camp with Plumwillow and the kits. He found the rest of his Clan huddled beside the fresh-kill pile. Their pelts were bushed-up and ragged; their voices sounded hoarse as they discussed the dog attack.

"Hawkwing!" His sister Blossomheart sprang to her paws and ran across the camp to meet him. "Are you okay? Are the kits okay?"

"We're all fine," Hawkwing replied wearily, setting Dewkit down and letting Reedkit slide off his back. "A bit scratched, and I've got a thorn in my pad. We had to hide in a gorse thicket."

"Thank StarClan!" Blossomheart exclaimed. "I was so worried."

"What about the rest of you?"

"We're okay," Blossomheart told him. "Clovertail got bitten, and one of the dogs ripped part of Firefern's pelt off, but Echosong has seen to them, and it's not serious. The rest of us are just a bit bruised. But we fought the vicious brutes off," she finished with satisfaction.

"That's good to hear," Plumwillow mewed, relief in her voice. "Hawkwing, I'm going to take the kits back to the nursery. They're exhausted."

Hawkwing nodded, seeing that she was right. The normally energetic kits could hardly put one paw in front of another as their mother herded them across the camp to the nursery. "They don't look scared anymore," he remarked. "They don't understand how close we came to something terrible."

Plumwillow sighed. "The sooner they forget, the better."

When they had gone, Hawkwing followed Blossomheart to join his Clanmates.

"The dogs are really a problem now," Birdwing was meowing as he padded up. "It's not safe here."

"Greenleaf is almost over," Leafstar responded. "We just have to move the camp further away from the dogs."

"Our camp *was* far away from the dogs," Sparrowpelt pointed out. "Or so we thought. If we move, who's to say that they won't find our new camp?"

"And it's not only the dogs!" Firefern protested, leaping to her paws. "They wouldn't be here if it wasn't for the Twolegs. They're a much greater danger!"

"That's right," Clovertail put in. "We settled here partly because it was peaceful, safe, and free of Twolegs. Now it's like we're living in the middle of a Twolegplace!"

"Hey, don't get carried away," Macgyver mewed, sounding much calmer than the she-cats. "Yes, there are Twolegs here now. But there's plenty of prey and unspoiled territory as well. And I've noticed that some of the Twolegs are packing up and leaving. Can't we put up with them for a bit longer? Maybe they'll all be gone by leaf-bare."

Parsleyseed nodded vigorously in agreement. "Twolegs are better than raccoons," he pointed out. "At least the worst they'll do is try to pet us."

"That's not true!" Echosong spoke up, her voice deeply serious. "Parsleyseed, you haven't lived long enough to see the evil Twolegs can do."

"You're right, Echosong," Leafstar meowed, dipping her head to the medicine cat. "But I think Macgyver's right, too, that the Twolegs are beginning to leave. I believe we can avoid the ones who remain by moving our camp."

Cries of protest rose from the cats who surrounded her.

"Wherever we go, there'll be Twolegs!"

"There's nowhere as sheltered as where we are now!"

Echosong silenced the objections with a wave of her tail as she rose to her paws and picked her way through the crowd of cats to stand in front of Leafstar.

"I don't know if moving our camp will help or not," she announced. "And I don't intend to stay and find out."

An even deeper silence rippled through the Clan as the cats exchanged shocked glances. Leafstar was staring wide-eyed at the medicine cat, as if she couldn't believe what she had just heard.

"What do you mean?" she asked.

Echosong let out a sigh; Hawkwing could see the distress in her eyes. "I've tried to see things your way, Leafstar," she began. "I really have. I want the Clan to settle down and become strong again. But I've just had another vision of a smoldering ember. The spark that remains. We're no closer to finding it, and now we're not even trying!"

"Has StarClan spoken to you again?" Leafstar asked urgently.

Echosong shook her head. "StarClan has *already* made it very clear that we're supposed to unite with the other Clans. The dog attack was a reminder of that—maybe even a sign. I can no longer ignore my feelings that we have turned our back on

StarClan and their instructions. There's only one way to dispel the darkness . . . and that is to find the spark that remains." She paused, taking a deep breath. "In the morning, I will set out to search for the lake in my visions, where I believe I will find ThunderClan."

Hawkwing felt as though a lightning bolt had appeared out of a clear sky and struck his Clan. He expected more protests, but every cat was silent, their gazes fixed on Leafstar. The unthinkable was happening, and no cat had any words.

"Why would you do this?" Leafstar asked quietly. "After we've lived together for so many seasons?"

"I know I have a duty to SkyClan," Echosong replied; Hawkwing thought she was having trouble keeping her voice steady. "But I have just as great a duty to StarClan. And I believe I haven't received any more messages from them because I'm not following their instructions."

"And what about your Clanmates?" Leafstar demanded, anger edging its way into her voice. "Clovertail was bitten today, and Firefern had her shoulder fur torn off." She angled her ears toward the two she-cats. "Who will look after them?"

"I thought of that, of course I did," Echosong responded. "And I spoke to Fidgetpaw. He will stay, and take good care of SkyClan."

"What?" Leafstar's voice rose. "Are you serious? Fidgetpaw is smart and he's learning quickly, but he's still only an apprentice! What if something terrible happened, and Fidgetpaw didn't know what to do?"

"That's the risk we have to take." Echosong flexed her

claws, digging them hard into the ground. "Believe me, Leaf-star, I've thought long and hard about this. But I know that drastic steps must be taken to save the Clan! And I believe that Fidgetpaw is capable. I've trained him as well as I can."

Fidgetpaw ducked his head where he sat on the edge of the crowd of cats. "I'll do my best, Leafstar," he mewed in a small voice, as if he was overwhelmed by the thought of taking responsibility for all of SkyClan.

He must be so nervous, Hawkwing thought sympathetically. *Echosong is asking a lot of him.*

For a few moments that seemed to drag out for moons, Leafstar and Echosong faced each other. Hawkwing could feel the tension in the air between them.

At last Echosong bowed her head. "Leafstar, you know that I must follow StarClan's wishes. They have saved us before."

For a long moment Leafstar remained in thoughtful silence. Then she gave a weary nod. "I know you believe that you have to do this. I'm not happy that you're leaving, and I have my doubts that Fidgetpaw is ready to take on this job. But if you're right, and this is truly the will of StarClan, then perhaps—one day—we'll be united again."

"I hope and pray that will happen," Echosong responded. Then she stood up straighter, letting her gaze travel around the Clan, and continued more briskly, "I would prefer not to go alone. Leafstar, will you allow some cats to come with me to find the lake I believe StarClan means us to find?"

Leafstar's ears twitched up, and for a moment Hawkwing thought that she would refuse. Then she dipped her head in reluctant agreement. "I know some cats might feel the same as you, Echosong," she mewed. "If any cat wants to leave with you, I will not stand in their way."

"Thank you," Echosong murmured.

"I'll come," Bellaleaf offered immediately, rising to her paws.

As she spoke Harrybrook half rose, seemed to change his mind, then got up to stand beside Bellaleaf. "I'll come too," he meowed. "I'm *sorry!*" he added, his eyes distraught as he gazed at his mother, Leafstar. "I don't want to leave you, but I think Echosong is right, and . . . and she can't just wander off without any warriors to take care of her!"

Leafstar's voice was tight as she responded. "You must follow your heart, Harrybrook."

Hawkwing felt his paws twitching. All his instincts were telling him to volunteer to go with Echosong. But there were too many arguments against it. *I have duties here! I have Curlypaw to train! And I owe so much to Leafstar!*

Aware of some cat's gaze on him, he turned his head and exchanged a long look with Plumwillow. He knew that she would never leave the rest of the Clan. *Besides, the kits are too young to travel.*

He knew too that the old hot-headed Hawkwing—the cat who had failed all the cats he loved—would have been the first one to volunteer to leave with Echosong. But even though he was still certain that this lake was the wrong place for SkyClan, now he felt strongly that the responsible thing to do was stay.

"Is that all?" Echosong asked.

Hawkwing felt that she was staring right at him. He looked away, but that meant that his gaze fell on Leafstar. He could tell—however hard the Clan leader tried not to show it—by the tightness of her muzzle and her bristling shoulder fur just how angry and upset she felt that more cats were leaving.

"Very well," Echosong meowed at last. "We will leave at sunrise."

As the sun rose, SkyClan gathered at the entrance to the camp to say good-bye to Echosong and the others.

"I understand what pushed you to go," Leafstar meowed to the medicine cat, "but it grieves me to the bottom of my heart to see the Clan split again. It was hard enough to lose Frecklewish, and the other warriors who stayed beside the gorge."

Echosong nodded; Hawkwing thought she looked regretful, but there was no sign of wavering in her decision. "I hope this will not be forever," she responded. "If—when—we find the other Clans, I'll send a messenger to find the rest of you. And the cats who stayed near the gorge, too."

Hawkwing's throat went dry at the thought of seeing his lost Clanmates again. *Are they okay? And what about Cherrytail and Cloudmist, back in Barley's barn? Maybe one day I'll see them again, too. And Pebbleshine . . . she* must *find her way back to us!*

Echosong slipped through the group of cats, saying a personal farewell to each of them. When she came to Hawkwing, she fixed him with a clear green gaze. "You have come so far," she murmured. As warm pride flooded Hawkwing's pelt, she added, "But you still have far to go. Remember who you are, Hawkwing." Then she touched her nose to his and moved on.

Startled, Hawkwing considered her words as he watched her go. *Remember who I am?*

But then tiny claws fastened into his pelt from behind, and he heard Dewkit squealing into his ear. "I'm a Twoleg dog! Fight me!"

I've found my family, Hawkwing thought. And even though Plumwillow wasn't his true mate, that was enough to fill his heart, for now.

CHAPTER 31

❧

Hawkwing poked his head through the ferns that sheltered the apprentices' den, only to find it empty. There was no sign of Curlypaw, and her scent was stale. Puzzled, he drew back and padded into the center of the camp, where Blossomheart and Sagenose were waiting for him.

"There's no sign of her," he reported. "I wonder where she's gone?"

Before either of his Clanmates could respond, Curlypaw came dashing through the camp entrance and skidded to a halt at Hawkwing's side.

"Sorry," she panted. "I had to go and make dirt."

Her pelt had an odd, harsh tang that Hawkwing couldn't identify, and the stale scent in her den suggested she had been away for longer than it would take to go to the dirtplace.

She's up to something, Hawkwing thought.

But he didn't want to question his apprentice in front of the others, and the rest of the hunting patrols had already left. "Okay," he meowed. "Let's go."

I'll talk to her later.

But as Hawkwing led the way through the woods, his

apprentice's weird behavior slipped out of his mind. He had too many other things to worry about.

Two moons had passed since Echosong and the others had left the Clan. A few days later, Leafstar had ordered the remaining SkyClan cats to move camp into a stretch of long grass at the far end of the lake.

But that had been no better. There were still disturbances from the Twolegs and their dogs, and the new camp was more exposed to the huge birds that had attacked Blossomheart and Curlypaw. Plumwillow had been terrified that they would carry off the kits.

So Leafstar had decided to move camp yet again, to an area of woodland on the opposite side of the lake from where they had first settled. They found a deep hollow surrounded by brambles and thornbushes; it wasn't as big or as sheltered as their first camp, but it was the best they could find.

At first the new place had seemed to work well. SkyClan was a long way away from the noise and activity around the water, and though there were a few Twoleg dens beside a Thunderpath on the far side of the trees, the Twolegs there didn't seem interested in the cats. Even so, their comings and goings, the roar of their monsters down the Thunderpath, disturbed the cats' peace and meant they had to be continually alert.

But what worried Hawkwing more than anything was that some of the younger cats weren't scared enough. They thought it was exciting to be so close to Twolegs.

And then there's Parsleyseed . . .

A few days before, as twilight was falling and the cats of SkyClan were eating together in the camp, the young warrior had risen to his paws in the midst of his Clanmates. "There's something I have to tell you," he meowed, sounding scared and determined at the same time.

Leafstar looked up, mildly surprised. "Go on," she responded.

Parsleyseed hesitated, gulping, and Hawkwing felt a prickle of uneasiness in his pelt. *What's the matter, that he could find it so hard to talk about?*

Then Parsleyseed seemed to brace himself. "I'm going to leave to become a kittypet!" he blurted out.

Yowls of disbelief and protest rose from the cats around him.

"You *can't!*"

"This is where you belong!"

"You would really betray SkyClan?"

Parsleyseed shook his head miserably, looking at his paws. "I don't want to betray any cat," he mewed, "but—"

Leafstar interrupted him, still calm, though Hawkwing could see that she was as shocked as any cat. "Why, Parsleyseed?" she asked. "What makes you want to leave us?"

"I'm scared all the time here," Parsleyseed confessed. "The territory is full of dogs and Twolegs. . . ."

"So you want to go and *live* with Twolegs?" Sparrowpelt snapped. "That's really smart of you!"

"It's not like that!" Parsleyseed defended himself. "I met these Twolegs—they live in one of the dens by the

Thunderpath—and they started to put food out for me. I tried it—and I really like the taste! And I let them stroke me, and I liked that, too!" The last few words burst out of him defiantly, as if he was ashamed and trying not to show it.

Now that Hawkwing thought about it, he remembered seeing Parsleyseed slinking off alone into the woods more than once over the last half moon. *I should have tried to find out what he was up to,* he thought, *and maybe it wouldn't have come to this.*

"Look, Parsleyseed." Macgyver, who had once been a daylight warrior, rose to his paws and padded up to the younger cat, laying his tail over the brown tabby tom's shoulders. "I know all about being a kittypet, and it's not as easy as you think. You only eat when the Twolegs give you food. You only go in and out when the Twolegs say you can. Is that what you really want?" When Parsleyseed didn't reply, he added, "And then there's the Cutter."

Parsleyseed looked sharply at him. "What's the Cutter?"

"I'm not exactly sure," Macgyver replied, "because my Twolegs never took me there, thank StarClan. But the Cutter does something. I know this because all the cats who went to him came back very lazy, not like proper cats at all. They got so *fat!*"

A few gasps of horror came from his listening Clanmates. "That's terrible!" Firefern exclaimed.

"I don't care," Parsleyseed meowed stubbornly. "I've made up my mind. Being a kittypet is easier. And safer."

Hawkwing saw the hurt in Leafstar's eyes at the young warrior's last words, but she didn't try to argue with him.

Because she knows that, these days, it's true.

He couldn't imagine ever wanting to leave his Clan for the life of a kittypet. It would feel like an insult to his parents, not to mention StarClan. But he could understand Parsleyseed's fear. *I still can't help feeling that something's wrong, and that something is coming that is even more terrifying than the dog attack. . . .*

The Clan leader had dipped her head. "Then may StarClan light your path, Parsleyseed."

And on the following morning, Parsleyseed had left Sky-Clan for good.

Now Hawkwing led his hunting patrol deeper into the woods, well away from the lake. Though the Twolegs weren't splashing around in the water anymore—*and why in the name of StarClan would any sensible creature* want *to get wet?*—they still roared around on their water monsters. Hawkwing had even seen them luring fish out of the water on strange sticks with long tendrils hanging from them.

"Hawkwing!" Curlypaw's whisper brought Hawkwing out of his thoughts. "Rabbit!"

She was angling her ears toward a mossy bank where Hawkwing could see the openings to several burrows. The rabbit was nibbling on a patch of sorrel, hopping slowly from one clump to the next.

"Okay," Hawkwing murmured. "Sagenose, Blossomheart, work your way around so you get between the rabbit and the burrows. Curlypaw, you're with me."

"The wind's blowing toward us," Sagenose pointed out. "If we do what you say, the rabbit will scent us."

"I know. I *want* it to scent you," Hawkwing explained. "But it won't be able to go underground, because you'll be in the way. The only way it can run is over here, straight into our paws."

"Brilliant!" Blossomheart breathed out.

When she and Sagenose had gone, circling around the rabbit from opposite directions, Hawkwing and Curlypaw crouched down in the long grass, a couple of tail-lengths separating them.

"Ready?" Hawkwing asked.

"Ready," Curlypaw confirmed, her eyes bright.

Several moments dragged out until the rabbit sat up, its ears quivering, then made a dash for the burrows. But Sagenose was in the way, bounding toward the rabbit with teeth and claws bared.

The rabbit veered away, letting out a thin squeal of terror as it saw Blossomheart, then doubled back and raced toward Curlypaw. Hawkwing almost sprang out of hiding, but stayed still, leaving the kill to his apprentice.

Curlypaw waited until exactly the right moment, then leaped out of the grass with a ferocious snarl and fell on top of the rabbit, biting down hard on its neck.

"Great catch!" Hawkwing congratulated her, padding over to give her prey a sniff.

"Yeah—fantastic!" Sagenose added as he bounded up.

"It was Hawkwing's plan," Curlypaw mewed, giving her chest fur an embarrassed lick at her father's praise. "I couldn't have done it without him."

Hawkwing gazed at her proudly. His apprentice was

becoming a great hunter, and he could imagine what an asset to her Clan she would be. *It's almost time to start thinking about her warrior ceremony.*

Later, as the hunting patrol was returning, laden with prey, Curlypaw hung back to let Sagenose and Blossomheart go on ahead. "Hawkwing, can I talk to you in private?" she asked.

"Of course you can," Hawkwing replied. He was surprised, until he remembered that Curlypaw had been gazing mistily at Rileypool for the past few days. *She's probably going to ask my advice about toms!* He hid his amusement. *Good luck with that,* he thought. *It's not like I'm an expert on love!*

Then his amusement faded as he remembered Pebbleshine, and how much he still missed her. *But I can't think of her now,* he told himself. *If Curlypaw needs me, I have to do the best I can for her.*

Before Curlypaw could tell Hawkwing what was on her mind, they heard a distant barking from the direction of the camp. *No!* Hawkwing thought. *Not again . . .*

Without a word all the patrol broke into a run, discarding their prey. Hawkwing led the way, hurtling through the trees until they were nothing but a blur as he sped past.

As he approached the camp, the direction of the barking changed, as if the dogs were moving off, farther into the woods. Briefly Hawkwing hoped that the danger was over.

But then Plumwillow burst out of the undergrowth, her fur bushed up and her eyes wild and distraught. "The kits are gone!" she exclaimed.

Hawkwing halted, horror turning his bones to ice. "What?"

"Dogs attacked the camp," Plumwillow gasped. "Only three—but they were so big. They managed to corner the kits, and they chased them out of the camp. . . ."

She broke off, her chest heaving as she fought for breath.

Hawkwing didn't need to hear any more. "Check the camp!" he ordered the rest of the patrol, then took off in the direction of the barking, with Plumwillow hard on his paws. Soon his lungs were burning, his legs aching as he forced his muscles to flex faster and faster. But he couldn't stop until he saw the kits again.

I'll flay those dogs if they've hurt one hair of their pelts!

At last Hawkwing and Plumwillow halted beside a line of bushes that enclosed a Twoleg den. The sound of barking ripped through the air. With a glance at Plumwillow, Hawkwing pushed his way through the bushes and into the Twoleg garden.

In the middle of a stretch of grass Hawkwing saw a tiny Twoleg den, striped in bright colors. Three huge black dogs stood outside it, barking so loudly they could be heard in StarClan.

"What *is* that?" Hawkwing murmured, half to himself. "It's too small for Twolegs."

"I think it's for the Twoleg kits. It's too small for the dogs to get in," Plumwillow murmured at his shoulder. "The kits must be in there—I can scent them!"

"Then they're safe for now," Hawkwing responded. "But how are we going to get them out?"

"We'll have to distract the dogs somehow," Plumwillow mewed.

Hawkwing gazed across the garden, imagining himself dashing out to draw the dogs off while Plumwillow rescued

the kits. *Yes, that could work!* he thought, flexing his claws excitedly. But before he could make a move the door of the Twoleg
den slammed open and a female Twoleg appeared, yowling
and waving her forelegs at the dogs.

The dogs ignored her, until she came close enough to grab
one of them by the collar around its neck and yank it back, still
yowling and waving her paw in the dogs' faces. Eventually the
dogs calmed down and backed off, whimpering.

The Twoleg peered inside the tiny den and her jaws
dropped open in surprise. She started to make soft, cooing
noises. Plumwillow and Hawkwing exchanged a glance of
alarm as the Twoleg reached into the den and lifted Dewkit
into her arms, then picked up Finkit and cuddled him. Reedkit followed her littermates into the open, staring in terror at
the Twoleg.

"We have to do something!" Plumwillow cried. "What if
she takes them inside her den? What if she makes them into
kittypets?"

"We won't let her," Hawkwing promised. "Listen—you bite
the Twoleg on her leg, and when she crouches down I'll leap
at her and claw her face. If that doesn't make her drop the kits,
nothing will!"

"Okay," Plumwillow mewed tensely.

Racing across the grass, she leaped up at the Twoleg and
sank her teeth into her leg. The Twoleg let out a yelp of pain
and stooped to bat Plumwillow away. Hawkwing dashed up
and aimed his claws at her face; the Twoleg started back in
alarm, dropping Finkit and Dewkit and letting out a frightened yowl.

"This way!" Hawkwing exclaimed, pushing all three kits in front of him toward the bushes. "As fast as you can!"

At the same moment a huge male Twoleg came running out of the den, yowling even louder than his mate and glaring in the cats' direction. The dogs started barking again, bounding after Hawkwing and Plumwillow as they helped the kits wriggle through the bushes and out into the woods.

Hawkwing turned to face the dogs, his claws extended as he snarled defiance, but before the dogs reached him the male Twoleg ran up to them, still yowling, and herded them back to the den. Hawkwing let out a gusty sigh of relief before thrusting his way through the tough branches to join Plumwillow and the kits.

Urging the kits on, Hawkwing and Plumwillow hurried deep into the trees before they dared stop to check on them.

"Are you okay?" Plumwillow asked anxiously, sniffing them all over.

"We're fine!" Reedkit panted.

"Twolegs aren't that scary," Finkit added.

Dewkit fluffed up his pelt. "It felt kind of nice when the female picked me up," he declared.

Hawkwing gave Plumwillow a serious look. "This is the second time the kits have been in danger from dogs," he meowed. "We can't risk it happening again."

"I know," Plumwillow agreed. "And I don't like the way they're not scared of Twolegs. You *should* be scared," she added severely to her kits.

"Then we have to do something," Hawkwing meowed.

Plumwillow gave him a long, serious look. "Are you saying

what I think you're saying?"

Hawkwing nodded. *I've tried my best to stay, but I can't deny any longer that the danger is getting worse. The dogs keep attacking, and the kits are growing up with no fear of Twolegs. This isn't our home. We need to find another camp.*

"We have to convince Leafstar to leave the lake," he responded. "She won't like it, but I can't see any other way."

When they were still a long way from the camp, Hawkwing spotted movement in the undergrowth. He tensed, then relaxed as a SkyClan patrol emerged into the open. Leafstar was in the lead, with Waspwhisker, Sparrowpelt, Tinycloud, and Rabbitleap.

"You found the kits!" Leafstar exclaimed, relief shining in her eyes as she halted in front of Hawkwing. "We were on our way to help you. Are they hurt?"

"No, we're all okay," Dewkit replied, fluffing out his fur.

"We ran faster than those stupid dogs," Reedkit boasted. "And we hid in a tiny little Twoleg den."

Finkit puffed out his chest proudly. "Those mange-pelts couldn't get us in there."

Hawkwing suppressed a *mrrow* of amusement. *Now that they're over their fear, they'll be telling the story for moons!*

"You were all very brave," Leafstar praised them. "And now let's get back to camp."

When the patrol returned with the kits, the rest of their Clanmates pressed around them, welcoming them back with yowls of joy.

"Give the kits space to breathe!" Plumwillow protested.

"They're exhausted—they need to eat something and go to sleep."

Soon the whole Clan settled down around the fresh-kill pile to eat and discuss the dog attack. The kits started to tell their story again—Hawkwing noticed that the dogs seemed to get bigger with every heartbeat—but before they got to the end their weariness overcame them, and they curled up next to Plumwillow in a purring, sleepy heap of fur.

As Hawkwing was finishing off a juicy vole, Curlypaw padded over to him and gave him a nudge. "Is it okay to talk now?"

Amid all the stress of the dog attack, Hawkwing had completely forgotten that Curlypaw had asked to talk to him. Now the last thing he wanted was to advise her about toms. He would much rather have burrowed into his nest in the warriors' den and gone to sleep. But he knew that he couldn't brush his apprentice off like that.

"Won't the morning do instead?" he asked.

Curlypaw shifted her paws uncomfortably. "It's kind of important."

Hawkwing suppressed a *mrrow* of amusement. *I guess toms are really important to a young she-cat!* "Okay," he replied. "Let's go over here where it's a bit quieter."

Hawkwing led the way to where a thornbush jutted out from the rocky bank which formed the edge of the camp. "Well, spit it out," he meowed.

Curlypaw gave him a nervous glance and then studied her paws. "I've given it a lot of thought," she murmured at last, "and I've decided to join Parsleyseed as a kittypet."

Hawkwing felt as if his heart had plummeted down into his paws. His jaws gaped open as he stared at his apprentice. *I thought this was going to be about Rileypool!* "What?" he spluttered. "I didn't see that coming!"

"That's because you didn't *want* to see," Curlypaw responded. "Whenever I've gotten the chance, I've been going down to the lakeshore, and I didn't much care if any cat saw me going. Most of the Twolegs are very nice. They stroke me and give me food."

"And you'd give up being a Clan cat for *that*?" Hawkwing asked incredulously. "You've been doing so well. You'll be a great warrior—a huge asset to your Clan!"

"I've tried my best to learn," Curlypaw sighed. "I know I'm good at hunting, and I do care about my Clan. But Parsley-seed is right; it's easier and safer to be a kittypet."

"You've been visiting Parsleyseed?" Hawkwing asked sharply.

"Yes. I went to Parsleyseed's new home first thing this morning and talked to him," Curlypaw replied.

So that's *where she was before our hunting patrol!* Hawkwing thought with sudden understanding. *That must have been some kind of Twoleg scent on her fur.*

"I met his Twolegs—Parsleyseed calls them 'housefolk'— and they were very kind," Curlypaw continued. "Parsleyseed says he has all the delicious food he can eat, and his housefolk let him out whenever he wants, except at night, because then it's his job to guard the Twoleg kit. He thinks he can convince his Twolegs to take in another cat, and I—" She hesitated, then finished defiantly, "I want to go!"

"But how can you abandon your Clan?" Hawkwing asked, still hardly able to believe he was hearing this. "How can you abandon *StarClan?*"

To his amazement, there was pity in Curlypaw's eyes as she gazed at him. "Why should I care about StarClan?" she asked. "Does StarClan care about us? Our medicine cat has left us. We haven't found the other Clans. What if everything we've been told about StarClan is just a . . . a pretty story? Because if StarClan really exists, why would they allow us to suffer like this?"

Hawkwing had no idea what to say. Her doubts reflected ones he had felt himself, but he had never realized that Curlypaw shared them. *It's my fault,* he thought. *I've failed her as a mentor.*

"Don't go," he mewed, his voice raw. *If she stays I'll do better,* he vowed. *I'll win her over. I'll share my doubts with her, and we'll talk about them together. I'll show her why being a Clan cat is important.*

Curlypaw rubbed her cheek against his. "I'll never stop being grateful to you, but I've already decided," she responded gently. "I'll leave in the morning."

"Does Leafstar know?" Hawkwing asked, reluctantly accepting defeat.

"I told Birdwing and Sagenose," Curlypaw replied. "They say they understand, and that they'll tell Leafstar."

She dipped her head and padded away toward the apprentices' den. Stunned, Hawkwing watched her stroll out of sight, then stumbled back into the center of the hollow. He didn't want to talk to any cat, but after a moment he found his paw steps taking him to the nursery, where Plumwillow had made a nest of moss and bracken underneath the low-growing branches of a hazel bush.

Inside he breathed in the warm, milky scent of the kits and began to relax slightly. Plumwillow was still awake, gently licking the sleeping kits. As Hawkwing approached she raised her head and blinked at him affectionately.

"Don't wake them," she murmured.

"I won't." Gently Hawkwing nuzzled each kit in turn. At his touch they gave a little wriggle, but didn't wake. "They're so beautiful. We must do everything we can to keep them safe."

Plumwillow nodded. "I'll see you in the morning."

Hawkwing retreated into the open again and spotted Leafstar sitting in the middle of the clearing, her head raised as she gazed at the moon. Her expression was unreadable.

Thinking of what he had to say to her on the following day, Hawkwing felt a tingle of apprehension in his belly. He knew that after everything the Clan had been through, Leafstar would probably react badly to his insistence that they finally leave the lake. *We must do this, though,* he thought, *for the good of the Clan.*

But how can I convince Leafstar of that, when even Echosong couldn't?

CHAPTER 32

❧

Hawkwing's heart was heavy as he padded out of the camp early the next morning with Curlypaw by his side. He still found it hard to believe that his apprentice was lost to him, and to the whole of SkyClan. It was harder still to be angry with her, after all the trouble SkyClan had suffered since Duskpaw's death in the fire and the arrival of Darktail.

How much more must we go through before we find our new home?

The dawn light was gray and dim, the clouds barely clearing the tops of the trees. Tall grasses bent over with the weight of dew, brushing the cats' pelts as they passed. The damp cold struck deep beneath Hawkwing's fur, and he shivered.

"You'll give me the chance to get to Parsleyseed's den?" Curlypaw asked. "I don't want any cat chasing me and trying to make me stay."

"No cat will come after you," Hawkwing promised. "If that's what you really want."

His belly cramped with apprehension as he imagined the reaction of his Clanmates when they found out she had actually gone. He didn't want them to think that Curlypaw was a coward, or just looking for a soft and easy life.

And what will they think of me? he asked himself gloomily. *A warrior who couldn't keep his apprentice. If I lose their respect, how will I convince Leafstar that we need to move on?*

The two cats halted on the bank of a small stream. Beyond it was a long slope covered with fern, and from the top of that, Hawkwing knew, Curlypaw would be able to see Parsleyseed's Twoleg nest.

"This is it, then," Hawkwing meowed. "You're sure you won't change your mind?"

Curlypaw shook her head. "I've thought long and hard about this, Hawkwing," she replied. "I know it's the right decision for me. But it's not like we'll never see each other again," she added, clearly trying to sound cheerful. "We still live beside the same lake."

We do for now, Hawkwing thought, still fiercely hoping that he could persuade Leafstar to change her mind and move on. But he didn't think that would make any difference to Curlypaw. "Good luck," he mewed. "And may StarClan light your path."

"Yours, too," Curlypaw responded, rubbing her cheek against his.

I'm really going to miss her, Hawkwing thought. *She's so smart and capable. And if SkyClan can't hold on to young cats like her, what kind of future do we have?*

With a final dip of her head, Curlypaw leaped across the stream and disappeared into the ferns. Hawkwing stood there for a long time, watching the movement of the fronds as Curlypaw climbed the slope. At last all movement ceased, and he knew she must have crossed the ridge and must be racing toward Parsleyseed's den and her new life as a kittypet.

And now I have to talk to Leafstar, he thought, turning away with a sigh.

When Hawkwing returned to camp, Leafstar and Waspwhisker were in the middle of arranging the dawn patrols. Hawkwing stood to one side until the groups separated and set out. Then he padded up to his Clan leader.

"Leafstar, may I speak to you in private?" he asked.

"What is this all about?" Waspwhisker asked.

Hawkwing gave the Clan deputy an awkward glance. He had wanted to discuss the Clan's future with Leafstar alone, but Waspwhisker was standing there as if his paws had grown roots, and Leafstar made no attempt to dismiss him.

Giving in, Hawkwing dipped his head respectfully. "I feel it's time to rethink our decision to stay here by the lake," he began. "Dewkit, Reedkit, and Finkit could have been killed yesterday. And we're losing young cats to Twolegs, of all things."

At these words, Leafstar exchanged a glance with Waspwhisker, and Hawkwing guessed that she had already told her deputy that Curlypaw had gone to join Parsleyseed.

"I understand we do not want to make the wrong decision," Hawkwing continued. "But I've had the feeling for a long time that there has to be a better place for us to be than this. And I can't ignore it any longer."

As Hawkwing spoke, Waspwhisker's eyes narrowed and his shoulder fur began to bristle. "You've got a *feeling*?" the deputy challenged him. "And because of this *feeling* we all have to set out again, going StarClan knows where?"

"Echosong didn't think it was right, either," mumbled Plumwillow.

"Isn't any other cat sick of traveling!?" Waspwhisker hissed.

"Waspwhisker, that's enough," Leafstar mewed with a twitch of her tail-tip. "I don't like what Hawkwing is saying any more than you do. But I have to admit that the same thoughts have been going through my mind."

A jolt of surprise throbbed through Hawkwing. *I expected a real argument with Leafstar. But here she is agreeing with me.*

"I keep expecting life to get easier here by the lake," Leafstar continued, "but . . . it doesn't. And I can see that some of our young cats are losing touch with StarClan."

Like Curlypaw, Hawkwing thought, remembering what his former apprentice had said the night before.

"And . . ." Leafstar went on, "Fidgetpaw hasn't had any visions since Echosong left. Now I understand what Echosong meant about losing her connection to StarClan. I can't help but think that if we were surrounded by other Clans, we would be better able to keep our faith in StarClan strong."

Waspwhisker had listened carefully to everything his Clan leader said, and now he gave a reluctant nod of acceptance. "What do you want to do, then?" he asked.

Leafstar hesitated, her eyes deep pools of thought. Hawkwing felt as though a whole family of mice were chasing each other in his belly as he waited for her decision.

Finally the Clan leader drew herself up and took a deep breath. "The only solution is to leave," she announced.

Waspwhisker's eyes stretched wide with amazement. "Leave *now*?" His shoulder fur began to bristle. "For StarClan's, sake, Leafstar, it's nearly leaf-bare. We had a terrible time traveling from the gorge to here, and that was in newleaf. What cat can imagine wandering in the wilderness for moons in the coldest weather, when prey is the most scarce?"

"But that's the worst that could happen," Hawkwing pointed out. "It's possible we would meet up with Echosong very soon, and find our place by the lake where the other Clans live, before leaf-bare. It's early yet—there's still a moon or two of leaf-fall ahead."

"Oh, yes," Waspwhisker meowed with a scowl, his voice heavily sarcastic. "This journey has gone really great for us so far—and you're saying the worst won't happen?"

Hawkwing winced. He realized how stupid he had been, after all the Clan had been through, to speak so optimistically.

"We mustn't lose faith," Leafstar insisted. "I know it will be a difficult journey, even if it is a short one. But we must remember what is at stake here: the future of SkyClan." Gazing at Hawkwing, her amber eyes softened. "It was brave of you to bring this up," she meowed. "A bit more like the Hawkwing I know." Before Hawkwing could ask her what she meant by that, she turned away. "I'll go speak to Fidgetpaw about preparing traveling herbs."

The sun had gone down, and twilight was gathering. Hawkwing watched as Leafstar leaped up to the branch of an oak tree that jutted out over the camp. His belly churned in anticipation of what was coming.

"Let all cats old enough to catch their own prey join here underneath this tree for a Clan meeting," she called.

In response to their leader's voice, the cats of SkyClan began to emerge from their dens. Waspwhisker bounded over to the tree and sat next to the trunk, looking up at his leader. Hawkwing padded over to join Plumwillow as she appeared at the entrance to the nursery. Her kits peered curiously around her, even though it was time for them to sleep. Sparrowpelt and Tinycloud sat nearby, their pelts brushing, while Fidgetpaw slid out of the medicine cat's den, and went to sit with Birdwing, Sagenose, and Macgyver.

As the rest of the Clan assembled they glanced uneasily at each other, whiskers twitching and shoulder fur beginning to rise. *And no wonder,* Hawkwing thought. *It's never good news when the Clan leader calls an unexpected meeting at this time.*

"The lake was never meant to be our new camp," Leafstar began. "It was simply somewhere to regroup, while we waited for a new sign from StarClan, or figured out once and for all what they were asking of us. And now, dogs and Twolegs give us trouble, and our young cats have begun to drift away from Clan life." She paused for a moment, closing her eyes briefly, then continued, "It is past time for SkyClan to leave this place, and resume our quest to seek out the other Clans."

A gasp of astonishment rose from the assembled cats. For

a moment they were stunned into silence. Then Sparrowpelt rose to his paws.

"I'm sorry, Leafstar," he meowed, "but if you weren't my Clan leader, I'd tell you there must be bees in your brain. *Leave?* When we finally have a decent place to live, and all the prey we can eat?"

"And monsters, and Twolegs, and dogs," his mate, Tinycloud, reminded him. "*Your* bees are swarming if you think this is where StarClan intended us to be."

"It's still a bad time to go," Birdwing pointed out. "Leafbare will be on us soon, and we don't even know where we're going."

"And worse things might happen if we stay," Leafstar responded. "My mind is made up. Our destiny has always been to be reunited with the other Clans. I am leaving in the morning, with any cats who want to come with me."

An uncomfortable silence fell at the Clan leader's words. Clovertail voiced what Hawkwing—and, he guessed, the rest of his Clan—was thinking.

"If we don't follow our leader, then it's the end of SkyClan."

"It might be the end of us anyway," Sagenose pointed out. "Who knows what dangers might be waiting for us out there?"

"We've had our fair share of danger," Rileypool agreed. "But if any cats stay here, they won't be part of our Clan anymore. Do you want to be a kittypet, Sagenose?"

The older warrior's only reply was an irritated lash of his tail.

"Of course we're coming with you, Leafstar," Waspwhisker

declared in a tone that didn't invite argument.

A murmur of agreement rose from the other cats, and Hawkwing sensed relief that the Clan deputy had made the decision for them. Some of them, like Tinycloud and Rileypool, even looked excited at the thought of seeking out other Clan cats.

Reedkit let out a disappointed wail. "But *why* can't we stay?" she whined. "I like it here by the lake."

Hawkwing, sitting with Plumwillow and the kits, bent his head and touched his nose to hers. "Don't worry," he mewed. "We'll live by a *new* lake someday. One with fewer Twolegs."

"But I heard that Twolegs like to leave out nice food for cats," Finkit piped up.

Hawkwing exchanged a concerned glance with Plumwillow.

"There'll be plenty of nice food where we're going," Hawkwing reassured Finkit. "And it always tastes better if you catch it yourself!"

"Will you teach us, then?" Dewkit asked eagerly. "I won't mind leaving if we can be apprentices and you'll be our mentor!"

Hawkwing gave a mock shudder. "Mentor *all three* of you? Oh, StarClan, no!"

"Mentors only have one apprentice at a time," Plumwillow mewed briskly. "Besides, you're too young to be apprentices yet. And now it's time for sleep," she added. "Tomorrow will be a long day."

When Hawkwing had helped Plumwillow settle the kits

in the nursery, he returned to the clearing to see Leafstar still sitting on the branch from where she had spoken to her Clan. Full darkness had fallen, and most of the other cats had already retreated to their dens.

"Leafstar, are you all right?" Hawkwing asked, leaping up to sit on the branch beside her.

Leafstar's gaze was fixed on the lake, just visible through the trees, her eyes luminous pools of regret. Hawkwing's pelt warmed with the depth of his respect for her, with a twinge of sadness as he recognized the massive burden of leadership resting on her shoulders in these dark times.

Being Clan leader must be like being a parent to all the cats in the Clan.

"I'm going to miss this place," Leafstar murmured. "I wanted so much for it to be our home forever. But it isn't."

Hawkwing nodded in agreement. "Perhaps something even better is waiting for us," he suggested.

"I hope so," Leafstar responded.

But Hawkwing could see the doubt in her eyes.

Hawkwing padded through deep woodland, where sunlight slanting through the branches dappled the ground with golden light. Though he didn't turn his head to see her, he could feel Pebbleshine's pelt brushing his, and smell her sweet scent. He felt filled up with happiness like a pool after heavy rain.

A sudden throaty roar disturbed Hawkwing's contentment. He glanced around sharply, half expecting to see a lion or a tiger from one of the elders' nursery tales. As he looked, the trees seemed to grow dim, their outlines blurred, and there was no trace of Pebbleshine.

"Don't go!" he yowled.

The roaring grew louder, and now Hawkwing recognized the sound of a monster. *But there shouldn't be monsters here!* he thought, his pelt prickling with the first onset of panic.

Hawkwing jerked awake, and raised his head to see dawn light trickling through the branches that sheltered the warriors' den, and his Clanmates stirring around him. The roaring continued, growing louder still.

I certainly won't miss that! he thought. *I wish we could find a camp far, far away from any Thunderpaths, so I never have to hear that sound again.*

Then Rileypool poked his head into the den. "Come out, quickly!" he meowed urgently. "There are Twolegs in the forest!"

"Then come in here and hide." Hawkwing's jaws stretched in a massive yawn. "That's what we usually do when Twolegs get too close. Twolegs are too stupid to see what's right in front of them!"

"No, this is different," Rileypool told him, his voice tight with tension. "There are too many of them, and—"

A yowl from outside interrupted him, followed by the heavy pounding of Twoleg paw steps. Hawkwing's neck fur began to bristle in alarm. Cautiously he peered out of the den, and cold horror shivered through him from ears to tail-tip at what he saw.

Five Twolegs were tramping into the camp. They wore

strange coverings on their paws and slick pelts the color of dandelions. Even worse, each of them was carrying a long stick with something made of interlaced tendrils, like a huge cobweb, on the end of it.

By now Hawkwing's Clanmates were pressing around him, trying to look out and gasping with fear at the sight.

"What are they doing?" Rabbitleap demanded, but no cat could answer him.

As Hawkwing watched, he spotted Fidgetpaw emerge from the medicine cat's den and stand there stunned at the invasion. Immediately one of the Twolegs swung his stick at Fidgetpaw, then lifted it with Fidgetpaw tangled inside the cobweb. The medicine cat struggled, but he couldn't break free.

Horror crawled like ants through Hawkwing's pelt as he watched. The Twoleg said something to one of his companions, and the two of them slapped paws. Then the second Twoleg rolled a tiny den into the camp, made of thin, shiny sticks. He opened one side, and the first Twoleg dumped Fidgetpaw inside.

"He's trapped!" Hawkwing yowled.

He hurled himself out of the warriors' den, his claws extended as he raced toward the invading Twolegs. His Clanmates poured out after him, snarling defiance.

But suddenly Leafstar was in their midst. "Don't fight!" she ordered. "We can't win. Run! Meet up in the long grass by the lake."

"But they have Fidgetpaw!" Hawkwing protested.

"There's nothing we can do!" Leafstar snapped back at

him. "Head for the lake!"

His heart wrenched at the thought of abandoning Fidgetpaw, but Hawkwing had to admit that she was right. These
Twolegs with their weird pelts and sticks were impossible for
them to fight. He dodged around one of the cobweb-things,
then halted as another Twoleg swung his stick around and
scooped up Waspwhisker.

This can't be happening! he thought as he stared at the Clan
deputy, who was screeching and fighting in vain as the Twoleg
carried him over to the shiny den.

"No!" Plumwillow yowled, giving Hawkwing a mighty
shove. "Run!"

Hawkwing pulled himself together. *We have to save the kits!*

He followed Plumwillow as she gathered her kits together.
All three of them were staring open-mouthed at the Twolegs,
as if they couldn't believe what they were seeing, or didn't
understand.

"What are they doing?" Dewkit asked.

"You can see what they're doing," Plumwillow snapped,
giving the little tom a shove. "Now go!"

Hawkwing helped her push the others along until the kits
finally realized the danger they were in and scurried for the
camp entrance. Once in the open they began to panic, scattering in three different directions.

"This way!" Hawkwing called.

Together with Plumwillow he managed to round up the
terrified kits and head toward the lake. On the way there they
spotted more Twolegs standing beside two monsters on a small

Thunderpath that led through the woods and down to the Twoleg dens. As Hawkwing and Plumwillow ran past with the kits the Twolegs let out a roar and lumbered toward them.

"Quick! This way!" Hawkwing gasped.

He veered toward an outcrop of rocks, and spotted the entrance to a rabbit burrow half concealed among the boulders. He pushed the kits into the opening of the burrow, then dived in himself with Plumwillow. Hawkwing gestured to the kits to be silent, and they crouched there, wide-eyed, listening to the Twolegs tramping around the rocky outcrop.

Finally the heavy paw steps died away; Hawkwing peered out cautiously and saw the Twolegs heading back toward their monster.

"Okay," he whispered. "We can go."

Keeping low, their bellies pressed to the ground as if they were stalking prey, Hawkwing and Plumwillow led the kits toward the lake. Hawkwing's fur was bushed up with fear, and with every paw step he expected to see one of the Twolegs' cobweb-sticks swooping down to envelop the kits.

I can't lose these *kits too,* he thought, remembering the lost Pebbleshine and her litter. *I have to save them!*

Hawkwing felt as if whole moons were passing as they crept along, until finally they made it to the tall grass and collapsed there, panting.

Rileypool and Sagenose had already arrived at the meeting-place, their fur bristling and a wild look in their eyes.

"They took Waspwhisker!" Rileypool exclaimed disbelievingly. "What will they do with him?"

"And Fidgetpaw!" Sagenose tore at the grass with his claws. "I have to save my kit!"

Peering out through the long stems, Hawkwing saw two Twolegs emerge from the trees, rolling the shiny den in front of them, with Fidgetpaw and Waspwhisker still trapped inside. The rest of the Clan was scattering, all of them making for the long grass, with the Twolegs in pursuit.

Hawkwing watched helplessly as they swung their sticks again and trapped Clovertail, then Birdwing, and carried the struggling cats over to the monster.

"Birdwing!" Sagenose howled as he saw his mate disappear into the belly of the monster. "Birdwing, not you too!"

Claws of pain gripped Hawkwing's heart; he knew exactly how his Clanmate felt. But he still blocked Sagenose's way as he tried to leap out of hiding and follow Birdwing. Sagenose tried to dodge around him, and Hawkwing had to dart to the side, anticipating which way his Clanmate would move, and stop him from charging into danger.

"No," he mewed, nose to nose with Sagenose. "You can't help them."

"I can at least go with them!" Sagenose panted, sliding out his claws to attack Hawkwing.

"No." That was Leafstar, appearing through the grass stems and resting her tail on Sagenose's shoulder. "SkyClan needs you, Sagenose."

"Birdwing and Fidgetpaw need me," Sagenose responded, bunching his muscles and preparing to leap out into the open.

Before he could move, Hawkwing slammed a paw down

hard on his neck. "Stop that!" he hissed. "Leafstar is right. We need you here."

For a moment Sagenose writhed in Hawkwing's grip, growling furiously. Then he collapsed with his nose on his paws and his eyes closed, not trying to fight anymore.

At last the remaining warriors of SkyClan made it to the tall grass, and watched as the Twolegs climbed back into the monsters, which awoke with a roar and sped along the Thunderpath, heading away from the lake.

"What just happened?" Dewkit asked plaintively. "Did they take them to be kittypets?"

"Maybe," Leafstar replied, though Hawkwing could tell by looking at her that she didn't believe it.

I don't believe it, either, he thought. *I know enough about Twolegs to be sure they don't treat their kittypets that way. Our Clanmates are prisoners.* Horror shivered through his pelt again as he added to himself, *What do they do to their prisoners?*

"They're gone," Leafstar meowed when the noise of the monsters had died away. Her voice was shaking with anger and grief. "The Twolegs are no longer willing to live in peace with us. This proves that we're right to leave."

"Leave?" Sagenose let out a desperate wail. "Surely we can't leave Birdwing and Fidgetpaw?"

"And Waspwhisker," Rabbitleap added.

"They are already gone," Leafstar told them gently. "Monsters can travel very far, very fast. Remember what happened to Pebbleshine!" As she spoke she cast an embarrassed glance at Hawkwing, as if she was sorry to have mentioned the name of his lost mate. Hawkwing didn't need the reminder. He was already reliving that terrible day. "She got trapped inside a monster that ran off with her. She never came back," Leafstar finished.

Rileypool let out a wail. "Are we going to lose *all* our Clanmates?"

"I know you're hurting," Leafstar meowed, "but you must be quiet. The Twolegs might hear you. And we must all be brave," she continued, gazing around at her Clan. "We have lost two special cats: our medicine cat, Fidgetpaw, and our deputy, Waspwhisker. We can only pray to StarClan to send Echosong back to us, but we can and will have another deputy."

A stir of surprise traveled through the remaining cats of SkyClan, as if none of them had thought of replacing Waspwhisker so quickly. *But it has to be done,* Hawkwing thought regretfully. *I wonder who Leafstar will choose.*

Leafstar stood silent for a few heartbeats, gazing down at her paws, as if she was deep in thought. Then she raised her head again. "I speak these words before StarClan," she announced, "that the spirits of our warrior ancestors may hear and approve my choice. Hawkwing will be the new deputy of SkyClan."

Hawkwing stared at his Clan leader, stunned. He couldn't have been more astonished if the ground had opened up and swallowed him. "Me?" he gasped. "But I—"

"You, Hawkwing," Leafstar interrupted him. "I can think of no cat better suited to help me lead our Clan through these dark days."

Hawkwing couldn't agree with her. *I failed my Clan . . . I've failed time and time again! I couldn't even keep my apprentice.* But as he gazed around at his Clanmates, saw their eyes shining and heard their approving murmurs, he realized with even more amazement that they wanted him to be their deputy.

"You'll do a marvelous job," Firefern assured him. "Remember how you saved the whole Clan back in the Twolegplace."

Plumwillow's gaze was warm as she turned to him. "Leafstar couldn't have made a better choice."

"That's right," Sparrowpelt added. "You'll be a great deputy, just like your father was."

Hawkwing couldn't agree with that. *I'll never be as good as Sharpclaw.* But his Clanmates were murmuring their agreement with Sparrowpelt's words. Even though it was too dangerous for them to chant his name, he couldn't have hoped for a better sign of their support.

"Then . . . thank you, Leafstar," Hawkwing stammered, his voice hoarse. "I swear that I will be loyal to SkyClan, and spend my last drop of blood defending it."

Leafstar dipped her head. "And now we must go," she meowed. "It is a difficult journey ahead of us, but we must make it, to have any chance of saving our Clan."

With a wave of her tail she ventured out of the long grass, checked that no more Twolegs were lurking, then led the way back into the trees in the direction Echosong had gone, a little more than two moons ago. Her Clan followed.

Hawkwing, his mind still reeling, took up a position in the rear. At the edge of the woods he halted and took a last look back at the lake. *We should never have stayed here,* he reflected. *Echosong was right.*

Then with a deep breath he turned and padded into the shadows after Leafstar and the tattered remnants of his Clan.

CHAPTER 33

✿

Hawkwing sat on a rock overlooking a shallow stream bubbling over stones, and surveyed his Clan's temporary camp. A moon and a half had passed since they left the lake, and though they thought they were going in the direction they had seen Echosong take when she left, they had seen no sign of her or the cats who went with her.

Every cat was weary of traveling, growing thinner as the weather became colder and prey scarcer. Finally Leafstar had decided to camp here, where the ground had fallen away into rocky hollows that offered at least a little shelter. But the landscape that surrounded them was bleak, with only a few wind-twisted trees; Hawkwing's heart sank right down to his paws at the thought of being caught here by leaf-bare.

Wind buffeted his fur as he sat on watch and let his mind travel back to the beginning of their new journey, just after Leafstar had made him deputy. The Clan had sheltered for the night in a copse on the side of a hill, where wind rustled the branches of the trees and sent clouds scudding across the sky. Unable to sleep, Hawkwing had padded out of his makeshift den and crouched among the roots of an oak tree, watching the sky. Soon, Leafstar had slipped through the shadows to join him.

"What convinced me to make you deputy," the Clan leader had meowed, "wasn't anything to do with what happened in the Twolegplace. It was remembering when you were brave enough to tell me that you thought we should leave the lake. That showed me that you have grown, and learned to put the needs of your Clan above your own."

Hawkwing had been flattered that Leafstar thought so, but privately he wasn't sure that he agreed. He still felt that he didn't deserve to be deputy. He had begun to grow used to his duties, though he found it strange to have his Clanmates defer to him and see the look of respect in their eyes. "I'll do my best, Leafstar," he had promised. "But if Waspwhisker should come back to us, I'll step down."

"That's in the paws of StarClan," Leafstar had murmured, though Hawkwing could tell that she had no hope of the former deputy returning.

Now he faced his secret fears that there wouldn't be a Clan for much longer. They had wandered through woodland, across open ground, keeping well clear of Twolegplaces, and if Leafstar had a purpose in the path she chose, Hawkwing didn't know what it was. Now that they had no medicine cat, they had no visions from StarClan to guide them. All they had was blind faith, and the hope of finding either Echosong or the lake she had dreamed of, where the Clan cats lived.

We could be traveling in entirely the wrong direction, Hawkwing thought despairingly. *And how many more cats can we lose before*

SkyClan is gone forever? Will Twolegs take more of us, like they took Wasp-whisker and the others?

Hawkwing was distracted from these dark thoughts by the appearance of Macgyver, who emerged from under a rocky overhang where he had made his den.

There isn't even room here to make a proper warriors' den we can all share, Hawkwing thought. *We have to split up. That's not right for a Clan camp.*

Macgyver padded over to Hawkwing, swaying a little on his paws.

"I'm hungry," he announced. "I'm going hunting."

Hawkwing gave a disapproving twitch of his whiskers. "The hunting patrols have already gone out," he mewed. "You said you were a bit tired, so I told you to get some rest."

"Well, I feel better now," Macgyver told him. "And I'm *starving!* So I'm going hunting."

Hawkwing leaped down from his rock and leaned in closer to the black-and-white tom. "Are you okay?" he asked.

Macgyver looked up at him, his eyes strangely blurred. "Never better," he muttered, and folded up to collapse at Hawkwing's paws.

"Macgyver!" Hawkwing gasped, appalled. He bent over his Clanmate, prodding him in a desperate attempt to rouse him. Macgyver only grunted, but at least that proved he was still alive.

Instinctively Hawkwing looked around for a medicine cat, but he realized in frustration that SkyClan didn't have one anymore. He raised his voice in a yowl. "Leafstar!"

* * *

"Tansy is for fever, I think," Hawkwing mewed uncertainly.

"No, it's borage," Firefern argued. "And there's a clump of it right there." She pointed upward with her tail to where plants tumbled from the lip of the bluff above the rocky hollow.

Two sunrises had passed since Macgyver had collapsed, and since then Blossomheart and Rileypool had succumbed to the same mysterious illness. All three cats lay together in a nest of moss and dried grass, curled up and seemingly unaware of anything that went on around them. Their pelts gave off a dry heat, though they still shivered with cold, even huddled together for warmth in thick bedding.

Hawkwing fluffed up his pelt against the stiff breeze that probed into it with claws of cold. The sky was gray, the bulging clouds getting ready to release their rain. *Leaf-bare is almost on us,* he thought, *and that's only going to make it harder for any cat who falls ill.*

"Even if you're right, it's not just fever," Hawkwing pointed out to Firefern. "They have bellyache as well, and you need juniper or watermint for that."

"Well, we *don't have* any juniper or watermint!" Firefern snapped. "And we do have borage."

"And what good will that do, if it's the wrong herb?" Hawkwing felt the heat of anger spreading through his pelt. "Firefern, are you completely mouse-brained?"

The ginger she-cat stared at him, shocked into silence. Hawkwing instantly realized how unfair he was being, to take his frustration out on a cat who was only trying to help.

"I'm sorry," he meowed, feeling close to his breaking point. *What right have I to tell Firefern she's wrong when I haven't the faintest idea which are the right herbs? We're all just guessing. It's hopeless, when we don't have a medicine cat.*

"It's okay, Hawkwing," Firefern responded. "I know how you feel. And look—even if the borage doesn't help, it can't do any harm, right? I'm going to fetch some."

While Firefern leaped nimbly up the rocks, Hawkwing gazed down at the three sick cats. Though Macgyver had been the first to get sick, Rileypool seemed to be the weakest; unconscious most of the time, and finding it difficult to eat even if some cat chewed his food up for him.

Hawkwing could hardly bear to look at Blossomheart, his bright, brave sister, lying there so limp and still. *Oh, StarClan, after all the cats I've lost, I can't lose the only littermate I have left!*

Firefern returned clutching some stems of borage in her jaws and started chewing them to a pulp. "If only we knew what this illness is," she mumbled around a mouthful.

"Well, Macgyver admitted he was so hungry he ate some crow-food," Hawkwing mused. "That might have caused it. And the others caught whatever it is from him, I guess. But that doesn't help."

"No," Firefern agreed. "The only thing that will help is to find Echosong."

She prodded Macgyver to rouse him and began pushing some of the pulped borage into his mouth. Macgyver lapped at it, muttered something inaudible, and lapsed back into unconsciousness.

"Hawkwing!" A cry sounded from across the camp.

Hawkwing whipped around to see Plumwillow heading toward him, supporting Finkit, who tottered along beside her on uncertain paws. Sagenose was helping to steady him on the other side; Dewkit and Reedkit followed, their eyes wide and scared.

"Finkit has the sickness!" Plumwillow wailed.

Hawkwing felt as if a dark fog had descended on him, blotting out the last traces of light and hope. The fear and tension that he felt were like claws in his belly, tearing him apart. *Not Finkit!*

"He was so good yesterday, soaking moss and fetching it so the sick cats could drink," Plumwillow went on as she and Finkit reached Hawkwing's side. "But I should have kept him away from them!"

"Every cat needs to keep away from them." Firefern looked up from treating the other patients. "Except for you and me, Hawkwing. We'd better make that a rule. Come on, Finkit," she added, "eat some of this nice borage."

"My belly aches," Finkit whimpered, but he bent his head and ate the borage without protesting.

Firefern nudged him into the nest with the others, and Blossomheart stirred slightly, wrapped her tail around him, and drew him closer.

"I'll stay and look after him," Plumwillow mewed.

Hawkwing stepped forward to block her with his tail. "No," he told her forcefully. "You have to take care of your other kits."

Plumwillow stared down at Finkit, then glanced over her

shoulder at Reedkit and Dewkit. The anguish in her eyes told Hawkwing how she was torn between them.

"Reedkit and Dewkit need you," he meowed gently. "I'll do the best I can for Finkit. You do trust me, don't you, Plumwillow?"

Plumwillow locked her gaze with his for a heartbeat, then dipped her head. "Yes, I do," she whispered. "But, oh, Hawkwing, you have to save him!"

Hawkwing wished he could promise her that Finkit would live, but he couldn't lie to her. They didn't know what the sickness was, and that made it nearly impossible to cure. He could see gratitude and grief in Plumwillow's eyes as she turned away, gathered her other kits closer with a sweep of her tail, and headed back to the crevice in the rocks where she had set up her nursery.

I can't promise anything. But I'll do everything I possibly can to save Finkit!

Hawkwing watched Plumwillow go, then spotted movement downstream: Leafstar was returning at the head of the hunting patrol that had gone out earlier. Their paw steps listless, their tails drooping with discouragement, the cats carried their prey over to the fresh-kill pile.

Such meager pickings! Hawkwing thought. *That'll never keep the Clan alive.*

Leafstar paused for a moment, gazing down regretfully at the scanty pile, then seemed to gather herself and padded over to the nest where the sick cats lay.

"How are they—" she began, then broke off as she saw that

Finkit had joined them. "Oh, no. Where is it all going to end?"

"We're doing the best we can," Firefern mewed.

Sagenose, who had stood by in silence all this time, turned to gaze at the ginger she-cat; Hawkwing thought his eyes looked blank and dead. "You know you're likely to catch it, right?"

"Tell me something I *don't* know," Firefern snapped.

"Every cat knows it," Sagenose meowed. "The more you treat the sick cats and get close to them, the more likely you are to get sick too."

"That may be true," Hawkwing responded, remembering what had happened to Finkit. He was nettled by his Clanmate's defeatist tone, though he reminded himself that Sagenose had lost his mate and his remaining kits by the lake. *I know how terrible that must have been.* "But medicine cats always treat the sick, no matter what they're risking," he finished.

Sagenose turned that blank, stone-cold stare on Hawkwing. "Right. But you and Firefern aren't medicine cats. None of us are. If we were, we might have some chance of curing the sick cats. Instead, we'll probably all get it, eventually."

Leafstar's shoulder fur had begun to bristle as Sagenose spoke. "What are you saying?" she demanded with a lash of her tail.

"I'm just pointing out that we have a choice here," Sagenose retorted.

"And what is that choice?" Leafstar hissed.

"We could split up," Sagenose replied. "Or send a group of cats to find Echosong."

Leafstar's lips drew back in the beginning of a snarl. "And just where do you suggest we do that?" she asked.

"I don't know," Sagenose admitted. "But a group of healthy cats moving around would have a better chance than we will if we just sit here waiting to die."

Leafstar's anger faded and her eyes were full of pain as she gazed at Hawkwing. "No," she meowed. "We will stay together. There are so few of us now. And isn't this what defines a Clan: that they stay together, even when things are hard? We have to believe that things will get better. We have to believe we will survive this. We have *no* choice, Sagenose!"

With that, she turned and stalked away. His gaze following her, Hawkwing tried not to let his misgivings show, for the sake of his Clan. But he couldn't be sure that they would survive this new challenge.

Two sunrises later, gazing down at the nest where the sick cats lay, Hawkwing was even less certain. True to Sagenose's prediction, Firefern too had fallen ill, the disease attacking her so fiercely that her paw steps were already leading her toward StarClan.

She exhausted herself helping the others, Hawkwing thought, *and now she hasn't the strength to fight the sickness.*

The other sick cats were no better. Rileypool seemed barely alive; Hawkwing had to watch carefully to see the faint rising and falling of his chest. He couldn't eat anymore, or even lap at soaked moss for a drink.

"Come on, Finkit," Hawkwing murmured encouragingly. "Look, I've some lovely mouse for you."

To his relief, the kit began licking at the mouse. Still keeping an eye on him, Hawkwing began to treat the others with borage, chewing up the leaves into a pulp and crouching beside each of his sick Clanmates until they licked it up. As he finished, he realized that Leafstar was standing beside him, looking down at the nest despairingly. She bent her head and touched her nose to Firefern's shoulder. "Oh, my daughter . . . ," she whispered. Then she straightened up and gave her pelt a shake. "I've been thinking about what Sagenose said," she began. "I hate to consider dividing the Clan, but I can't deny it any longer—we could all die of the sickness if we stay here together. The best chance we have is to split off some healthy cats to go look for Echosong."

"But what will happen to them?" Hawkwing asked, angling his ears toward the sick cats.

"I will stay with them," Leafstar replied, her voice full of love and sorrow. "They are my cats. I am sworn to protect them."

Hawkwing stood silent for a moment, hardly able to believe that it had come to this, that his Clan leader was forced to make these terrible decisions, without even StarClan to guide her. It had been so long since their warrior ancestors had spoken to them, even before Echosong had left.

I don't know whether I can bear to leave Blossomheart, or Finkit. He's like my own kit.

"You must lead the rest of the Clan," Leafstar continued, as if she knew what Hawkwing was thinking. "It's the only chance SkyClan has."

"Then we'll come back if we don't find Echosong within

three sunrises," Hawkwing suggested.

Leafstar shook her head emphatically. "You can't come back. Not until you find Echosong."

Hawkwing felt his throat burn as he had to accept his leader's order—the decree that meant he might never see Finkit and Blossomheart again.

"You must help me convince the others," Leafstar urged him. "It's SkyClan's best chance of surviving. And when you agreed to be deputy, you agreed to put SkyClan first. That's what we do, Hawkwing. It's the sacrifice we make."

Hawkwing dipped his head. "You're right, Leafstar. I'll do as you say."

Leafstar leaped up onto a nearby rock and let out a yowl. "Let all cats old enough to catch their own prey join here for a Clan meeting."

The cats of SkyClan began to creep into the open from cracks in the rock or tussocks of long grass where they had set up their makeshift dens. Pain gripped Hawkwing's heart at the sight of them: their ribs showing beneath tattered pelts, their eyes dull with despair. Prey had been scarce ever since they'd left the lake, and they were exhausted from constant travel. Hawkwing could see every one of Sagenose's ribs, while Tinycloud's pelt looked as if she hadn't groomed herself in a moon. Dewkit and Reedkit, who had once been strong and sturdy, looked so frail that a puff of wind could have blown them away.

Every cat gathered around Leafstar and waited in silence to hear what she would say.

"Cats of SkyClan," the Clan leader began, "you all know how desperate our plight is. Our Clanmates will die unless we can find Echosong, and if we stay here, sooner or later we will all catch the same sickness."

"What?" Plumwillow let out a cry of disbelief, her burning gaze fixed on Leafstar. "You can't mean you want the rest of us to leave our Clanmates?"

Leafstar returned Plumwillow's gaze solemnly. She didn't answer the warrior's question, but Hawkwing heard Plumwillow gasp as the truth sank in.

"You expect me to leave my own kit?"

Before Leafstar could respond, Hawkwing's ears pricked at the sound of a cat approaching.

Please, not an attack. StarClan, not now. The wind was blowing away from SkyClan, so there was no scent to tell him what might be approaching. He slid out his claws.

"Hello?" A familiar voice reached Hawkwing's ears.

Oh, StarClan, I can't believe it! I think I'll die of relief!

Hawkwing felt his entire body go slack. His Clanmates too were stirring around him, looking for the source of the sound, sudden hope in their eyes.

A silver tabby she-cat stepped out from among the trees, with two other cats trailing behind her. Hawkwing let out a triumphant yowl of welcome. *Oh, StarClan, thank you!*

"Echosong!"

CHAPTER 34

❧

The SkyClan medicine cat splashed through the stream, followed by Bellaleaf and Harrybrook, and padded up to her Clanmates. She, too, was thinner than when Hawkwing had last seen her, but her eyes were bright, and she looked strong. The healthy cats all crowded around her enthusiastically, purring and brushing their pelts against hers.

"Greetings, Echosong!"

"Welcome back!"

"Thank StarClan you found us!"

Hawkwing stared at Echosong, wondering if he was having some kind of weird waking dream. *After all the terrible things that have happened, I can't believe Echosong would return to us just when we need her most!* Then he reflected that if this wasn't real, all his Clanmates must be having the same dream. *It must be true! Echosong is really here!*

"But *how* did you find us?" Leafstar asked, struggling through the crowd to Echosong's side. "We've been looking for you for at least a moon."

Echosong's green eyes were brilliant as she replied. "It was easy! StarClan showed me where to go."

Warmth spread through Hawkwing's pelt, as if sunlight had broken through the storm-laden clouds overhead. *Then StarClan hasn't abandoned us!*

"I had a dream," Echosong continued. "A brown tabby tom spoke to me . . . I think he must be a medicine cat from the first SkyClan. He told me that my Clan had need of me, and that he would guide my paw steps."

"We certainly do need you," Leafstar responded. "We have sick cats, and we don't know what to do for them without a medicine cat."

"But you have Fidgetpaw. . . ." Echosong glanced around, her eyes puzzled. "Wait . . . no! Where is he?"

Several cats chimed in, telling Echosong how Fidgetpaw and more of their Clanmates had been trapped beside the lake, by the Twolegs with the weird cobweb-things on sticks. Hawkwing shuddered at the memory, imagining for a moment that he could still hear the harsh voices of the Twolegs and the terrified wails of his lost Clanmates.

"That's terrible!" Echosong exclaimed. "And our Clan deputy, too."

"Yes, Hawkwing is deputy now," Leafstar told her.

Echosong shot Hawkwing a pleased look. "Well, well. I can see I've a lot to catch up on," she mewed. "But first, show me the sick cats."

Hawkwing led Echosong to the nest where the sick cats lay. Harrybrook and Bellaleaf still followed her, and Bellaleaf let out a piercing wail as she saw her brother Rileypool curled up motionless among the moss and leaves. "*No! He's dead!*"

Echosong held her paw close to Rileypool's nose, and Hawkwing saw the faint ruffle of her fur that showed Rileypool still breathed.

"He lives," Echosong said in a grave voice, "but barely."

"Oh, thank StarClan! Please help him!" Bellaleaf begged.

"I'm going to do just that," Echosong reassured her. "Hawkwing, what have you done so far?"

"We gave them borage," Hawkwing replied, pointing with his tail to a heap of the herb beside the nest. "That's right, for fever, isn't it?"

"Yes, it would be right, if that was borage." Echosong turned over a few of the stems with one paw. "But it's not, it's comfrey."

Hawkwing felt as if all the blood was draining from his heart, and he saw black sparkles in the sky. "StarClan, no!" he gasped. "Have I been poisoning them?" *It's like everything has to go wrong for SkyClan, even when we try our best,* he thought, his pelt growing hot with guilt.

Echosong shook her head. "No, we use a poultice of comfrey root for wounds," she explained. "The leaves aren't good for much, that I know of, but they wouldn't do any harm. But now I need to find some real borage."

Hawkwing sent Sparrowpelt and Tinycloud with Echosong into the trees in case of trouble. The patrol returned quickly, Echosong carrying a bunch of herbs in her jaws.

"We're lucky that so far there hasn't been a frost," she mewed as she dropped the stems beside the sick cats' nest. "That kills off herbs quicker than anything."

Hawkwing bent his head to examine the herbs Echosong had brought. He saw that the leaves of borage looked very much like comfrey, but the scent was quite different. *A medicine cat would have known that.*

Echosong chewed up the leaves and managed to force the pulp between the sick cats' jaws. Hawkwing watched intently, hoping for some sign of improvement, even though he knew it was far too soon to expect any change.

"They will get better, won't they?" Bellaleaf asked; she had stayed crouched beside her brother ever since she returned.

"That's in the paws of StarClan," Echosong replied, but then added, "I've seen cats recover from worse illness than this."

"I wish there was something I could do," Bellaleaf meowed.

"There is," Hawkwing told her briskly. "Lead a hunting patrol, and bring back some prey for them when they wake up."

Bellaleaf glanced at Rileypool, clearly reluctant to leave him, then rose to her paws. "Right away, Hawkwing. I'll find some other cats."

"You're right to keep her busy," Echosong mewed to Hawkwing when Bellaleaf had gone. "I wouldn't say this in front of her, but I'm not hopeful for Rileypool. Firefern, too. They're both very far gone."

A heavy knot of dread gathered in Hawkwing's belly as he braced himself to ask the next question. "And Finkit?"

Echosong sighed, looking at the kit's frail chest as it rose and fell. "It's hard to say. He has youth on his side. But he's so tiny. . . ."

Hawkwing felt like his heart was being squeezed so tightly it might burst. He had to look away.

Please, StarClan, if anything I've ever done has pleased you . . . please, spare that kit.

The last warriors of StarClan were fading from the sky as the dawn light strengthened. In the middle of the rocky hollow the cats of SkyClan crouched around the bodies of their Clanmates, stiff and cold in death, with frost sparkling in their fur.

Hawkwing tried to find some consolation in looking at the cats who had survived the sickness. Macgyver and Blossomheart were out of danger, though still weak and shaky. And Finkit looked desperately small and skinny beside his robust littermates, but he was gaining strength every day. A small spark of joy kindled inside Hawkwing as he remembered the moment when Finkit had opened his eyes, wailing plaintively for his mother and complaining about how hungry he was.

But his joy was quenched when he looked at the bodies of Rileypool and Firefern, who were lost to the illness. *They'll never hunt again, never have an apprentice to mentor, never take a mate or have kits. . . .*

As the sky grew flushed with rose and amber where the sun would rise, Echosong rose to her paws and took a few paces forward to stand beside her dead Clanmates. "May StarClan light your path, Firefern and Rileypool," she mewed, using the words which medicine cats had spoken beside the dead for seasons upon seasons. "May you find good hunting, swift running, and shelter when you sleep."

Her words signaled the end of the vigil. Cats began to rise and stretch the stiffness out of their muscles. With no elders remaining in the Clan, Hawkwing was wondering who to choose to take care of the burial, when Leafstar also rose and came to stand beside Echosong.

"We have lost two valuable Clanmates," she began, then stopped as her voice quivered on the last few words.

Hawkwing understood how difficult this was for his Clan leader. It was her duty to inspire her Clan, and yet she was also grieving as a mother. Only Harrybrook remained of the kits she and Billystorm had together, and Billystorm himself was gone, buried in a remote place where Leafstar would never set paw.

The Clan leader took several deep breaths and gave her pelt a shake. "Yet it's important that we go on believing in our Clan," she went on, in command of herself again. "Rileypool and Firefern believed, and I believe, that StarClan will guide us to a brighter future."

"I'd like to believe that too." Plumwillow spoke up from where she sat beside her kits. "But if StarClan wants to guide us, why hasn't Echosong had another vision?"

It was Echosong who replied. "I had the dream that led me back to you," she pointed out. "And that means that StarClan has broken their silence."

"Then why hasn't StarClan just told you where to find the lake and the other Clans?" Sagenose challenged her.

"Visions don't work like that," Echosong told him, a hint of regret in her voice. "StarClan shows me what it wants to show, when it wants to show me. We must all have faith."

"We've had faith ever since we were driven out of the gorge," Plumwillow meowed bitterly. "If StarClan cares for us, surely they would have given us some better guidance by now? We've been tramping through barren territory for so long!" She let out a contemptuous snort. "Does StarClan *enjoy* seeing us suffer like this? How can we still be loyal to them?"

Gasps of dismay came from some of her Clanmates, but others were nodding and murmuring agreement.

"You mustn't talk like that," Hawkwing protested.

"Yes, StarClan must have a reason for what they tell us—or don't tell us," Echosong agreed.

"Maybe their 'reason' is that they've forgotten us!" Plumwillow snapped. "Wouldn't we all live better lives if we gave up the idea of finding the lake? We've had no home for so long—are we truly a Clan anymore, or just a tattered, undernourished group of rogues?"

Yowls of protest arose from some of the cats around her, though Hawkwing could see that others still agreed with Plumwillow. *And I'm trying desperately hard not to be one of them.*

"We are and always will be a Clan." Leafstar's voice cut through the noise. "I will never lose faith that eventually we will find the other Clans and the home where we are meant to live."

"Leafstar is right," Echosong added. "StarClan has sent me one dream, and I know others will follow."

"We might wait for that until our tails drop off!" Sagenose huffed.

Hawkwing rose to stand beside Leafstar and Echosong. "Rogue cats only look out for themselves," he pointed out. "Clan cats help each other, and that's what we've been doing all along. Of course we're a Clan, and we must go on believing there are better times ahead."

Plumwillow gave him a furious glare. "You've got bees in your brain, Hawkwing!"

I can understand why she's angry with me, Hawkwing thought. *And in a way she's right. I wish I didn't see so much truth in her words.*

Even though Hawkwing knew he had to support his Clan leader and his medicine cat, he was inwardly torn. He could easily imagine the kind of life he could have with Plumwillow and her kits if they abandoned the rest of the Clan and found a cozy cave, or perhaps a barn like the one where Barley lived. If they had only themselves to feed, they would all get more prey.

Plumwillow has never been my mate, but it's been so long now since Sandynose and Pebbleshine disappeared. . . . Maybe she and I could be together, someday.

Hawkwing pushed away the enticing vision. *No, my first duty is to my Clan.*

While Hawkwing was thinking, the argument had raged on around him. He began to realize that it didn't matter what he or any cat said: Most of his Clanmates were too beaten down by the onset of leaf-bare, the endless wandering, the losses of their Clanmates, and the silence from StarClan to have any hope for the future.

"SkyClan is dead," Plumwillow stated flatly. "It has been, really, ever since we were driven out of the gorge. Are we trying to revive something we should have given up on long ago?" She lashed her tail; her kits were staring up at her with huge, bewildered eyes. "Nothing lasts forever," she continued. "The original SkyClan died out, too."

Hawkwing could see Leafstar's anguish in her eyes and the drooping of her shoulders. For a few moments she was silent, and the conflicting voices died away as every cat turned to her.

"I can't hold cats hostage if they want to leave." Leafstar's words were forced out. "But let us not decide while tempers are high and the bodies of our Clanmates lie beside us. Tomorrow I will call a Clan meeting and we will discuss this again."

To Hawkwing's relief, murmurs of agreement met his leader's suggestion. Even Plumwillow had nothing more to say.

Hawkwing glanced around the group of cats and beckoned with his tail to Sparrowpelt, Sagenose, Bellaleaf, and Rabbitleap. "Please carry Firefern and Rileypool out of camp and bury them," he directed.

He watched the cats he had chosen carefully lift the bodies of their Clanmates and bear them away, padding downstream to where a hawthorn bush hung over the water. The rest of the cats began to disperse. Clan life continued on, but Hawkwing's heart was still heavy.

Is this the end of SkyClan?

"Great StarClan, you're alive!"

The joyful yowl roused Hawkwing from sleep. The pale

sun of leaf-bare was shining through the branches of the thornbush where he had made his den, and there was a stir of movement outside in the camp. He sprang to his paws, scattering moss from his nest.

It's so late . . . I should have sent out the patrols! And what is going on out there?

Hawkwing bounded out into the camp and halted as if he had slammed into a tree. *It can't be! But . . .*

Across the rocky hollow, Sandynose was standing just outside the nursery, with Plumwillow beside him, purring ecstatically. The two cats had twined their tails together, and Sandynose was covering Plumwillow's head with loving licks.

A rush of emotion shook Hawkwing like a leaf in a gale. He felt wonder and relief that Sandynose was still alive, and had found his Clan again after so long, but warring with that was grief at the way Plumwillow was greeting him so happily.

Hawkwing stood still for a few heartbeats, grappling with the hurt he felt at being forgotten. Since the kits had been born, Plumwillow had often turned to him for advice or support, but she had never looked at him with that blaze of happiness in her eyes. *Of course she didn't,* Hawkwing thought to himself, feeling foolish, *Sandynose is her real mate. Her Pebbleshine.*

At the thought of his own mate, his breath caught. Then he asked himself how he would react if Pebbleshine suddenly came back to him, alive.

Plumwillow rubbed her cheek against Sandynose's, purring loudly enough for Hawkwing to hear it across the hollow.

Yes, it would be just like that.

"But what happened to you?" Plumwillow asked, when their first joyous reunion was over.

"Fallowfern and I were trapped in a Twoleg den," Sandy-nose explained. He waved his tail, and for the first time Hawkwing noticed that Fallowfern was standing a couple of fox-lengths away. "The stupid creatures wouldn't let us out, and it took us a half moon or so to outwit them and get away. We went back to the gorge, but it was full of rogues, so we went into the Twolegplace to find Ebonyclaw. She told us you were heading for Barley's barn, and we decided to follow."

"Did you get there?" Blossomheart asked urgently as more cats crowded up to greet the newcomers. "Did you see Cherry-tail and Cloudmist?"

Hawkwing waited tensely for the answer.

"Yes, and they're both fine," Sandynose replied. "Getting nice and fat on Barley's mice! So then," he continued his story, "Barley showed us the right direction, and we've been wandering, trying to find you, ever since."

"But how did you?" Tinycloud asked. "We've traveled so far!"

"Finally we came to a lake," Sandynose replied. "The hunting was good, so we settled there for a while. We met a kittypet—he said his name was Max—and he told us cats had been living there for a while, so that gave us hope we would catch up to you sooner or later. And now we can't believe our luck!" he finished, with a loving look at his mate. "Plumwillow is alive—and our kits. Oh, StarClan, can I meet them?"

Her eyes shining proudly, Plumwillow turned back to the

nursery and called to her kits. They emerged drowsily into the open, and Hawkwing could recognize the uncertainty and confusion in their eyes as they gazed up at Sandynose.

"Kits, this is your father," Plumwillow explained.

Reedkit blinked in bewilderment, glancing from Sandynose to Hawkwing and back again. "But . . . I thought Hawkwing was our father," she mewed.

Plumwillow gave her chest fur a couple of embarrassed licks. "No," she responded. "Hawkwing has helped me look after you since you were born, and he loves you very much, but he isn't your father. Sandynose is your father."

Sandynose turned his head to look at Hawkwing, surprised and not entirely pleased. His eyes narrowed and the tip of his tail switched. Hawkwing's pelt grew hot as he shared Plumwillow's embarrassment, and his heart began to pound as he wondered what Sandynose would say.

"It's okay," Plumwillow meowed rapidly, before her mate could speak. "Hawkwing helped me when I had a hard time at my kitting, and he's been a huge help with the kits ever since. He lost his mate, too, so we had lots to talk about—just as friends."

Hawkwing nodded, feeling how weird this was, and how he wanted to make it absolutely clear to Sandynose that he hadn't stolen his mate. *And now, I'm never going to.* "That's right, just as friends," he confirmed.

Sandynose relaxed. "Thank you, Hawkwing," he murmured. "I can never repay you for keeping my family safe."

"Uh . . . don't mention it," Hawkwing responded. He was

trying hard to hide the hurt he felt, as he remembered all the good times he had spent with the kits, playing and telling stories and beginning to teach them all they would need to know.

There'll be times like that again. Hawkwing tried to believe that, but he knew he was deceiving himself.

Watching the kits chatting eagerly with their real father, Hawkwing felt the truth settle over him like a weight on his chest. *It will never be the same.*

By now all the cats were awake, vying to tell Sandynose about their experiences since they left the gorge. Hawkwing watched sadly as Fallowfern struggled with the news that her mate Waspwhisker had been taken by Twolegs at the lake.

"So what's next for the Clan?" Sandynose asked eventually. "Do you have any idea where you're going?"

Hawkwing remembered that Sandynose had already been lost when Echosong had her vision of the Clan living beside a lake. Sandynose's eyes grew wide with wonder as she told him about it.

"At first, we thought the lake where you met Max was the place in my vision," the medicine cat explained. "But we were wrong. Too many Twolegs came there in greenleaf, and there was nowhere left for cats to live in peace."

"So we moved on." Leafstar took up the story. "But we haven't found the lake of Echosong's vision, and now we've come to a . . . a place where a decision must be made. Some cats are losing hope, and there are still moons of leaf-bare to come. Do we keep going, or do we split up and admit that SkyClan is . . . dead?"

"I'm sorry, Leafstar." Plumwillow turned to her Clan leader, hope sparkling in her eyes. "For everything I said yesterday. Seeing Sandynose and Fallowfern again has given me a change of heart. How could we ever have found each other again if we weren't all destined to be together?"

"That's right," Sagenose—who had been almost as certain as Plumwillow that SkyClan had no future—agreed. "If Sandynose and Fallowfern could find us, then there's hope that the others who stayed by the gorge, or even the cats who were lost by the lake, might come back to us someday." He raised his head and let out a triumphant yowl. "Long live Sky-Clan!"

"Long live SkyClan! Long live SkyClan!" his Clanmates chorused around him. Their eyes shone with enthusiasm and commitment, and Hawkwing felt that he was part of the strong SkyClan that he remembered, not a ragtag band of cats who were scarcely better than rogues or loners.

Hawkwing saw the relief that flooded into Leafstar's amber eyes. He shared it, and yet he found himself struggling with conflicting emotions.

I'm glad that SkyClan lives on. But what is my place in it now?

Hawkwing led out a hunting patrol, and returned to find Plumwillow and Sandynose playing with the kits outside the nursery. Sandynose was tossing a ball of moss to each kit in turn, catching it when they batted it back to him.

"Hey, Hawkwing, come and join us!" he called as Hawkwing padded past.

Hawkwing deposited his prey on the fresh-kill pile, then bounded over to the nursery. All three kits leaped up as he approached, jumping on him with mock growls and battering at him with their soft paws.

"Stinky badger!" Finkit snarled. "Get out of our camp!"

"Yes," Dewkit added. "Get out or we'll rip your fur off!"

Hawkwing rolled over and pretended to be terrified. He caught a glimpse of Sandynose, who was looking a little hurt as he watched the game.

How would I feel, he asked himself, *if I was reunited with my kits at this age? I'd be very jealous of any cat who raised them in my place.*

"Sorry, kits," he mewed, rising to his paws and shaking them off gently. "I have to go and speak to Leafstar."

Padding away, he felt as much pain as if they had really ripped his fur off, but he knew that he was doing the right thing.

Tiny paws were prodding Hawkwing all over, and he blinked himself awake. Shaking off sleep, he realized it was still the middle of the night; in the faint light of the moon he made out Dewkit, Reedkit, and Finkit standing over him.

"What are you doing here?" he asked. "You should be in the nursery with Plumwillow."

"*He's* there," Reedkit mewed with a disdainful flick of her tail.

"We want you to tell us what's going on," Finkit explained. "*You're* our father, not this stranger."

"Yeah, can't you send him away?" Dewkit asked. "You're

Clan deputy; every cat has to do what you tell them."

Hawkwing stared at them; for a moment he didn't know where to start. "Plumwillow would be very sad if I sent Sandynose away," he began at last.

Reedkit shrugged. "She didn't seem like she was all that sad before he came back."

Hawkwing beckoned the kits to come and snuggle down with him in the moss and bracken of his nest, away from the frosty night breeze.

"Now listen," he meowed. "Plumwillow chose Sandynose to be your father, not me, and—"

"Then she's a stupid furball!" Finkit interrupted.

Hawkwing gave him a gentle tap on the nose, his claws carefully sheathed. "That's no way to talk about your mother," he scolded, then went on, "I had a mate, too, and she was expecting my kits. Her name was Pebbleshine, and I loved her very much. But a Twoleg monster carried her away, and I lost her."

All three kits' eyes were round with dismay; Hawkwing realized this was the first time they had heard the details of what had happened. "That's terrible!" Reedkit breathed out.

"If I found my kits now," Hawkwing continued, struggling to keep his voice even, "I would want the chance to be a father to them, even though nothing could make up for the time we lost. Can you understand that?"

"Sort of . . . ," Reedkit replied.

"And Sandynose loves all of you very much, just as I would love my kits if I could meet them. But he's only just getting to know you. You have to give him time."

"But does that mean you *can't* be our father anymore?" Dewkit asked. "Can't we have two?"

Hawkwing suppressed a *mrrow* of laughter. "I'm not sure," he meowed, his amusement giving way to sadness. "Sandynose is a great cat. I want to give you space to get to know him."

Reedkit hunched her shoulders with a mutinous look. "I don't *want* to know him!"

"That's unkind." Hawkwing stretched out his tail and gave the little she-kit a gentle flick around her ears. "You don't want to hurt Sandynose, do you?"

"No, but . . ." Reedkit gave her pelt a shake. "It's not fair!"

"Everything was fine before Sandynose came," Dewkit agreed. "Why does it all have to change?"

Hawkwing took a deep breath, trying to find some way of persuading the kits to trust Sandynose. "Your father and mother make each other very happy," he began at last. "And they want you to be part of that happiness. You can't do that if you won't give Sandynose a chance. He'll be a really good father, I know he will."

"I guess he's okay," Finkit muttered doubtfully. "But he's not *you*, Hawkwing."

Hawkwing felt that love and pain were going to tear him apart. "I'm not your father. But that doesn't mean I don't care for you," he reassured the kits. "I'll always be here to help you if you ever need me."

The three kits exchanged disappointed glances. "I guess we can be nicer to Sandynose," Reedkit mewed. "But he doesn't know about being a badger and all the other games you play with us."

"Give him time," Hawkwing responded, touching noses with each of the kits in turn. "Now, off you go, back to the nursery before Plumwillow misses you."

Wriggling out of his nest, the kits scampered off. Hawkwing watched them across the camp, his heart feeling hollow and empty.

Will I ever be able to raise kits of my own?

CHAPTER 35

❧

SkyClan spent a few more days in the rocky hollow, until the sick cats had recovered enough to travel, and Sandynose and Fallowfern had rested from their wanderings. Then Leafstar gave the order to move on.

"You lead us this time," she meowed to Echosong. "StarClan guided your paws to find us; perhaps they'll guide you to the lake and the other Clans."

But if that was true, Hawkwing thought, StarClan was taking their time about it.

A few days later, the Clan emerged from a narrow valley to see the dens of a Twolegplace spread out in front of them. The air above it looked hazy; a faint, harsh tang reached them on the breeze and in the distance they could hear the roar of monsters.

"I don't want to go that way," Plumwillow meowed. "I don't want to be near Twolegs ever again!"

Hawkwing, standing beside her near the front of the group, rested his tail-tip reassuringly on her shoulder. "I know," he murmured. "But maybe we have to."

"But we might meet some of those weird yellow Twolegs," Finkit objected.

"Yes, and they'll scoop us up in their cobweb-things and take us away!" Dewkit added, his eyes huge with apprehension.

Hawkwing saw that Leafstar and Echosong were deep in conversation, though he was too far away to hear what they were saying. A moment later Leafstar leaped up onto a nearby rock and raised her voice to address the rest of the Clan.

"Echosong says this is the way we must go," the Clan leader meowed. "But we'll try to pass alongside the Twoleg dens, so we don't risk meeting many Twolegs or monsters."

"*One* Twoleg is too many," Sagenose muttered.

"We can travel by night," Echosong pointed out. "That way most of the Twolegs and their monsters will be asleep in their nests."

"So we'll rest here until the sun goes down," Leafstar continued. "Every cat should hunt and then try to get some sleep."

The rocky valley didn't offer much prey, but Hawkwing managed to catch a rabbit and Sandynose caught a shrew while Plumwillow found a sheltered spot where the kits could take a nap. They all settled down together after they had shared the fresh-kill, Hawkwing a short distance away.

He found it impossible to sleep. The lake where they were to meet the other Clans had never seemed so far away.

The sky was streaked red with the last traces of sunlight when the cats of SkyClan set out again, padding cautiously across the open space that separated them from the Twoleg-place. The acrid tang in the air grew stronger and harsh yellow light spilled out onto the ground as they approached the dens. Monsters roared up and down the Thunderpaths, beams from their huge eyes slicing through the gathering darkness.

Leafstar and Hawkwing kept their Clanmates bunched together as they slipped between the dens, darting from one clot of shadow to the next, crouching in a shivering cluster as monsters or Twolegs passed by. Hawkwing couldn't forget his lost Clanmates' despairing wails as the Twolegs carried them off from the lake camp.

After what seemed like a moon, he felt himself relax as he and his Clanmates left the last of the Twoleg dens behind and headed out across a stretch of open ground covered with coarse grass and scrubby bushes. The grass stems were stiff and spiky, furred with frost, pricking the cats' pads as they trudged over them. But in spite of the discomfort, and a cold wind buffeting their fur, Hawkwing sensed the easing of tension among his Clanmates too.

The sky was beginning to grow pale with the light of dawn, showing a belt of woodland crossing their path, the leafless branches outlined against the sky.

"Trees!" Sparrowpelt exclaimed. "Thank StarClan!"

Sandynose swiped his tongue around his jaws. "And where there are trees, there'll be prey."

But when the cats arrived under the trees, they found that there was little undergrowth, and the scanty prey-scents were faint and growing stale.

"I think all the prey is hiding away down their holes," Tinycloud grumbled.

Plumwillow managed to track down a mouse, which she gave to her kits to share, and Sparrowpelt caught a squirrel after a frantic dash through the branches, but none of the other cats had any luck.

Then Hawkwing caught sight of a few rabbit holes in a steep bank on the far side of the trees. His whiskers twitched at the scent of rabbit. "Look over there," he murmured to Leafstar. "I could go down one of those holes and scare the rabbits out."

"You will *not*," Leafstar replied decisively. "I don't want my deputy stuck down a rabbit hole. If we wait, maybe they'll come out on their own."

Hawkwing sighed. "Okay."

As the dawn light strengthened, most of the Clan settled down at the edge of the wood, their gazes fixed on the rabbit holes. Plumwillow and Sandynose kept their kits well back among the trees, so the kits wouldn't make a noise and scare away the prey.

Eventually Hawkwing saw a flicker of movement at the mouth of one of the burrows, and a rabbit hopped into the open. It halted a fox-length away from the opening and began to nibble the grass.

"Wait a few moments," Hawkwing whispered, his jaws beginning to water. "Let it come out a bit further before we attack."

He had scarcely finished speaking when a flash of ginger erupted from the top of the bank. A ginger tom leaped straight onto the rabbit, pinning it down with his claws and cutting off its squeal with a bite to the neck.

"Hey!" Macgyver called out, jumping to his paws. "That was ours!"

The ginger tom paused in the act of stooping to pick up his prey. "Yours?" he snarled. "My claws. My teeth. *My* prey."

Macgyver stalked out into the open, followed by the rest of the Clan. "Shove off, flea-pelt!" he snapped.

The ginger tom's fur bristled and he crouched over the body of the rabbit, ready to spring. He didn't look at all intimidated by the number of cats surrounding him.

Hawkwing exchanged an uneasy glance with Leafstar. The tom was no full-fed kittypet; he was clearly a rogue or a loner, and he looked just as thin and desperate as the SkyClan cats.

"We can't risk a fight," Leafstar murmured. "We've enough problems without that. Besides, he *is* the one who caught the rabbit."

"I'll deal with it," Hawkwing responded, an idea slipping into his mind.

He padded forward, gesturing with his tail for his Clan-mates to keep back. "Okay," he meowed to the ginger tom. "You can keep the prey if you'll answer a few questions."

The tom narrowed his eyes. "What questions?"

"Is there a big lake around here?" Hawkwing began. "One that's so big you can stand on the shore and hardly see the other side."

The tom's hostility began to fade, replaced by confusion. He shook his head. "There's nowhere like that around here."

A chill of despair began to creep through Hawkwing's pelt, but he went on. "Then do you know about any Clans of cats nearby?"

The ginger tom twitched his whiskers, puzzled. "Clans?"

"Cats like us," Hawkwing mewed.

The tom raked his gaze across the SkyClan warriors and gave a disdainful sniff. "Mange-ridden prey-stealers, you mean?"

A low growl came from Sparrowpelt's throat, but Hawkwing glared at him and flicked his tail at his Clanmate for silence.

"Clan cats live in a group together," Leafstar explained, padding up beside Hawkwing. "We look after each other and train our young ones."

"Really?" The ginger tom sneered. "That doesn't seem to have done you much good, does it?"

Hawkwing winced at the truth behind the tom's words. "Have you seen any cats like that?" he asked.

"No. Never heard of *Clans* before. Never want to hear about them again. You've all got brains full of feathers!"

Without waiting for a response, the ginger tom snatched up the rabbit, bounded up the bank past the burrows, and vanished from sight.

"That went well," Hawkwing sighed.

"We'd better move on," Leafstar meowed, above the angry muttering of her Clan. "It sounds like we've still got a long way to go."

Finally, after more than two moons, the cats of SkyClan made camp in a copse of oaks and gorse bushes, where the ground was covered with bracken and bramble thickets, offering some shelter from the cold.

"We'll rest here for a few days," Leafstar decided. "Tonight is the full moon, when StarClan draws closest to us. Perhaps they will send us a sign at last."

Every cat was too exhausted that night to do more than curl up where they stood. The following morning, Hawkwing began to make a proper nest for himself in the bracken. As he pulled at the dead brown stems, he noticed tiny new fronds beginning to uncurl in the depths of the clump. The biting green color brought a sudden surge of hope in his heart.

Maybe this long, miserable leaf-bare is coming to an end at last.

Looking up, Hawkwing spotted Echosong speaking urgently to Leafstar across the makeshift camp. He hardly had time to wonder what that was all about before Leafstar raised her head and let out a yowl.

"Let all cats old enough to catch their own prey join here in the middle of the camp for a Clan meeting!"

Cats slid out of the bracken where, like Hawkwing, they had been making their nests. Plumwillow's kits bounced to the front of the crowd, with Sandynose and Plumwillow just behind them. Bellaleaf sat beside Fallowfern and Blossomheart, while Sparrowpelt and Macgyver padded up from the opposite side of the camp. The rest of the Clan gathered around; Hawkwing could feel a sense of tension in the air, as if every cat was expecting something to happen.

He bounded over to join his Clanmates, noticing that Leafstar's amber eyes were glowing and her whiskers quivering.

She's excited about something, he thought, *and she's doing a poor job of hiding it.*

When the entire Clan had assembled, Leafstar let her gaze travel over her cats. "Echosong has had another vision," she announced. Raising her voice to carry over the eager exclamations from the rest of the Clan, she added, "Echosong, please tell us about it."

The medicine cat stepped up to Leafstar's side and raised her head; her beautiful green eyes were full of joy and gratitude. "I was tempted to lose hope, after we had been traveling for so long," she began. "But last night, under the light of the full moon, I begged StarClan to send me a sign that we were still on the right track—that SkyClan had a future to share, and not merely a past."

"And they answered you?" Tinycloud asked.

"Yes, I had a vision," Echosong replied. "I saw Skystar, the pale gray tom who first appeared to me in the Whispering Cave, and told me to find the spark that remains."

"What did he say this time?" Sparrowpelt asked eagerly.

"He told me, 'Embrace what you find in the shadows, for only they can clear the sky,'" Echosong announced to the Clan.

"Well, that's *really* helpful!" Sagenose exclaimed with a disgusted twitch of his whiskers.

"Yes, why does StarClan have to be so *vague*?" Plumwillow demanded. "Would it hurt them to tell us *clearly* so we can understand?"

More cats jumped in with their comments and suggestions, and as the arguments rose Echosong had to wave her tail vigorously for silence. "Skystar showed me a five-pointed maple leaf," Echosong told the Clan, "and said that now SkyClan is scattered like leaves, blown by the wind."

"We *know* that," Sagenose muttered.

Echosong ignored the interruption. "But then he told me to look at the leaf."

Hawkwing's pads prickled with irritation at this incomprehensible message. Glancing around, he realized that his Clanmates were just as bewildered as he was. Confused murmuring arose from them as they exchanged puzzled glances. Hawkwing felt as though he was wandering in a fog, and that StarClan's sign had made it even harder to decide what path they should take.

Then Hawkwing noticed that a look of understanding was spreading over Leafstar's face, her amber eyes glowing with sudden excitement. "I see!" she exclaimed. "A leaf with five points—and including SkyClan, there are five Clans! We *are* on the right track. StarClan wants us to find the other Clans."

Cats turned to each other, eagerly discussing what they had just heard. Then Blossomheart spoke up. "That's all very well, but that's what we already thought they meant. And it doesn't exactly tell us what to *do*."

Echosong dipped her head. "True. StarClan never makes it easy for us. But I asked for a sign that we were on the right track—and we are! StarClan hasn't forgotten us."

Her Clanmates nodded in agreement. Hawkwing's gaze fell on the tender new fern fronds uncurling in the midst of the dead brown growth of previous seasons. Beside them was a single yellow flower of coltsfoot, glowing like a tiny sun. *Maybe new hope is coming after all. Maybe SkyClan will be rewarded for surviving this miserable leaf-bare.*

All morning a stiff breeze had been blowing, driving gray clouds across the sky. Now rain fell in a sharp, freezing shower, sending the SkyClan cats diving for shelter in the bushes. Hawkwing crouched underneath some thickly growing holly branches, licking the icy drops from his fur and struggling to hold on to his earlier optimism.

StarClan has chosen to speak to us again. I must hold on to that.

When at last the rain had passed, Leafstar called the cats back into the middle of the camp.

"There is one more thing to do," she announced, "and one of the most important duties of a Clan leader. Dewkit, Finkit, Reedkit, come here."

Exchanging wondering glances, the three kits padded up to stand in front of Leafstar, while Plumwillow let out a soft wail.

"Just *look* at them! It's as if they'd been pulled through the bushes backward! Why does Leafstar never give us any notice?"

"Today it is my task to make three new apprentices," Leafstar went on. "And I can think of no better way to commit ourselves to the future under the guidance of StarClan." Beckoning Dewkit with her tail, she continued, "From this day forward, this apprentice will be known as Dewpaw. Macgyver, you gave up your life as a kittypet to follow SkyClan. I trust you will pass on your commitment to Dewpaw as his mentor."

A look of pleased surprise gathered on Macgyver's face as

Dewpaw trotted up to him and stretched up to touch his nose.

"Dewpaw! Dewpaw!"

Hawkwing joined in as his Clanmates chanted the new apprentice's name, then watched proudly as Leafstar apprenticed Finkit to Blossomheart and Reedkit to Bellaleaf.

"Finpaw! Reedpaw! Finpaw! Reedpaw!" the Clan called out, while the new apprentices glowed with excitement.

Hawkwing felt a moment's pang that he wasn't to mentor one of his beloved kits, then reflected that if he had been the mentor for one of them, the other two would have felt left out, and discontented with their own mentors.

Leafstar has chosen well.

He thought back over all the moons of their journey, remembering the effort it had taken to keep the kits safe and together—not to mention keeping the rest of SkyClan safe, too, so that they would see this day. *Dogs, Twolegs, sickness . . . we have survived them all.* Now he felt that SkyClan was waking from a bad dream, and these eager young cats were its future.

He spotted Plumwillow casting him a grateful look, and dipped his head in acknowledgment. He could see in her eyes that she recognized how hard this was for him. Since Sandynose's return, Hawkwing hadn't tried to speak to her alone, not wanting to get into the middle of their happiness. But he felt a warm glow inside at the thought that Plumwillow remembered what he had done for her family.

All three apprentices were crowding around Plumwillow and Sandynose, eagerly discussing their ceremony. "Wasn't it amazing when the whole Clan called out our names?" Reedpaw meowed.

"It felt great!" Dewpaw puffed out his chest. "I'm going to be the best apprentice ever."

"No, you're not! I am!" Finpaw insisted, swiping at his brother's ear.

Sandynose separated the two young cats with a gentle paw before they could start tussling. "That's enough of that," he told them. "You have to behave yourselves and listen to your mentors. Then you'll *all* be great warriors one day."

"We will!" the new apprentices promised him fervently.

Hawkwing could see that they were well on the way to accepting Sandynose, and he determinedly crushed down a small pang of regret.

Then the kits broke away from their parents and came scampering across to him.

"We're apprentices now!" Finpaw announced. "Isn't it great?"

"I'm very proud of all of you," Hawkwing told them. "You've survived incredibly difficult times to become apprentices. And I truly believe that you will see SkyClan flourish again."

"I believe that, too!" Dewpaw assured him.

At last the kits left, scurrying off excitedly to join their mentors.

"I want to catch a mouse!" Reedpaw squealed, flinging herself at Bellaleaf. "Show me how!"

"Stop squealing like that, for a start," Bellaleaf responded, wryly amused. "Come on, I'll teach you the hunter's crouch."

"Us too!" Finpaw demanded, bouncing up to Blossomheart, while Dewpaw skidded to a halt in front of Macgyver.

All three mentors led their apprentices to a flat grassy area at the side of the camp, where Blossomheart began demonstrating the hunter's crouch.

As he watched them go, listening to their eager chatter, a familiar hollowness swelled inside Hawkwing. *These are not my kits,* he reminded himself. *They will always have a place in my heart, but they can't truly fill the hole Pebbleshine and our kits have left behind.*

His paws led him to the top of a rocky bluff overlooking the camp. Wind ruffling his fur, Hawkwing raised his head to gaze at the sky, where the clouds were rapidly clearing.

What will fill my heart, then? Hawkwing asked himself. He didn't feel the despair he had struggled with all leaf-bare, but he also didn't have any answer to his question.

"My brave warrior, with the wings of a hawk." Echosong padded up beside him and settled down with her paws tucked under her. She met his gaze, curiosity in her green eyes. "What do you see when you look at the horizon?" she asked.

Hawkwing gazed out across the vista of rolling hills and trees, and considered the medicine cat's words. There was only one honest answer. "The future," he replied.

"That's no small task," Echosong responded, "after the tragedies we've all suffered. It takes a strong cat to see the future, instead of getting lost in the past."

Hawkwing looked down at her. "Do you think we'll find the other Clans?"

"I *know* we will, for StarClan has told me so," Echosong replied. "And they've told me something else, too."

Hawkwing waited curiously, but for a few heartbeats Echosong didn't go on.

"After I went back to sleep," she continued at last, "I had a vision of a young she-cat who looked exactly like you, Hawkwing. At her paws was a maple leaf, and she nodded down to its five points. Do you know what that means?"

Hawkwing stared at her, stunned. *What could that mean?* "She looked just like me?" he stammered. "Then . . . she . . . could she be my kin?"

Echosong nodded sagely. "Your kin . . . or perhaps even your kit."

A wave of fierce emotion washed over Hawkwing, almost carrying him off his paws. *Could my kits really be part of my future? It's what I want most in the world—but I never dreamed it could be possible.*

"You deserve happiness, after everything you've suffered," Echosong meowed. "It has been a long, difficult journey, but it has made you into a very strong cat—the very cat your Clan needs most."

"Thank you," Hawkwing meowed fervently.

Side by side, he and Echosong turned to look out at the sky. The clouds had cleared away, and the sun shone in a vast expanse of crystal blue.

A fragile hope began to bloom inside Hawkwing. *If one of my kits is alive, then surely Pebbleshine is, too.* For the first time he began to believe that everything his Clan had suffered would prove worth it in the end.

We aren't home by the lake yet, Hawkwing thought, *but for the first time in a long while, I believe we will be soon.*

READ ON FOR AN
EXCLUSIVE MANGA ADVENTURE . . .

CREATED BY
ERIN HUNTER

WRITTEN BY
DAN JOLLEY

ART BY
JAMES L. BARRY

SKYCLAN!

THIS IS AS GOOD A PLACE TO STOP FOR THE NIGHT AS WE'RE LIKELY TO FIND.

TIME TO MAKE CAMP!

ARE YOU THREE READY?

YES!

UH-HUH!

LEAD THE WAY!

LEAFSTAR... I'M TAKING THESE THREE ON A HUNT.

WE'LL BE BACK WITH SOME FRESHKILL BEFORE YOU KNOW IT!

I'M GONNA CATCH A SQUIRREL!

BET YOU WON'T!

JUST WAIT AND SEE!

HAWKWING...ARE YOU ALL RIGHT?

WHY WOULDN'T I BE, PLUMWILLOW?

THE SIGHT OF THOSE THREE...SO ATTACHED TO THEIR FATHER NOW. INSTEAD OF TO YOU.

NO, NO. I ENJOYED TEACHING THEM WHEN THEY WERE YOUNG.

BUT THE ROLE OF FATHER SHOULD BE FILLED BY THEIR ACTUAL FATHER.

ECHOSONG DID HAVE A VISION OF ONE OF MY KITS. BUT...

WAS WHAT SHE SAW TRUE? WAS ANY OF IT TRUE? IT SEEMS LIKE A LIFETIME AGO THAT SHE LEFT US.

YOU COULD STILL MEET YOUR KITS ONE DAY, YOU KNOW.

PERHAPS STARCLAN WILL LEAD YOU TO THEM. OR THEM TO YOU.

HOW ARE WE SUPPOSED TO FOLLOW HER VISIONS, WHEN SHE'S NOT HERE TO GUIDE US?

I KNOW THE ANSWER. "HAVE FAITH." EASY TO SAY. DIFFICULT TO KEEP DOING.

• • •

HE DID IT! HE DID IT!

DEWPAW CAUGHT A SQUIRREL!

LEAFSTAR...YOU KNOW YOU HAVE MY CONFIDENCE. BUT, I CAN'T HELP BUT THINK...

THAT IT WOULD BE BETTER IF WE HAD A FIRM DESTINATION?

YOU MUST HAVE FAITH, SANDYNOSE.

STARCLAN WILL LEAD US.

AT THAT INSTANT I SEE IT.

A LEAF AS BRILLIANT RED AS A TONGUE OF FLAME. RIDING THE WIND.

A WIND STORM IS BLOWING UP!

EVERYONE FIND SHELTER UNTIL IT PASSES!

ECHOSONG SPOKE OF A LEAF SHAPED LIKE A FIVE-POINTED STAR...

COULD THIS BE WHAT SHE MEANT?

I HAVE TO FIND OUT.

HAWKWING!

HAWKWING, WHERE ARE YOU GOING?

HAWKWING!

I FEEL THE WIND DIE.

THE LEAF I'VE BEEN CHASING LIKE AN OVEREXCITED KIT DOES WHAT EVERY LEAF DOES.

FALLS TO THE GROUND. FAR BELOW.

HAWKWING! WHAT WERE YOU THINKING, DASHING OFF LIKE THAT IN UNFAMILIAR TERRITORY? YOU COULD HAVE BEEN HURT!

BUT AS I RAISE MY EYES, WORDS SOUND OUT IN MY MIND. LEAFSTAR'S WORDS.

AND ECHOSONG'S.

"HAVE FAITH. YOU HAVE TO HAVE FAITH."

"FOLLOW THE BLOOD TRAIL."

THE END

PROLOGUE

The dazzling plains seemed to stretch forever. Even Windrider, a vulture soaring high above the savannah, struggled to see where Bravelands reached its end.

Narrowing her ancient eyes, she let her gaze trail over the great yellow-grass sea, and pinpointed at last where it met the endless blue sky in a shimmering line of light. A wingtip twitched, and she banked, riding the warm air downward in a broad, graceful spiral.

Her flock followed her lead, calling out to one another in harsh, guttural voices, but Windrider was silent, scanning the savannah. Far below, herds of animals as small as ants moved across the land, following the paths beaten by countless generations. A gash in the land marked the muddy, trickling river; a horde of wildebeests was teeming into the gully and galloping up and over the sheer bank. Zebras and gazelles, grazing

1

together on the far side, glanced up incuriously at the wildebeests' approach. Then they dipped their heads to graze again,
ambling and milling peacefully.

A dark spot on the landscape caught Windrider's keen
eye—a creature separate from the others, and not moving. She
flew lower, adjusting her path with great beats of her broad
wings.

"There, my flock. There."

The others followed her down, in swooping circles. "May
Windrider's eyes be forever sharp," cried Blackwing, as the
others took up the chorus of gratitude. "She has found us flesh
once again."

It was just as Windrider had hoped: the corpse of a gazelle.
Its old and tired spirit had gone; its eyes were blank and dead.
Perhaps a cheetah had brought it down. It lay half hidden
between ocher rocks, barely visible to wingless rot-eaters; and
though its killer had fed, much of its torn flesh remained on
its bones. The gazelle had enjoyed its time and its life; now it
would nourish the vultures—just as they, in their turn, would
one day become food for others. All was as it should be . . . or
at least, so Windrider hoped.

"We must test the flesh, brothers and sisters," she called.
"Then we can feed in peace."

Windrider tilted her head, banking sharply in to land, the
other vultures flapping and clamoring behind her. Her claws
touched the gritty ground, and she hopped a couple of paces
toward the gazelle. With a glance to the birds on her right and
left, Windrider nodded once.

"A bad death will linger with the fallen."

"May the Great Spirit always grant good death," chorused the rest of the flock.

Each vulture tore a thin strip of meat from the carcass's flank, gulping it down. They all paused, looking to Windrider for the final judgment. She closed her eyes briefly.

"The kill is clean," she reassured them at last. "Feed, my flock."

When the carcass was picked bare, its bones stripped of the last tattered remnants of flesh, Windrider stepped back. Beating her wings, she launched herself skyward once more. Every vulture, sated, followed her in a chaos of feathers and rasping cries. It felt good to return to the air, to soar higher and higher into the fierce blue, knowing that the flock had eaten well and survived for another day.

When she was high enough to catch a broad current of warm air, Windrider let it take her, twitching her wings, gazing down once more. From the shimmering horizon to the dark sprawling forests, to the low range of mountains far beyond the plains, she surveyed the land. Ahead lay a cluster of slender, flat-topped acacia trees; at their edge, just within their shade, shifting golden-yellow shapes were visible against the dry earth.

Lions, she thought, *lounging in the heat of the day.*

"They will not hunt, for now," remarked Blackwing, following her gaze.

"No, not until dusk," Windrider agreed.

Then they will feast. And we will follow.

Windrider had mixed feelings about the great prides of Bravelands. Lions meant food, unsullied and copious; like all the creatures of the land, they followed the Code, killing only to survive. But she loathed their arrogance. They were among the few creatures who would not follow the Great Mother, leader of all the animals, and give respect to her wisdom.

Two cubs were romping and play-fighting, full of energy and mischief even in the heat of the high white sun. As her shadow passed over the smaller of the two, he started and looked up. His golden eyes met hers, and he opened his small jaws.

She was still high above him, but the sound of a roar buffeted the air around her. With astonishment, Windrider felt her wings tremble, and she was momentarily rocked off her course.

"Windrider?" came Blackwing's concerned voice.

Glancing back, Windrider realized none of her flock had felt the impact of that roar.

No. It was not the little lion's voice. That is not possible!

"It is nothing," she told Blackwing curtly.

Half angry, half fascinated, she forced her wings to readjust, balancing her flight once more. *No grown lion's roar could reach the heights of the sky, let alone a tiny cub's. There is more here to know.*

Windrider tilted in the air, seeking out the little lion once again. He still stood there, stiff-legged and defiant, his golden gaze fixed upward. At last, his tail whisking with triumph, he turned away. The other cub followed him as he bounded back to his pride.

Lost in thought, Windrider veered east. What she had just seen—it was an omen, she was sure of it; though she could not imagine what its message might be. *A tiny cub, with a roar to make the sky shudder. This is a vision, a portent!*

She led her flock higher and farther into the clear blue sky, until the small pride of lions and even the huge herds of the savannah were lost in the beautiful vastness of Bravelands.

CHAPTER 1

Swiftcub pounced after the vulture's shadow, but it flitted away too quickly to follow. Breathing hard, he pranced back to his pride. *I saw that bird off our territory,* he thought, delighted. *No rot-eater's going to come near Gallantpride while I'm around!*

The pride needed him to defend it, Swiftcub thought, picking up his paws and strutting around his family. Why, right now they were all half asleep, dozing and basking in the shade of the acacia trees. The most energetic thing the other lions were doing was lifting their heads to groom their nearest neighbors, or their own paws. They had no *idea* of the threat Swiftcub had just banished.

I might be only a few moons old, but my father is the strongest, bravest lion in Bravelands. And I'm going to be just like him!

"Swiftcub!"

The gentle but commanding voice snapped him out of his

dreams of glory. He came to a halt, turning and flicking his ears at the regal lioness who stood over him.

"Mother," he said, shifting on his paws.

"Why are you shouting at vultures?" Swift scolded him fondly, licking at his ears. "They're nothing but scavengers. Come on, you and your sister can play later. Right now you're supposed to be practicing hunting. And if you're going to catch anything, you'll need to keep your eyes on the prey, not on the sky!"

"Sorry, Mother." Guiltily he padded after her as she led him through the dry grass, her tail swishing. The ground rose gently, and Swiftcub had to trot to keep up. The grasses tickled his nose, and he was so focused on trying not to sneeze, he almost bumped into his mother's haunches as she crouched.

"Oops," he growled.

Valor shot him a glare. His older sister was hunched a little to the left of their mother, fully focused on their hunting practice. Valor's sleek body was low to the ground, her muscles tense; as she moved one paw forward with the utmost caution, Swiftcub tried to copy her, though it was hard to keep up on his much shorter legs. One creeping pace, then two. Then another.

I'm being very quiet, just like Valor. I'm going to be a great hunter. He slunk up alongside his mother, who remained quite still.

"There, Swiftcub," she murmured. "Do you see the burrows?"

He did, now. Ahead of the three lions, the ground rose up even higher, into a bare, sandy mound dotted with small shadowy holes. As Swiftcub watched, a small nose and whiskers poked out, testing the air. The meerkat emerged completely, stood up on its hind legs, and stared around. Satisfied, it stuck out a pink tongue and began to groom its chest, as more meerkats appeared beyond it. Growing in confidence, they scurried farther away from their burrows.

"Careful now," rumbled Swift. "They're very quick. Go!"

Swiftcub sprang forward, his little paws bounding over the ground. Still, he wasn't fast enough to outpace Valor, who was far ahead of him already. A stab of disappointment spoiled his excitement, and suddenly it was even harder to run fast, but he ran grimly after his sister.

The startled meerkats were already doubling back into their holes. Stubby tails flicked and vanished; the bigger leader, his round dark eyes glaring at the oncoming lions, was last to twist and dash underground. Valor's jaws snapped at his tail, just missing.

"Sky and stone!" the bigger cub swore, coming to a halt in a cloud of dust. She shook her head furiously and licked her jaws. "I nearly had it!"

A rumble of laughter made Swiftcub turn. His father, Gallant, stood watching them. Swiftcub couldn't help but feel the usual twinge of awe mixed in with his delight. Black-maned and huge, his sleek fur glowing golden in the sun, Gallant would have been intimidating if Swiftcub hadn't known and loved him so well. Swift rose to her paws and greeted the great lion affectionately, rubbing his maned neck with her head.

"It was a good attempt, Valor," Gallant reassured his

daughter. "What Swift said is true: meerkats are *very* hard to catch. You were so close—one day you'll be as fine a hunter as your mother." He nuzzled Swift and licked her neck.

"*I* wasn't anywhere near it," grumbled Swiftcub. "I'll never be as fast as Valor."

"Oh, you will," said Gallant. "Don't forget, Valor's a whole year older than you, my son. You're getting bigger and faster every day. Be patient!" He stepped closer, leaning in so his great tawny muzzle brushed Swiftcub's own. "That's the secret to stalking, too. Learn patience, and one day you will be a *very* fine hunter."

"I hope so," said Swiftcub meekly.

Gallant nuzzled him. "Don't doubt yourself, my cub. You're going to be a great lion and the best kind of leader: one who keeps his own pride safe and content, but puts fear into the heart of his strongest enemy!"

That does sound good! Feeling much better, Swiftcub nodded. Gallant nipped affectionately at the tufty fur on top of his head and padded toward Valor.

Swiftcub watched him proudly. *He's right, of course. Father knows everything! And I will be a great hunter, I will. And a brave, strong leader—*

A tiny movement caught his eye, a scuttling shadow in his father's path.

A scorpion!

Barely pausing to think, Swiftcub sprang, bowling between his father's paws and almost tripping him. He skidded to a halt right in front of Gallant, snarling at the small sand-yellow scorpion. It paused, curling up its barbed tail and raising its pincers in threat.

"No, Swiftcub!" cried his father.

Swiftcub swiped his paw sideways at the creature, catching its plated shell and sending it flying into the long grass.

All four lions watched the grass, holding their breath, waiting for a furious scorpion to reemerge. But there was no stir of movement. It must have fled. Swiftcub sat back, his heart suddenly banging against his ribs.

"Skies above!" Gallant laughed. Valor gaped, and Swift dragged her cub into her paws and began to lick him roughly.

"Mother . . ." he protested.

"Honestly, Swiftcub!" she scolded him as her tongue swept across his face. "Your father might have gotten a nasty sting from that creature—but *you* could have been killed!"

"You're such an idiot, little brother," sighed Valor, but there was admiration in her eyes.

Gallant and Swift exchanged proud looks. "Swift," growled Gallant, "I do believe the time has come to give our cub his true name."

Swift nodded, her eyes shining. "Now that we know what kind of lion he is, I think you're right."

Gallant turned toward the acacia trees, his tail lashing, and gave a resounding roar.

It always amazed Swiftcub that the pride could be lying half asleep one moment and alert the very next. Almost before Gallant had finished roaring his summons, there was a rustle of grass, a crunch of paws on dry earth, and the rest of Gallantpride appeared, ears pricked and eyes bright with curiosity. Gallant huffed in greeting, and the twenty lionesses and young lions of his pride spread out in a circle around him, watching and listening intently.

Gallant looked down again at Swiftcub, who blinked and glanced away, suddenly rather shy. "Crouch down," murmured the great lion.

When he obeyed, Swiftcub felt his father's huge paw rest on his head.

"Henceforth," declared Gallant, "this cub of mine will no longer be known as Swiftcub. He faced a dangerous foe without hesitation and protected his pride. His name, now and forever, is Fearless Gallantpride."

It was done so quickly, Swiftcub felt dizzy with astonishment. *I have my name! I'm Fearless. Fearless Gallantpride!*

All around him, his whole family echoed his name, roaring their approval. Their deep cries resonated across the grasslands.

"Fearless Gallantpride!"

"Welcome, Fearless, son of Gallant!"

ERIN
HUNTER

is inspired by a fascination with
the ferocity of the natural world.
As well as having great respect for
nature in all its forms, Erin enjoys
creating rich, mythical explanations
for animal behavior. She is also the
author of the Survivors, Seekers, and
Bravelands series.

Download the free Warriors app at
www.warriorcats.com.

ENTER THE
BRAVELANDS

Heed the call of the wild in this brand-new,
action-packed series from **Erin Hunter**.

A LION
cast out from his pride.

AN ELEPHANT
who can read the bones of the dead.

A BABOON
rebelling against his destiny.

A NEW WARRIORS ADVENTURE HAS BEGUN

1

2

3

4

Alderpaw, son of Bramblestar and Squirrelflight,
must embark on a treacherous journey
to save the Clans from a mysterious threat.

HARPER
An Imprint of HarperCollinsPublishers

www.warriorcats.com

WARRIORS : THE NEW PROPHECY

THE NEW PROPHECY
WARRIORS
MIDNIGHT
ERIN HUNTER
#1 NEW YORK TIMES BESTSELLING AUTHOR

THE NEW PROPHECY
WARRIORS
MOONRISE
ERIN HUNTER
#1 NEW YORK TIMES BESTSELLING AUTHOR

THE NEW PROPHECY
WARRIORS
DAWN
ERIN HUNTER
#1 NEW YORK TIMES BESTSELLING AUTHOR

THE NEW PROPHECY
WARRIORS
STARLIGHT
ERIN HUNTER
#1 NEW YORK TIMES BESTSELLING AUTHOR

THE NEW PROPHECY
WARRIORS
TWILIGHT
ERIN HUNTER
#1 NEW YORK TIMES BESTSELLING AUTHOR

THE NEW PROPHECY
WARRIORS
SUNSET
ERIN HUNTER
#1 NEW YORK TIMES BESTSELLING AUTHOR

In the second series, follow the next generation of heroic cats as they set off on a quest to save the Clans from destruction.

HARPER
An Imprint of HarperCollinsPublishers

www.warriorcats.com

WARRIORS: POWER OF THREE

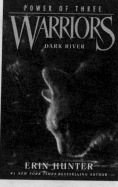

In the third series, Firestar's grandchildren begin their training as warrior cats. Prophecy foretells that they will hold more power than any cats before them.

HARPER
An Imprint of HarperCollinsPublishers

www.warriorcats.com

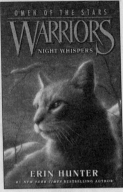

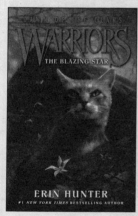

WARRIORS: SUPER EDITIONS

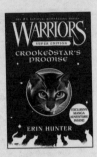

These extra-long, stand-alone adventures will take
you deep inside each of the Clans with thrilling tales
featuring the most legendary warrior cats.

WARRIORS: BONUS STORIES

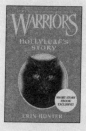

Discover the untold stories of the warrior cats and Clans
when you download the separate ebook novellas—or read
them in four paperback bind-ups!

HARPER
An Imprint of HarperCollinsPublishers

www.warriorcats.com

ALSO BY ERIN HUNTER:
SURVIVORS

Survivors: The Original Series

The time has come for dogs to rule the wild.

HARPER
An Imprint of HarperCollinsPublishers

www.survivorsdogs.com